FATHOMLESS

FATHOMLESS

GREIG BECK

COHESION PRESS

MAYDAY HILLS LUNATIC ASYLUM

BEECHWORTH, AUSTRALIA

FATHOMLESS

Greig Beck © 2016

Cover Art/Design © Dean Samed
Layout © Geoff Brown

ISBNs:
Paperback: 978-0-9946304-0-7
eBook: 978-0-9946304-3-8

Cohesion Press
Mayday Hills Lunatic Asylum
Beechworth, Australia

ACKNOWLEDGEMENTS:
Thank you to my test pilots –
Matthew Summers, genre expert,
and ex-Coastie, Paul Scott.
Good insights, gentlemen.

And also a big shout-out to my editor, Amanda 'AJ'
Spedding – my wizard who turns lead into gold!

DEDICATION:
To the men and women of the Coast Guard – alert,
responsive, adaptive, and always there – thank you.
Semper Paratus.

CONTENTS

CONTENTS

RETURN OF THE MONSTER

"I fear all we have done is to awaken a sleeping giant,
and fill him with a terrible resolve."
Isoroku Yamamoto

BODY OF WATER FOUND BENEATH CANADA IS LARGER THAN ALL THE GREAT LAKES COMBINED

Huge reserves of the oldest water on Earth are locked deep within the planet's crust and could be home to new forms of life, according to scientists. Geologists have revealed they have found water that is up to 2.7 billion years old in sites all over the world. They now estimate that there could be around 2.5 million cubic miles of this water buried beneath the ground.

RICHARD GRAY, DAILY MAIL UK. Dec 2014

PROLOGUE

THE LEGEND OF BAD WATER

Baranof Island, Southern Wilderness,
Gulf of Alaska,
1952

Jim Granger stood on the rock ledge and looked out over the glacier valley that would feed into the bay miles to the west. It was October, and though the magnificent blue water from Indigo Lake sparkled from the autumn sunlight, after dark it would be bitterly cold, and deadly. He needed to be back at the camp long before then.

He turned to scan the rock face – about fifty feet further along the narrow ledge he perched upon, there was a crack in the stone that displayed nothing but a dark void, a cave entrance, *the* cave entrance he hoped.

It had taken him months, no, years to find his way here. Ages ago he had done some field work for a mining company, and had developed a relationship with some of the local native Nantouk people.

The Nantouk were an old race and had lived in the Alaskan territory for over ten thousand years. They were still distrustful of strangers, as first contact with Europeans hadn't gone well – in the 1700s they had met and traded with both Russian and Spanish explorers – epidemics of

1

smallpox and other infectious diseases quickly followed, near decimating the people. Then came the hunters, traders, land grabbers, and finally the miners, of which he was one.

Getting them to open up had been a long and patience-stretching task. And it had all started when one evening an elder had talked of a legend called *Bad Water*, and then shown him a tooth, broken, but a big one, bigger than anything he had ever seen. The old tribesman had hinted that he didn't *find* the artifact, but instead, in his youth, had battled the creature himself.

No matter how hard Granger had pressed him for a sea location, the old man had evaded, obfuscated, and just as Granger was thinking he had misunderstood him, the old man had suggested it wasn't from the open ocean at all, but instead from some dark, hidden place.

Granger had been patient, coming back time and again, and working hard to become a trusted friend of the tribal group. Eventually the Nantouk elder had told him of an ancient and nearly forgotten custom. Granger had listened eagerly as the old man talked. It seemed that before gaining manhood, the young men of the tribe would be required to enter a secret place that was older than the world according to the Nantouk. It was the place of Bad Water, and using only a length of rope and harpoon, they were to catch something fantastic, and then bring their prize back to the tribe.

The old man had then held up the broken tooth – serrated, seven inches long; it was the proof of his fearlessness, gained more than a half-century before.

The Nantouk were first and foremost hunters and fishermen, and didn't know the meaning of deception, so if an elder said he caught something fantastic, Granger believed him.

Granger grinned, wiped at his dripping nose, and then leaned out to gaze at the rip of darkness in the sheer rock face. He was a geologist by profession, but he was also a fossil hunter and fanatical caver. The legend of the Bad Water was irresistible to him. He knew from his experience, whenever there was a legend there was always some germ of fact behind it. You just needed patience, good forensic skills, and sometimes a good dose of insanity to ferret it out.

Granger's laugh was lost in the freezing wind. He leant out further. Where he was heading was isolated, unknown and would be difficult to get to, and therefore perfect; perfect, because all of those factors might mean he'd be the first European to ever enter it.

He eased along the ledge, being careful to balance the pack on his shoulders, and try not to look down. It was an eight hundred foot drop to the water, but even if by some miracle he survived the fall, then that cold blue liquid would freeze-burn his skin, and more than likely stop his heart in an instant.

He reached out; a few more feet to the rip in the rock wall, and then he had its edge. He rested, waiting for his heart rate to come down as he felt the jagged stone under his palm. The cliff side was primarily diorite batholith – hard, damned hard. As a geologist, he knew that any rock, no matter how dense, under the right pressures became as elastic as rubber or could fracture like glass. One huge tectonic shift could rip open a section of the earth, and then the next shift could close it off, land-locking all manner of life forms in either a safe-harbor, or their grave. And that was exactly what he hoped for.

Granger was buoyant, and also confident that today he would find something really memorable. Not far away from where he stood, there were rich Miocene shale layers, where abundant fossils had been found. At one time, this area was underwater, as another amateur, just like himself, had uncovered fossilized clam beds and evidence of early cetaceans that placed the site as being an ancient sea floor around the Miocene period. Jim had a theory – as the water-covered landscape began to shrink when more and more ice formed during another glacial epoch, the last giants of the waterways needed to retreat to warmer currents, or risk being stranded. And if they had become stranded, then their bones awaited him, somewhere beneath his feet.

Granger thought of the elder's story of catching some huge living creature. He didn't think the Nantouk elder had purposely misled him, but that maybe time and imagination had meant things weren't exactly as the man remembered them. At the least, Granger expected to find some sort of prehistoric bone yard, protected from the elements with high quality specimens prized by museums, universities and private collectors from Boston to Berlin.

He ducked inside – there was blackness, and depth. Excellent, just what he hoped for. He knelt to check his equipment in his pack: rope, water, brandy flask, miner's chalk, a carbide miner's lamp, a new type of incandescent flashlight, candles as back up and most importantly, waxed matches. There was also a single picture of Violet – *Vie* – his wife. Jim stared at the pretty young woman, the pretty young *patient* woman, who waited at home with their baby daughter. Vie was his strength, and his biggest fan. She'd sit for hours, listening to him as he told her of his latest finding or exploration. There was real interest in her eyes. Sometimes he wondered whether he was here because of his own hobby-interest, or simply to bring back fantastic stories to amuse that beautiful woman.

Jim kissed the picture and stuck it in his breast pocket, patting it. He finally pulled free his favorite mining helmet – cast iron, yellow and battered, and with his name and title engraved across the front. He'd had it for years, and it had brought him luck for every single one of them. He put it on.

Satisfied, he stood and drew in a deep breath. Jim Granger stepped forward, but then paused. He'd told the group what he was doing, but few knew exactly where he was going. He looked around, and then crouched to pick up a shard of stone. He used it to scrape and scratch at the hard granite wall just inside on a flat surface, going over his lettering again and again until the sheet of diorite now carried his message deep enough not to be obliterated by the weather. At least for a century or two; after that, *I'll just be another fossil*, he thought, grinning. He finished and leant back to admire his work.

Jim Granger went in here – 12 Oct 52.

"If I'm lost, a good signpost for my searchers, and if I'm not, an unforgivable piece of graffiti."

He tossed the rock over his shoulder, not waiting to hear it strike stone or water, hundreds of feet below.

"Wish me luck, Vie." He started in.

His first impression: old, very old, and though dry at the cave mouth, he could smell salt and dampness further in. He readied his carbide lamp, carefully turning a small knob to allow water to drip onto the carbide pellets in its base. The lamp immediately started to release trapped acetylene that was then piped to a wick. He hated using the carbide lantern as the gas was highly flammable, and worse, the temperamental bastards were prone to exploding – not great in an enclosed environment. But they were the most reliable lamps available, and also their illumination lasted many hours. He'd save his flashlight for emergencies, as the batteries ran out within a few minutes.

Granger eased himself along the fissure for the first twenty feet. It was narrow and steep, and he found he was quickly descending at an angle of about forty degrees before it flattened and opened out. He walked slowly, stopping often, a smile on his face as he lifted the lantern high to examine the indentations in the wall. The striations showed different lines of sediment that had compressed down to layers of color in the stone.

"Hello." He stepped in closer, his smile widening. "Mr Amphistium, I believe." He held up the lamp to the plate-sized fossil pressed in the stone. "And you, sir, are proof of evolution." Jim knew the species was an ancestor of the flatfish, but where the modern variety had an asymmetric head with both eyes on one side, this fossil fish had one eye in the center of the head, and the other near the edge – evidence that evolution had only half finished her job.

He wished he had his camera, but the device was way too bulky, and he had needed to pack light for the journey to the cave. He satisfied himself with digging out his notebook and quickly jotting down some details, and doing a quick pencil sketch that he would enhance back at the camp.

Jim waved the lamp around – two cave entrances. He'd stick to the left, and pray it didn't branch too many times. To help, he reached into a pocket for a fat stick of caving chalk, and wrote directions and a short message on the wall.

He stepped in further, and exhaled, looking around and whistling – on the wall there was cave art. Some of the images were faded by countless centuries, but others were more recent, perhaps only decades old. There were small figures, standing on the dark water's edge, spears held high. There were drawings of water creatures – fish, sharks, turtles, and strange shapes Granger couldn't recognize. There were men pulling the creatures onto stone shorelines, or in turn, they being pulled into the water. The final ones showed the unlucky ones in the dark sea being ripped to pieces, shredded and consumed by the denizens of that dark water.

Granger had been following the ancient tableau as he continued on, moving ever lower, the temperature, strangely, getting warmer, *much* warmer. He entered a large flat room; *must be nearly a hundred feet around,* he thought, judging by the way the multiple echoes bounced back at him. He was about to continue on when a melon-sized rock caught his eye. He squatted before it, and rolled it towards himself. He drew a small pick from his belt and looked for a fracture point. He tapped it several times, the echoes mimicking his sounds before the rock split neatly in two.

Jim's eyebrows shot up and he snorted softly. Like a window on a world long past, the ancient continent gave up its secrets to those it deemed worthy. He smiled, and lifted one half of the stone. There was an enormous tooth embedded in the matrix. He placed his hand upon it and spread his fingers – the triangular, serrated blade extended well beyond his palm and fingertips. It was just like the Nantouk elder's tooth, but bigger and age darkened.

Jim loved his fossil hunting, but was by no means an expert. And this was something new to him. He tapped again at its edges, and was delighted by the tooth falling free. He lifted it.

"You must be made of damned hard material." He turned it in his hands. "Some sort of dinosaur... probably aquatic." He stuck it in a pouch at his waist, looking forward to researching the find when he got back.

Granger stood slowly, and wiped his brow. It was even warmer now. There was some volcanic activity in this area, as this was a tectonic collision point, but mostly it was just the odd shimmy and shake from minor earth tremors. He shone his light up at the ceiling, but saw nothing to worry him in the cave structure above.

He crossed the huge room to then ease himself into another tunnel. As he turned sideways to wedge himself into the crevice, he noticed that some of the stones were raw, as though newly broken. He shone his light beam upwards again – there was a lighter patch on the ceiling – the rock had fallen recently. He exhaled, indecision freezing him for a second or two. In geological terms, *fallen recently*, could have meant any time in the last five minutes or fifty thousand years.

He shrugged and decided to press on, travelling ever

lower. The going was easier, but the slope was getting steeper, and he knew he had descended quite far by now, and well below sea level. Even with a light pack, it would be a wearying climb back out. He stopped to mark some more chalk messages on the cave wall, and he would do so again at the change in the geology.

Minutes passed, and then more minutes. Granger knew he wasn't being mindful of the time when he came to another split in a rock wall. He checked his wristwatch. *Last one,* he thought, aware now that he had exceeded his planned descent timing. He eased through, walking side-on for several uncomfortable minutes until he popped out the other side, and into another large chamber. He held the lamp up, and then sniffed – dampness, but not the damp smell of moss, mould or slime, but unexpectedly that of seawater. He walked slowly forward; his arm outstretched holding up the lamp. His foot kicked a small piece of rubble that bounced several times before disappearing into one of the numerous holes in the cave floor. He frowned, hearing the rock carry on bouncing as it continued its descent.

At the center of the cave floor there was one hole, larger than the rest. This one had what looked like the remains of a rope ladder still clinging to wooden pegs at its edge.

Granger quickly approached, and then lowered himself to his knees, holding the lamp over the hole. A warm breeze caressed his slick face, and the smell of water was even stronger. It wasn't the sharp tang of mineral salts that can build up at the edges of subterranean thermal pools, but more the smell of salt marshes, weed and exposed rock on a tidal edge.

It didn't make sense. The Arctic Gulf waters were currently around ten degrees, but this smelled like tropical water, and besides, the ocean itself was miles away. Could there be a breach somewhere below him? But even that defied logic, as he must have been half a mile below sea level by now, and the pressure should have caused an upwelling. Where he was now, should have been submerged.

There might be another explanation – this was the home of the *Bad Water*. He squinted down into the hole, but could see nothing with his carbide lamp's base shielding the illumination. He placed the lamp to the side, and pulled his pack off his shoulders so he could retrieve his flashlight. He lay flat and pointed the weak yellow beam downward. Nothing but more blackness, but he was sure he could hear the lapping of a surf, or perhaps it was the ocean sound one hears when pressing a seashell to their ear.

He got to his knees and shone the light in an arc over the cave floor; there were several more of the holes – *Swiss cheese*, he thought, with some trepidation. He rose to his feet too quickly, his knee knocking over the lamp.

"Damn it all," he cursed and righted the lamp, but immediately smelt the unmistakable acrid odor of acetylene gas. He looked down at the simple brass and tin mechanism; it fizzed, and there was what he feared – a leak.

"No you don't, you temperamental sonofabitch!"

Granger knew he had only seconds, and swung the lamp hard, flinging it to the end of the cave, and turned preparing to sprint for the crevice he had slipped through. For the briefest of seconds, he heard the clang of the brass and steel striking stone, before that small sound was quickly absorbed into the roar and flash of an explosion.

The blast was enormous, laying him flat, and before the first echo could reverberate, Granger felt a ripple run through the stone beneath him. He lay still in the utter darkness for a second, and then felt around the cave floor for his flashlight, thankfully locating it quickly. He placed the small string loop at its end over his wrist and then switched it on. The sepia beam swirled with dust.

The smell of burned gases, ozone, and choking dust were strong. Granger coughed as he got slowly to his feet, wincing at the pain in his knees, and knowing he was surely missing the skin on both.

There came an odd tickling vibration beneath his soles. "*Please, no more*," he whispered. Grains of sand and pebbles began to rain down, making a plinking sound on his steel helmet.

"God, no."

He was frozen, waiting, listening, reaching out with all his senses and hoping that what he feared wasn't about to occur. There came a faint sound that reminded him of the great ice sheets cracking as the first thaws of spring calved off huge bergs from the Arctic glaciers. Suddenly, in the dim yellow glow of his flashlight he saw a black line running towards him across the cave floor. Almost immediately, it started to open like a giant zipper.

Jim Granger felt like he was on a sinking ship, where the deck was beginning to tilt. He ran, but slid, and then fell. He suddenly found himself floating. His flashlight wasn't in his hand anymore, but the string loop kept it close, and the weak yellow beam illuminated a rush of meteorites falling with him. He smelled the saltwater, and above the crushing sound of cracking rock, he thought he could hear ancient surf far away in the dark void.

It was impossible to determine how long he fell through the darkness, but after an eternity he started to hear the crash of large stones hitting water, and then he too hit the surface. The impact stunned him, but thankfully the broken rock falling just ahead of him, had churned the water taking the lethality from the surface tension.

He lay on his back, floating and groaning softly. He tasted salt, or maybe blood, and opened his eyes to look around. He saw nothing, and knew he floated on a black sea, in a dark world.

"*Help!*"

help – help – heeelp – heeeel – heeeee…

The echoes continued for many minutes, and told him that the cavern was enormous. He eased upright and began to tread water. He felt a tug of string at his wrist.

"Please god." He fiddled with the flashlight, and it rewarded him with an orange glow. It was weak, and its beam only illuminated about a dozen feet, but never had he been so happy to see a light in his life.

He spun one way, and then the next, but there was nothing but walls of blackness. At the far edge of his light he could just make out a spot of bright yellow, his helmet, slowly turning on the dark water after its drop from above. It looked like a tiny lemon turtle on its back. For some reason, it comforted him. "*Get help*," he sputtered to it, and then turned away.

I need to find one of the walls. If I can do that, perhaps I can find a way up. Jim Granger had been in caves and cave-ins before, and the one thing he knew, if there was a way in, there was usually a way out.

"*Hello!*"

The echo bounced back again and again – it was long and hollow – and told him he was a long way from anything solid. He needed to find a wall, so turned off the flashlight to save its power and began to stroke eastward for no particular reason.

"*Hello!*" he tested the cave depth again, hoping he would receive a shortened echo, telling him he was closer to an obstacle. But there was still a vast emptiness in the repeating sound.

Jim swam for thirty minutes before stopping to tread water and catch his breath. He felt the first pressure wave then, and was initially buoyed by the sensation – *a backwash for sure*, he hoped.

"*Hello.*" Strangely, the echoes were still as long and hollow as ever. He began to swim again, but immediately felt the next pressure wave push him in the water. This time it had come from another angle. He stopped and floated, his brow furrowing.

There came another push of water, from one side, and then the next. It reminded him of the time he swam in the lake at home, and one of the big boats came close. He felt another surge, and another, this time from behind him –

it felt like something was going around him. He felt his testicles shrink, even in the warm water.

Jim Granger lifted his flashlight, and switched it on. He slowly swiveled, holding the light up. The oil-black water was as flat as glass, with just the hint of a mist lifting from its warm surface.

"What are you?" he whispered, but knew he didn't really want to know. The memory of the old man jumped into his head – him, and his prize – *the tooth.*

The impact hit Jim Granger from the side, dragging him for a dozen feet, and knocking the wind from him. He swirled and bobbed in the water, suddenly unable to stay on the surface. His control over his body seemed gone, and even though he was a strong swimmer, he feared his legs or back had been broken as his lower half refused to obey him.

He used his arms to break the surface, thrashing in his panic and gulping air. He raised the flashlight, and in its dying glow saw that the water that dripped from his hands was red. Jim reached down, and whimpered. He now knew why he couldn't tread water – both his legs were gone from the thigh.

"What are you?" his scream was weak, and his head felt light as his life was rapidly gushing from his body. Shock was setting in. *I'm dead*, he thought, as he let his body sink. The last thing he saw was a lemon yellow turtle spinning madly on the surface.

Jim Granger was consumed whole before he even made it to the bottom.

CHAPTER 1

Stanford University, Stanford
Lecture Room M106
Today

Cate Granger stood on the podium looking out over the mostly empty room. She was finishing up her lecture, and paused as the rear door opened a crack and a figure slipped through. The person saluted and then slipped into a back seat.

She smiled and nodded once. It was Greg Jamison, her colleague and friend who, like her, was a professor of evolutionary biology at Stanford University. He was thirty, and just a few years younger than her, but with a mop of blonde hair that made him look more excited teenager than academic.

Both of them specialized in adaptive changes to marine life, with their current research centered on collapsing fish stocks, and how some species were able to adjust through evolution and flourish, sometimes to the detriment of the existing creatures in the habitat. *Adapt or Die,* they'd call their paper when they finally got around to finishing it.

She changed the screen image behind her. It now showed a grainy picture of a forest, probably from some decades back – there was healthy oak and birch trees, some shrubs and open grass fields. There was also a couple of deer just peering from the underbrush, and between the tree canopies, a few birds were caught mid flight – it was an idyllic forest setting.

"Not all introduced species are invasive," Cate said, pausing to look around the room at the shiny, youthful faces. Most stared at the screen, but a few young men stole glances at her when they thought she wasn't watching. She suppressed a smile and continued.

"And some species we don't even realize are, or even could be, invasive until it's too late." She changed the image to one of the same setting, but obviously taken years later. The forest looked melted – *green melted* – everything smothered under a thick mat of strangling plant life. The trees, the bushes, even the areas that had once been grassy clearings were crushed beneath the living mass.

"And then when we do find out, sometimes these biologicals are so embedded, and the damage so advanced, that all we can do is surrender and learn to live with it." She looked over her shoulder at the screen. "This is the kudzu vine – *Pueraria montana var. lobata* – grows up to seven inches per day. We introduced it in 1876 as an ornamental plant to drape over our sunny porches. Kudzu's real leg-up came in the late '30s when it was said to be a 'miraculous' gift that would fix nitrogen into overburdened southern soils. So we planted it everywhere."

She sighed. "It was once dubbed, the savior of the south. Now, it's eating the south."

She changed the slide, showing images of zebra mussel infestations in rivers and lakes, then moved onto thirty-foot boa constrictors eating anything moving in the Florida Everglades. Finally, she stopped at an ancient looking drawing.

"This painting is called Fish Swimming Amid Falling Flowers. It was painted during the Song dynasty, around a thousand years ago by a man called, Liu Cai. Peaceful, *huh*?"

The watercolor showed some sort of variety of carp in a pond, swimming through colorful floating blossoms.

"The Chinese have been cultivating the carp species for

centuries – has a great reputation for being hardy, and a talent for eating pond weed, which was a huge problem for us in many of our waterways." She shrugged. "You can eat them, they look attractive, low maintenance, and some can live for nearly a century." She changed the slide to two men holding a single fish in the air – it was a giant.

"The problem was, they liked our waterways so much, they multiplied, and grew big – up to one hundred pounds each. And then they decimated every other living thing in the waterways. In fact, in the Illinois River today, they account for ninety per cent of the entire biomass. Bottom line: once the carp moves in, everything else either moves out, gets eaten, or starves."

She gave the room a flat smile. "Forget climate change; the estimated damage from invasive species worldwide totals more than $1.4 trillion – *annually.*"

Cate leant forward onto her knuckles. "A habitat that took millions of years to become established can be irretrievably altered in twelve months." She paused a beat, drawing all eyes back to her. "That's why today, there are such rigorous checks and balances on what we allow into our country, into our forests, and our airways, and into our rivers." She looked at each of the students. "I'm your original green warrior, but even I know that there are some creatures that do not deserve to exist in some areas – they're aliens, deadly invaders. And if they can't be moved on, then eradication is the only solution. Or one day, we might find something moves in, that even threatens us."

Cate let the silence hang for a second or two, before shutting the images down. She then took a few questions, set an assignment, and finally dismissed her class.

Greg jogged down the steps towards her. "Professor Granger."

She grinned. "Professor Jamison. What brings you to my class? Trying to spark a few ideas for your own sessions?"

"Great presentation." He leaned on her desk. "I would

have mentioned the Australian cane toad or the gray rabbit waves of the 1800s. Still, overall I think you covered the topic in excellent detail." He held up a finger. "But *I am* here to remind you not to forget our meeting with Bill later today."

"Sure. Got a few errands to run, but I'll be there. You know how I love bureaucracy." Cate pretended to put a finger down her throat.

"Hey, who doesn't?" Greg rolled his eyes. "Just don't be late; you know how Bill gets. Besides, he said he had something important to discuss with us."

"Let me guess; a new water cooler in the entrance foyer." She snorted. "Don't sweat it; I can deal with Bill. He doesn't mind if I'm a few minutes late. You just deal with marking all those student papers on time." Cate smiled, turning away from her colleague to pack. They had a good boss in Bill Harris, and besides, she knew she could twist him around her little finger.

"Yeah, well, you might want to be in on time today." From behind her, Greg sounded like he was grinning as he spoke. "Because overnight the new satellite data came in from NASA."

Cate stopped and turned. "Quadrant 43?"

"Oh yeah," he said cheerily. "We got the entire west coast of Alaska this time."

"Yes." She fist pumped. For Cate, the university role was a dream job. She got to study evolution's mysteries and indulge her first love of exploring, something she guessed she inherited from her grandfather who went missing exploring the Alaskan coastline over sixty years before.

Her thoughts quickly turned to Violet, her grandmother, the tiny bird-like woman who smelled of lavender and mothballs. Violet had shown her the letters her husband had sent her nearly three quarters of a century ago. It was all that was left of him; his magnificent letters, decorated with hand-drawn pictures of fossilized creatures, that and a few old photographs. Violet, or *Vie* as her mother called her, used to read them to Cate when she was a little girl, telling of the great and brave soul who had the heart of a pioneer. She once said to her, that she hated him going into his caves, and had told him that one day he'd go so deep, he'd come face to face with the devil himself. She had laughed softly, but there was sadness in her eyes.

"*I'll find him for you,*" Cate had said to her with all the solemnity a six year old could muster.

"Hey, still with me?" Greg leaned towards her.

"*Huh?* Oh yeah, sure." Cate started to hurriedly pack, sliding books, pens and notes into her satchel. She grinned; Jim Granger was her very own family mystery. It still left her wondering what ever happened to the man with that explorer's soul – just like hers, she bet.

She'd find out one day, for herself, *and* Violet, she thought, daydreaming now. One day soon.

"See that?" Cate Granger pointed at the screen, showing image data of the Alaskan southern wilderness taken from about two thousand miles above the continent.

"Sure, Indigo Lake." Greg shrugged. "So what?"

Cate tapped the screen. "Look, look."

"You mean there's something else?" Greg leant over the back of her chair, squinting. "Not… really… sure what am I supposed to be looking at." He straightened. "But the lake's very blue, and…" He leaned around to look at her face. "Did you know the color is a bit of a mystery?"

"Yes, thank you, Greg, and the pretty blue is why they call it Indigo Lake." She gritted her teeth, "I meant this; focus, here." She tapped the screen harder, over a section of sheer cliff wall. The granite and diorite batholith wall of Indigo Lake on Baranof Island was about eight hundred feet high, and even from the great distance, its edifice looked intimidating.

The image itself was nearly drained of color, and some aspects were highlighted. One being the lake, a deep blue, others were paler blues and grays, with dots of orange speckled around.

"It's got a thermal overlay; what we're looking for is hotspots. Anything that's above air-temp normal." She raised an eyebrow. "So, now, does anything look a little strange to you; maybe leap out?"

There were specks of warm yellow and orange dotted about, which most probably represented some larger wildlife like caribou, but there was a larger flare she knew caught his attention. He folded his arms, nodding. "Yep, there's something hot on the wall."

"Bingo." She pointed, gun-like at his chest, and then turned back to the screen. "But not *on* the wall, instead, *in* the wall. There's sure something hot in there. My bet is there's a cave entrance that's pushing out heat from somewhere below the lake." She jiggled her eyebrows. "Maybe another lake."

"Mineral springs. Hey, have you ever heard the legend of *Bad Water*? It's supposed to be haunted."

She scowled him to silence. "No, the whole area is called Bad Water by the locals, and not even they remember why. It's not the lake." She waved a hand. "And before you even say it, there's no way some local wildlife is big enough to generate that much of a heat signature, and if something has flown in, it'd have to be the size of a damn ostrich."

"Damn, I was just going to say ostrich." He grinned. "So, a geothermal vent then. This area is still active, minimally, sure, but still. I know the geology, Cate. Plate tectonics in those parts are a huge generator of the wild Alaskan structures." Greg unfolded his arms and made shapes in the air. "The North American Plate is still riding over the top of the Pacific Plate – the valleys are sinking and the mountains are growing taller at a rate of about an inch or more a year." He smiled, looking self-satisfied.

"Bullshit," Cate said over her shoulder.

He snorted. "Well, thank you for your professional rebuttal, your honor."

"I mean, bullshit to it being just some sort of thermal vent. I think it's a vent all right, but not leading to deep magma, or steam from super-heated rock, or even heat from subduction friction." She turned to him. "I think it opens to a body of warm water."

"Your mythical secret lake?"

"Yup." She nodded, smiling. "And my studies lead me to believe there's a body of water bigger than all of the great lakes combined – and all right under our feet, well, *their feet*. And all we need to do is prove it's there, and more importantly, prove it can be accessed." She grinned. "So, someone needs to go in and take a look."

Greg paced away for a moment. "Cate, your grandfather disappeared around those parts didn't he?"

"Oh yeah, long time ago," she said distractedly as she fiddled with the cliff-face images.

"Ah, and now you seem to be in the same area, like you're looking for him." He stopped pacing and faced her.

"No; just a coincidence is all." Cate turned slowly in her seat.

"You know, the scientific community believes that water might be suspended within the geology, caught up in the rock, like some sort of deep earth sponge." He tilted his head. "It'd be primordial soup, *thick*, primordial soup."

"Movile Cave." She raised her eyebrows.

"Huh?" Greg's mouth twitched into a smile. "*Ah*, Romania." He nodded. "You think it's something like that?"

"Maybe. Why not?" She tilted her head. "The Movile was only discovered in 1986. Cut off from the outside world for nearly six million years. Had a whole ecosystem of unique species that had evolved in there… and not just blind shrimp, but big things like cave spiders the size of your hand."

"*Ooh*, they sound like fun." He grinned.

She turned back to her screen. "I just need more data." She leaned in closer to her screen, elbows on the desk. "I've got an old pal up there who owes me a favor or two. We can grab a quick peek of the opening in the cliff wall without getting our hands dirty." She spoke over her shoulder. "No mess, no fuss. Sound like a plan?"

"Sure… then what?"

"Then, if there's something interesting there, we get approval for a full expedition." She held out her hands, shoulders hiked. "See? Easy as A-B-C."

Greg gave her a broad smile. "You know me; I'm all for doing a little preplanning before jumping right in and doing something expensive, career ending, or just plain dumb."

She laughed softly. "Always good to have you onboard, Mr Jamison."

Three days later, Cate, Greg, and Abigail Burke, a newly minted PHD straight out of the geology department, sat in Cate's office – their Home Base, as Cate called it. An enormous curved computer screen was center stage, and several computers were set up in a horseshoe shape on the tiered desks before them. They waited on a communication link to be established between Frederick Wan Ling – a friend of Cate's doing some research on migrating Arctic birds – and their in-house system.

Greg brought in the coffees as Cate checked the speaker on the desk for the fourth time. She checked her watch again and then turned to Abigail. "We'll record everything, but keep your fingers crossed the link holds. This is costing me the last of my exploration budget, and a truck-load of goodwill with a friend."

"You must have pull. I didn't think anyone was getting extraneous budget allocations anymore." Greg took his seat.

Cate wiggled her eyebrows. "I *knows* people." She swallowed; truth be known, there was no exploration budget. Getting funding to go on questionable treasure hunts in today's razor-thin funding environment was near impossible, especially at a time when university departments were being shut down or downsized.

Even if there was the prospect of finding any money, it'd take weeks to procure its release. Cate had no time or patience for university political maneuvering, so had dipped into her own savings for the project. Getting a result was now damned personal.

"Professor Cate Granger... *Cate*? Are you there?" The voice was scratchy, and as disembodied as she expected.

"Freddie!" Cate scooted forward in her chair. "You made it. How is it?"

"How is it? *Fucking freezing.*" His yell competed with the sound of a rushing wind in the background.

Greg leaned towards Cate, whispering. "Remind him he's in the Gulf of Alaska."

Cate turned and scowled before spinning back to the speaker. "I owe you big time, Freddie. Did you get all the kit?"

"Yep, top of the line; spared no expense. And had a nice meal as well. Spent every penny you gave me." There was grating laughter.

"And another nice meal when I see you again, Freddie, promise. Are we just about ready?" Cate held up her hands, fingers crossed on both.

"Sure am, ran a test flight, and am just preparing to attach the spare relay beacons. Nice piece of tech, if I do say so myself."

"What'd you get?" Greg sat, sipping and listening.

"The DJI Phantom 2 with HERO4 GoPro – eye in the sky, baby." Freddie's voice bubbled with excitement.

Abigail mouthed, *wow*, then leaned forward. "Hi Frederick, this is Abigail Burke. Is that the quad copter version?"

21

"Hi Abigail. Call me Fred or Freddie; only mom calls me Frederick, and that's only when she's pissed at me. And you bet it is; Phantom Quadcopter v2.0, with gimbal control dial and built-in battery, compass, thermal reader, full hour flying time, and relay drop-crane for WiFi buoys – means when it enters zero line-of-sight areas like a cave, it can drop the relays, and continue to send and receive signals so we don't lose him."

"Cool, very cool," Greg said. "No wonder he blew the budget."

Cate clasped her fingers together on the desk. "Okay, Freddie, we're ready when you are."

"Then let's do this, and before I lose all feeling in my fingers and toes." There was muffled sound over the comm-link as Freddie fiddled with something, followed by a small electronic whine.

"Camera up."

Immediately the curved screen on their desk popped to life, showing nothing but a close up of rock, a scattering of snow, and some hardy lichens.

"Here we go." Cate sat back.

The image vibrated for a few seconds before stabilizing and lifting higher. The quadcopter swiveled in the air to show a freezing landscape, thankfully with manageable wind gusts. It continued its slow turn until they could see a young, Asian man on a small foldaway chair, heavily bundled up in a bulky parker, beanie, and with a large hood pulled up over the lot.

He had a box on his lap that contained two joysticks, numerous dials and toggles, and a small screen, whereby he was seeing the same feed as they were.

"Can you see me?" Freddie lifted a hand and waved.

"Can see and hear you loud and clear, Freddie. This is great." Cate grinned, waving back.

"Then we're good to go." He looked up at hovering drone. "Buzz, you ready?" Freddie made the camera tilt up and down as it whined mosquito-like above him.

"Okay, he's ready, so…" He pointed. "…to infinity and beyond."

Greg groaned.

Freddie kept the quadcopter hovering above him, and Cate shrugged her impatience.

"Cate, just remember, we have limited time. And if the drone loses power somewhere inaccessible, then it's staying."

"So go for it; we're just along for the ride," Greg said, pulling up his chair, and sipping coffee as if he were at a movie matinee.

"Along for the ride and paying the bills." The grating laugh again.

Greg mouthed: *I love this guy.*

Cate rolled her eyes and leant back in towards the screen. Abby had a pad on her lap, and pen poised. The images coming through were so sharp they looked more like they were seeing out of a window rather than an image feed from over ten thousand miles away.

"Status check, ladies and gentlemen." Freddie's voice became business-like. "We have a slight breeze of three knots from the south-southeast, temperature is a bracing three degrees, and time is 10:20 hours and counting."

The drone rose higher, and then moved towards the cliff edge. It lifted rapidly for a few seconds as it was caught in a sudden updraft, but the gyros kept the image balanced. It moved out over the lip, and then the drone started to drop.

Cate clicked her fingers at Greg. "Start recording."

"Will do." Greg crossed to one of the computers and hit a few keys and then returned to his seat. "Going to E-Drive. We can clean it up later."

The drone hovered for a moment more at the edge, turning back to Freddie one last time, who lifted an arm to wave goodbye, and then the drone turned back, and began its descent.

"Diorite batholith, quartz and some granite – damned

hard rock," Greg said, turning to Abby and raising his eyebrows.

"Very good, Professor Jamison." Abby smiled. "And it's old; there's exposed Jurassic-age plutonic rock I can see there. That's the result of the magmatic arc most probably created by the northwest-directed subduction. What I can see is hornblende gabbro through quartz monzonite, tonalite and quartz diorite." She smiled, disarmingly. "But like you said, damned hard rock."

He nodded, mock serious. "I was just going to say all that."

"Quiet, you two." Cate threw the words over her shoulder as she frowned at the screen.

There was a soft moan rising from the speakers as the wind moved across the cave mouth as the drone approached. The cave itself was a vertical tear in the rock, about ten feet high, and three wide – narrow.

"We going to fit in that?" Cate asked.

"Just." Freddie's voice was distracted.

The drone eased towards the dark opening, and immediately its brilliant lights blinked on. The darkness inside the cave was pushed back and the hovering machine moved carefully into the tear.

"Hold it there... *back up, back up*." Cate stood, sat back down, and then half stood again, her neck craned forward. "Slow, slow, rotate ninety degrees to your left."

The drone backed up to just inside the cave, and the turned in the air. The lights illuminated a large flat wall. The scratched message was still clear. She breathed the words as she read.

"Jim Granger went in here – 12 Oct 52."

Greg sat back. "So, this is not about your grandfather, huh?"

"I knew it." Cate made a fist. "I knew he came this way."

Freddie's voice filled the room again. "Interesting; outside it's just on three degrees, but temperature inside the cave mouth says it's fifty. That's a massive jump. Got a real hot zone in there somewhere. Okay guys, we're burning time, so gotta get moving. I'm taking Buzz in."

The drone moved slowly, the images now compressed down to the width of the cave entrance, until it opened out into a large flat room. Freddie swiveled the drone through a full three-sixty-degree turn.

"Looks to be about a hundred feet in here, give or take." The drone hung in the air for another few seconds, before zooming ahead. "There's another opening on the far side – going in." Freddie now whispered his words as if worried about being overheard. "You should be seeing a thermal readout beside your screen – temperature now about seventy degrees. I'm dropping a relay beacon, so we don't lose contact with Buzz."

The drone lowered for a moment, gently rose, and then tilted forward to show a small box on the ground with a green blinking light.

"Relay beacon 1, away. Good to go." The drone moved on, and they heard an intake of breath from Freddie as they approached another narrowing in the cave. "Jesus, going to be tight; if we get wedged, we're done. Cate, give me a go/no-go on this; after all, it's your kit."

Cate didn't hesitate. "Go for it; that's why were all here." She checked the timer on the side of the image – they'd been flying for twelve minutes – so far so good. The drone eased in, the internal gyros keeping the small four-prop craft rock-steady.

"Going down now. Angle of descent is about twenty-five per cent. Cave now opening out. Thank you, oh god of the caves. Hey, guys, who was the god of the caves?"

"Lots of them," said Abigail. "Mostly minor Greek goddesses like Nyx, Hypnos, and Eileithyia, come to mind."

"Cool, all goddesses. I like it," Freddie said.

"And don't forget Hades... but he'll be deeper where it's nice and hot," Greg said, turning and winking at Abby.

"Hold it. Swivel left." Cate sat forward and then broke into a smile.

On the wall they could see an arrow and underneath, the initials 'J.G.'. Cate exhaled with satisfaction. "This is it."

"You said he went missing…" Greg glanced at her. "… so, um, Cate, you've got to be ready for what we find. He could still be in here – or what's left of him."

Cate stared straight ahead. "Even if he was there, it would be closure, nothing more." She gripped the desk edge. "*Whoa…*"

"Well, well, well, looks like your grandfather wasn't the only one in here; this place was a regular Central Station." Greg straightened in his seat.

The drone illuminated the cave wall, showing ancient rock art images of small human figures, fish, sharks, turtles, and other creatures that were unidentifiable. Natives either speared them, or were themselves pulled into the water, and attacked.

"Awesome," Abby breathed. "And old."

"Must be Nantouk," Greg said. "But this looks almost prehistoric. How long have they been here?"

"Around ten thousand years, but before them, who knows." Cate's mouth hung open in an awed smile.

The next narrow fissure took five full minutes to navigate, but this one opened to a large flat room with evidence of a recent rock fall at its edges. But that wasn't what held their attention – at its center was a dark, gaping hole in the cave floor.

"You seeing this, Cate?" Freddie sounded breathless. "The wall, do you see?"

"Yes." Cate had her nose only inches from the screen. "Blackened. There's been an explosion of some sort… and fairly recent."

"Yep, and it's also damned hot in here. There's an updraft coming from that big cavity." The drone went and hovered over the hole, and it was buffeted slightly, even with the gyros working to keep it level.

"Can't get a reading. No idea how deep it goes." Freddie let out a huge juddering breath. "It's freezing."

"The cave? The hole?" Cate frowned.

"No, but I wish I was in that nice warm cave. I can't feel my fingers anymore."

They could hear another exhalation, and Cate pictured her friend blowing on his fingertips.

"Guys, we now have ten minutes of time left... and we'll need most of that to get Buzz back to us. Sorry, time's up." Freddie started to back the drone up.

Cate sat staring at the screen for a few more seconds, her mind working. There was no other exit from the cave other than that hole. There had been an explosion and the edges of the hole looked raw, new, so she bet her last dollar that her grandfather fell in, or travelled into that damn pit.

"Why?" she sat back.

"*Huh*, why what?" Freddie asked.

Cate shook her head, sitting forward. "Freddie, you know what? I don't really want a drone. What I really want is to know what's in that hole, and why Jim Granger went in there." She folded her arms, knowing she was about to kiss her investment goodbye.

"But..." Freddie sighed. "Wow, okay Professor, you're the boss lady. Dropping the last relay beacon."

He moved the drone to the edge of the hole, and let another of the small boxes fall to the cave floor at its edge. Then he lifted over the stygian dark void. He tilted forward, but there was nothing but blackness filling the screen.

Cate imagined this was what it would be like if you were in deep space, and came across a black hole – no light, no sound, no nothing – there was just the absence of everything.

Greg nudged her. "If you gaze long enough into an abyss, the abyss will gaze back into you." He grinned. "Ready?"

She nodded dreamily. "Let's do this. Freddie, take it in."

"Aye aye, Captain, taking her in." They passed over the lip of the hole, and continued to drop. "Going to use full illumination as I guess we don't need to save any power for a return journey."

Extra lights came on, but there was still nothing but darkness. Numbers scrolled up on the side of their screen showing descent rate – fifty feet, one hundred, five hundred, six… the rate of drop was accelerating as Freddie let gravity take over.

"*Whoa*, we're now well below the lake's water level. Must be some sort of partition between it and what's down there. And this cavern is big, real big! Buzz has pinged it and estimates it to be about a mile long and half that wide – and that's just above the water line."

"Plenty of humidity," said Abby, pointing with a pencil to the scrolling numbers.

A glowing set of bars appeared on the bottom of their screen – there was ten – eight were red, and only two green. It was a warning, and while they watched one more went to red.

"Shit, we're gonna lose Buzz. We're getting too far from the last signal relay buoy," Freddie said.

"Good, it's been boring as hell; wall to wall darkness," Greg added. "Hey, Freddie, what happens if we do lose contact with the drone?"

"We'll either just drop out of the sky, or Buzz flies away by himself." Freddie laughed. "He'll be free from us clumsy humans to sail away into the wild black yonder of a brave new world."

"Thank you, Freddie, very dramatic. But how much time have we got left?" Cate frowned at the screen.

"Time? I'm guessing another few more minutes, and then it's bye bye Buzz." Freddie sounded like he blew more air on his fingers. "We'll probably lose rotor and navigation control first, because it feeds off the strongest signal. But we'll have some of the sensor and analytics for a little longer."

"What about our eyes – the HERO4 GoPro camera has a separate signal, doesn't it?" Abby asked. "Will that continue to function?"

"Yeah, good question, Abby. As it's got its own WiFi frequency and battery, maybe that might still record and transmit, after everything else is gone. We'll find out real soon, won't we?"

The drone continued to drop, its level at eight hundred and fifty feet when the screen began to fizz with snow.

"Okay, I'm losing him. Going to switch over the HEROs frequency and try and lock the controls so it simply continues to drop without sailing off into a rock wall or something. Here goes..."

The screen went from static filled darkness, to complete dead black and there was nothing but the sound of Freddie breathing. Then suddenly the drone's small halogens came back on, lighting nothing but walls of dark. Half the data readouts on Cate's screen had vanished, with just chemical analysis, sonar and the camera still working.

"Worked, but we've lost thermal, sound and navigation. At least we can see, taste our environment, and also work out how big it is. But I've got no idea how fast we're dropping or where we are at the moment. We've got visual markers only from now on... that's if we get any at all."

They waited, and then there came a crazed jostling from the screen images.

"I think we've hit something, or landed," Freddie said.

The image stabilized, and then they could make out the black water, washing up over the camera lens. Cate hurriedly read off some of the details.

"Salt water, I knew it." She turned and high-fived Greg before turning back to her screen.

"Holy shit, look at that sonar readout." Cate whooped again. "The cavern above is only about a mile wide, but this body of water is not even returning a signal on two of its sides – it's off the goddamned charts... and it's deep. A few hundred feet deep here, but drops down thousands farther in."

The water level that had been half way up the lens, and the only indication of something visual on their screen, bubbled for a moment, and things went dark – not solid black like last time, as there were still tiny flecks illuminated in the beams of the halogen lights.

"Dammit, we're sinking," Freddie groaned.

The rest of the readouts disappeared, and just the camera's signal continued to send images that were strong enough to be received by the relay buoys high above it. But mostly there was silence and darkness with the occasional tiny glowing fleck scudding by.

"Look!" Cate's loud voice was so sudden, it made Greg and Abby jump in their seats.

Her fists balled at her chest as she lunged forward, grinning madly. A tiny krill-like organism flicked itself past the screen. It looked like a striped slater bug, but its tiny arms rowed like a set of oars past them and continued on past their line of sight.

"Life," Cate whispered.

"No big deal," Greg said softly. "Many cave pools and underground lakes have some sort of albino shrimp or water nymphs. If we're lucky, we might come across some tiny blind eelettes as well."

"Yes, I know, but many of my esteemed colleagues who agreed there could be giant bodies of water hidden deep below the earth thought they'd be some sort of thick chemical sludge, and way too toxic to support life. But there it is, and notice something? That small creature has fully functional eyes, and is color banded. Means it can see and is subject to some sort of light source. We have no idea what the environment is like down here yet." Cate turned. "Buzz's sonar said there wasn't even a return signal on some sections of the submerged cavern – do you know how big something has got to be, to not return a sonar ping?"

Greg rolled his eyes. "Yeah, yeah, miles, I know."

"Sixty thousand feet give or take." Abby put her pencil down. "About twelve miles, before horizon drop."

"Thank you, Abby, and that's only where it loses strength. My satellite mapping has the thing charted at hundreds of miles – trillions of gallons of pristine seawater. That's no lake, that's an underground sea." She sat back, feeling a dreamy light-headedness.

"Was this what you were looking for, Pop? This hidden sea world?"

"Cate, Buzz is fading fast; losing signal strength," Freddie said in a rush. "And just as well I guess. I need to get home and thaw out my little bits before they all drop off."

"Sure." Cate slumped back, sighing. "I wish I was there."

"About to lose image." Freddie spoke distractedly as if he was focusing on something else. "Going to switch on all lights, as any remaining power is useless anyway. Okay Buzz, thanks for the show, and so long buddy."

Immediately the dark water with the milky halo of light flared brighter and wider. More detritus snow filled the screen, and more scudding miniature shrimp. Cate half smiled, and began to sit forward, her chin resting on her palms, intent on savoring the last of the live images from the deep subterranean sea.

"*Shit!*"

Freddie's yell burst from the speakers, and was like an electric shock jolting her from her seat, making Abby scream, and causing Greg to spray a mouthful of coffee onto the desk.

A cavernous maw opened in front of them, coming out of the stygian gloom like an express train, to gape wider and wider. There were flashes of white, and then the signal died. It didn't just fade or whiteout, instead it was abruptly shut off.

The three of them sat in stunned silence for several seconds, mouths hanging open, and eyes round.

Cate shut her mouth and swallowed. "What... just... happened?" She got slowly to her feet.

"Did you fucking see that?" Freddie's voice was several pitches higher. "*Did you?*"

Cate's mouth worked but no words came.

"Yes, but what *did* I just see?" Greg also stood, his eyes going from the screen to Cate and then back.

"Did we just get sucked into another cave?" Abby frowned, her bottom lip pulled into her mouth.

"No, I don't think so," Cate said softly, feeling her scalp tingle. "I think, more like the cave came for us." She turned to Greg. "I think we just got eaten."

It was late, 9:00pm, and the university halls were empty save for the distant throaty roar of a vacuum cleaner in one of the other rooms.

Cate rewound and re-ran the drone's footage over and over – enlarging, enhancing, and freeze-framing the images. When she had the clearest frame she could extract, she sat back in her chair, exhausted, but exhilarated, and stared hard at her result – the triangular shape, the serrations, the color, she knew what it looked like to her, but dared not give voice to her thoughts.

She wished there was some way to get some scale, but there was nothing to benchmark it against – the item could be an inch or a foot long. Still, it seemed to have swallowed Buzz whole, and the drone was nearly as round as a manhole cover. She folded her arms, clicking her tongue against her teeth as she weighed up options. Bottom line, she needed to be there. She also needed advice, and knew just the person she should get it from – Jack Douglas Monroe.

She hadn't spoken to Jack for over three years. He had

been her best friend, companion, confidant, and once lover – her face went hot as an image of them intertwined flashed into her mind.

At the time, she thought he was going to be *the one*. He was *supposed* to be *the one*, she thought. But he was never there; being a marine biologist he was forever out on the blue water somewhere. He had often wanted her to go with him, but, well, her own work and ambitions took precedence. She never went, even once. And then she saw the photos in the Spanish newspaper of the latest dive he was on, the new ray species he had found, and of course, next came the pictures of the bikini girl draped all over him. While she thought he was *the one*, seemed she was probably the *one of the many*.

She let her mind float her back on a daydream to that last time they had been together. She had invited him over, but not for what he had expected. Jack had turned up at her door with a bottle of wine, and his usual silly grin. She let him in, and he leant to kiss her but she turned away.

"What's wrong?" he had asked, eyebrows up.

She had been ready, locked and loaded, and she strode to her desk, spinning her computer around that displayed the image of him and the girl on the boat. "Nothing's wrong… if you think I'm an idiot."

His face closed down, and he put the bottle on her desk. "That's Angelina, she's only a friend. A biologist who was working with me on—"

"I know what she as working on." Cate quickly pulled up the woman's Facefriend page, showing her posts about the dates she had with the tall and handsome American marine biologist. Cate spun back to him, folding her arms and feeling her anger rise to volcanic levels.

Jack saw it. "Oh, good grief." He threw up his hands. "We had a few drinks; that's all."

"Bullshit." Her arms tightened across her chest as though locking her fury in tight.

He shook his head. "No it isn't, and you know what? I asked *you* to come, but you never did… in fact, you *never* do."

"Lucky for you, it seems." She loathed his deflections and his lies.

"This is stupid." Jack's brows snapped together as his own storm began to brew. "If you just wanted to vent, you could have done that over the phone."

"Get out before I say something I'll really regret." She nodded to his wine. "And take your cheap booze with you."

"Keep it. You can drown your sorrows, alone." He spun, and headed for the door, slamming it behind him. She had saluted his departure by launching the bottle from her window, missing him by mere inches. "*Don't come back,*" she had screamed.

Cate titled her head back and exhaled long and slow through compressed lips as she returned to the present. In the blink of an eye, it was over. She hated him then. And then later hated herself for losing something she valued so dearly. Both of them had been too stubborn to reach out to the other, and then their roads split. She hadn't seen Jack in years, but the ghost of their past love still haunted her. Her face went hot all over again, and she was surprised the old anger was still there.

Never, ever again, she thought. That was one bridge she had burned, blown up, and then buried a mile deep. She'd find another shark expert.

Cate saved the image of the tooth to her local drive, and shut her computer down. She stood and stretched, feeling the fatigue settle heavily on her limbs. She needed sleep; she needed to be sharp. Tomorrow there was one more person left to convince if she was going to get funding to enter that body of water before anyone else.

CHAPTER 2

Cate ended her presentation, leaving up the image of the tooth on the large screen behind her.

"All indications are it's a mega predator, *we think*. In a significant body of water, deep below the surface, and sealed off from environmental interference." She smiled confidently at her boss, Bill Harris, the only person in the room. "Imagine what this can tell us about climate change, evolution, and ancient species. This is what we've been looking for, Bill – proof of life – *pristine, ancient life.*"

Bill Harris had been the Faculty Head of Biology for twenty years, and been Greg and Cate's boss for the last three. He sat stone still, his large hands clasped together on the desk before him.

"Certainly interesting." He nodded slowly, keeping his eyes on the image.

She felt a knotting in her stomach. He wouldn't meet her eyes – a bad sign. "Just interesting? It's damn astounding is what it is." She hiked the corners of her mouth up, trying to radiate enthusiasm.

He sucked in a deep breath, and then winced. "*Yeeah,* I'll grant you, it's probably a life form, but what you've shown me is indistinct, impossible to verify, and—"

"And I think it's a whole world down there; untouched and waiting for us to explore. This could change our knowledge about everything. We need to get back there and do a full exploratory – before anyone else. I've put some basic numbers together." She hurriedly turned to her computer and called up a spreadsheet. She spun back to him.

Bill had a single hand up. "I think that's enough for today, Cate. Thank you."

"If I get a modest draw down, a hundred thousand, I can assemble a team, and be up there within a month." She knew she was beginning to talk too fast.

"Cate..." His sounded fatigued.

"Everything we find will have Stanford U's name on it." She was losing him.

"*Cate...* there is *no* funds to be drawn down on." His expression was grave.

She felt deflated, and searched his face, looking for anything encouraging. There was nothing. "So, you're saying, just not now, then?"

"No Cate, not now, and not ever, I'm afraid. There's something else." A muscle in his jaw twitched. "There's no demand for evolutionary biology anymore." He sighed. "I'm sorry; the board has already decided... we're going to have to shut down your Department."

Cate pushed open the door so hard it slammed into the wall, knocking out a chip of plaster.

"I knew it. *The bastards.*" She gritted her teeth.

"Well, that doesn't sound promising." Greg frowned.

"*Bastards!*" Cate repeated, feeling a tension headache coming on.

"Let me guess; budget cuts?" Greg had to jog to keep up with her.

"Budget cuts? More like fucking Cate and Greg cuts." She banged a fist into her leg as she strode down the hallway, her face like thunder. People stepped out of her way, students and staff alike parting like the Red Sea before her. She pulled up, stopping so suddenly Greg banged into her back.

"Hey, what did you mean about *Cate and Greg,* cuts?" He tried to get in front of her.

"Nothing, like you said; budget cuts." She couldn't bring herself to tell him just yet that he was also out of a job. There had to be another angle she could pursue, and her mind worked furiously.

She clicked her fingers. "I'm an idiot; I should have said we were going to explore the effects of climate change on newly discovered species." She went to turn around, head back into his office, but Greg grabbed her arm.

"Forget it, Cate. We should have known this would be low priority when there are dozens of researchers fighting for funding. Besides, a hundred grand was going to be well short of what we really needed. Think about it; we'd need to be there for at least a week, maybe more. We'd need an underwater camera on some type of submersible platform, new computer equipment, food, accommodation, flights, and on and on." Greg sighed. "We would have been capital-light by a mile to begin with."

Cate stood hands on hips, her eyes sharp. "Maybe, but it would have gotten us there… and gotten us there *first*."

"No maybe. *Definitely*. And then we'd be spending days just filling out paperwork and reports. Stanford would own everything." He began to turn away, but paused and then eased back. "You know what you really need? Some sort of sponsor, or funding partner, independent of the university."

Cate straightened. "A partner?" she stared off down the hall, the gears in her mind turning again.

"Sure," Greg said. "I bet Bill was onboard with the concept, but just doesn't have the funds. If we…"

Cate turned so quickly, Greg flinched. "I could kiss you."

"Uh, thanks?" he smiled, brows knitted.

She sped off, half turning as she went. "Meet you back at the lab. I've got to send someone an invitation they can't refuse."

Cate sat in the foyer of the gleaming silver spire that rose a hundred and ten floors above the center of New York City. She licked her lips and her hands gripped the armrests of the soft chair, and beneath her, her feet tapped insistently on the dark marble floor. The reception desk was like the floor – marble, and expensive she bet. There was glass and chrome everywhere, and on walls and pedestals there were works of art with small nametags underneath, each bearing the moniker of artists she had never heard of or could even attempt to pronounce.

She sighed, heart hammering in her chest. If the opulence was designed to make someone feel intimidated, it was sure working on her.

The person she had come to see was Valery Konstantin Mironov, a Russian-born businessman who didn't exactly have a rags-to-riches story, rather a riches to even more riches story. He was one of the Russian oligarchs who made too many enemies in his homeland and decided to emigrate. The guy was worth billions and was now reputed to be the eighth richest man in the country. That made him interesting, but of little relevance to Cate. However, what did make him an outstanding person for her to seek out was his passion and hobby.

Mironov was the only person anywhere, anytime, to have a fish tank in one of his homes that was the size of two Olympic swimming pools. What made the tanks astounding was what he had in it – two coelacanths, the living fossil fish found in the Indian Ocean shallows and thought to have been extinct for sixty-six million years. The man's hobby was fossil hunting, collecting, and anything to do with the Earth's primordial past

Cate had sent the Russian a letter containing a polite request – all included with the film she had shot in the subterranean sea recently. She'd taken a risk sending proprietary university property, but she knew it was the only way to get his attention. And after all, as her grandfather always used to say in his letters, *without risk there was no reward.*

"Ms Cate Granger?"

Cate swung around at her name. The young woman was exceptionally tall with perfect cheekbones and eyes that were a luminous blue. She immediately made Cate feel like an ugly duckling. Another way to intimidate guests, she thought, beginning to detest Valery Mironov already.

"Yes." She got to her feet, smoothing her jacket. "*Professor* Cate Granger."

"Of course. I'm Sonya Borashev, Mr Mironov's personal assistant." She held out a hand that Cate shook quickly, noticing how calloused the tall woman's palm was. She then she motioned to the private elevator. "Mr Mironov will see you now."

Cate nodded, swallowed and followed the woman, noticing that every item of clothing she wore was designer and immaculate. She bet the woman's pay as an assistant outstripped Cate's own as a tenured professor by a country mile. But was Sonya happy? Cate wondered, her mouth curving into a smile.

"Ms Borashev, Valery Mironov; can I ask where you met him?" Cate looked away, expecting Sonya Borashev's answer to be from some professional executive pool, while she waited for her name to go up in lights on Broadway.

"I was recruited by Mironov Enterprises five years ago," Sonya said, slowing as they approached an elevator door. She stopped and turned. "Straight from Harvard, where I was majoring in physics."

Cate suddenly felt even smaller beside the woman. Sonya smiled briefly and then nodded to the two men standing beside the elevator, who turned and both inserted a key into an identical slot either side of the doors at the same time. The doors *shushed* open, the car already waiting, and Cate and Sonya stepped in. Inside it smelled of lavender, wood paneling, and the tall woman's expensive perfume.

As the car rose, Cate worked hard at slowing her breathing. She was already made nervous by the displays of wealth and power, and was determined to project confidence to Mironov, not some sort of freshman skittishness. The elevator glided higher without a sound and only a hint of increasing gravity. She shut her eyes for a moment, thinking over her pitch. If it failed, she had no idea what other options she might have.

Cate tried to think of something calming and immediately Jack Monroe's face popped into her head. He always knew what to say. She sighed and opened her eyes, noticing Sonya looking down at her.

Cate cleared her throat. "So, he's a good boss?"

Sonya's glossy lips curved slightly. "The best." She continued to study Cate for a moment. "He is also a very busy man, and needs to be on a plane in a few hours. You must be brief, and to the point."

Cate nodded, feeling suddenly under pressure. "He gets a lot of these, huh?"

Her face softened. "No, in fact, he gets *none* of these. He never sees anyone like this; you must have really piqued his interest."

Cate brightened as she felt the elevator slow. The door shushed open again, and just like on the foyer, another pair of enormous men waited either side of the door. *Valery liked his security.* Must be a Russian thing.

The statuesque assistant led Cate to a huge set of double doors, with 'AKM' in calligraphic-style crest on a band of gold across the panels. She paused, giving Cate a genuine smile.

"You'll do fine. Good luck." She pushed open the door and stood back, not entering herself.

Cate sucked in a deep breath and walked in.

The first thing she noticed was the echo of her heels in the cavernous space. The lighting was soft, and the decorations sparse. There were a few islands of furniture –

a huge antique desk that must have been twenty feet long, and a dark burgundy leather couch. But what drew her eyes was one entire wall was made of glass, a shimmering blue, and behind it, there were all manner of strange creatures gliding past. It must have contained an enormous amount of water as further into its depths clarity was lost in a deeper blue haze. Sea grasses swayed in an artificial current, and sand floored one side, building to weed-covered boulders in another, giving the whole scene a natural habitat quality.

Two eel-like fish sinuously approached the front of the tank to eye her, and Cate stepped closer to return the examination.

"Incredible," she whispered. Both creatures were a little over a foot long, and had thick scales like armor plating. Along their backs was a tall, serrated dorsal fin like some sort of ancient dimetrodon dinosaur.

"*Polypterus Senegalus.*" The voice was deep, with the hint of a Russian accent.

Cate nodded without turning. "The dinosaur eel; very rare, very aggressive."

"What else?" the voice asked.

Cate smiled, enjoying the game. "Native to tropical African waterways, and have primitive lungs – they can leave the water for short periods of time. A true evolutionary transitional form." She felt the man come up behind her, and examined his reflection in the tank. He was tall, thin, and younger than she expected, and with a perfectly manicured Hemmingway-style beard.

"Very good, Professor Granger."

"Was that a test?" she asked, turning.

Mironov shrugged. "Only a handful of people in the country could have recognized those fish for what they are."

He stuck out his hand, and Cate grasped it. His palm was leathery, dry, and told of a man who worked with weights, wood, or maybe even rope – a sailor, she bet.

"Valery Konstantin Mironov – call me Valery." He turned and motioned to the couch. She saw there was a coffee pot waiting.

Cate stole one more look at the tank, and then followed him to sit. Mironov lifted a remote from a slot in the armrest and pointed it at a wall. A panel slid back and then a screen appeared. The image flickered, and then came to life. It was her footage. He froze it at the image of the tooth, and laced his fingers in his lap.

"And this was taken in a sealed subterranean cavern, deep beneath the surface of the west Alaskan coast?" He watched her carefully. "And no one else knows about this?"

"The local Nantouk people have probably known about it for ten thousand years." Cate tilted her head. "But other than my close colleagues, then no, no one else is aware of what this potentially is."

"And what is it?" Mironov's ice-blue eyes were unblinking.

She turned back to the screen. "An alpha predator, living in a massive body of water that is of tropical temperature, and one that could have been sealed off from the outside world for hundreds of thousands or maybe even many millions of years."

"A mutation then?" Mironov tilted his head.

"Perhaps, but I think it is more likely something caught in an evolutionary cul-de-sac. A creature has been frozen in time by a benign and unchanging environment… a remnant species."

Mironov stared for a moment. "Sometimes evolution…" he turned to her. "…or maybe God himself, tries things out. Sometimes they don't work, or God realizes He has made a mistake." He turned back to the screen. "And then these things get cancelled out. Some for good reason." He turned to her with a flat smile. "And now it is back."

"It never went away… just like the coelacanths you have at home." She raised an eyebrow as she sipped her coffee.

His mouth lifted into a smile. "Yes." He raised his cup, saluting her. "So, Ms Granger, this sounds like something you would kill for, *hmm*? Why aren't you already there, exploring, filming, negotiating television rights to a documentary?"

"You know why I'm here," Cate said, feeling irritation at the man's knowing smile. She bet he had done more to check on her bona fides than ask a few questions about rare fish. "My university hasn't the capital to fund an expedition right now. At least not in my lifetime."

"Perhaps not in a thousand lifetimes, I think." He smiled again.

She scoffed. "You know what?" Cate got to her feet. "I didn't come here to play games. This site could potentially hold Lazarus species that have been extinct on the surface world. There may be secrets of evolution that could be beyond anything we can ever imagine."

Mironov opened his hands and held them wide. "But you can't get there, and soon someone else will find the site, and then..." He made a small popping noise with his lips, and shrugged.

Cate looked back to the fish tank. "We know there is life there, and I believe a helluva lot bigger and more interesting than a dinosaur eel." She tilted her head, her lips curved into a confident smile.

His mouth turned down, and he turned back to her image of the serrated tooth on the screen. "Maybe, but without scale, it might be nothing more than a few blind salmon trapped in a cave."

Cate shook her head. "Well, that blind salmon took out all our equipment. So no, I think it's something damned substantial." She narrowed her eyes. "And so do you... or I wouldn't be here. Whatever it was, we need to check it out – fully map the location, document what we find and do a hands-on exploratory. Be first in, so we can save the habitat, before someone else exploits it."

Mironov's eyes narrowed. "Hands on? You want to go in; scuba tanks?"

Cate shook her head. "No. This body of water is so huge it has its own horizon. It'd be a cave dive of unprecedented proportions, and way too big for a free dive. I'm betting it will also have a million places to get lost or hooked up, so a remote vehicle would more than likely become snagged and lost." She shrugged. "But, the only way to get any sort of accurate sonar mapping and research done, and have immediate decision-making capability is to be there, in person. And yeah, sure, I want to go." She shook her head again. "No, *I intend to go.*"

Mironov's smile returned. "Those that lead and do not take risks themselves, cannot truly expect their followers to also take risks." He steepled his fingers and leant forward. "And what type of budget did you have in mind? Ballpark?"

She inhaled deeply. *Think big.* "A million dollars."

He nodded slowly, his brows up. "A million dollars?" Mironov eased back into his chair. "And you will need a submarine. *Hmm?* Or do you already have one?" One eyebrow remained up.

Cate tried to appear relaxed as she also eased back into the soft leather. She shook her head slowly, but smiled. "We have nothing but our expertise, and the location."

He tilted his head. "I already know the location. It took me all of a few minutes to have your communication traffic accessed and then pinpoint the conversations you had with your colleague, Mr Frederick Wan Ling, on Baranof Island."

She stood, anger flaring. "Listen, I didn't come here with a begging bowl. I came here because I admire your dedication and interest in ancient species. I assumed you'd be an ideal and enthusiastic sponsor. I'm thinking now I was wrong."

Mironov never flinched. "What's in it for me?"

Cate paused, analyzing the question. She had assumed that just being involved was enough for the man. After all, he didn't need fame, money, recognition, or a new circle of friends. She folded her arms. "Knowledge, *unique knowledge*. To a man like you, a million dollars is a small investment for that type of payoff."

"A million dollars?" Mironov rose from the couch. "So, I think you would need a multi-man submersible with potential deep-sea capability, a crew, specialists, and supplies. You would need to excavate into the cavern void with sophisticated mining equipment – you'd need a team of specialists for that. You would also need to sink communication relay silos along the way. You would need transportation costs for personnel and equipment, and also be undertaking your project in an extreme environment. All up, I estimate an initial investment requirement of one hundred and fifty million US dollars." He shrugged. "And possibly a lot more when it comes to retrieval." He turned an unblinking gaze on her. "Expensive price for knowledge, even *unique knowledge*."

Cate licked her lips, realizing he was right, and she had been thinking like an amateur in regard to her projections. *I've got nothing to lose.* "Yeah, one fifty million, expensive, sure, but not for you. So, in or out?" Cate held his gaze.

Mironov turned and walked to a huge window of darkened glass that overlooked the city. He clasped fingers together behind his back. "Those that lead and do not take risks themselves, cannot truly expect their followers to also take risks."

Cate smiled, immediately understanding. "You want to come."

He turned. "Like you said, we have a lot in common, Professor Granger."

"Cate." Her smile broadened, and she joined him at the window.

"Cate." He held out his hand. "Here's to unique knowledge."

She nodded. "Welcome aboard, Valery."

Valery Mironov sat staring into the depths of the huge, blue tank, watching the pair of dinosaur eels coil around each other. One slowed, its bony eye socket swiveling to regard him momentarily before it vanished into the deeper recesses of the contained lake.

"What do you think?" Sonya asked, standing beside him.

"Interesting." He pursed his lips.

"Interesting enough to spend all that money?" She asked her voice carrying a hint of caution.

He looked up and saw the concern in her eyes. "Sonya, I spend that much money on construction every year. And for that, I just get more buildings. But how many times do you get a chance to travel back in time?" He smiled, raising one eyebrow. "Yes, I think the investment is warranted."

"Full check?" She tilted her head.

"Yes, please. Full background check on Cate Granger and everyone close to her." He stood. "I'll have a hardware list for you soon."

"Valery, this will be very high risk." She reached out to place a hand gently on his forearm. He covered it with his own.

"I know, but when we feel our hearts racing fastest, then we know we are living life to its fullest." He patted her hand. "Go now, we have work to do."

Cate was back in California with Greg and Abby hovering over each of her shoulders as she typed up plans. "We need him."

Greg was pacing, but stopped and turned. "A Russian exile – are you kidding me? We need his money, sure, but we don't need him."

"Inseparable," Cate said without hesitation. "For the amount of exploration we want to do, and to do it properly, would require a good-sized submersible. I didn't even stop to think how we were going to get the submersible into that underground sea – Valery pointed out that we'd need a damn big hole to lower it into. That's engineering on a grand scale, with costs running into nine figures."

"But can't we assemble the submersible there? Drop it down in sections?" Greg asked.

Cate turned to him. "We're not talking about a flat-pack Swedish dining table, Greg. We need a hi-tech machine that will house several crew for up to twenty-four hours and be able to take us deep, even down to a potential crush depths." She turned back to the screen. "And as the digging is taking place over a cavern it needs all the excavation expertise we can muster. Or rather all the experts Valery Mironov can muster... and pay for."

"It's going to take time to source," Abby said. "Most civilian submersibles are only two-man operations, and deep-dive vehicles have a battery life of around twelve hours, max. So, where's he getting it?"

Cate shrugged. "Mironov said he had contacts and could organize it within sixty days; I trust him. Besides, what choice do we have? I did some quick research; if we wanted to get a sub that was suitable, it'd need to be built to spec – it'd cost us at least a year in wait time alone. I stopped counting when the numbers screamed past forty million."

"And that's his golden ticket, huh?" Greg asked.

Cate looked over her shoulder. "*Uh-huh*, but I get to pick my own crew... well, most of them."

"And that includes Mironov." Greg's lips came together.

"Get over it." Cate turned back to her screen. "This is really happening, so everyone better just lock and load, or step out of the way."

Abby grinned. "I can't believe you're able to stay so calm."

"Experience." Cate faked a smile, perspiration running down her sides.

CHAPTER 3

Brogidan Yusoff, head of the Russian Ministry of Resources and Agriculture, leaned in closer to Uli Stroyev – his second in charge – as he flicked through the printed folder of the satellite images intercepted from their American counterparts. The final one was a deep-earth penetration shot taken with a high-energy strategraphic sonar imager and then enhanced with computer graphics. It showed the vast body of liquid extending under Alaska, and well across the Bering Sea.

"So, Mr Stroyev, I think now we know what Valery Konstantin Mironov wants with one of our deep sea submersibles, *hmm*?"

"A little ocean trip, I think, Minister." Uli Stroyev smirked, watching as Yusoff's large head bobbed in enjoyment. The Minister had oversized, fleshy features, and heavy epicanthic folds over each eye giving him a slight Asian appearance that betrayed his Mongolian heritage.

Stroyev knew of the hatred Yusoff harbored for the wealthy defector. Valery Mironov had many run-ins with the Russian business and political establishments, but managed to stay on the right side of President Volkov through huge donations to the man and employing many of his children in prestigious, high-paying jobs. It was smart, and the only thing that saved his skin. But old enmities ran deep. The people who ran rival companies, and supported other politicians, detested Mironov for his inflexible approach to competition, and his willingness to bring rival's aberrant behavior to the attention of Volkov. In turn, the President got to be seen as stamping down hard on corruption, and made himself popular with the masses. The transgressors had their assets seized, and ended up in jail, while Mironov went from strength to strength.

Stroyev looked into the large, fleshy face of the minister, seeing the venomous hatred twisting his features. Brogidan Yusoff had been caught up in a foreign currency transaction that helped move the ruble, making him millions, but losing the country billions in export revenue. Mironov found out, reported it, and President Volkov paid Yusoff a personal visit. The minister had only stayed out of prison by signing over his hugely-profitable national construction business to the president, and also blaming his son for the illegal trading. The young man was still rotting in one of their forced labor camps.

Yusoff kept his job and his skin. All this while Mironov moved to America, with Volkov's blessing, and his own children got green cards?

Yusoff had lost a lot of political capital, money, and credibility. What remained was a hatred that burned deep. He had personally ordered Mironov's assassination, but the man had fled with his billions to the west, and while he was there, he was relatively safe. But once outside of his guarded towers, well, then his head belonged to Yusoff.

"It seems his hobby draws him out. He mounts an expedition to somewhere in Alaska, and now, at great expense, he has bought a Priz Class submersible, and hired a crew." Yusoff clasped one fist in another. "We must find out where."

"He gives us many clues. Mironov is also organizing an engineering team – miners and geologists." Stroyev tapped the screen's satellite image of the colossal body of subterranean water. "I think maybe it is not in Alaskan waters he plans his mission, but somewhere inland."

"What clues?" One of Yusoff's eyebrows lifted a folded eye a little wider.

"I have a friend… a miner. He told me once that the deeper you go into the earth, the hotter it gets – in fact, one-degree increase for every seventy feet you travel down. It is called a thermal gradient, I think, and it is why some deep mines are like blast furnaces. This underground body of water Mironov seeks is very deep in some places and will be much warmer than the outside temperature." Stroyev stroked his chin. "So we look for warmth in a frozen land; where it comes close to the surface, it will give itself away."

"Good." Yusoff's big head bobbed again. "Once the spider crawls from his hole, then he can be trapped. On the surface he will be guarded. But once he is in the submarine he is alone. You said he is hiring a crew? Maybe we should assist in picking that crew, *hmm?*"

"My thoughts exactly, Minister." Stroyev grinned. "But Mironov will be vigilant in running background checks on his chosen team members. Our man must be inserted later – perhaps as a substitute?"

"Go on." Yusoff leaned closer.

"There is someone, a commando who was a submariner. He is awaiting execution for murder. He could be adapted to our needs. He would be the perfect assassin," Stroyev assured.

"I want Mironov brought to me. I want to look him in the eye, and then blow his brains all over the wall, personally." Yusoff glared.

"You wish to do it yourself?" Stroyev's brows knitted.

"Yes. I have waited decades for this opportunity. This man we send, he must be prepared to do anything, everything, for this mission. Will he?"

"He could be made to kill for us," Stroyev said evenly.

"Not enough." Yusoff leant so close that Stroyev could smell beer and onions on the man's breath. "He must be prepared to go to hell and back, and bring that pig to me, alive. We need to ensure we have the right levers to pull to make this submariner dance to our tune."

Stroyev nodded, and rubbed his chin. "He has a family... poor. Perhaps we could tell him that when he has completed his mission, his record will be wiped clean, and his family will be well looked after – a new house, medical care?"

"If he thought there'd be a happy ending, then anything is possible." Yusoff sat back in his chair, his fingers steepled on his stomach. "But of course, once he has given us Mironov, then he is a risk. No one can be left alive – no loose ends."

Stroyev held his hands open. "Of course."

Yusoff grinned. "I don't care what it costs – make it happen."

Uli Stroyev typed his plans on his computer. He made lists: what skills he would need, from where, and how much it would cost to procure his assets. He also had to factor in which government officials and other bureaucrats he would need to bribe... or threaten. Yusoff had said he didn't care what it cost. That made success the only factor to consider.

He sat back, thinking through the logistics. One difficulty was getting his man inserted onto Mironov's crew list without being detected. But once that was achieved, then he could take control and steer the vessel to wherever was required. The other challenge was extracting Valery Mironov from a submersible in an underground sea.

Stroyev knew people could be transferred safely from a submersible even at extreme depths. They had docking tubes, and the larger models even had facilities built in to jettison a lifeboat pod.

But how would you extract someone from below the water that was also below the earth? He rubbed his chin, his mind whirring furiously now.

Yusoff owned a petroleum company that had a small

fleet of oil exploration ships. They needed to bore into the seabed all the time, and then extract oil from the depths. The technology was already there; it just needed to be adapted.

He would call an emergency meeting with the mining engineers. It might be possible – *no* – it would be. If Mironov could be extracted alive, then good. And if he died, well, Yusoff would be pissed but at least he would have the pleasure of knowing his old foe died while being crushed in a pipe miles below the ocean.

Stroyev reached for the phone; it was time these overpaid technocrats pushed some technological boundaries.

CHAPTER 4

Two Months Later

"All right, I'll bite, so, other than me, who made the cut for the Fantastic Voyage team?" Greg asked.

Cate stopped entering data on her screen, and sat back. "Sure, you're on the list, but it's going to be dangerous, so this is a voluntary gig. Could be a one-way trip."

"*Pfft.* Is that some sort of pre-mission pep talk? Sign me up." He grinned. "And think of all that overtime."

"I'm serious Greg." She swung around, staring into his face.

He held her gaze. "I am serious. As an evolutionary biologist, this is probably the biggest opportunity that will ever come my way. I'm definitely in."

"Good." Cate smiled and reached out to squeeze his arm.

"So, who else?" Greg tilted his head, brows raised.

"There will be a crew of seven. There'll be me, of course, and now you. And seeing it's a subterranean mission, we'll need a geologist, so Abby Burke is available to come. Valery Mironov is coming as a passenger, and he's already selected one other – a specialist."

Greg silently counted. "Okay, that's five; you said seven."

Cate swung back to her screen. "Valery obtained a new Russian Priz Class submersible – apparently the biggest, toughest Deep Sea Vehicle going around. He even managed to get a two-man engineering crew as part of the deal. So that makes seven."

Greg whistled. "Okay, I am now officially impressed." He leaned over her shoulder. "So, this new Russian boyfriend of yours; he's single?"

Cate laughed softly, but had wondered what it would be like to date a billionaire. "Don't be ridiculous, Professor Jamison; we're just friends." *But who knows what the future holds.*

"And the expert?" Greig straightened.

She turned to face him again. "Mironov suggested someone he knows, maybe a fellow Russian, with a unique skill set; a marine biologist who specializes in *Selachimorpha* – sharks."

CHAPTER 5

Kodiak Island, Kodiak Archipelago,
Former Russian Settlement

The submarine engineer downed another glass of vodka and checked his watch. He had plenty of time. Early next morning he was to board a helicopter that would drop him on Baranof Island to meet with his crewmembers, and another Russian submariner.

He snorted; he'd never worked with Americans before. He heard they were brash and loud, but soft. A little like children who had eaten too much sugar at a birthday party. He chuckled, and downed his vodka. Checking his watch again; he'd have another, and then get some sleep.

The Russian engineer's cabin was on the outskirts of a small settlement that was little more than a few dozen houses, a landing strip, and miles of jagged coast. He groaned and stood – he needed to piss first. He headed to the outhouse, unbuttoning his fly as he went. In the single toilet room, he pulled open his pants and was about to let a stream of urine go when the loop of wire slipped around his neck. It pulled tight in an instant, and his breath, blood flow and thinking was immediately cut off.

The last thing he knew was a pounding in his temples that was like monstrous drumbeats, and then someone whispering in Russian for him to be quiet, to relax, and let go.

He did.

The agent opened the door a crack; seeing no one outside, he quickly dragged the body back to the submariner's cabin. He sorted through the man's travel documents and identification, substituting his own for those that needed new facial photographs.

He then quickly sent a confirmation back to his controller – *mission was go*.

He grinned as he saw the small glass of vodka already poured, waiting. He lifted it, saluting, and downing it in one. He wiped his mouth, and then set to prising up the wooden floorboards. He'd bury the body under the cabin. With the coming winter, it would be months before the ground was warm enough to give up its stinking secrets.

He had hours before the helicopter to Baranof Island. He poured another vodka.

CHAPTER 6

The Bering Sea,
Ten miles west of the Baker-Shevardnadze Line
168 deg 58' 37'

Captain Boris Gorkin flicked the thick, unfiltered cigarette over the railing, where the freezing, iron-gray sea quickly swallowed it in its cap of froth and foam. The Russian drill ship, the *Viktor Dubynin*, was attached to the ocean floor by six sea anchors each weighing thirty thousand pounds and connected to the ship by steel cables two inches in diameter.

They were designed to hold it in place even in the roughest of conditions. But still the vessel bucked and pulled like a stallion refusing to be broken. The *Dubynin* was in an area of the Bering Sea that was just ten miles from the Russian-USA Maritime boundary, and in water that was shallow at only five hundred feet. Twelve thousand years ago this area was a land bridge between what is now Russian and Alaska, and had been honeycombed with caves.

Captain Gorkin looked westward, out over the freezing chop. Below the water, he would normally have feeder pipes already laid down and ready for them. The pipeline would be thirty inches in diameter and allow millions of gallons of under-pressure liquid to be extracted and then transported per minute. But that was for a standard petroleum extraction project.

The job their masters had told them to execute would be one of retrieval, and the pipes they used would be stouter, wider – fifty inches overall – and the pumping would be of a single object. It sounded to be more like sucking a tablet through a drinking straw; he grinned at the madness of it.

About two thousand feet below the sea bottom, they had been told to seek out a huge liquid bed the size of Lake Baikal. And now, the specialised ship was already penetrating the sea floor, its tungsten-tipped drill pushing through the hundreds of feet of ancient mud that had been laid down many millions of years before, and then on into the super-hard matrix that lay below it.

Blowout collars and numerous seals protected the drill shaft, as the liquid they expected to encounter would be under extreme pressure, and the risk of leakage was high. So far, the presence of the *Viktor Dubynin* raised no eyebrows, even so close to the Baker-Shevardnadze Line, as these roving ships either explored, sampled, or drilled on the shelf of their own continent every month of the year.

Gorkin pulled open the door, entering the warmth of the cabin. The subterranean liquid bed would soon be breached. The drill ship's crew of fifty men and women were confident they would be ready to accept the object within the next few days – provided it was in the right place. The entire operation would eventually cost many, many millions, but the promised bonuses would be huge.

Gorkin smiled; everything was going to plan, and the only thing left to consider was how to spend his money.

CHAPTER 7

Baranof Island, Granger Base Camp

Cate finally felt that her ass was coming back into shape after several hours on the unforgiving seat of the helicopter. She stretched her back again and looked out over the swarms of people, tents, and furiously-working machinery. It was hard to believe this was the site of the conversation they'd had with Freddie only a few months back. Now it more resembled a circus, complete with its own big-top – a gigantic, hundred foot tent-like structure erected over the hole that was being cut, drilled, and excavated down to the huge cavern she knew existed below them.

Getting approval to excavate, let alone be here, was something Cate hadn't even thought about. And when she did, she assumed it would be impossible to achieve. But Valery Mironov had contacts, and his assistant, Sonya Borashev, had the ideas. It turned out that getting an exploration license for geothermals was relatively easy – you tell the Alaskan government you're looking for oil, they'll tell you to go to hell. You tell them you're looking for a cheap, renewable energy resource, and they'll invite you to dinner.

She smiled as she watched the workers move about quickly and efficiently, all in bright red high-visibility coveralls, looking like some sort of gigantic swarm of army ants crawling over their nest.

Cate was the last of the team in. Valery Mironov, his specialist, Sonya, Greg and Abby, plus the two submersible engineers were already onsite... somewhere.

She grimaced at the sound of grinding that could be felt as well as heard, as diamond-tipped cutters made short work of the diorite and granite layers. She nodded, satisfied, and turned to flip back the door flap of their tent. Greg and Abby turned to nod to her, and Sonya continued to stare at a small screen.

"Excellent work." Jack Monroe turned to her. "You've managed to take a shot of something using the same camera they must use to snap pictures of Bigfoot and Nessie." He gave her *that* grin she both hated and loved.

She stared, feeling like a bolt of electricity ran right through her. Her mouth hung open, and she had to consciously snap it shut.

"What... the hell... are you doing here?"

"He's my specialist, of course." Valery Mironov entered the tent. He was whip-thin, but looked fit and elegant in his coverall uniform. "I'm sure I told you I'd be bringing one."

Cate rounded on Mironov, jerking a thumb back at Jack. "But not *that* one."

"Thanks, and no offence taken." Jack still grinned.

"I wanted the best, and Mr Monroe *is* the best." He looked from Cate to Jack, and then back to Cate, a single eyebrow raised. "I hope you two professionals won't find working together a problem?"

Jack held up his hands. "I'm fine with it."

I'll *bet* you are, she thought and steamed, feeling her heart race. The damned thing was she couldn't yet tell if it was from anger at being ambushed, or from excitement. She decided to play it cool, and worked at relaxing her features. She smiled. "No, no problem at all." She held out her hand to Jack. "I was just a little surprised is all. Good to see you again."

"Same." Jack grabbed her hand, and shook it.

His hand felt hot, and her heart rate went up another few beats.

"Excellent." Mironov clapped, and then turned. He spoke quietly in Russian to Sonya who nodded and laughed softly. He then crossed to the others. "Greg Jamison and Abigail Burke, I believe." Mironov shook hands with each and then returned to Cate, taking her by the arm and leading her away a few paces. He bent and lowered his voice.

"It is good to see you again, Cate. I hope I didn't embarrass you, but time was short, and I needed the best. There simply is no time to worry about emotional politics."

She waved it away. "Forget it; when did you get here?"

"Hours ago; I've been checking on a few things, making sure that our submersible was shipshape. As you know, this investment is expensive, and I'm sure we all want to get the maximum benefit from it." He checked his watch. "And I still have a few things to coordinate. So I'll leave you to it." He saluted her, and his mouth just curved into a smile as his eyes slid to Jack. Mironov nodded to the rest of team and then left. Sonya followed him out.

"So, that was the boss, huh?" Greg said as the tent flap closed.

"No," Cate said, turning to him, and then Jack. "On this trip, *I'm* the boss."

Jack also saluted. "Sir, yes sir." He pointed back to the computer screen. "Now, about that drunken picture of yours." Seeing her scowl, he waved her down. "Just pulling your pigtails, Cate. It's an exciting image, especially given it's from some sort of troglodytic species." He straightened coming to his full six feet two inches. "There's a lot of motion blurring, but if, as you said, this camera took the footage at fifty frames per second, then whatever that is, must have been coming at you at significant speed. Definitely a tooth though, and from the shape, I'd swear it was a Great White."

"I knew it was a tooth." Cate made a fist.

"Oh yeah." Jack nodded. "Triangular shape, serrated

edge, definitely an upper tooth of the Carcharodon species. This thing is used for cutting up large prey. We've got no perspective to judge proportions, so it could be any size."

"Sharks don't live in caves. So what else could it be?" Greg's brows were drawn together.

Jack shrugged. "Something I've never seen, maybe. Can't tell all that much from a few blurred frames. But, just to walk you back there, Mr Jamison, nurse, epaulette, horn, to name just a few sharks, can all live in caves, and many shark species only hunt in the dark. These things are amazing creatures. They're very ancient, and been around for hundreds of millions of years. They can adapt quickly to changing environments – light versus dark, salt versus fresh, warm versus cold." Jack folded his arms across his chest. "In fact, the bigger guys who hunt at great depths have to quickly adjust to changing cold, light, salt, pressure, almost instantly."

Greg shrugged. "So do whales."

Jack nodded. "But the sharks have an advantage – they don't need to surface. Big ol' whale dives deep looking for squid, instead finds a hungry Great White already down there."

"I always wondered about that." Abby came closer. "In the depths it's always permanent darkness, so how exactly do they see what they're going after? Sense of smell?" Abby tilted her head; her eyes glistened as they fixed on the tall and handsome marine biologist.

Abby's attention irritated Cate. But she also saw that Greg's eyes narrowed, and he eased forward before Jack could respond. "Super senses." He smiled confidently. "Sure, they have eyes but don't need them to hunt. They can sorta feel electrical impulses and vibrations in the water. Right, Jack?"

Jack nodded. "Very good, Mr Jamison; the shark's snout is a veritable factory of sensory organs, many of them we are only just now working out what they do and how they do it."

"It's Greg; just call me Greg." He gave a slight bow, his eyes on Abby.

Jack grinned. "Greg it is then."

"And Abby." She gave him a wide grin and stuck out her hand.

Jack shook it, and the young geologist hung on for a few seconds longer than Cate liked. Suddenly everyone seemed gathered around Jack, while she, the mission leader, was standing by herself.

"Okay, when you three have finished bonding," Cate glared momentarily at Greg and Abby, and then looked down at the image on her screen. "Bottom line, which no one here is disputing, is it's probably a unique species, living in a remote and untouched environment. We need to ensure it stays that way."

"Works for me," Jack said.

"If we can find the creature again and document it, then we can seek a protection order over the entire subterranean body of water – have it set aside as a no-go zone like we've done with some of the last pristine reefs and estuaries. Then as the primary discoverers, we can apply for a solitary research license – it'll be all ours for years."

Cate stood and looked at her wristwatch. "Okay, lets' move this along. Jack and I will check on excavation work. It's due for completion within the next six hours. Once that's done, we'll be preparing for the drop. As we discussed on the chopper, the sub's being checked over now – I don't need to tell you how critical this is, because on a deep dive, if we spring a leak, the force of the water could cut through us like a laser, and the pressure will crush us down to the size of soda cans."

"Nice." Greg grimaced. "I've been thinking about that, The Priz class is a Russian design, but I'm assuming there'll be English instructions, because…."

"Nope, I asked, but not available," Jack said. "And no time to get them translated. But I can manage most of the controls, and any specialist equipment or operations can be handled by the two Russian crew."

Cate nodded. "Good, and those crewmembers are both marine engineers, and should already be here somewhere, wandering all over the camp. We need to find them, organize them, and work with them." She grinned. "And yes, they speak English."

"Thank god for that," Greg sighed.

"Greg – Dmitry Torshin, and Yegor Gryzlov – find them, give them a hot coffee, and then get them to work. *Capice?*" Cate's brows went up. "Like now."

"Did you say, Igor?" Greg grinned, hunching over and swinging one arm.

"No, *Yegor*, and be nice, our lives will be in their hands." Cate picked up her computer pad.

Greg saluted. "You got it, boss." He hesitated for a moment, and then quickly looked over his shoulder to where Jack was hunched over a computer screen. He stepped in closer to her and lowered his voice.

"*Um*, Jack… is having your old flame here going to be a problem? A minute ago, you looked like you'd just seen a ghost."

Cate's rolled her eyes. "Oh please, I'm thirty-two not sixteen, and professionalism is my middle name."

"I feel better already. And by the way, your middle name is Corinne." He glanced quickly over his shoulder again. "Seriously, I'm not sure about him. I remember when you two were an item; your relationship with Jack was like a rollercoaster – one day it was all dancing in the sunlight, and the next it was an emotional MMA fight to the death."

Cate continued to type on her pad, not wanting to look up at him in case he saw the doubt in her eyes. "That's all history. This is purely business logic, and I agree with Valery; Jack is a qualified sub pilot and has the necessary skills for the expedition. Valery made the right choice." Her typing got harder as she felt the need to justify herself.

"Good, after all, don't want us all to be trapped in a small metal room if you two decide to have another of your legendary fights." Greg leaned even closer, his brows up. "Or one of your even more legendary, make-up sessions afterwards."

"Now who's acting like they're sixteen?" She pushed him back a step. "And besides..." she looked over his shoulder. "I don't think it's me he's interested in."

Greg turned in time to see Abby giggle at something Jack was telling her, and his expression dropped.

Cate lifted her chin. "Okay people, we meet back here in two hours for final briefing." She turned to Jack. "Mr Monroe, let's go check on our front door."

"More than two years," Jack said as he walked beside Cate. "Then out of the blue, I get a call saying I'm needed for a job. Working with a certain Stanford professor."

"You must have thought all your happy days had come at once." Cate stared straight ahead.

"I said, no," Jack said softly.

She snorted. "And yet, here you are."

"Yeah, well, Valery is very persuasive..." He turned and lifted his eyebrows. "...and very rich. It seemed money was no object to him, but speed and secrecy was." He looked down at her. "Besides, I'd be lying if I said wasn't curious about you."

They walked in silence for a few more moments, and then Jack leant across to her. "I tried to contact you; about a year ago."

She could feel him looking at her.

"I even left a message... left several actually."

She stopped and faced him. "Jack, it's just a job."

"*Just* a job; that's it?" He gave her a crooked smile.

"That's it," Cate said, feigning indifference. "We had

our time, it was fun, but that's all in the past now. However, for all your faults, and there sure are millions of them," she smiled. "…you were damned good at what you did."

"Thanks… I think. Well, that's fine with me then." Jack pulled in a cheek. "So, that image; that's important, huh?"

"Sure is." She glanced at him. "You said size was hard to estimate, but it took out our probe…" she opened her arms about three feet wide. "…and my gut tells me it was no minnow."

Jack nodded, as they continued on. "Recognizable predatory behavior – some sort of shark species. But is it an old one or new one?"

"Well, I think it's something that's been trapped there for perhaps millions of years, and I need a classification. It makes sense to get that from an expert."

"Ah, so you get to use me. Add my name to the report to lend it some legitimacy?" He nudged her. "Well, I'm glad to be here. I'd hate to think you went on this crazy-ass mission without me. At least this way I can keep an eye on you. For all my million faults, I still worry about you." He looked from under a lowered brow. "Maybe that's another of my faults – make it, one million and one."

"Well, that one's not a fault." She smiled. "But I'm a big girl, and I can look after myself now." Cate looked up at him. "We also need a pilot, and I know you can work just about every type of submersible on the planet. Besides, you think I'm totally going to entrust my life's work, and life, to a couple of Russian engineers I've never met before? I'm happy to take risks, but I'm not suicidal."

She turned back to the huge tent-like structure that had its own plastic canopy entrance walkway. Cate pushed aside the heavy flap, releasing the monstrous sound of grinding rock.

Just inside there were tables of hats, gloves, protective goggles and earmuffs. Jack and Cate kitted up, and walked to a railing that ran around the edge of the pit. Together they peered down into the deep, fifty-foot circular hole.

The railing creaked and Cate quickly leaned back, feeling a sudden rush of vertigo. "*Whoa.*" Beneath her feet she felt the juddering of the rock drills and hammers as they pounded the dense material below her. Normally for mining, they'd use explosives, but given they knew there was a drop of around a thousand feet underneath them, the work was carried out in layers – the rock cut and drilled, excavated away, testing done, and then another layer carved out.

The foreman rose from the pit in a drop-cage, waved, and took off his glove to shake Cate's hand. He nodded to Jack.

"We're down to the last sections, Professor Granger. The equipment will be withdrawn and then we're going to pin-blow the bottom layer of diorite; let it drop into the cavern below. It'll give you a nice neat hole with a strong structure at its edges."

"How deep?" Jack asked.

"We had to cut in two hundred and twenty-five feet… all within a few weeks." The foreman tilted his hard hat back on his head. "Not bad if I do say so myself."

Jack whistled. "We could have just used Heceta Island's Viva Silva Cave, that's only a few dozen miles south, and is one of the deepest caves in the continent – drops down about eight hundred feet – would have saved a lot of digging."

"I know it." The foreman said. "And that cave narrows down to cracks – we'd never get equipment into its basement. Better to start here with room to work. Just take the top off; bit like eating a boiled egg – break through the shell, and the rest is breakfast." He winked at Jack.

Jack grinned. "Guess so."

The grinding intensified, making Cate and Jack wince.

"How long until you break through?" Cate yelled.

The foreman turned and looked back down into the

hole. Small backhoes, mobile cutters and jackhammers were moving slowly up ramps and into lift cages. Bore holes had been drilled around the edges of the pit, each the size of a soda can, and ready to have an explosive charge packed into them.

"Ten minutes," he said. "No need to leave, as the charges are rigged to blow downwards. Just keep your safety glasses on, and lean well back."

"Great. I'll stay." Cate looked to Jack and nodded – she meant both of them.

Klaxon horns blared, and the remaining crew rose slowly in cages, leaving nothing behind on the rock floor. Cate marveled at how clean the surface looked. Though it was rough-hewn flooring, it was mostly swept clean, probably, she thought, to keep the chance of flying debris shards to a minimum. The explosives ringed the hole, each had a flashing red light on top, the wires to each and then all the way up to a console inside a toughened Perspex booth, set up a few feet from where they stood.

The foreman called them in, and each placed new padded earmuffs over their head, these ones with two-way radio built in. The foreman checked the line of connections and switches on the panel, like a DJ about to play a dance party's favorite tunes. He turned to Cate and gave her a thumbs-up, and then lifted a microphone to his mouth.

"Area is clear and secure, charges are set, and we are good to go." He took one last look around; satisfied he clicked on the speaker again. "Ready on ten-nine-eight-seven…"

Cate adjusted her earmuffs, and instinctively grabbed Jack Monroe's arm gripping it tightly.

"Four-three-two-one… fire in the hole."

The explosions were almost an anticlimax, as the red lights on the charges turned green, there was a muffled line of thumps accompanied by puffs of smoke from each tiny hole. What happened next wasn't.

Like a monstrous granite coin, the entire circular floor of the pit just fell away. It dropped silently and smoothly, as though an elevator travelling to the lower floors. The strong lights set up around the perimeter of the pit followed it for a few dozen feet, before it vanished in the blackness.

"Holy shit." Cate pulled off her earmuffs, straining forward until Jack grabbed and held her. No sound came back up for what seemed like ages, until there was the distant whump of one heavy surface striking another.

"Dr Granger, you now have your hole." The foreman dipped his hard hat to her, and then turned to the tent's entrance.

"Where are you going?" she asked.

"Got to check in with the boss." He waved and left.

"I thought you were the boss," Jack said, with an expression that was quizzically amused.

"Far from it." Cate watched the foreman go. The man's job was done and done well. Next would come the drop crew, who needed to first rig up the huge crane they would need to lower them all to the water's surface, over a thousand feet below.

That'd probably be done before they even had a working submarine that, at this moment, was still somewhere back on the wind-scoured cliff tops of Barnoff Island.

Jack grunted. "Well, that was the easy part. So now let's go and see how Greg and his new Russian comrades are getting on."

"*Da, comrade.*" She grinned and followed.

Greg shook hands with the two men, introducing them both to Abby and vice versa. Dmitry Torshin was a born submariner, an engineer, and would also be their navigator. The man was of average height, broad Slavic features, with a distinctive gap between his front teeth. He never stopped smiling, and Greg liked him immediately.

The other man, Yegor Gryzlov, was taller; six-two, six-three, maybe, which surprised Greg as he expected someone who spent his life working in a submarine would be more... *compact*. The big man had experience piloting a Priz class deep sea submersible, albeit an older model, and he would support Jack Monroe who was to captain the vessel. He didn't talk much and didn't seem capable of smiling at all. In fact Greg picked up nothing but an air of dour, ill-humor, and of wanting to be anywhere else but here.

Perhaps working with Americans was not his ideal job, Greg thought, not warming to him at all.

Yegor's saving grace was that he was polite, and seemed to take a shine to Abby, bowing and offering his hand to shake. He held onto hers as a basement-deep voice rumbled out.

"I once have parakeet called Abby. You like birds? Like little pretty sparrow, I think so."

She looked bemused, but smiled and continued to shake his huge hand. He hung on until she answered. "Yes, Yegor, I like birds."

Greg turned to the submersible. It currently sat in a huge wooden cradle, with rails tracks leading to the edge of the newly-excavated drop pit. The biggest crane Greg had seen in his life sat idle just a few dozen feet back from the dark hole, waiting to lift and lower the submersible into the void. The crane would then remain there, waiting for them to return, hopefully within twenty-four hours. As Greg watched, men still crawled over the sub's hull, checking seals and banging on the superstructure.

There was a name written on its side in Cyrillic lettering – Русалка

"Hey, easy with *Prusalka*," Dmitry yelled up at them.

"Prusalka?" Greg's brows shot up.

Dmitry nodded and grinned. "*Da*, Prusalka; is big fish, but...' He leaned closer. "...name means, mermaid." He winked, and then pulled back on seeing Greg's expression. "You got anything better?"

Greg thought for a moment and then shook his head. "I got nothin'. So, Prusalka it is then. Hey, do we need anything?"

Dmitry rubbed his chin. "Tools we have, cranes, welding, supplies, and once all checked should be air and water tight." He grinned again. "Hopefully."

Greg grimaced. "Only hopefully?" He turned to the dour Yegor. "Anything else you need, big guy?"

"Big luck." The big man turned away.

Greg nodded deeply. "*Ooookay*, well, we all need that – big and small."

Abby cleared her throat. "This is going to be in a subterranean environment – it'll be totally dark. You've piloted this type of submarine in those conditions before, right?"

"In deep water, always dark." Yegor nodded. "As long as rivets hold, chemical adhesives and welding holds, instruments work and dozens of other life-sustaining operations do their jobs, then we probably be okay. Don't worry, little Abby sparrow."

"Probably? Still not building confidence, Yegor." Greg sighed and turned away just as Cate and Jack pushed into the tent.

"All okay?" Cate had a quizzical look on her face, as if picking up on some uneasiness in the room.

Greg tilted his head towards Yegor. "Our crew friends were just telling us that we'll *probably* be safe as long as we have some luck."

"He's right," Jack said. "The Priz Class is designed to be broken down and then reassembled. It's big, but it was created to be a rapid-response submersible." He straightened to his full height, looking the big Russian in the eyes. "Should be ready to go. Are you telling me this isn't the case?"

Yegor just stared from under bushy brows, and Greg could feel the tension go up a few degrees. *That's just great,* he thought; they'd have two big guys, who might not like each other, trapped together in a tin can, in water thousands of feet deep and blacker than night. What could possibly go wrong?

Dmitry waved a hand. "No, no, not any real problems. My big friend is just overly cautious. We will be fine." He turned to Yegor and his jovial expression hardened momentarily, before turning back to Greg. "But we must do final checks now if you wish to launch soon."

Greg exhaled, but still felt the awkwardness remain.

"Please, you show us where we can work. We assume the hydraulic lifts are all in place." Dmitry waited.

Cate nodded. "All just waiting on you two gentlemen." She strode forward, sticking out a hand. "I'm Cate Granger, mission leader."

Dmitry's brow went up. "Is not Valery Mironov...?" He then quickly grinned. "Oh yes, of course, of course. Sorry to not greet you, but things are moving so quickly." He gave a huge theatrical shrug. "You are in charge; we are ready when you are."

"I got this," Jack said. "Let me show them the way. I might like to hang around for the final system's check; I might learn something." He turned to wink at Greg.

"Well okay, all good then." The three men left, and Greg stood staring at the tent flap, his mind whirling. "Is it too late to tell you I suffer from claustrophobia?"

"It sure is, little buddy." Cate smiled. "Besides, where would I be without you, Gilligan?"

"Thanks, Skipper." Greg turned to Abby. "That makes you Mary Anne."

"Ginger." She lifted her chin and smiled.

The temperature outside the colossal tent was near freezing, and cutting winds carrying furious snow stung exposed skin and seemed to cut right through the thickest of materials. It moaned and battered the canopy walls and roof as Cate, Greg and Abby stood at the edge of the massive pit, staring down, noses running as the three thawed out.

There was no heating in the tent, but inside it was an unbelievable 60 degrees. The temperature differential was achieved solely by the rising warm air from the massive, underground body of water.

Cate inhaled. Normally freezing weather made aromas impossible to detect, as the colder it got the more the aromas became locked away from the senses. But in here, so close to the dark hole, she could smell rock moss and sea grasses, warm sand, and when she closed her eyes she imagined she was standing on the shoreline of some dark beach, its surface glinting under a moonless night.

She opened her eyes and leaned forward, wishing she could get a glimpse. They had lowered cameras and recording equipment, but even with lighting there had been little to see. Movement sensors had picked up small density changes and vibrations, but for the most part, far below them it seemed like there was nothing but dead water. *Not surprising*, she thought, as when that huge slab of rock hit the water, it would have scared anything living away for miles.

"Why have we never found this?" Greg asked, leaning over the railing.

"It doesn't surprise me that it remained hidden," Abby said. "After all, Alaska not only boasts the biggest land size, but also holds the smallest population of the fifty states. Only six hundred and fifty thousand people call Alaska home." She turned. "You'd have to stumble onto it, or fall into it."

Cate's head jerked up.

"*Ouch*." Greg grimaced.

Abby momentarily put a hand over her mouth. "Oh god, sorry Cate, I didn't mean like your grandfather, *um,* might have."

Cate waved her away. "Forget it. And for the record, we know the locals must have been aware of it. The native Nantouk people called Baranof Island *Sheet'-ká X'áat'l* – The Forbidden Island. And the general understanding is that the pretty blue lake outside was simply known as *Tlagoo Khwáanx'i* – Bad Water. Or at least that used to be what we understood."

Cate stared into the dark void. "But there was another legend. One much older." Cate remembered her grandfather's letters. "The Bad Water was not named because it was undrinkable, but because it was dangerous for some reason. Remember the cave drawings – either the Nantouk or some other ancient people knew about the body of water, and fished from it." She turned to face the group. "What if the Bad Water, *Tlagoo Khwáanx'I,* they referred to wasn't the blue lake at all, but instead this subterranean sea."

"Maybe it's haunted," Greg said. "You know, some sort of ancient curse, or it's taboo."

Cate shook her head slowly, not really listening to anymore as she stared into the blackness. A ghost walked up her spine, making her shiver. She still found it hard to believe she was going to be dropped into that dark hole within the next few hours. She turned, beside her both Abby and Greg looked drained of color, and she knew exactly what they were feeling – trepidation, doubt, and fear. Same as she did, but she kept telling herself it was really just excitement and exhilaration. She knew it was a lie – she was scared shitless.

Cate gathered herself, and grinned, and then slapped Greg on the shoulder making him jump. "Okay team, let's go suit up. It's party time."

Cate zipped up her coveralls, and swung her arms a little. The loose material was comfortable and designed to keep them warm while giving them full a non-restrictive movement in the confined space.

Abby zipped hers up, with Greg watching from the side. The young woman was smaller than Cate, but had an impressive set of breasts that Greg seemed to find mesmerizing. She managed to catch his eye and gave him a mock stern look. In return, he simply wiggled his brows, and crossed to Abby.

"All set there? Let me check your collar." He turned her around and ran his fingers along the top turning the collar out from where it had accidently folded inwards against her skin. "There; snug as a bug in a rug." He stood back a pace, one hand on his chin. "It suits you."

"Thank you." Abby spun as if modeling. "I call it the baggy submariner look."

Greg held his arms out, and then flexed them. "And I call mine the action romper suit – ready for anything."

Cate sniggered. Greg would have weighed about ten stone, dripping wet. She turned to see Jack Monroe enter the tent, his huge body in his own suit bulging at the arms and chest, testimony to hard work on an athletic physique. She found it hard to look away, and her eyes travelled up and down his body. *Stop it,* she thought, angrily.

There was a small smile on his lips as he nodded to her. "We're ready. Sub's all sealed and we've done a full power check; all good there. Crane will be lifting it into the hammock any moment, and then…" he pointed down with a single finger.

"And then, next stop hell." Greg grinned at Abby.

"Or to a wonderland." Valery Mironov entered the tent with Sonya. Cate noticed his coverall uniform was similar to theirs, but had a gold crest of his initials on the breast. His silver beard was perfectly trimmed as always, and he grinned a perfect smile.

"Welcome back," Cate said. "Everything in order?"

"Of course, Cate. We've been introducing ourselves to Dmitry and Yegor. As you know, this investment is expensive, and I'm sure we all want to get the maximum benefit from it. We also want to come back safely. And now..." Mironov held his arms wide. "...it looks like we're just about ready to go."

"*Ah*, speaking of that." Greg had his hand up. "Safety, I mean. Not that we're expecting any trouble, but we already know that the thickness of the granite shell over the lake makes communications impossible. But what if we, *um*, need to call home in an emergency?"

Cate rolled her eyes, and went to respond, when Mironov came and stood beside her.

"If I may?"

Cate nodded. "Please."

Mironov turned back to Greg. "Good question, Mr Jamison, because when you plan for things to go right, you must also plan for when they go wrong. We'll be entering zones that are well over a thousand feet below solid rock, and then entering water that is even deeper. The combined pressure will make it what they call abyssal zone water. Unfortunately, there is no way a signal will get through that much geology, and given the size of the subterranean sea, we may be well away from any signal relay buoys we drop. So..." He smiled, seeming to enjoy the suspense. "I have taken the trouble of having communication pipes drilled down right across the Alaskan continent – all the way down to the water. My engineers will be lowering a goodies package of extra supplies, plus two-way communication silos. We'll be moving between those, periodically checking in with our surface support personnel. If we need to call home urgently, then we make our way to one of them."

Cate couldn't hide how impressed she felt. "I'd say we certainly backed the right guy."

"How many, and how far apart, are they... the buoys I mean?" Abby asked.

"Twenty overall, and first one is close, just fifteen miles," Mironov responded smoothly.

Greg scoffed. "That's close? We're talking underwater distance here."

"I'm guessing you needed to find suitable geology for drilling," Jack said. "Also some parts of the subterranean body of water are deeper than others. Right?"

"Exactly, Mr Monroe." Mironov looked along the faces of the small group "Now if—"

"One more thing." Greg held up his hand again. "If we're in trouble and need to get out quick, I don't suppose climbing up one of your communication silos is a possibility?"

"No." Mironov began to look bored.

"We'll be fine," Jack said. "The Priz Class submersible is basically an underwater tank. It's low tech, and slow tech, but its got plenty of room, is tough and reliable... at least now it is."

"Now it is?" Greg's eyebrows shot up.

"Early models suffered implosions at depth. But its seals were strengthened with the new models." Jack grinned as Greg pretended to faint.

"Anything else?" Cate tilted her head back slightly. There was silence, and she looked to Mironov, who nodded.

"Okay, people, then we're good to go." She led them out.

Cate hugged her arms tight to her body, trying to squeeze out the cold attempting to needle its way in through the fabric of her clothing. They stood staring up at the vessel sitting in a cradle awaiting lift off. They would need to enter it before it was lowered into the cavern and then on into the water – there would be no intermediate platform or pontoon waiting for them below.

Once they arrived down on the water, the two Russian crewmembers would then decouple them. The cables would be left dangling, and awaiting their return, hopefully within twenty-four hours.

"Where's Yegor?" Cate asked, turning.

Greg shrugged. "He said he had to use the bathroom, but..." he checked his watch. "That was ten minutes ago. Maybe he's got the runs; nerves and all." He wrinkled his nose. "And we're gonna be stuck with him in a small metal room – *yech!*"

"I think he's gone home." Dmitry frowned for a second or two, and then brayed with laughter, holding up a hand. "I joke; he will be back. Maybe he call his wife or something. He always do things by himself."

"Go and find him," Jack said, and then stared into the distance. "Forget it; here comes the big grizzly bear now."

Yegor jogged back to the group. "I'm here, and ready."

"Where've you been?" Jack's voice was sharp.

Yegor scowled, and then waved an arm out at the cold landscape. "I never see Alaska before. I go looking around." His gaze was unwavering. "I here and ready now."

Jack grunted, holding his gaze. After another moment, Yegor turned to the submersible, walking to it and laying a hand on the cold steel of the hull. "And you are ready too, my Prusalka *Kpacota*." He stood back looking up, admiringly.

Mironov smiled, and said something in Russian to Yegor. The big man nodded and grinned sheepishly. Mironov turned to the group. "*Kpacota* is an old Russian word, for beautiful woman." He raised his brows. "Let us hope it is not one of the temperamental ones, yes?"

Cate and Abby groaned, but Greg nodded vigorously.

Cate turned to the *Prusalka*; it was the first time she had seen the vessel in its entirety. The craft itself was a stubby, bulbous-looking vehicle, finished off with striking orange and white bands. Along each side were three fist-sized glass panes – not portholes, but cameras, Cate knew. The rear had a powerful curved-blade propeller with three controlling struts, and there was a small conning tower on top. Underneath was a set of folded mechanical arms, making it look like some sort of praying mantis awaiting its next meal.

In between the arms was a capsule – a mini submersible that was an escape pod of sorts. The problem was, it was no bigger than a coffin, and was designed for one, maybe two people. Jack had told her the Priz class had been modified in the last decade to give it a sleeker design, and more safety features – the pod being one of them. This was following an incident in 2005 where an older model had got itself entangled in cables on an underwater hydrophone array off the coast of the Kamchatka Peninsula. Six hundred feet down, the thick steel cables defied being untangled, moved or cut.

The men were trapped on the seafloor for seventy-six hours before a British remotely-operated vehicle with advanced equipment only just managed to sever the coils of steel with only a few hours of air remaining. Looking at the pregnant, vitamin-capsule shape, she couldn't imagine what it looked like before its slim-down makeover.

Cate went to step up onto the first rung of the ladder, when Sonya held up a hand.

"Wait."

"*Huh?*" Cate jerked back a step.

Sonya was already scaling the steps like a monkey, and quickly dropped down through the hatch.

"What's with that?" Cate asked Mironov, feeling pissed off by his assistant.

Mironov shrugged, and grinned. "It's okay, Cate. Ms Borashev just likes to be thorough in regards to security."

Yeah right; like what's she going to be able to do, anyway? Cate wondered. She folded her arms, tight, and glared at Jack for no reason.

In another minute Sonya climbed back out and down. She spoke softly to Mironov, and the Russian billionaire nodded as he listened. He then turned to Cate and graced her with a small bow. "Mission leaders first."

"*Thank you.*" Cate climbed the ladder, and was about to drop down in through the hatch, when she looked back down at the crew. There were smiles, grins of excitement and some of nerves. She also saw Valery still talking softly to Sonya. He reached up to brush a strand of loose hair from her forehead. She could clearly see the look of adoration in Sonya's eyes. *Definitely something there*, she thought, as she dropped down into the cabin.

Cate was immediately assaulted by the smells – oil, stale air, and ancient body odor. The submarine was as cramped as she expected. It looked like a combination of spaceship and electronics workshop with walls of equipment, small screens everywhere, and the lighting inside was a dull red. The design was probably practical and functional, but the Russians sure didn't believe in aesthetics or comfort.

There were two seats at the front, and five in the belly of the craft. An open area at the back could have contained extra equipment or passengers, as the submersible could pack in twenty if it needed to undertake a deepwater rescue. But for now, the space had some modest supplies stacked neatly at the rear, but also a larger chair, with its own control panel – Mironov's personal seat. They all had to hunch slightly to fit, Jack, Yegor and Mironov especially, but at least they wouldn't have to crawl over each other.

Yegor and Jack sat at the front, and Cate, Greg, Abby and Dmitry, all took the seats in the main compartment, with Mironov easing back into his own, and crossing his long, thin legs. He looked relaxed and at ease, as if waiting for a movie to start in his private theatre. Dmitry immediately set to checking monitors and dials, and Cate, Greg and Abby started to prepare their own sampling and recording equipment.

Each of the team had multiple screens in front of them, including a viewing screen, as the only glass was at the front. The window was in a curved convex-design, based on the eggshell-dome shape – it was the strongest structure in nature and allowed the massive forces applied to it to be spread across the entire surface. Deep-sea submariners found out the hard way that flat portholes blew inwards at greater depths. For now, Jack and Yegor had a view, and those at the back of the bus would have to be satisfied with remote viewing, or leaning back to see around the two pilots.

Dmitry turned to speak a few words in Russian to his big colleague, who nodded and gave a deep, *"Da"* over his shoulder. The smaller man then rose to his feet, and leant over Cate.

"Get ready for lift. I must close hatch for descent." He grinned, patted her shoulder and then climbed the ladder, pulling the heavy metal circular disc down over his head and spinning the wheel on the primary hatch. He leapt down, and then sealed the interior bulkhead hatch. They were now sealed in.

An image of a blood-lit steel coffin flashed into Cate's mind, but thankfully, small spaces never worried her. However, with the bracing external air shut out, the cocktail of old and new smells crowded around them, threatening to overwhelm her senses. She hoped she got used to them as the voyage progressed, and new air was pumped in.

Yegor pulled a headset over his large head, and pointed to another sitting on the console waiting for Jack.

"Okay, bridge is yours, Captain Monroe."

Dmitry also pulled a set of earphones over his head and began to speak softly. Cate couldn't make out whether it was English or Russian.

Jack switched on his microphone. "Confirm systems check, confirm hatch seal, confirm crew readiness; we're all good to go here, Base Control." Jack turned in his seat. "Hang on everyone; the first step is a big one."

"Always is." Cate picked up the seat belt and pulled it over her shoulder, buckling it at her waist. Greg and Abby did the same. She noticed Dmitry didn't, and she leant across.

"Buckle up."

He nodded. "Soon, I need to make some adjustments. Besides, I trust your ground crew to lower us safely." He shrugged. "And if they drop us a thousand feet, a seatbelt is not going to make much difference, *Da*?"

"*Da*," Cate said slowly.

Cate heard the clank of steel on the hull and she clasped the edge of the desk-like console before her. Beside her, Greg's face might have been drained of color, but it was hard to tell as small green flaring screens and the overhead red light gave him a ghoulish appearance. She looked over her shoulder, behind them, Abby's eyes moved from screen to dial, and then back, her face wide-eyed with excitement. At the rear Mironov smiled, his legs still crossed. He nodded to her, relaxed, confident, and she wished she could borrow some of his nerve.

Dmitry still unbuckled, hovered over differing pieces of equipment, making adjustments and tweaking controls. He finally eased back, and then swiveled in his seat.

"Up, up and away." He finally strapped himself in.

The craft groaned, shuddered, metal strained, and then it lifted.

"If seals break, I think happen now." Dmitry held up a finger, his eyes on the roof of the ship, as he listened for several seconds. "Wait, wait..." he dropped his hand. "I think we okay."

They could hear the rumbling of the enormous tractor-like sled even through the reinforced hull of *Prusalka*, and there was only the slightest sensation of movement inside as they were conveyed to the edge of the hole. Cate held on tight, knowing this should only take a few minutes, and then they could expect the drop to the water below would take at least sixty more nerve-racking minutes.

Dmitry turned in his seat. "Dr Granger, all my life I have loved the ocean. But this is new for me. Please tell me more about this body of water we are about to enter." He shrugged. "It was all hush-hush, so our superiors tell us little. Now we are all locked in, and all friends, you can share some more please?"

Still clinging to the console top, Cate leaned back and turned to Mironov. The Russian billionaire just shrugged, and she guessed he thought like her; there was no reason to keep this a secret now they were all about to plunge into this mission together. Besides, it'd be a useful distraction for her, for all of them, during the drop.

She let go of the console, and swiveled in her seat. Her fingers ached, and it was only then she realized how tight she had been hanging on.

"Well, we have, and haven't seen it. We have strategraphic images taken from satellites, and some sonar readings, but as for seeing it physically, we only had glimpses of a dark water environment." She decided to withhold the image of the tooth, as she didn't want to worry the Russian crew, and didn't have all the answers to questions she knew they would ask.

"I understand it is a huge body of water. Do you think it is a dead sea?" It was if Dmitry had just read her mind. He waited, his grin still firmly in place.

"Dead? No." She thought for a moment or two, choosing her words carefully. "No, I don't think it will be a dead body of water. But as for fully understanding and classifying the life forms, if there *are* any life forms, will be one of the tasks we will undertake while we are mapping the hydro-geology."

Cate felt Abby and Greg's eyes on her.

"If there are any life forms?" He leant forward, his eyes going briefly to Mironov, and his voice dropping to a conspiratorial level. "Did you know we now have the ability to direct an extra strong electrical discharge pulse over the skin of the submersible? Was done at Mr Mironov's request." He bobbed his head. "So, I also think it is not a dead sea. I also think maybe not everything down there is friendly." He leant back his voice returning to its normal timbre. "But maybe we don't need it then."

Cate could feel him assessing her. She just shrugged. The pulse was news to her, and she turned to Mironov, who just smiled, obviously enjoying allowing her to do all the work. She spoke while keeping her eyes on the Russian billionaire. "I guess Valery just likes to be careful and prepared for anything." She raised her eyebrows and Mironov nodded in return.

"Good." Dmitry sighed. "Sorry, I have so many questions. I'm excited about our trip." Dmitry spun back to his console for a few moments before half turning. "But must be something down there." He frowned as though wrestling with a thorny problem. "Because, you have one geologist, but two biologists and a marine shark specialist. Plus Mr Mironov, who is interested in ancient living things. So maybe you expect something down there, yes? Something big." His brows came together. "One more thing; if something down there, how did it get there?"

It was a good question and one she sought answers to herself. "*If* there are life forms." Cate exhaled slowly. "Well, maybe there was an opening to the ocean a long way back. The creatures entered, and then an earth movement sealed them all in and cut them off from the outside world. Many times in the past, the ocean levels were much higher than they were today. Pretty much all of the coast, from Alaska down to California was submerged for twenty to fifty miles inland. It was nothing but shallow seas and coastal swamps. When the water receded, maybe some of the deeper pockets remained, and then somehow became landlocked." She shrugged. "It's one theory."

"But living in darkness?" Dmitry tilted his head. "I know of cave lakes in Ural Mountains; but things there are little." He made his finger inch along in front of her.

Cate remembered the image of the tooth – Jack had said it was hard to judge size. Somehow, she didn't think it was some sort of tiny blind eel down in those depths. She looked back to Dmitry. "Well, that's what we hope to find out." She spun back to her console, gripping it again as she heard a metallic clunk, the groan of steel and then the submersible swung slightly in its cradle.

Jack put a hand to his head, pressing the microphone cup in tighter for a second or two, before turning in his seat.

"Get ready, ladies and gentlemen, the drop is about to commence. Next stop Seatopia."

"*Seatopia?*" Greg chuckled. "I like it."

Abby stopped making notes for a moment, and turned to Cate, grimacing. "I'm nervous." She held up a hand; it shook slightly.

Cate wanted to hug the younger woman, but held up her own hand. The fingers also trembled. "I wouldn't worry about it if I was you."

There came a jolt, and then nothing. Cate knew the crane was now lowering the vessel. They would descend at about four miles per hour – little more than walking speed. It would take a full hour to drop all the way down to the inky black sea, where the hydraulics would slow, easing them gently into the water like an old man easing into a hot bath. It was then up to Dmitry to climb up and detach the tethers that would remain dangling in place. They'd all get to say one last goodbye and then they'd submerge and head east towards the vast body of the underground sea.

Cate drew in a deep breath, momentarily feeling overwhelmed by the millions of tons of rock pressing down on top of her. She guessed there'd be air pockets along the way that they could surface into if need be, and some of them would be huge dry caverns, perhaps with dark rocky beaches lapping at stygian bays. As the oxygen content of the water was high she had to assume that any air pockets they came across would be breathable. They had more than enough air for the trip, but it might be nice to take a breath of something other than canned air.

Cate closed her eyes, and listened to her heartbeat. In what seemed just another few minutes she felt a settling of weight in her body, and knew that meant they were being eased into the water. She turned and saw Jack listening to a voice high overhead, or perhaps they were sitting back in some comfortable office somewhere.

"Okay Base, we're down." He turned. "Dmitry, unhook us."

"Yes, Captain." Dmitry swung in his seat, and headed to the laddered hatch, spinning the airtight seal, and climbing to then open the next.

Cate leant back as a draft of warm, wet air billowed into the cabin.

Jack spun in his seat. "We need to run a final check on the equipment, so we all get a few minutes to say farewell to the surface, and say hello to our new home for the next twenty-four hours. Then it's bon voyage." He looked to Cate. "So who's first?"

Cate unbuckled her belt. "That'd be me." She crossed to the ladder and waited at its base. The conning tower was small, little more than the width of the hatch. It was designed to facilitate entry and exit of personnel, and if need be, to allow docking of another submersible in the event of underwater transfers.

Dmitry slid down and nodded to her, and turned to Jack. "Tether uncoupled, Captain."

"Good work." Jack turned to Cate, and motioned to the ladder. "Enjoy. You've got three minutes."

Cate went straight up the rungs and as soon as her head lifted above the rim of the tower she inhaled deeply and was assailed by the humidity and amazing smells of the monstrous cavern.

She shut her eyes, just using her other senses to take in the ambiance. She felt a giddy excitement as her mind created mental images of mossy rocks, beaches, drying kelp, sponges and sea grasses. She tried to blank out the small sounds coming from below and concentrate on the dark. Slowly it came – first there was the plink of dripping water, followed by its corresponding tiny echoes. Minute scratching came from some rock surface hidden away in the darkness that may have been some sort of crustacean feeding on lichen. The humidity against her skin was salty, pleasant, and like a balmy tropical evening.

She felt the *Prusalka* submersible rise gently on a swell. She was initially confused, but the scientist in her kind of expected it – even though there was no pull of the moon to create tidal surges, and there was no weather to whip up waves, the deeper water was probably warmer than the surface water. That would mean there would be a constant upwelling and circulation of warm to cooler water, resulting in a current. It would have also generated an oxygenation effect, making the water more habitable and hospitable to life. *It all stacks up*, she thought excitedly.

Cate opened her eyes and looked skyward. Above here there was a near microscopic dot of light, the cut-hole they had been dropped into. Two cables dangled nearby, rising up into a dark infinity, and for one crazy moment, she imagined herself climbing up one towards the surface, and the safety of the sunlight.

"Is it my turn yet?"

Cate grinned and looked down. Greg's red-lit face stared up at her.

"Sure." She carefully eased herself back down. "Just think of it as a moonless night over a tropical sea." She quickly looked back up at the glowing dot in the cave roof. "No, in fact, if you look up, you might just see a moon after all."

"Sounds romantic, but, I wish I packed my fishing rod." Greg shinnied up the ladder, and Cate continued to stare up after him, already missing the open air.

"Cate." Jack called her up front, and Yegor stood out of his seat for her.

"I also would like to go up to top." He eased around her to get in line.

Cate sat. "So that was the boring bit out of the way," she said, smiling. "Now for the interesting stuff."

He grinned. "Sure, boring, but probably the most dangerous. If we had dropped, even from a hundred feet up, the sub would have been fine, but we would have been plastered all over its insides." Jack waved it away. He then pointed to a screen in front showing a sonar map of their environment. There were cliff walls behind them to the west, but for the other quadrants, it ran on for miles.

There was a course plotted already on his screen. "We follow this route, and hopefully as we travel, the sonar will give us more terrain as the signals bounce back to our onboard computer for it to map and record our findings." Jack traced the map with his finger. "Here, the cavern roof seems to drop right down to the water line. So, from that point, we dive deep. Might not be any low stalactites, but best not to take any chances."

"Works for me. We should get some great readings along the way." Cate felt the ball of excitement and trepidation in her gut bounce a few times. "And then we dive deep." She couldn't take her eyes from the screen.

CHAPTER 8

Brogidan Yusoff, head of the Resources and Agriculture Ministry, read the transcript from their field agent – they were in the subterranean lake and proceeding. Everything was going to plan.

He nodded, satisfied, but wished he had thought to have some sort of video link established from inside the submarine; he would pay a million dollars just to see the look on Mironov's face when the man realized what was happening.

He rubbed stubby hands together and then opened the link given to him by his second in charge, Uli Stroyev. On the screen it now showed a satellite image of the Baranof Island landscape. A red dot was centered just on the Western coast – *a bullseye*, he thought. He knew that as they moved deeper he would lose the signal. It didn't matter; Mironov was nearly in his hands, and everyone else onboard the submarine was already dead and soon to be buried, as far as he was concerned.

"A ghost ship." Yusoff pushed the screen away and clapped his hands. "Good... a good day."

CHAPTER 9

"Rig for diving." Jack Monroe checked dials and flicked switches. Along with Cate and the rest of the crew, he now wore a headset. Even though they were only a dozen feet from the pilots, it was critical that commands and instructions were heard fast and clearly – in an extreme environment like a deep-sea submersible, reacting correctly could be the difference between life and death.

"Ladies and gentlemen, everyone to their positions, please." Jack flexed his hands and then grabbed one of the u-shaped steering wheels.

Beside Jack, Yegor Gryzlov's hands also worked furiously. Cate could hear Dmitry working at his own console, and everywhere she looked, walls of technical equipment sprung to life.

"Bridge is clear, all crew to their positions, Captain," Yegor responded in his Russian baritone.

"All valves, hatches, intakes to close," Jack said mechanically.

Yegor would repeat the instruction when the order was confirmed.

Jack continued down his checklist, his voice calm and professional. For some reason, Cate felt a flush of pride, and wished it were she that had decided to bring him in.

"Pressure in the boat," Jack intoned.

Once the submarine had been fully sealed, Yegor released air pressure into the hull, and Cate felt her ears pop. The hull-opening indicator board showed all green lights, indicating the pressure levels were steady and the craft was airtight.

"Hull is secure. Pressure maintained." Yegor turned to Jack.

Jack nodded. "Okay then, open main vents."

A gushing, gurgling could be heard from underneath their feet as the ballast tank vents were opened, allowing them to fill with water.

Dmitry leant back, speaking over his shoulder. "Air in the banks, shit in the tanks, ready to dive, comrades." He giggled.

Greg laughed, Cate groaned, and Abby stuck her tongue out in distaste.

"Increase diving speed, Mr Gryzlov; take us down to forty-five feet and level off."

"Yes, Captain." Yegor pushed his own wheel forward, and Cate knew from her own homework, that the tiny bow planes, which were kept folded up against the superstructure to prevent damage while surfaced, were extended, and angled for full dive. The stern planes, close to the huge angled propeller, would also be tilting to control the boat's angle.

Cate turned from her own view screen to look past Jack, and out the front-view window. She saw the dark water begin to rush up and over the convex glass as the last bubbles were left behind.

"Dmitry, give me some external readings," Jack said.

"Aye, Captain." The Russian grinned into his phosphor green screen. "External temperature at seventy-five degrees. Chemical content..." he bobbed his head for a moment. "...a little high in calcium and organic material, but okay." His head jerked back a notch. "Oh, interesting... external radiation at eighty miliseverts."

"That's high," Greg said.

Cate nodded. "Yes. Normal background is about two miliseverts."

"Dangerous?" Jack swung to look at Cate.

Cate shook her head. "No, and we should expect it the deeper we go. The Earth's skin is a great barrier against radiation – both atmospheric from above, and deeper down, the rock gives back radiation from heavy metal impregnation. The count will probably get higher the deeper we go. Won't be a problem as long as it's below five hundred miliseverts."

"Good." Jack turned back to the curved window. "Dmitry, keep a watch on the count."

"At forty-five feet, Captain," Yegor intoned.

"Close vents, reduce speed." Jack took the earphones off his head and swung in his seat. "Ladies and gentlemen, we are now at cruising speed, and steady as she goes. Take over Yegor."

Cate grinned. "We're underway." She felt a little giddy excitement.

Jack unstrapped his belt. "Feel free to move around… but stay off the jogging track." He rose, but couldn't quite straighten in the cramped compartment. "Cate, not much to see, but want to sit up front as we head in?" He stepped aside.

"You bet." Cate slipped out of her seat, and burrowed forward, sitting down and swiveling frontward. Jack leaned over her shoulder.

There was near complete darkness. However from time to time, small specks of light drifted past, or larger flashes pinged from out of the darkness.

"Bioluminescence," Cate breathed.

"That's right. This will be exactly like a deep-sea environment. The things down here will have seen no sunlight so use the bio-light to attract prey, or a mate, or even as a sign of distress."

Cate looked down at the controls. "Does the sub... *Prusalka*, have any external lights?"

Greg and Abby crowded up behind them, causing

Yegor to momentarily turn, his huge brows coming down like a might bushy shelf over his eyes. "Give room, please."

"*Ouch.*" Cate hunched her shoulders, as bodies crushed in on her. It seemed no one was prepared to give up an inch of viewing space.

"Lights won't do much down here," Greg said. "Too much dark depths, and without any points of reference or solid objects to illuminate, you'll get nothing but black on black."

Yegor snorted. "Maybe with American lights. *Prusalka* has most advanced LED technology on planet with titanium housing for long-term immersion durability." He turned to Greg. "Tested to full trench-depth at twenty-six thousand feet." His big brows went up.

"LEDs? I thought they were tiny things used in desk lamps," Greg said, crowding closer.

"Not these babies." Jack kept his eyes on the curved window. "New LED technology is far better able to tolerate depths by having an internal oil pressure compensation system." Jack turned to Greg. "Added to that, a conventional incandescent light bulb emits around fifteen Watts of light, and standard fluorescent lights emit up to a hundred Watts. But, these Russian LEDs can give us up to three hundred Watts plus we have a spot light that can throw out a beam of over five hundred." He shrugged. "But that generates a little too much heat to run for too long." Jack turned to Yegor. "Sound about right, big guy?"

Yegor grinned in return. "You do homework. Good." He nodded. "Like I said; Russian lights best in world."

"Well, then..." Abby gripped Cate's shoulder. "...let's see what we've got down here."

Cate felt Mironov sidle up behind them and lean his long frame forward to see over her shoulder. She turned from Jack to Yegor.

"Let's do it."

The big man's hand reached for a bank of switches on the panel before him, flicking them up one after the other.

Immediately a ring of high power LED lights around the outside of the convex glass window burst into life, opening a broad white path before them.

Cate slumped back into the seat. "Oh my god."

CHAPTER 10

In Valery Mironov's outer office, Sonya Borashev read the CIA report, and ground her teeth. She dropped it to the desk. *Svoloch!* She had warned Valery that this might happen. Their CIA contact had intercepted communication chatter between Kodiak Island, near Baranof Island, and the Russian mainland.

She had immediately dispatched a covert team to Kodiak Island, and they had found a body – murdered. There'd been a switch, and one of those Russian crewmen was not who he said he was.

Sonya looked at the bank of clocks on the wall, showing the time zone for every major city on earth. The submersible had dived and gone dark by now – she was too late to do anything about it.

The report crumpled in her fist. She should have demanded to come along. On paper she was an assistant, but Sonya was one of Mironov's personal guardians, recruited by Valery from Harvard for her mind, but then sent to Israel for bodyguard training in the Mossad combat camps. She'd excelled, and had been with him now for eight years. It was no secret that she loved him, and she'd die for him… and if need be, she wouldn't hesitate to kill for him.

Sonya pushed thick blond hair back from her face, and continued to stare at the clocks. Her mind worked; what would they want? Money? Valery was worth billions. Influence? He was also involved in numerous business dealings in too many countries to count.

She touched her lips as her mind worked. In a way, they already had taken him hostage. So if he wasn't dead yet, then they wanted something else. Sonya looked again at the bank of clocks on the wall. There was nothing she could do, until she knew more. Until then she must wait, listen, and watch. When they made their next move, she would act.

Her hand curled into a fist, and her stomach knotted. One thing she knew; if they harmed him, she would follow them to the four corners of the world and kill every one of them, personally.

CHAPTER 11

Huge jellyfish, five feet across, their clear bells hung with bulbous, red chandeliers drifted like dirigibles in a night sky. In amongst them, scudding about was what looked like scrolled seashells, trailing small tentacles that reminded Cate of Chinese lanterns.

"There are no secrets that time does not reveal." Mironov clasped his hands to his chin, as if in prayer.

"Well, anyone still want to ask if down here might be a dead zone?" Greg said, a grin splitting his face.

Dmitry was on his feet. "But this is impossible. How could things like this survive?"

Jack couldn't take his eyes off the window as he leaned on Cate's shoulder. "Life will adapt or die."

Cate looked up at him briefly to nod and then turn back as something like a tiny shrimp stuck momentarily to the curved window. "And if the water remains warm, oxygenated, and circulating, then the life forms will thrive. Heat is all they really need to do just fine."

"But so many… and so big." Dmitry's mouth gaped.

Mironov leant forward to examine the small creature. "It is unusual, but has its precedents. There's a cave in Brazil called the Olonga-Ringa cavern that has a sunken lake; there's a species of nine-foot eel that hasn't been seen on the surface for twenty million years."

Jack tapped Cate on the shoulder. "Time to go to work." She turned and rose from the seat, and he slid back in.

Cate stayed just behind him. "And we're still at mid water – let's take it down and have a look at the bottom."

Jack nodded and turned to Yegor. "Down fifty feet, Mr Gryzlov."

"*Da*... yes, sir." Yegor pushed the u-shaped wheel forward a half-inch and *Prusalka* angled down a few degrees, and began to plow through the forest of jellyfish. The huge bells bounced soundlessly off the curved window.

"Anyone know what type they are?" Abby asked.

Cate's eyes remained firmly fixed on the window. "No, but Jack might have a clue; he's our expert on all things underwater."

"I can recognize most," Jack said. "Growing up I had a voracious appetite for all things to do with sea life – past and present. Aquatic paleontology was my first real hobby." He stared. "But no idea on the jellyfish – not modern, and as they're so soft, they never really left any fossil record trace behind. As for the seashells, I'd say nauteloids – those were around for hundreds of millions of years, and still around today – just not at that size."

"Nautiloidea is an ancient class of cephalopods – related to squid and the octopus," Mironov said evenly. "Most died out prior to the Ordovician period."

"Cephalopods? Great, hate to be stuck in a dark cave, underwater, with anything with too many arms," Greg said.

"You and me both," said Cate. "I'll tell you about a nightmare I had once after reading a book about being trapped under the dark Antarctic ice."

Jack half turned. "The giant man-eating squid thing again?"

"Great," Abby said.

Cate squeezed Jack's shoulder, hard. "Don't worry, Abby, even I know that nothing like that exists in the fossil record."

"Leveling off at ten feet above sea floor... I mean cave floor," Yegor said.

"Fantastic," Cate breathed. "And it *is* a sea; just one no one knows about."

Outside the underground sea floor was a plain of grasses, with huge fans waving their gossamer wings, and the odd bulbous sponge poking up like brown cabbages. In amongst the plant life, creatures that resembled tiny many-legged skateboards were busily darting about.

"*Ha*, trilobites," Abby pronounced. "One for me."

"Yes. They were our world's first real survivors, existing for nearly three hundred million years. Some were the size of your thumb, and others, like these guys, as big as a loaf of bread." Jack smiled. "My first fossil was a middle Cambrian trilobite – four hundred and ninety million years old."

A cloud of darker fluid puffed up from out to their side, drawing their attention. One of the trilobites was caught in the claws of a foot-long creature that looked like a long flat lobster.

Jack frowned. "*Heeeey*, that could be a sea scorpion." He grinned. "It was one of the apex predators in the shallows of the primordial seas." He half turned. "Did you know they were the first creatures to leave the water, and they were big? The Eurypterids grew to nearly nine feet, and over half a billion years ago, they crawled up onto desolate Cambrian shorelines. The fish only followed them millions of years later. But they were a little smarter, evolving more efficient lungs and then turning into amphibians. The result was they pushed the sea scorpions back into the ocean, and went on to grow big and then rule all the lands."

Abby blew air through compressed lips. "Imagine what our world would have been like if the scorpions had won the race – makes you wonder, if we, humans I mean, would even exist."

"Sure we would," Greg said, cheerily. "We'd just have exoskeletons and eyes on stalks."

"*Gaak.*" Abby stifled a giggle.

"Look." Greg pointed at something easing its way up behind the dining sea scorpion.

"Attracted by the blood," Jack said.

"That is *truly* weird." Abby tried to lean out over Jack's shoulder, and Cate pulled her back.

"It's more than that," said Mironov softly. "It is a breathtaking wonder." He leaned forward. "*Anomalocaris*, I believe. What do you think, Mr Monroe?"

Jack's forehead furrowed. "*Anomalocaris* – impossible, impossible, impossible." He exhaled slowly. "But if that's what it is, it is a ghost from Earth's earliest time, and one of evolutions marvels." He turned briefly to Mironov, before going back to the strange creature. "Nature trying its hand at the weird and wonderful – nothing like it exists today, and nothing has for hundreds of millions of years." He folded his arms, still shaking his head, as he remained staring at the thing.

The three-foot-long creature slowed as it approached the sea scorpion. It seemed to hover, its stealth approach unmistakable as it glided in and out of the thicker grasses. It had an oval ribbed body with flaps on the edge that gently undulated; golf ball sized glossy black eyes on stalks, and armor plating. But its front end seemed the work of a mad artist commissioned to design the most terrifying predator he could imagine. Below the head, two long appendages were tightly coiled as it came nearer the scorpion, then each began to slowly unfurl like a double elephant trunk.

Jack eased the submersible to a full stop, and the entire crew crowded in at the curved window. The team could see now that the coils had spikes on the underside and were in fact arms used for gripping and holding prey.

Jack carefully turned to Cate. "Thank you for bringing me." He slowly eased back around as though worried a sudden movement might send the monstrosity darting away into the dark. He leant on the u-shaped wheel. "My bucket list is now officially empty."

Cate just nodded and smiled, not letting on it wasn't her decision to bring him at all. She kind of liked that he thought it was.

When the Anomalocaris was within a few feet, the hovering creature lunged, its long appendages fully extending to wrap around the sea scorpion. The thick glass allowed no sound to penetrate to them, but all could imagine the crunching of the carapace that was taking place in the dark water. The Anomalocaris, scorpion now held tight in its spiked embrace, resumed its slow hovering as it carted away its meal to be dined on in peace in whatever lair it occupied.

"Holy shit," Greg said. "That was intense."

"The rule of tooth and claw." Mironov turned and went back to his seat.

"Predator becomes prey." Jack ran hands up through his hair. "Let's take her forward Mr Gryzlov; five knots."

"Did you see those tooth-like things on its arms?" Abby asked. "Could that have been the thing that attacked our drone?"

Cate watched, transfixed, as the weird creature disappeared into the utter darkness of the subterranean sea. Abby's voice only just registered. "*What?* No, no, different structure." She could feel Jack's eyes on her, and knew what he thought, but obviously decided to keep to himself.

"Good," Abby said. "Because that thing freaks me out."

"*Shit!*"

Jack's yell was just as startling as the giant that loomed up out of the darkness. He twisted the wheel, hard, swerving *Prusalka* out of its way.

"*Jesus...* all stop." He laughed nervously. "I should have expected that." Jack exhaled loudly. "Fuck... sorry."

The *Prusalka* slowed, then stopped, and Jack switched on the halogen lamps.

The forest of huge stalagmites rose from the sunken floor like giant Easter Island carvings. Things darted in and out of the waving plant life on their surfaces, and long spiny-limbed crustaceans clung to their crusted surfaces.

"Stalagmites... under water?" Greg scoffed.

"The only way they could form is if this cave had been dry once... or at least this section of it," Abby said.

"They're enormous." Greg leaned over Jack. "I can't even see where they begin."

"This lake or sea will probably contain trillions of gallons of water, but it's either just seepage from above, or this massive empty cave system was dry, and an earthquake ripped it open and allowed seawater to pour in, dragging all the sea life with it."

"Or at some time, part of it drained," Cate said. "Maybe leaking its contents to the outside world before it refilled and then was sealed again."

"Makes sense," Mironov added from behind them. "If this ocean world had at one time opened to allow these things in, then it stands to reason it can reopen to let them out... or has at some time in the long distant past." He stroked his silver beard. "That might be why we see evolutionary remnants reappear that we thought were long extinct."

Cate smiled. "Like your coelacanths?"

Mironov nodded, and then turned to his small screens.

The submarine eased past the monolith forest. Everyone's head turned as they watch them pass by the window.

"That was a close one. We need to keep a lookout, there's sure to be others." Jack swung in his seat, finding Dmitry hovering behind Yegor. "I think we need eyes on the sonar screen, permanently, from now on."

"Aye aye, Captain." Dmitry rushed to take his seat.

Jack wiped his face with his forearm. "We got distracted – can't let it happen again. Everyone back to their seats."

As they sat down and buckled in, Cate felt a pulse move through the skin of the submersible. She felt her stomach do a little flip. "What was that?" She noticed everyone had frozen momentarily, waiting.

Dmitry turned in his seat, head titled as though listening. "Pressure pulse."

"I felt it too," Jack said.

There came a soft clang against the skin of the submarine, and then from outside the window, they saw debris come raining down – silt and stones, most no bigger than a fist.

"I think there's been a pretty good sized tremor down here." Jack leaned forward, looking up from under the curved window, and then out over the seafloor. "Most of the beasties look to have headed home."

Greg snorted. "You'd think they'd be used to that – living in a giant cave I mean."

"Maybe they are," Abby said. "And that's why they've learned to get the hell out of here when the rocky rain starts to fall."

"Let's hope no big pieces, yes?" Yegor said slowly.

"*Very*, yes," Greg responded.

They continued on, the grasses now strewn with what looked like snow from the overhead rain of debris. However it didn't take long for small crustaceans to reappear from their nooks and crannies and begin to pick over the new morsels of moss and lichen on the fallen rocks.

"I think... something," Dmitry said.

Jack half turned. "You got something back there?"

"A ghost maybe – strange. I thought I saw big sonar shadow." Dmitry exhaled through his nose. "Gone now. But there is a geology change coming up."

"Ahead slow, Yegor." Jack leaned one arm over the chair. "What have you got?"

"Cliff coming up – five hundred feet to starboard," Dmitry responded, head down over his screen.

"Barrier wall?" Jack asked, and turned back to the window.

"No, a cliff, and we are on top of it. Deep water, falling away to depths," Dmitry responded.

Jack eased *Prusalka* back another few knots. Out of the window, they could see the fields of grasses and sea life began to disappear, and then the seafloor became a barren plain of dark rock. In another hundred feet, the bottom just ran out and fell into a darkness their powerful light couldn't hope to penetrate.

"Very deep," Yegor said.

"Hey, is back – our ghost." Dmitry hunched forward, but clicked the sonar to speaker. They could all hear the pings.

"Where? What? Speak to me, Dmitry." Jack stopped the submersible.

"From over the cliff edge, four thousand feet and moving parallel to *Prusalka*. Big, *big signature* – sixty feet, maybe more." Dmitry frowned. "I don't like this."

"Light it up," Jack said.

"No…" Cate spun in her seat. "*Leave us dark.*"

Dmitry held up a hand. "Wait. Going deep… deeper." He licked his lips, listening for a few more moments, his forehead puckered. He began to relax. "Gone."

They sat in silence, listening to the soft ping of the sonar. Cate could feel her heart thumping, more from excitement than fear. Jack turned in his seat, to find Cate's eyes.

She simply stared back at him.

"*What, was that?*" Abby asked, eyes round.

Dmitry shook his head. "If in ocean, I would say, whale. But down here…" He made a popping sound with his lips, and then shrugged.

"Slow to stop." Jack turned back to lean forward on the wheel, as the Priz Class deep-sea submersible glided to a halt on the edge of the precipice. Cate and the others craned to see out, but there was nothing but darkness.

"Yegor, let's light it up – we'll be fine." He turned to nod briefly to Cate. "Give me a quick rotation with the spot light."

The big Russian grunted and flicked up a few switches. The powerful beam on the top of the submarine came to life, and a huge tunnel of white light created a corridor reaching far out into the depths. Still, there was nothing to see but more utter blackness.

"Behold, the abyss." Greg's voice was barely a whisper. "I've never been in water so deep."

"Or dark," Abby said softly.

Dmitry stood so he could see over the top of his huge Russian compatriot. "So, we go in?"

There was silence for several seconds.

"Of course," Cate said. "It's why we came."

"Good." Dmitry clapped his hands once and sat down again. "I think now we will see if our submarine is water tight, yes?"

"How deep is it?" Greg asked.

"Deep,"' Jack said. "I'm getting a reading of about two thousand feet, stays like that for a few miles, and then drops off my scanners." Jack read some more numbers off his screen. "But the predictive analytics says based on the geology profile, it probably falls away to eight thousand feet – well outside our crush tolerance."

They continued to stare in silence for several more moments. Cate could feel the fluttering of excitement in her belly and something else, a weird feeling of foreboding she couldn't quite settle.

"Anyone else get the feeling something down there is staring back at us?" Greg looked from Abby to Cate.

"I don't like it," Yegor said.

"It's not unusual to fear the unknown." Mironov's calm voice turned their heads. "But like Professor Granger said; it's why we came."

"That's right." Cate swallowed, her mouth dry. "The first signal buoy is ten miles to the southeast – that way." She pointed out into the darkness, out over the shelf. "We're here to do a job – to map, analyze, record, and understand an environment that is unique in the world. We need to understand it, so we can save it. So..."

Jack moved the spotlight around, the tunnel of light finding nothing but blackness.

"It's like being in space, but without the stars," Abby breathed, her eyes shining. "The ocean is more ancient than the mountains, and freighted with the memories and the dreams of time." She turned to Greg, grinning. "HP Lovecraft, in one of his more lucid moments."

"Cool." Greg beamed back at her.

"Okay, people." Jack nodded to Yegor. "Take her along the edge of the cliff, Yegor. We'll keep using the spotlight for now."

The steady thrumming vibration of the propeller shaft only just overlaid the soft ping of the sonar as it reached out to try and touch on anything moving in the miles of darkness.

Jack turned in his seat again. "Dmitry, I want a full sonar scan – three hundred and sixty degrees."

Dmitry sat straighter. "You want to look out for columns of stone even from behind us?"

Jack seemed to think for a minute. "No, just, anything at all out there. Your ghosts, maybe."

"Okay, you got it, Captain." Dmitry adjusted his headphones, made some adjustments on his control panel, and then hunched over his phosphor-green screen.

"Holding at twelve fathoms." Yegor's voice was deep and calm.

Abby leaned around Cate to Greg. "A fathom is about six feet."

"*Duh.*" Greg rolled his eyes.

"Read it off in feet, Yegor." Jack laughed softly. "Don't want our land lubbers having to mentally convert the depth bands we are passing through every time you call it."

Yegor groaned, but then nodded. "Okay. We are steady at seventy feet." He half turned to look at Greg. "Oh, yes, and one knot is one nautical mile per hour, okay?"

"Yes, yes, thank you, and by the way, I'm no land lubber," Greg scoffed.

"Land lubber?" Abby chuckled. "What the hell is a *lubber* anyway?"

"Contact." Dmitry's voice was loud in the small craft, and made Cate jump in her seat.

"Shit, what is it?" Cate swung around, leaping from her seat to look over Dmitry's shoulder. "Is it the thing you saw before?"

"Cate, back to your seat." Jack's voice overrode her curiosity, but she remained on her feet. After all, she was in charge.

"*Sit down*, Professor Granger." His voice had an edge.

Professor Granger? She snorted, and sat, but only because she wanted to. She continued to face the Russian engineer.

"No, smaller signature." He listened and calibrated his sonar scope. "Maybe six feet long, moving fast, bearing forty-five degrees... still at a distance of five hundred feet." He listened some more. "Closing."

Greg leant back, trying to see over Jack and Yegor's shoulders. "Which way?" he whispered to Abby.

Cate turned to see Abby holding up her hands, pointing.

"Zero degrees is dead ahead." She swiveled. "One-eighty is behind, ninety degrees was right-side starboard, and two-seventy degrees left was port side. Okay? And everything else is varying degrees on that. You get it?"

"I think so. That way?" Greg pointed out into the darkness, between the front and the right side starboard.

Abby nodded. "Bingo."

"Only a hundred feet out now – I think is coming in for a look at us." Dmitry looked up and out the front window.

"Too small to worry us," Jack said. "Turning three degrees to face it. Yegor, switch off the spot and window lights and we'll see if we can draw it in close for a look-see."

Yegor flicked switches and immediately the blinding spotlight followed by the ring of halogen lights surrounding the convex window went out.

The sonar pinged, and something else ticked softly above them as the group sat and waited. Cate saw that

Dmitry sat hunched over his sonar, his face ghoulishly lit by the phosphor green of his screen as he calmly read out data.

"Fifty feet, thirty, twenty, ten..." he looked up. "It's here."

"Lights up," Jack said.

The big fish was framed in the glaring lights outside the window. The skin of the creature was pink and wrinkled, like that of a newborn baby. It had a shark-like shape but an elongated, flattened snout above protruding jaws that were filled with nail-like teeth.

"Now that is one ugly mother," Greg said

"Yech; looks sorta boneless... ancient," Abby said.

The thing swam more like a snake than a shark, its long sinuous body sliding up and over the underwater cliff.

"Looks ancient, because it is." Greg leaned towards Abby, looking delighted for the opportunity to impress her with his knowledge. "Been around for over one hundred and twenty million years. But if we went deep diving to about three hundred feet into one of the Atlantic sea canyons, we might just run across one today. It's called a goblin shark." He looked back at the sinuous shark's face. "For a very obvious reason; it's damn ugly."

"Incoming!" Dmitry's yell made them all cringe.

In the glare of the halogen light ring, the goblin shark was struck by something fast, and big enough to completely block the window. Once their vision cleared, they were left with a maelstrom of flesh fragments, blood, and the remaining front third of the goblin shark, severed from the rest of its body.

It all occurred so quickly, that the jaws of the goblin shark still worked as if the thing hadn't realized it had been bitten in two.

"Jesus Christ; what the hell just happened?" Jack kept a grip on his wheel, and yelled into the glass. "Talk to me, Dmitry."

"Sorry, could not see it. This thing came up beside the cliff wall… sonar blind spot." His eyes remained fixed on his screen. "Big, over thirty feet, circling." He looked to Jack. "Now coming back… *fast*."

"All right, brace everyone," Jack yelled again, his forearms bulging as he gripped the wheel.

Once again the viewing window was momentarily filled as something large, flannel-gray and armor plated swept by. When it had passed, the head of the shark was also gone.

"Come back for rest of meal," Yegor said. "Big fish."

"Yegor, give me the spot, follow it." Jack flicked switches as the big Russian lit up the darkness; the glaring spotlight flared to life. Yegor swiveled the tunnel of light towards the retreating creature.

"Holy shit. I take it all back… *that* mother is the ugliest thing I've ever seen." Greg's mouth hung open as he watched the massive fish swim away.

At the far reach of the spotlight the fish started to turn.

"It's covered in something – big scales," Yegor said. He watched the huge fish from under lowered brows. "Coming back."

"Placoderm," Mironov said, with a little awe in his voice. "Should have expected it. They were very prevalent in the early seas."

"Placoderm," Jack repeated. "Predator, and you're right, Yegor, it is covered in big scales, but on this thing they weren't just for show, they were actual interlocking armor plates. Its name means armored fish… and judging by the size, I'd say this guy is one of the biggest – *dunkleosteus*."

The armored fish passed by the front of the submersible, and one of its baseball sized eyes swiveled in the bony socket, to fix on them. They each could see it clearly now; the powerful-looking creature was about thirty-feet long, and looked to be made of overlapping sheets of steel all plated together. Even its mouth and eye sockets had plating around them.

"The mouth," Cate said. "The force that thing must have." The jaws hung on the face, and resembled nothing more than a massive bear trap complete with huge shearing teeth, some over a foot across.

"This monster hasn't been around since the late Devonian period." Jack turned to Cate. "Big predator."

Cate pushed hair off her slick forehead. "I don't get it; these things are far older than the life forms we were expecting."

Greg shrugged. "C'mon Cate, we've theorized about this type of habitat in our research. In this ocean-sized goldfish bowl, the environment might never alter. And if there's plenty of food, then as long as there's a biological balance, there would be no reason for anything trapped in here to go extinct." He pointed. "That bad boy can eat anything, and I'm sure those jaws could make fast work of those big sea scorpions... make fast work of anything."

They watched, spellbound, as the armor-plated fish circled them for another second or two. Its front end was like that of a tank, but its rear end was surprisingly slender, trailing away to a thin, almost whip-like tail.

"Back us up, Yegor," Jack said. "Let's get out of that cloud of chum floating all around us."

"Question," Abby said. "Why does it need all the armor? If it's an apex predator, why does it need so much protection?"

"Maybe it needed to protect itself from others of its kind," Cate responded, feeling uneasy about the way the fish was staying close to them.

"Looks like a living battering ram," Greg said.

"I think we should leave this area." Mironov carefully eased back in his seat and pulled the strap over his shoulder.

The group watched in silence for a few moments before Jack slowly looked over his shoulder at Cate; she could see the look on his face – he knew they weren't safe.

At the far reaches of their illumination, the huge fish turned, and started coming back at them

"Yep," Jack said. "I think we've seen enough. Twenty degree starboard, Yegor; ahead half speed."

Jack switched off the spotlight as the submersible eased around, and headed out over the dark water.

Jack half turned. "Dmitry..."

Dmitry grunted. "Yes, is still following us."

"Cate, get on rear camera. We need eyes on this thing." Jack leant across to Yegor. "Let's take it up to three-quarter speed."

Cate hunched over a secondary screen, and looked quickly to Mironov, who also leaned in close to a control panel beside his chair that delivered a feed from all external camera feeds. He also watched the armor-plated fish's approach.

"Will it attack us?" Abby asked.

Cate looked back to her screen. "This thing is a hyper carnivore, but look at the tail – it's fast and aggressively territorial. It'll basically try and eat anything it can fit in its mouth." She looked up. "It's gaining on us."

"Do you, *um*, think it can bite through the hull?" Abby's voice had gone up a few notes.

"*Ha!*" Dmitry spun in his chair. "Impossible; the *Prusalka* is titanium hull, and can take the pressure of the deep trenches. This little fishy will just break its teeth."

Cate looked away from her screen. "I'm not worried about that," she said. "The dunkleosteus' jaws are just like a giant compacting machine. But what I'm more worried about is—"

The impact threw Dmitry off his chair, and an alarm sounded from all around them. Sparks came from equipment panels overhead, and from beside Cate. "Shit." She momentarily covered her face.

"Goddamn thing just rammed us." Jack spun, yelling to Dmitry. "Get up and put that out before it chews up our oxygen."

Dmitry rolled, got to his feet, and grabbed at a small

extinguisher. "Hold breath." He blasted the panels with a cloud of the white gas.

Cate waved a hand in front of her face, trying to find her screen. "I can't see it."

Mironov pursed his lips. "It's coming around again – circling."

Yegor pointed out the front window, as the huge powerful fish went past them, heading out into the dark.

"That hurt us," Jack said. "Don't want to take too many more of those impacts. Taking her down – full dive, Mr Gryzlov."

"Down?" Greg's head snapped around. "Fuck that. We just had our bones rattled, and you want to take us down deeper? We should be surfacing."

Jack spoke over his shoulder. "Cool it, Greg. Placoderms usually hunt in the shallows to midwater – above a few hundred feet. There is only one place it can't follow us, and that's down. Yegor, increase ballast compression, angle down at ten degrees, and ahead full."

"Aye, Captain." Yegor flicked switches, and turned dials, but stared straight ahead from under his shelf-like brows.

There was a low frequency thrum coming from under their feet, and the angle of the cabin changed as they headed downwards into the dark void.

"Still out there." Dmitry shook his head. "Much faster than we are. I think is going to… *brace!*"

The second impact came from the rear this time, and the *Prusalka* yawed in the water, sliding sideways for a few seconds before Jack corrected the course. From somewhere overhead there came the sound of a high pressure hissing.

"Jesus, I hope that's not water coming in." Greg's voice was several octaves higher.

"*Sonofabitch.*" Jack gritted his teeth, his forearms bulging on the wheel. "Hang on everyone." He pushed the wheel further forward, increasing their angle of descent.

The crew gripped shelf tops, railings or anything they could hold onto as the floor dipped to forty-five degrees. Cate turned to look at Mironov, who sat gripping his armrests, and watching his view screens, his face as untroubled as if he were simply catching a movie in his private theatre.

Jack's voice brought her head back to him.

"Talk to me, Dmitry."

"I can't see him." The Russian grimaced. "No sign."

"I don't think we've lost him," Jack yelled. "Everyone keep a lookout."

Cate stared at the small screen in front of her that displayed the dark starboard water, and little else. Her head hurt from concentrating, or perhaps from the lingering gas Dmitry shot from the mini fire extinguisher.

"Nothing here." She turned in her seat to Greg sitting opposite, and viewing the port water side. He must have felt her stare, because he shook his head. "Nothing; all clear on the left, uh, I mean port side."

"At two hundred feet," Yegor intoned.

"Clear here," Abby said.

"It's nighttime in a licorice factory – anything on sonar, Dmitry?" Greg asked.

"Not really, sure. Maybe up on shelf, or staying close to cliff wall. But not showing on sonar." The Russian's brows were knitted, his face bathed in the green glow of his sonar screen

"Eyes on – everyone," Jack said, keeping the wheel pushed forward as they dived. He leaned forward to look out and up through his curved front window. "Valery, anything back there?"

Mironov looked from screen to screen, and then slowly shook his head. "Looks clear on all quadrants, Jack."

"Three hundred feet," Yegor said mechanically.

"Yes, coming now," Dmitry yelled. "Straight down on us."

The impact was like being in a huge bell that was being rung. Greg was thrown into his console, and for one terrifying moment, there came the sound of popping and complaining steel.

Yegor snorted, his bristled top lip turning up in a smile. "*Prusalka,* she doesn't like it, but she will hold. We okay, unless…"

"Unless?" Jack turned to him.

"Unless, bonehead fish hits our propeller, and make deformed. And then…" He shrugged.

"Ah fuck." Jack leant back in his seat. "Then, we row home."

Dmitry groaned. "Bad news; very bad. It is coming again, too fast for us."

He then spoke rapidly in Russian to Yegor, who half turned and yelled back in the same fashion. The two men argued for several seconds.

"That's enough!" Jack yelled.

Yegor spoke softly. "Dmitry say, maybe we should go back up."

"And what do you say?" Jack turned to the big man.

He bobbed his huge head for a moment. "Don't want to be hit in propeller. But, I think if fish can't go deep, then we should go deep."

"I agree; we keep going down."

"Jack, switch all external lighting off. Our glow could be attracting it." Cate gripped her console top even harder, but felt her fingers slipping due to the perspiration on her hands.

"Good idea; we run dark." Jack and Yegor flicked switches, and the external lights blinked out. "Ladies and gentlemen, rig for silent running. No one even breathes until I say."

"No, no, no." Dmitry went to get to his feet, but Cate turned and used two hands to shove him back into his seat.

"Stay still and stay silent." She held a finger to her lips.

Jack turned slowly, only the dim red glow of the *Prusalka's* interior on his face as he whispered. "Just read the sonar, Dmitry. Don't want to run into anything, now do we?"

Dmitry nodded and turned back to his control panel. His own face was green-lit, making him seem goblin-like. "Okay, okay... our friend is dropping in and out of the scope – still out there, looking for us, maybe."

"Four hundred and fifty feet," Yegor intoned softly.

Jack nodded and gestured with a flat hand – keep going down.

"*Svoloch!*" Dmitry hissed the Russian curse and gripped his console. "Something else now, big, very big – coming up from deeper water."

"What is it?" Abby whispered. "Is it something... worse?"

Dmitry's eyes bulged, but then he forcefully blew air from his lips. "Going past us... heading for hard-head fish."

"This is it," Cate said. "I know it." She turned to Mironov who smiled briefly, and then turned back to his monitors

The small Russian stared hard at the screen, and he held a hand to the cup over his ear. "Is strange, the signatures came together – then merged as one." He frowned listening, looking like he was trying to tease more meaning from the sonar pulses. He finally sat back. "Nothing – gone – both gone."

"Five hundred feet," Yegor said.

"Leveling off at five hundred," Jack said. "Everyone remain in their seat and stay quiet until we've put another mile on the dial."

"Still clear," Dmitry whispered.

"What the hell just happened?" Greg's forehead was creased with anger.

"Big fish get eaten by even bigger fish, I'd say." Mironov's brows were raised.

"Very big fish, I think," Dmitry said, nodding. "Maybe something big down here after all, yes?"

"Lights back on?" Yegor asked.

Cate nodded. "I think we can—"

"No, not yet," Mironov said quietly. "Let's just wait a while, and see what happens."

Cate's lips compressed, but Mironov simply nodded towards the front.

A luminous ribbon snaked out of the darkness and passed by the curved window. It was dotted with green and blue lights, and two antenna hung over disc-like eyes that each held a glowing bulb of yellow. The thing looked to be about twenty feet long, and only an inch wide. Further out, other creatures pulsed and blazed.

"More bioluminescence – not unexpected down here," Cate breathed, rising from her chair, Mironov's rudeness already forgotten.

Jack opened his mouth when he saw her approach, but then smiled, and turned back to enjoy the show himself.

"That could be an oar fish," Mironov said.

"Or was once," Greg responded, also getting up, quickly followed by Abby.

"They're quite rare you know." Mironov leant forward in his throne-like chair, leaning on his knees. "Maybe this variety has adapted for a dark-water lifestyle."

"Very possible; it takes thousands of generations to evolve a new capability... or lose one. But the stranger thing is, we are not at any great depth just yet. In the ocean, varieties such as the flashlight fish, bristlemouth, anglerfish, and viperfish, all use bioluminescence for capturing prey, attracting mates, or signaling. But they operate well below this level. We're still at mid-mesopelagic, and that reaches down to six hundred and fifty feet. Below that is the bathypelagic, where we'd expect the real deep-sea life."

"How deep can they go?" Abby asked.

"I have seen them before," Yegor rumbled. "But, yes, much deeper than this."

Cate rested one hand on Jack's shoulder, but snatched it away, and folded her arms. "They can get down to the abyssopelagic – the abyssal zone – that's about thirteen thousand feet down. Down there, you might find little more than Isopods, tube worms, snail fish and a few other soft-bodied organisms. Most of them grow extremely large."

"Deep sea gigantism," Greg said. "For example, in the deeps, normally tiny Isopods are ten times normal size, and very aggressive. They're usually scavengers, but when they're big, they'll attack and eat live prey."

Cate nodded. "When food is scare, I guess you gotta be prepared to fight for it..." She straightened. "...and be big enough to win those fights. But then that's it for most sea life. Below that we have the hadopelagic – the hadal zone – the deep-sea trenches. Down to twenty-eight thousand feet and counting. Who knows what's really down there."

Cate pulled at her collar, feeling a run of perspiration down the center of her back and under her arms. She leant forward again. "Jack, it's getting real hot in here; what's the outside temperature?"

Jack looked down at a small screen on his panel, quickly reading off some of the numbers. "Eighty-two degrees – *yeah*, damned warm." He turned to her. "But there're no coolers in here, only some internal heaters. Deep water is usually cold, so no one expected they'd need to stay cool."

"Five hundred feet, leveling off." Yegor leaned across to them. "Maybe we can increase the dehumidifier load. This will make it dryer in cabin and at least make it feel cooler."

"Good idea." Jack nodded. "But what about power usage; they're damned hungry aren't they?"

Yegor bobbed his large head. "*Da*, yes, but they can run for thirty hours before impacting on battery life. We should be back home in less than that."

"Let's do it," Jack said, winking up at Cate. "Make us a little more comfortable, anyway."

Dmitry spoke to his screen. "Nothing on sonar now – all quiet." He half turned to Jack and Yegor. "I think we lose it, or them."

"Good." Jack exhaled and straightened in his chair. "All stop. Dmitry, give me a damage report." He swiveled his chair to face back into the cabin. "Let me know if there's any structural impact on hull integrity. I'd prefer not to find we had a hairline crack when we are travelling down into the high pressure layers."

Jack looked up at Cate again. "Okay, we can stretch our legs, but keep the noise to a minimum. That rock-headed bastard's fossils were found in fairly shallow water so it doesn't usually hunt this deep – which is only a guess, as everything we know about Placoderms is from fossils. But..." he grimaced. "...we need to decide, as a group, about our next course of action. We could have been incapacitated, or worse, holed. Regardless of the toughness of the *Prusalka*, it was never built to sustain that type of attack."

Jack gave Cate a tight smile. "Sorry; you wanted a responsible captain, and unfortunately, like it or not, that's exactly what you got."

Cate's jaw jutted. She couldn't believe what he was doing. "You know, what I wanted, and what I expected was a captain who would navigate the risks – expected and unexpected. I never wanted some sort of millpond boating enthusiast, but someone with fortitude. We'll be fine."

Jack held her eyes for a moment. "Wow."

"Hold it together, Jack." She gave him a tight smile, then turned on her heel and sat heavily.

"That's what I intend to do." Jack swiveled in his seat, facing back towards Cate, Greg, Abby, Dmitry and Valery Mironov. Yegor continued to monitor the sensors as the submersible hovered in the water, dark and silent, as glowing life forms moved around them. But the others watched him, sensing some sort of growing conflict. Only Valery Mironov looked amused.

"Listen up, people. We need a vote on whether we proceed or return to base. The attack we sustained was *unexpected*." His eyes slid to Cate. "And I mean so far out of expectations that it creates exceptional risk. It immediately calls into question all our other expectations on risk management." Jack raised his chin. "Dmitry, report?"

"There is no damage," the Russian responded proudly. "Hard-head fish, not as hard as *Prusalka*'s hull; no fishy is going to break in. So, no problem."

"There you are." Cate turned back to her console.

Yegor grunted from beside Jack. "Yes, no problem... maybe, this time."

Jack half turned. "You have something to add, Mr Gryzlov? Everyone gets a say here."

The big Russian shrugged. "*Prusalka* is able to take crush-depth pressure." He looked briefly at Dmitry. "But is designed to accept pressure in a contiguous form along the entire superstructure, not just in any one place." He glared at Dmitry.

Dmitry's eyes were steady, and his grinning persona had vanished.

Jack looked from Dmitry to Yegor. "Yep, that's what I thought."

"So, all over pressure good, point-pressure, bad, huh Yegor?" Greg raised his brows.

"That about sums it up," Jack said, his expression earnest. "We've only been down here a few hours, and already come under attack. We survived through quick action and a lot of luck. But we are about to head into the absolute unknown." He paused, looking along each of their faces. "What happens when we head into the deep canyons? We could be attacked by something a lot bigger and a lot more powerful. Is everyone ready for that?"

Cate swung back around. She knew Jack was right to lay out all the risks, but still, she couldn't help feeling betrayed. It was like they were suddenly pulling in opposite directions all over again. If they got back to the entry point, and the engineers above ground said they'd need to haul them up for modifications, it'd be weeks or even months before they got back – *if* they ever got back. After all the cost, time and effort of even getting to this point – *fuck that.*

"I disagree. I think we've just had the worst of what this place can throw at us… and we survived with nothing more than a few bruises. You heard our engineer – no damage."

"Wait a minute." Greg's eyes went from Cate, back to Jack. "What did you mean by something a lot bigger and a lot more powerful?"

"Don't you dare, Jack." Cate felt a tension headache coming on.

Jack clasped his fingers together and sat forward, ignoring her. "Depends on when this place was created and isolated from the outside world's oceans. The things we've seen so far are old, damned old, and it makes me think they've been locked away in here a lot longer than we anticipated." His eyes went to Cate as he spoke. "For all we know this biological pocket was created when the super continent, Pangaea, was around. That existed from about three hundred million years ago, and then pulled apart, just under two hundred million years ago."

He looked down at his shoes momentarily. "And if that was the case, then it might have captured some of the world's oldest and most powerful predators."

"Like… what?" Abby's lips had tightened into a little ring.

Greg reached across to pat her shoulder. "Well, during the cretaceous, about one hundred and fifty million years ago, we saw the rise of the giant marine reptiles." He shrugged. "There were huge things, called mosasaurs that grew to fifty feet, easy. They were fast, powerful and very aggressive – think giant streamlined alligator. Let's hope none of those monsters are in here."

"Oh great." Abby turned. "Cate, are we going to be okay?"

"I think it's extremely unlikely anything like that could

still exist in here... and I'm not sure campfire horror stories are what's needed right now. We're scientists, remember?" Cate's jaw set. "Most of the ancient life forms we've seen to date are relatively small – even the Placoderm. I think a few people just need to stiffen their spine."

"What about the ghost Dmitry saw on the sonar?" Greg pointed at the Russian engineer. "He thought it was huge."

Dmitry grinned and hiked his shoulders.

"Siphonophore colonies – jellyfish," Mironov said, then uncrossed his legs, and smiled at Jack.

Jack stared back for a moment, but then scoffed, and shook his head. Dmitry bobbed his head. "Oh yes, I have heard of this happening. Is possible."

"What? What does that even mean?" Greg's head turned from Dmitry to Jack. "That the ghost you saw was a jellyfish?"

"No." Jack sighed. "But there is a phenomenon that was detected during World War Two, whereby false ocean bottoms, walls, and even large objects were detected by sonar. They were false readings that turned out to be masses of..." he held out a hand.

"Jellyfish." Cate answered. "And we've seen some big bastards down here already, haven't we Jack?" *Checkmate.*

"I don't believe that's what it was." Mironov's lips just quirked up a fraction. "Our object was under significant locomotion."

Cate's mouth hung open; *what the hell is his game?* Mironov pursed his lips and went back to looking at his several screens.

Cate exhaled, and turned to the group. "Look, I know as much as you guys, but there could be a hundred explanations for the sonar shadow. Might have been a jellyfish wall, or for all we know, there could be more modern creatures in here. My gut feel is this enclosed body of water has had periods of open and closure to the outside world. Maybe when the subsurface plates slide and rip apart, and then re-zip – things might have gotten in and out then." She turned to Abby. "Abby; you're our geologist, when was the last major crustal disturbance along this coast line?"

Abby looked to the roof, as if searching her memory. "That would be during the Miocene Epoch, around the Langhian Stage – fifteen million years ago, give or take. Significant geological changes right across the North American continent. That was a big one – it was even thought responsible for the Yellowstone hot spots."

"There you go." Cate slapped her thigh. "My guess is it might be some sort of primitive whale." Her eyes slid to Jack, who simply stared in return. *Yeah, I'm lying, so what?* Her glare said to him.

"I agree with Professor Granger." Mironov continued to stare at his screens, looking relaxed as always. "I doubt the ancient sea reptiles would still exist in here, and it is more likely to be a cetacean or some such species from that time. But does it really matter?"

Greg scoffed. "Like, yeah. The less giant things down here that might eat me the better."

"Well, I'm hoping for a whale," Abby said. "Whales I can deal with."

"*Ah* yes, the gentle bovines of the sea… but not always." Mironov smiled. "Just remember, even if this body of water was sealed only recently, geologically speaking of course, there was once a type of ancient whale that could have burst straight from the pages of Melville's novel, and that once hunted the oceans about fifteen million years ago. In fact, it was called the *Levyatan Melvillei*, after the great author. It grew to sixty feet, had foot-long teeth, and unlike todays whales, it had a fully functioning jaw that allowed it to rip free car-sized chunks of flesh. It probably preyed on other whales, and anything else it could catch."

"Like that really helped, Valery," Cate sighed and sat back.

The billionaire smiled back at her, seeming to enjoy the agitation he was creating.

"Okay, okay, so a hundred and fifty million years ago, bad... and fifteen million years ago, probably just as bad. But what if this place was open and closed only a few million years ago – say just two or three million?" Greg winked at Abby, looking like he was beginning to enjoy the game as well.

"Weeelll." Jack shook his head. "That's no better. In fact, many would say, it gets a lot worse. You see, just over a million years ago, we had the worst of the worst." Jack's mouth twisted as he leaned back. "Didn't we, Cate?"

Cate's brow was furrowed in thought as she stared at the submersible's floor.

Jack continued. "Then, we had the largest and most fearsome predator to have ever lived in our global oceans. It ruled for about twenty million years, and then, depending on which expert you talk to, mysteriously vanished between one and two million years ago."

"Megalodon. Of course," Greg said softly. "The tooth, *the tooth* we saw." He rocked back in his chair. "Oh, fuck."

"We don't know that." Cate lunged forward, but Abby leaned around her.

"You mean *the* tooth? The one from the image the drone took?"

Jack folded his arms. "You told them, right Cate? Told them that's what we think is really down here... and *why* we're here?"

Cate felt both annoyance and exasperation. "Sort of." She turned slowly to Greg and Abby. "I specifically said there could be a super predator down here. But how could I know exactly what type? You're the expert, Jack, and even you could only guess. In fact, we're all guessing about what that tooth was."

"I kinda get the feeling you two have an idea what it is we are looking for." Greg pulled in a cheek. "Right, Cate?

Might as well share, we're not exactly gonna walk out now, are we?"

Cate's lips compressed into a line, and Yegor turned his large head. "I think I also would like to know what we can meet down here."

"A type of shark… a big one," Jack said.

"A shark; that's it?" Abby tilted her head, her eyes narrowed.

"Yes and no," Mironov said. "If it's what we think it might be, it will certainly be a shark, but no ordinary representative of the species." He smiled benignly at Cate. "We believe it is *Carcharodon Megalodon* – the name itself means big tooth in ancient Greek. It averages sixty feet, and as wide around as a bus. Some scientists believe it could have gotten even bigger. What they all agree on, was this beast was territorial and once staking a claim, would have decimated entire marine communities. Today, its smaller cousin, the Great White, causes consternation when it comes too close one of our beaches. But imagine something four, five, six times its size." He sighed. "It's one of the ocean's mysteries, as there's no compelling reason, that I have ever seen, to account for it becoming extinct."

Mironov steepled his fingers. "Actually, I've been waiting for an opportunity to ask, Mr Monroe – the Megalodon – extinct or not? It was extremely tolerant of temperature changes, pressure changes, could hunt in light and dark water, and would have been certainly fast enough to catch even the swiftest prey, so, where is it?"

Every head swung to Jack. He seemed to think for a moment or two, and then his lips lifted to a small smile. "Extinct in here, or out there?"

"Extinct anywhere," Greg shot back.

"Eventually all things are revealed; all mysteries become truths." Jack's mouth turned down momentarily. "But if there's one place that holds its mysteries longest, that place is our oceans. They are as deep, dark and fathomless as the night sky. I've studied shark species all my life, and even been on expeditions before looking for signs of the Megalodon, the dinosaur shark. Never found any proof, conclusive proof, anyway."

"But you found something, didn't you, Mr Monroe?" Mironov smiled, confidently.

Mironov's insightful probing made Cate wonder just how much the billionaire knew about all of them – *everything*, she bet. Otherwise he might never have come.

She saw Jack's jaws working, and remembered it was something he did when making a decision. She bet he was weighing up what to tell them, and what to hold back.

"What we found was a lot more questions." He looked up slowly. "In 1918, on the eastern coast of Australia, fishermen refused to go to sea when a monster shark turned up and started taking the lobster pots. These guys were used to big sharks, but this one frightened them so much that they refused to put to sea – and remember, in those days, no fishing meant no food and no income. Eyewitnesses claimed the shark was over fifty feet long, with a dorsal fin, taller than a grown man."

"*Je-zuz* Christ." Greg tilted himself back in his chair.

Jack's mouth lifted into a lop-sided grin. "In March 1954, the Cutter called the *Rachel Cohen* supposedly ran aground in the middle of the Pacific. When they hauled it up into dry-dock, they found there was an enormous bite mark around the propeller beams that was way too large for any modern shark to make. The tooth marks were about five inches wide…" Jack held his hands apart. "… the largest Great White has teeth only measuring two and a half inches."

He sighed. "More recently, in 1975, during a deep-sea dredging exploration, the HMS *Challenger* brought up two teeth from deep water – turned out they were Megalodon teeth – no surprise, as the shark was a global predator, and hunted in deep water. But what did shock the scientists was that these teeth seemed to only date to fifteen thousand years ago." He shook his head, his eyes locked on Mironov's. "Those teeth should not have been so, *young*." He sat back. "The list goes on."

"That's enough, Jack, and thanks… for unnecessarily worrying the crap out of everyone, I mean." Cate got to her feet. "Look, I know everyone's scared. Hell, I'm scared. That Placoderm frightened the shit out of me. But I was nervous and excited before we came, and I think that's how we all should be down here. We're explorers, pioneers – in fact, probably the first modern humans to be in these waters. Not only will we go down in history, but think of the things we'll see? Think of what we've *already* seen."

She looked to Mironov. "Now would be a good time for your input, Valery."

Mironov's eyes were still on Jack. "One thing Jack's story tells us, is that there are just as many wonders to be found in our deep oceans, as there are in here." He smiled. "And in many ways, we are safer in here, than out there."

"How do you come to that conclusion?" Abby asked, her brows drawn together.

"We made some modifications to the submersible. Some countermeasures if you like." He shrugged. "Just improvements to some existing capabilities. You see, these deep-sea vehicles can run into all manner of things in depths that take a fancy to the lights and noise."

"Like giant squid?" Greg asked.

"Like the squid, yes. Though the soft-bodied cephalopods can't damage the hull, they can certainly become fouled in the propeller or tangled in the superstructure. As Dmitry has already mentioned, the Priz Class is able to run a mild electric shock over the hull to discourage these unwelcome visitors." He smiled. "We simply gave the discouragement factor a bit more juice – five million volts more juice in a short burst. Wouldn't want to do it too many times, or we might drain the batteries. But it'll see off the largest of inquisitive visitors, I would imagine."

Dmitry grinned. "*Prusalka* is now largest electric eel in world."

"Exactly," Mironov said easing back in his chair.

Jack grunted, his eyes on Mironov. "That's good... if we ever get grabbed." He turned to the big Russian beside him. "Yegor, can the *Prusalka* sustain another attack like the one we just experienced?"

His big head bobbed for a moment. "Yes, sure, we can take another few hull hits from big hard-headed fish. But that is not really what I worried about. Submarine is unlikely to be holed by this type of attack. But if big fish thing strikes our propeller and bends shaft or breaks blades, maybe we can surface and repair it, here with big cavern, but..." He grimaced.

"But..." Jack rubbed both hands up through his hair. "Of course." He looked at Yegor who simply nodded. Jack sat back. "But what happens if we get crippled in an area of the cave that is fully submerged? We'd be dead in the water, and no surface above us."

"We'd be fucked," Greg said.

"That's enough of that," Cate shot back.

"Very unlikely," Mironov said, picking something from his sleeve.

"The propeller is a point of vulnerability, and now I'm not sure we're fully prepared. We need to take a vote." Jack sighed and then mouthed *sorry* to her.

Cate couldn't help her jaw tightening. "We proceed."

Jack's expression drooped, and Cate could tell his pragmatism was probably fighting against any old loyalty he felt to her. Finally he shook his head. "I vote we go back. Talk to topside. See what else we can do to ensure we have a safer mission. We've run into too many unknowns and we only just started. We have a chance to recalibrate. Next time we might not, and it could be fatal."

Cate steamed, her eyes on Jack. He wouldn't look at her.

"I agree, we get some extra armor, firepower or something. Then full speed ahead." Greg shrugged, as he looked at Cate. "Just a detour."

"We should go on," Dmitry said. "I think Professor Granger is good idea to continue adventure now. Besides, what else can we do to *Prusalka*? Stick harpoons on her, or maybe we go in battleship?" He grinned sheepishly, and made a pointing motion – down.

Yegor spoke without turning. "We go back; create shielding for propeller, at least."

"We'll burn through resources going back, I believe, for nothing." Mironov raised a single eyebrow. "We can expect to be tested, but I do not think that we run home every time that happens. This submersible can deal with anything now. We are already better for the experience. My vote; we proceed." He smiled at Cate.

"Three for three." Jack looked to Abby. "You're the decider."

The young geologist suddenly looked panicked as her eyes darted from Greg, to Jack, then to Cate.

"I don't know what to do." The woman's eyes glistened.

Cate could see the inner turmoil written large on the young woman's face. She was being torn apart... *by her*. Cate sighed, noisily, feeling a momentary bloom of anger, but then dampened it down, knowing Abby was scared out of her mind.

"*Ah fuck.*" Cate looked heavenward for a moment, feeling defeated. "It's okay, Abby, don't say anything." The corner of Cate's mouth quirked up. "I change my vote; I think we should go back as well. It wouldn't hurt to at least see what we can do to protect the propeller shaft – an obvious potential point of failure."

Abby looked down. "Thank you."

Jack nodded to her, and immediately turned his seat back to the curved window. "We'll move well out of the area before coming full about. If that Placoderm is as territorial as we think, then it should remain around here. Mr Gryzlov, stay at depth, and proceed one mile before coming about. We'll stay low, keep our heads down, and then loop back," Jack said.

"*Da*, Captain." Yegor pushed the wheel forward. "Good idea."

Jack half turned. "I think we should all stay quiet and in our seats for a little longer. No need to invite something in for a look-see."

"Gets my vote," Greg said, swinging back in his seat and hunching over his viewing screen. "Plenty to look at."

"Steady as she goes, Yegor." Jack half turned. "Dmitry, eyes open back there… and everyone else, keep watching your port and starboard screens. I want to know the minute you see of hear anything interesting."

They travelled in silence, the minutes turning into hours, as Yegor took them far out to the northeast, before slowly coming around in a gigantic arc, and heading back towards the underwater cliff face.

"Cliff wall coming up,"' Dmitry said. "Five hundred feet."

"Take her in close, and then all stop. We'll float up, slowly, see if anything is above the cliff line, before proceeding… at speed."

"Aye, Captain." Yegor glided in to about twenty feet from the sheer cliff, and then shut down the engines. He increased pressure in the ballast tanks, and *Prusalka* slowly rose in the black water.

Dmitry counted off the depths. "Coming up to four hundred feet, three hundred, two hundred, coming up to cliff edge."

"Slow now, hover at the lip. I want to take a peek first," Jack said.

Dmitry nodded, grinning. "A few small physical signatures, but nothing significant."

"All clear, here," Greg said quickly.

"Nothing as well." Cate looked up.

"Clear and clear." From both Abby and Mironov.

"Okay, ease us forward, Yegor. We'll proceed at three-quarter speed; take us about an hour to get back to the drop area. We stay quiet, and we move fast."

Cate felt herself sink back in her seat as the powerful propeller spun faster, giving them an extra kick under the dark water. After another few minutes, Jack re-engaged the front viewing lights.

"Nothing." He frowned. "There's nothing out there other than a few jellyfish. Where's all that weird and wonderful life we saw on the way in?"

"Maybe the dunkleo-thingy scared everything off," Abby said, slightly rising in her chair.

"Or we did," Greg added.

"Maybe," Jack said. "Coming up on drop zone. We'll surface and hook straight up to the comm line. See if the engineers can give us some advice on the prop shielding."

"Wait." Cate craned towards her small screen. "*Slow down, slow down...* what's that on the bottom, about fifty feet out on my side, *um*, I think at about forty degrees, starboard."

They had passed by the object, but she was sure she had seen something that wasn't there the first time. She got to her feet, as Jack eased the submersible around. Cate went and stood behind him.

"There was something on the bottom. Something, I think not... natural."

"Yegor, slow to two knots; we'll do a quick scan and..." Jack sprang forward. "*Holy Christ!*"

The first thing they saw was the bright red coveralls. The human body, or the remains of it, was missing its legs, and now hundreds of tiny creatures that looked like spindly scorpions feasted on the stumps. The tattered remnants of its clothing were ragged and burned.

Not far away was another body. This one, eyes wide and looking waxen, and anchored to the bottom by wrist-thick worms that had risen from the ooze, their heads buried deep into the dead flesh.

"The ground crew," Cate said, barely above a whisper.

"My engineers," Mironov added.

"Something really bad happened up there," Cate put a hand over her mouth.

There was rubble everywhere, and the water began to become cloudy. Jack flicked on the spotlight, immediately revealing the twisted spiderweb of steel and cable.

"Oh god no," Jack grimaced. "That's our goddamn crane."

"They're all dead," Abby said softly.

"I don't understand," Greg crowded in beside Cate. "What the hell happened?"

The mountain of tangled remains of the crane was piled on the bottom. Rock, soil and fallen bodies created small islands everywhere.

"That tremor we felt a while back..." Jack stopped the submersible and it hovered in the dark water. "That must have been an earthquake. Maybe we weakened the cave roof, and it collapsed."

"*Hmm*, then why would everything look scorched?" Mironov asked.

"We have topside camera." Dmitry waved Cate over. "Look, hole is bigger."

Cate rushed to look over Dmitry's shoulder at the top camera's feed. At first, it was hard to make out – the circle of light was still there, but instead of the pinpoint of light she remembered, it now looked ragged, uneven and much bigger.

"We should surface," Cate said. "Maybe we can still get a signal out. Or at least pick one up, and see what happened."

"Is that a good idea?" Greg asked. "Some of those boulders on the bottom are the size of trucks. What happens if one more decides to drop down on top of us?"

"We risk it," Jack said. "Take her up, Yegor."

The big Russian was frowning so deeply, his brows formed a single massive shelf over his dark eyes. "I don't think so." He turned his head slowly to Jack. "You look." He pointed one of his blunt fingers at the radiation counter on his console. It was registering off the scale for plutonium particle count.

"What...?" Jack sat back, rubbing both hands up through his sweat soaked hair. He turned as Mironov cleared his throat.

"Now I think it becomes clear," the Russian billionaire said evenly. "Why the bodies were burned up, why all the destruction, and why the localized tremor we felt. I suggest, there has been a detonation of some sort of tactical nuclear weapon on the surface – small, compact, undoubtedly low yield, of maybe even less than a single kiloton. But enough to totally obliterate the surface crew."

Mironov looked at his own monitors, which were duplicates of many of Yegor's and Dmitrys. "And by the look of that heavy particle count, I'd say it was an enhanced radiation weapon – a dirty bomb – designed to maximize the ionizing particles. Poison the area."

Cate sat down before her legs gave way. "They didn't want to just destroy our means of escape, they wanted to salt the earth to ensure we never could." Cate folded her arm tight cross her chest, feeling chilled even in the humid cabin. "Even if we got scrubbers in, it'd take months or even years to clean it up." Her eyes welled up. "We've got days."

"Very bad." Dmitry rubbed a hand up over his shaven head. "Someone wanted to cut us off."

"Someone *did* cut us off," Greg shot back. "But why? Why would they do that?"

"Why and who?" Jack's lips compressed.

Cate noticed Mironov ease back in his chair, his eyes narrowed as his vision seemed to have turned inward.

"Does that mean we can't get home?" Abby's chin wobbled. "Are we trapped?"

There was silence for many minutes, before Dmitry

leaned towards Cate. "We need to find out what happened. Every minute is important."

"Dmitry is right. And we can't stay here." Cate looked across to Jack. "How far did you say it was until we hit that first communication buoy?"

"Fifteen miles," Jack responded slowly.

Cate saw the worry in his eyes. She also felt the knot of panic in her gut, and a thousand questions tumbled over each other in her head. But she knew that voicing them now was less than useless, and might just panic the team.

"We have no choice now; we go forward – head to the next communication buoy. Find out what happened, and work on a plan to get ourselves out of here." She looked along their faces; only Jack met her eyes. She smiled back. "And I guess, in the meantime, we get to do the job we were sent down here to do – nothing has changed in that regard."

"Whether we like it or not – that's just freakin great," Greg said sourly.

Cate rounded on him. "Listen, buster; you got an alternative to just sitting there worrying about your ass? And maybe becoming so poisoned from the radiation, your eyes start to bleed?"

Greg held up a hand. "Easy there, Cate. I'm sorry, but I'm just a little nervous, is all. Remember we came back so we can get ourselves better protection from those placasaurs."

"Placoderms," Jack corrected, softly.

"Yeah, whatever, and now we've got to cross its front yard again… without extra shielding." He hiked his shoulders. "That's all."

Cate stared at the floor, feeling exhaustion drag on her bones. "And my response is the same; what's the alternative?" She exhaled, lifting her head. "Look, this is a shitty outcome, and I'm betting it was a lot shittier for those poor guys who just got blown away. We could have been topside, or even underneath the explosion and been crushed. Fact is, we're alive, and we have a plan. So as far as I'm concerned, it's been our lucky day."

Greg nodded, but Cate saw his eyes were still evasive. She didn't want to fight with him or anyone else right now. She turned slowly to Jack. "Can you get us to the communication buoy via a different route?"

"Sure, no problem,"' Jack said, his mouth set in a tight line.

She looked to Mironov, who nodded and sat back. She saw no more questions behind anyone's eyes, so just pointed forward.

"Then let's do it."

CHAPTER 12

Brogidan Yusoff stubbed out his thick cigarette, and grinned into the receiver as he listened to Uli Stroyev, his ministerial aide, relay their progress.

"The Baranof Island entrance has been obliterated and has a radioactive seal. It will take two years to bring it to a level of contamination repair that would permit people to work there without full protective clothing." Stroyev laughed softly.

Yusoff grunted. "And what about diplomatic blowback? Did you cover your tracks?"

"Of course. We even planted some communication chatter online from our Middle East agents, hinting at a terrorist cell. They'll be chasing their tails for years. It's over, Minister; they're sealed in." Stroyev laughed again. "No one will be climbing out of that hole anytime soon."

"Then our friend Mironov is trapped and sealed in a tin can with our agent. Today is a good day." Yusoff poured some vodka into a small glass.

"Well, Minster, maybe not trapped… just yet." Stroyev's words halted Yusoff's glass at his lips.

"What?"

"Our agent has informed me that the Americans have drilled secret communication and supply tubes down to the underground sea all across the Alaskan continent. I think it would be good if we got to them before Mironov does," Stroyev said.

Yusoff laugh was like grinding stones. "Trust that wily old fox to ensure he has a few rat runs hidden in his maze." He put his glass down. "Listen carefully; you find those communication pipes. You make sure that if Mironov ever makes it to them, he is given nothing but dead air, understand?"

"Of course, Minister." Stroyev's voice had the appropriate level of servility.

"Contact me when you have news." Yusoff disconnected the line and sat back. He quickly lifted his glass, downing the shot in a gulp. "So, we move our chess pieces around, Valery. But there is a difference; I have all the time in the world, and for you, the clock is ticking."

Yusoff poured himself another glass and lifted it. "Salute, Valery."

Sonya Borashev was on her feet; throat raw from screaming into the phone at subordinates, FBI insiders, colleagues, and anyone she thought needed an extra dose of urgency.

The nuclear explosion on the cliff-top site was centered directly over the access hole they had drilled. It was a tactical nuclear device, packed down to around one-point-one kilotons. But still, the size wasn't the issue, it was the contamination – the detonation's particle footprint meant it was a neutron bomb, a low-yield thermonuclear weapon where a burst of neutrons generated by a fusion reaction is intentionally allowed to escape the device's housing, poisoning its surroundings.

Sonya paced, working through the options outlined to her: they could vacate the site, seal it, and leave it for the elements to clean up over a generation. Next option was a standard decon-job – that would shrink the time to make it habitable down to a few years. But then they'd need to rebuild the crane and other superstructure required, plus do all the work in Level-A HAZMAT suits.

She leant forward on her knuckles on the desk.

Last option was a rapid decon – scrub and remove the contaminated debris, work around the clock, and forget about making it habitable, instead just make it bearable. It would mean they could get back in there within a few months.

"Fuck it!" She swept a pile of folders and pens from her desk. It had been her job to screen the submersible crew, and somehow a switch had taken place. She screamed her frustration, and snatched up a heavy crystal clock, drawing her arm back and preparing to throw it.

Sonya stopped her arm – Valery was still alive, but he had days and hours, not months. She dropped the clock and sat heavily, closing her eyes and feeling her heart beat rapidly in her chest. She used her training to ease it back, like a racing car driver throttling down as they came into a bend – if not there would be an imminent crash.

"Who are you?" She mentally ran through the list of Valery Mironov's known enemies. It was a long list, but only a handful wanted him dead. Her brows furrowed. But only one she knew of wanted him punished first, and then dead. Her eyes flicked open.

Brogidan Yusoff, head of the Russian Ministry of Resources and Agriculture – could it be him? Only he had the resources, the reach and determination, and also the psychology to undertake such an attack... and he had tried before.

She sat stone still for a moment, her ice blue eyes unblinking. "I can't contact you, Valery, but if you urgently wanted to contact me, you would make your way to..." her eyes widened. If they knew about the mission, then they'd soon know about the communication silos. She launched back from the desk so quickly the chair flipped backwards several times.

She pulled open her desk drawer and reached for the gun – a Glock 27 – small compact, and deadly. She tucked it into her belt and then sprinted for the door.

CHAPTER 13

The *Prusalka* hovered at the edge of the chasm. No one spoke, or seemed to even breathe. Cate stood behind Jack and Yegor, and everyone else crowded up behind her to stare out through the curved glass window at the darkness beyond the submerged cliff drop-off.

She knew there were things down there that wanted to attack, and if given the chance, eat them alive. Not that that was likely to happen, because once at depth, any puncture to the hull, and they'd all be dead in a few seconds, compacted down to the size of soda cans by the thousands of pounds of pressure that relentlessly worked on the skin of the vessel. She was staring trance-like, until Jack's voice made her start.

"The first communication silo is directly under Hobart Bay, fifteen miles eastward. But to get there we'll need to go deep this time," Jack said.

"Past hard-head fish." Dmitry nodded, and then went back to his scope.

"And that other thing," Greg said. "Whatever that big blip was – either a shark or a whale, it came up out of the depths, and luckily for us, went after the dunkle-whatever."

"Wasn't interested in us." Jack briefly glanced at Greg. "We don't really have a choice. Think of it as walking through a jungle – there might be a tiger in there, but we know it can't be everywhere, and if we're quiet and smart, it won't even find us."

"As quite as we can be in a fifty ton clunker of a submarine," Greg said.

The huge Yegor turned and glared, and Greg immediately hiked his shoulders. "Not that *Prusalka* is a clunker."

Yegor muttered and faced the window again.

"What are you thinking?" Cate asked Jack.

Jack looked back out at the dark void. "We descend to five hundred feet again – run hard and fast at those depths. Should keep us below any surface predators, and above anything rising up from below." He turned in his seat. "But there's a shelf that pushes down a thousand feet; we'll need to dive deep to get under it." He turned back. "There's no other way to the first comm-buoy."

Cate nodded slowly, and got to her feet. She walked forward, and stood beside Jack, arms folded. She could feel his eyes on her.

After moment, he reached up and placed a hand on her forearm. "We'll be fine."

"Of course we will." She patted his hand, but then turned slightly, pulling away from him. "So, let's go for it. We need to find out what the hell happened... and where we can find another way out."

"Gets my vote," Greg said. "Full speed ahead, Captain Nemo." He reached back to high-five Abby.

Yegor turned to Jack, waiting.

"Let's take her down to five hundred feet again, maximum speed until we close in on the shelf." He half smiled. "And if we're still in one piece, then we'll dip under it and head for Hobart Bay."

Yegor nodded and pushed a t-shaped joystick forward. The thrumming of the engine vibration tickled the soles of their feet as the propeller shaft spun ever faster. Jack pushed the u-shaped wheel forward, and they begin to descend down the side of the cliff.

"Take your seats and strap-in everyone." He turned and grinned. "Coffee and tea will be served shortly."

"But how long, until...?" Abby's voice was barely a

squeak. She cleared her throat. "*Um,* how long have we got, thinking about, you know, food, water, air…?"

Yegor turned in his seat. "Don't worry, little sparrow. We can stay down one hundred and twenty hours, but I do not think this will be necessary. There will be air pockets in the caves, so we can surface and replenish the tanks if need be. We have food for a week, and…" He waved a huge arm at the window. "…there is plenty of fish. Also, we have water and water purification device." He turned, his lips curved up in a lopsided grin. "I think our big problem is not having deck of cards if we get bored."

Abby smiled, and nodded. "Thank you."

"All the comforts of home; but if we do get stuck down here, forever…" Greg leaned towards her. "…we might need to start thinking about populating the inner Earth, and, well, I'm single."

She wrinkled her nose. "Not if you were the last man on Earth… or below it."

Greg reached into a pocket, and held up a half eaten bag of M&Ms. "I have chocolate."

"*Ooh,* then that must make you the chief." Abby pushed him back towards his chair.

Dmitry laughed. "You see? We'll be fine."

"Five hundred feet, leveling off." Yegor eased back on the wheel, and the bulbous craft slowed in the water like a deep-sea dirigible in a pitch-black sky.

CHAPTER 14

Hobart Bay, Alaska
57°27'11" North, 133°23'36" West
Population: 12

The stealth chopper dropped the two black-clad men a mile from the Bay's village. It was a scoured area gouged out of the pristine wilderness, and sat on the edge of a moonlit bay that was as still as dark blue glass.

There were just three permanent resident families this time of year, and as the outside temperature was currently hovering around zero degrees, all of them would be inside their respective cabins preparing for hot evening meals.

The men now moved quickly to the edge of the clearing, where they crouched – there was no movement, sound, or alert dogs watching the village grounds.

One used night vision glasses to slowly scan the perimeter, and then focused back on the tiny, unremarkable structure. It was constructed of old wood and designed to blend into its surroundings. But they knew what it housed was far from the ordinary.

He lowered the glasses. "External motion sensors, infrared cameras, and acoustic detection devices – we'll need a pulse."

The other man grunted, and pulled a squat-looking device from his backpack. The pulse generator would direct a short but powerful electromagnetic wave over the structure, temporarily disabling any electronics.

"Clear…" He fired it. The pulse was invisible and powerful. There would be no clues for Mironov's teams this day.

He quickly packed it away, and then the duo sprinted hard to the small building. The door was closed but the electronic lock was now disengaged – one pulled it open, turned to the other and grinned.

"After you, comrade."

Inside it was dark, but they could easily make out the huge cylinder that protruded from the earth. There was a three-foot access panel flush with the skin of the communication silo. Inside it was a feat of engineering mastery, as the long tube stretched down thousands of feet to the subterranean sea below. The six foot bore hole was then lined with pre-made tubing that was a ribbed design to allow flexibility so the whole pathway could move as the surrounding geology breathed and flexed with every tremor, quake, or seismic shudder the earth could muster in these parts.

Inside the access panel there were thousands of feet of fiber-optic threads, plus a type of hydraulic dumb-water to transport any urgently-required materials to below ground. The communication buoy and support package was gone, now thousands of feet below, mute and patiently waiting for its guests to arrive.

One of the men waited at the door, holding it open a crack, and keeping an eye on the silent village, while the other dropped to one knee shrugged off his backpack and removed a loaf of bread-sized package. He removed a waterproof wrapping and then set to working on some dials and buttons. Immediately, a blinking green light went red, and a digital readout began to count down. He stood, and placed the package inside the shaft, letting it drop into the dark.

"Let's go."

They were out the door and sprinting to the tree line,

retracing their steps for another hundred feet, before the deep thump of the explosion shook some early snow from tree branches down onto their heads.

One grinned to the other. "Sorry Mr Mironov, no letters from home today, *Da?*"

The other laughed. "We need to hurry. Fifty miles to our next target, in Sheslay Canada – and now they know we're here."

They began to sprint back to their pickup point. One paused to look back. Behind them, a column of orange erupted from the roof of the small building sending a mushroom cloud of vaporized fiber-optic cables and plastic into the air. He grinned again, and ran harder.

CHAPTER 15

Now at three thousand feet." Yegor's voice was deep and calm as ever, despite the intermittent sound of metal popping and groaning under immense pressure.

Jack ignored it; he knew the sounds a submersible made in deep water, and nothing he heard worried him in the slightest. Hours back, he had switched off the ring of halogens around the window, and they rarely saw any luminescent life forms appear out of the darkness. Dmitry reported the odd anomaly on the sonar, but whatever they were, they never came close enough to concern them

"Wow, *this* is deep,"' Greg said. "Bottom of the ocean stuff."

"*Nyet*, far from it," Yegor said, without turning. "Now we are approximately at a level that is usual bottom of continental shelf. Long way down to real ocean bottom."

"How deep?" Greg said, leaning around to stare out into the dark void beyond Jack and Yegor.

"In this cavern, or in the oceans?" Jack asked.

"Both," Abby said, leaning back.

"Well, in here, our soundings having it drop to below eight thousand feet in certain places – that certainly is deep – crush depths for sure. But it's nothing compared to what's in the ocean trenches." Jack spun in his seat to face the group. "Cate mentioned the different depths we have in the ocean. It's actually a bit like the Earth's geology and can be defined in layers – the crust, the mantle, outer core and inner core – so too can the world's oceans be thought of as existing in layers."

Jack used his hands, to make layers in the air. He started at the top. "Most everything we know lives in the upper-most layer, called the pelagic zone; that's above the continental shelf. But below that are several more layers that are largely unexplored." He grinned. "Did you know that ninety-five per cent of the underwater world remains unexplored? Down in the deep and dark, are three more zones – below three thousand feet, we enter the Bathyal Zone – it's also called the midnight zone as it's the first layer totally devoid of light."

Yegor grunted. "We can dive to this depth in the *Prusalka* if need be."

Jack nodded. "But the ocean goes even deeper, dropping down farther to below thirteen thousand feet or so, and into the abyssal zone – the abyss – home of the giant tubeworm and giant squid, and that one goes all the way down to twenty thousand feet."

Cate leaned forward resting her elbows on her knees. "But there's one more zone to go – the Hadal – my favorite, and named after the realm of Hades. That one drops down to thirty-six thousand feet, and touches the deepest ocean trenches on Earth. We have no real idea what's down there. And when our deepest submersibles make it down, they can only spend a few minutes looking at about a dozen square feet of the environment. Imagine dropping into the Amazon jungle for a few minutes, at night and in a coffin, with a flashlight and tiny window to see through." She took a small sip from her water bottle. "We don't know what lives down there... if anything even could."

Jack nodded, holding her gaze and hoping she was thawing to him again. "That's right, and for that matter, we aren't even sure what really lives in the dark layers above either. The world still has plenty of mysteries, and the ocean is the prize winner for keeping the most."

"Well, thank god, we're in this cave, where it's nice and safe," Greg said, grinning.

Another pop and groan from the hull seemed to punctuate Greg's comment, making everyone look at the steel ceiling above their heads.

"Safe-*ish,*" Greg added.

Dmitry smiled in the red-green darkness. "A little pressure is good – makes diamonds, yes?"

"Look – there's a light out there," Abby said, pointing out of the front window.

The group turned as one, immediately seeing the dot of blue light in the darkness. It hovered for a moment, like a star in the night sky before beginning to close in on them.

"More bioluminescent fish, I'll wager," Jack said.

As they approached, the thing hovered again, seeming to watch them. It lengthened, and they saw that the blue glow ran the length of an eel-like body, with dots of blue, and a bulb at one end.

"Light it up," Jack said.

Yegor flicked a switch and the ring of lights around the front window threw a pathway out into the dark. The fish was an eight-foot silver ribbon with a hair-like tail. But the other end of the fish was where the nightmare began.

"Jesus," Greg said softly.

It had a box-like head that seemed all boney and angular. Large, bulging black eyes and a massive needle-filled mouth with the teeth seeming way too large for the jaws that hung open like a trap. Extending out over its mouth was another bulb, a lure, which had been flaring blue until the light had landed upon it.

The thing whipped its tail and vanished.

"Oh wow," Abby said. "Nightmare."

"Deep-sea dragonfish," Mironov said. "Member of the *Stomiidae* family – but this species is quite a way up. They usually permanently live out their lives at about ten thousand feet... and they're rarely over a foot long."

"Everything is bigger down here." Greg pushed long hair from his forehead.

"Why not?" Cate put her water bottle down. "This place has had hundreds of millions of years all to itself. Bigger things do better in the game of competition. And if the environmental conditions remain static, and no new species are inserted, then there's no reason for anything to die out. The existing species just continue to grow."

"And it's also free of us nasty, predatory human beings," Abby said.

"Yeah, like we're the scary things down here," Greg scoffed.

Cate used the back of her hand to dab at perspiration on her forehead. "If this thing usually lives at ten thousand feet, why was it up here?"

Jack shrugged. "Might just be another adaptation. Or something chased it out of its normal hunting ground."

"Thank you, Jack; like that just settled my nerves." Greg got to his feet and tried to pace, but there was only room for a few steps before he had to turn. His head struck a pipe above, ringing through the submersible. "Ouch."

"Sit down, and be quiet," Cate said. "You're making us all nervous."

"I'm making *you* nervous?" Greg forced a smile. "Am I the only one who thinks it's getting smaller in here?" He approached Jack and Yegor. "Hey, guys, do you think we can surface soon? Just to get a breath of fresh air?"

Jack turned to study the young scientist for a moment. "Not just yet, Greg. Why don't you sit down, buddy? Take it easy for a minute or two."

Greg grimaced, looking like he was about to object.

"Greg, *please* do as your told." Cate scowled.

He stiffened, turning to her. "Will you stop talking to me like that? You're not Captain Bligh, you know." He pointed at Jack. "And we've already got a captain."

Cate's eyes narrowed. "I'm the mission leader—"

"Yeah, yeah, and I'm thinking we're a bit top-heavy on the management layer in here – we've got a captain, a mission leader, and also Mr Money Bags at the rear who seems to be pulling the strings." He began to pace.

Mironov looked up and smiled. Jack swung in his seat.

"Greg... *Greg!*"

The young man stopped moving.

"Just... take it easy, buddy." Jack waved him down, but continued to watch him. He'd seen claustrophobia before, and even though the man was of slight build, the last thing anyone needed right now was someone having a panic attack in a confined space. "We got this, Greg."

Greg grimaced and wrung his hands for a moment, and then headed back to his seat. Jack turned to Dmitry.

"What's our oxygen level like? Still damned hot and thick in here."

Dmitry read from his instrument panel. "Oxygen levels are normal, but is still hot – eighty-one degrees. But not just in here; it's eighty-five degrees outside – very tropical waters." He looked up. "Should we increase dehumidifiers? Tough on batteries, but..." He shrugged.

Jack thought for a moment. "Hold off for now, but keep an eye on that temperature gauge. If it gets above eighty-five in here, we'll cool it down. Otherwise we'll be losing too much fluid." Jack spoke over his shoulder. "Make sure everyone is drinking water."

"Got it," Cate said, sipping again.

"Big canyon coming up; deep," Yegor intoned. "Also ceiling is dropping down – we need to go deeper."

"I see it." Jack swung back to the screen. "Let's take it down slow." He stared hard out the window at the darkness, occasionally sprinkled with pinpoint blue lights like distant stars, in the fathomless dark. "How deep does it go?"

"Very deep here; eight thousand two hundred feet." Yegor half turned to Jack. "We are at four thousand feet – we can go to five thousand, but not deeper – is not just the pressure, but also the heat. Must be volcanic vents down there."

Jack checked the computer projections – the heat was just under a hundred degrees outside now, and climbing to two hundred deeper down. "You're probably right. Let's stay close to the canyon wall, and drop down just enough to clear the ceiling. We pass under it, and then take her back to shallower water. Hopefully, we can find another air pocket once we pass through."

Yegor grunted his assent, and eased the wheel forward.

"Cate, can you come up here." Jack nodded her forward.

Cate left her seat and bent towards his face. "What is it?"

Jack momentarily smelled her perfume. He lowered his voice. "Getting damned hot – inside and out. Not sure how hot it's going to get, and we need to dive even deeper under the ceiling." His eyes flicked to Greg and Abby. "Things are getting a little tight, and I don't want claustrophobia starting to crowd us."

Cate nodded. "Don't worry; I've got some of my best travelling songs set to go."

"That's the spirit." Jack grinned. "But no dancing."

She crouched. "But this answers a few questions though. The main one being why there's so much life in this sunless water –the heat, and the minerals from whatever geothermal activity below are the basis of a food chain."

"I know, I've dived to thermal vents that support abundant hydrothermic communities miles down in the deep. The extremophile bacteria form huge mats near the hot vents, which attracts organisms such as amphipods and copepods that graze upon it. Larger organisms, feed on them, and so on, until you have a fully-functioning food chain. The things down here don't need sunlight; they just need warmth."

"There's something else that bothered me," Cate said. "Most everything we've seen has pigmentation, and eyes. Why would you still need eyes after so many millions of years if you lived in total darkness?"

"Yeah, I wondered that. The bioluminescent guys need them, but everything else?" He nodded. "Good question; either these things get exposed to sunlight, or there's another light source we haven't seen yet."

"At five thousand feet – maximum depth," Yegor said. "Also, we are at cave ceiling depths, and can pass under the overhang."

"Good; steady as she goes." Jack flexed his fingers for a moment. "We're still on silent running folks."

He switched on the spotlight beam, and angled it upwards. He couldn't help grinning in awe – it gave him a weird sensation, seeing what looked like a rocky sea floor hanging over their heads. Crags, ravines and jagged rock teeth reached downwards, some for a hundred feet, and Yegor deftly maneuvered in and amongst them. Dots of small, spindly crustaceans clung on tight, and ribbons of kelp-like plants hung like drab streamers. Jack momentarily angled the light downwards, but below, there was nothing but an endless dark void.

"How deep here?" Mironov's soft words floated from the back of the cabin.

Jack looked at his panel. "Here, this canyon falls to about eight and a half thousand feet."

"*Oh no*, Captain... is something," Dmitry whispered.

"Huh?" Jack switched off the powerful beam. "What is it, Dmitry?"

Dmitry stared hard at his glowing green screen. "Coming up, big, but moving very slowly. Still at sixty-two hundred feet, but drifting up."

"Towards us?" Abby's voice sounded little more than a squeak.

"Maybe," Dmitry said. "But it is like it is just drifting or floating up towards us. Maybe it is floating debris." He looked again at the screen, and then held a hand to one of the cups over his ear. "Fifty-eight hundred feet now; I think definitely coming up at us." He looked up. "Intersecting course."

"Hey, I have an idea – when it gets here, let's all be somewhere else," Greg hissed.

"Stay calm, Greg," Jack said evenly. "We're not sitting in a jet. This submersible is designed for deep-sea exploration, and has a top speed of three-point-five knots – around four miles per hour, walking speed, and we're doing that now. So we're not going to outrun anything."

Jack leaned towards Yegor. "Move in a little tighter to the ceiling."

"More closer?" The big Russian's brows went up, but he still eased the wheel back a few degrees, moving *Prusalka* to within a few dozen feet of the jagged granite ceiling. "I think this close enough, there are currents from below; that might push us onto rock."

"Currents; I knew it," Cate said. "The hotter water in the deep thermals will rise, the cooler water will settle. It basically creates a continual current, circulating nutrients and stopping the water from stagnating. This place is a fully-functional but contained environment."

"Drifting object now at fifty-three hundred feet." He looked up from the instrument panel. "Coming up out of the deep; that way." He pointed forward and slightly to the right side of the front window.

"All stop." Jack placed a hand on the spotlight, but didn't turn it on. "Everyone stay calm, and brace themselves." He spoke over his shoulder. "Keep talking, Dmitry."

"It is as big as we are. Now, just hovering in the water – when we stop, it stops. I think was waiting for us to come to it. Now at one hundred feet out."

The ring of halogen lights surrounding the window only illuminated a few dozen feet, but now it was further hindered by the upside down forest of crags and hanging mountains from the ceiling that cast deeper shadows behind them. Jack sucked in a deep breath and then flicked on the spotlight.

"*Christ!*" Greg's yell made Cate jump in her seat.

"Magnificent," Mironov said softly.

The huge squid hung in the water like a massive parachute; its tentacles dangled beneath it, and its shroud slightly open as its jets gently sucked in and then eased out water. Huge eyes the size of basketballs watched them with an intelligent curiosity that was both mesmerizing and unsettling.

"A fucking giant squid," Greg spluttered.

"Big one," said Yegor. "Maybe fifty feet across."

"Colossal or perhaps Architeuthis." Mironov had left his seat and now stood behind Jack's shoulder. "And why not? They've also been around for many millions of years. They just don't leave obvious fossils due to their soft bodies."

The massive umbrella glided closer, and one of the long tentacle-whips lifted towards the submersible. Jack eased the *Prusalka* back a dozen feet but the huge arm stretched and finally the four-foot pad gently touched the glass of the front window, tapping and caressing it.

"Probably just trying to understand what this hard-bodied creature is," Jack said, watching it closely.

"Yeah, or maybe trying to reach inside and get to the soft-looking beings it can undoubtedly see here," Greg countered.

The second long whip came forward to also feel along the glass.

"They can taste with their tentacle tips, you know." Mironov's eyes were fixed. One of the pads flattened on the glass, and they could all see the softball-sized circular suction mechanisms opening and then compressing flat on the convex glass. At the center of each was a talon-like structure that arced forward to scrape at the window.

"I think we've seen enough." Jack moved the stick back a few more notches. The tentacles stretched slightly, but then more of the stubbier gripping arms came forward, and the shroud enveloped the glass. The *Prusalka* stopped dead in the water.

Abby whimpered behind them.

Yegor turned to her. "Don't worry, little sparrow; it can't get in, or damage us."

The shroud completely enveloped them, and Cate suddenly felt like a skydiver that had become fouled in their parachute.

The huge bell of the mantle closed tight over the front of a vessel, and then the beak emerged – two-feet long, parrot-like and wickedly curved. It scraped against the toughened glass, and even inside the submersible they heard the grinding, squeal that set their teeth on edge. A long white gouge appeared on the super toughened glass.

"Okay; that's enough of that. We need that bastard off, now! If that thing gets itself caught in our prop, we'll be dragging it all the way to the communication buoy."

"Yeah, and I for one, do not want to damn well surface with the Kraken still hanging onto us." Greg's eyes were round and his mouth remained open.

Yegor half turned to Dmitry, speaking ponderously in Russian. Dmitry nodded and rubbed his hands together. He then flicked up a clear cover over an array of switches which he set on, and then calibrated a dial. "Priming charge – half voltage." He then looked towards the window. "Five-four-three-two-one…" He pressed a single flat button.

The cabin's lights flickered and then like a magician's trick, the glass immediately cleared, except for a swirling cloud of dark ink that was quickly left behind as the submersible powered backwards.

"Now that was cool." Greg clapped his hands, and then rubbed them.

Dmitry smiled. "You see? Even though big one; nothing to worry about. We have encountered squid before in the depths. Like big puppy dog; they are very inquisitive and smart, and more than likely it was curiosity that drove it to cling to us."

"That was big enough for me," Cate said. "I'd hate to be anywhere near one of those that was any bigger."

"They used to grow a lot bigger. Maybe they still do, in the depths." Mironov returned to his seat. "But like I said, nothing much exists in the fossil record; there are traces – big traces. Battle scars on fossilized whale skin indicate creatures potentially hundreds of feet across." He turned to Greg. "They'd be your original Kraken."

"And this place is a living fossil record," Abby said quietly. "It came from below, so maybe we *not* go any deeper."

"I second that," Greg said.

"We shouldn't need to go any further down; we're under the ceiling now," Jack said.

They glided on, just a gentle thrum beneath their feet, and a slick humidity growing around them. Their own moisture hung in the air, but Cate knew Jack was loathe to use any more cooling power until they knew how much longer they needed to travel.

She was now constantly aware of Dmitry's body odor – raw and acrid, like old gym clothes that had been left in a bag with a cabbage on a hot day. She ignored it, guessing she wasn't exactly a rose herself right now.

"We have passed under shelf," Yegor said. "We can rise now."

"Good, take her up to one thousand feet. Nice and slow. Dmitry let me know the instant anything decides to take an interest in us," Jack said.

"How much longer until we get to the Hobart Bay silo?" Cate asked, licking her dry lips.

"Three miles, give or take – we're nearly there." He smiled at her. "We'll find out what happened and make a plan."

Cate sank back into her chair, and turned to the small screen. Her seat on the starboard side of *Prusalka* meant she stared out into the abyssal deep of the dark trench. Once again indistinct stars floated in the distance, and could have been specks just hanging a few feet from her camera, or they could have been colossal beasts half a mile away in the darkness.

She discretely let her eyes slide to her crewmembers: Abby was scratching notes into a small book – a journal or diary perhaps. Her face was slick and she had her hair pulled back from a shining forehead. Behind her, Greg sat fidgeting, drumming his fingers, and trying to engage Dmitry in a conversation. The Russian waved him away or shushed him as he tried to concentrate on the small green screen, and sonar pulses bouncing back to him and relayed to his earphones. She turned to Valery Mironov, who was staring at her. He smiled and nodded, and went back to his own bank of screens, his lips pursed in contemplation.

"Coming up on Hobart Bay, people," Jack said, turning to flash them a smile.

Cate immediately smiled back, before she could check herself. *Involuntary action*, she thought. It was probably just the relief at getting safely to their destination, but there was always something about his voice that instilled calm and confidence in those around him.

"Blow tanks, Yegor, nice and slow."

The submersible slowed, and then with the hiss of compressed gasses rushing to the ballast tanks, the *Prusalka* began to rise.

"Coming up on the shelf," Dmitry said. "The communication silo's buoy should be three hundred feet directly ahead."

As they rose the last few feet, Yegor eased the vessel ahead slowly. They broke the surface, and Cate could just make out the splash of liquid against the front glass.

"We're up," Greg said, rising to his feet.

"Sit down." Jack's voice was low, but the authoritative tone, pushed Greg straight back into his seat. "We're going to need to locate the buoy – could be anywhere, so might take us a while."

"It's getting shallower," Yegor said. "Now at twenty feet."

"Bingo," Jack said, pointing. "Ten o'clock; up against that ledge."

There was a pile of rubble; the tumbled rock debris looked fresh cut, where the pipe had been drilled down into the earth. Amongst the mound of raw stone was a mess of cables that dangled down from the roof, ending in several steel canisters that looked like huge diver's tanks.

"Communication equipment will be in one of those pods. Yegor, bring us in close to that ledge just past the pipe. We can hold our position there." Jack spoke over his shoulder: "Cate, Greg, you're up."

"Yes!" Greg pumped one of his fists. Mironov also got to his feet.

Dmitry shook his head. "We should not all go." He bobbed his head. "Until we know is okay."

Jack nodded. "He's right. Sorry Valery, I need you to sit tight for the time being. We can all get out to stretch our legs once Greg and Cate have done a quick reconnoiter."

Mironov's face remained devoid of expression as he retook his seat, and the huge Yegor turned to look briefly at him, his shelf-like brows folded down over dark eyes. A look passed between them.

Cate turned and shrugged to the Russian billionaire then got to her feet. She saw something behind his eyes that was unreadable, and after a moment he gave her a small phlegmatic smile, and went back to his bank of tiny screens

She leant on the back of Jack's chair, staring out at the glistening rocks. She knew there'd be a cliff wall back in the darkness, somewhere, but *Prusalka*'s lights barely illuminated anything beyond the first fifty feet.

Jack looked up at her. "Be careful out there, okay?"

"I'll be fine," Cate said too quickly. She looked down and saw the genuine concern on his face, and felt like a heel. She put a hand on his shoulder. "Don't worry."

"Wait." Dmitry held up a finger. He went to a storage cabinet built beneath one of the metal desks and returned with two flashlights. They were the type where the handle could be split into a circle that could be worn on the forehead like a caver's light. He quickly tested both, and then held them out. "Very good luck." He grinned and bobbed his head.

Jack half turned. "Dmitry, you follow them up and keep watch."

Dmitry nodded, and then paused. "And what do I do if I see something?"

Greg paused. "See something?"

"What do you do?" Jack asked. "Well, one, you tell them to get back to the *Prusalka*; and two, throw a wrench." Jack grinned.

The submersible gently eased in beside the rock platform.

"Plenty of water – still fifteen feet beneath us." Yegor cut the engines. He sat back, and folded his arms. "Okay."

"You're good to go, people." Jack got to his feet, catching Cate's eye. "Find out what the hell happened up there."

Cate waited as Dmitry raced up the ladder to push open the heavy steel hatch, and then jumped back down, his boots clanging on the steel deck. Warm, peaty-smelling air swirled into the vessel, and Cate raised her chin and inhaled – *foreboding and inviting*. She placed one hand on the ladder, hesitated for only another second, and then was first up the steel rungs.

Cate climbed down the side of the vessel, and leaped across a two feet gap Yegor had left between them and the rock shelf. She had her flashlight on, and all around was a pervading darkness. Looking back at the *Prusalka*, she was taken by how alien the thing must have looked to the other creatures below the surface – the bulbous and striped submersible had a single, bulging eye that glowed a dull red from the inner lighting. From inside Jack waved at her, and beside him the huge motionless form of Yegor. Greg jumped down and joined her.

Cate lifted her light to the dark stretch of sea just past the submersible. Where it was illuminated by the sub there seemed an endless flat and oily-looking surface. Vapors of mist rose from it, testament to the warmth of the water. Even if she hadn't already seen the weird and wonderful things below its surface, it looked primordial and threatening, and the thought of being in that water, and not surrounded by all of *Prusalka's* armor plating made her stomach do a little flip.

"We're not in Kansas anymore," she whispered.

"Down here it feels like we're not on Earth anymore," Greg said floating the beam of his light back along the shelf.

She smiled. "At least not today's Earth." Cate closed her eyes and inhaled again. "I imagine this is what the world was like when it was young and raw."

"Ready?" he asked.

"*Huh?*" Her eyes snapped open. "Of course, and be careful. Looks slippery." She pointed her light down at the rocks. Small, ghostly, crab-like creatures scuttled away from her as she shuffled her way forward, careful not to crush any of them. Behind her, a crackling sound told her Greg wasn't so particular.

They had to cross a few hundred feet of the rock shelf to the pile of cables and pod-like containers sitting on a mound of fallen debris. Cate could see why they termed them buoys – they were like stubby, three-foot vitamin pills, each attached by cables that hung from somewhere up in the dark high above them. She marveled at the skill of the engineers who had managed to drill through the thousands of feet of rock, and then place them right where they were supposed to be.

Closer now, she saw that one of the buoys had an image of head phones stenciled on its surface, and additional cables sheathed in rubber attached – these would be the optical fibers that would relay messages back and forth between them. Cate knelt beside it, her mind whirling –

she'd need to be succinct, and organised her thoughts in preparation. She wondered who it would be up there waiting for her.

She unlatched a small door, and then also an inner watertight compartment. There was a panel of dials and a single switch, also a headset she immediately placed over her head. She switched it on.

Nothing.

She frowned and moved the dials, slowly, like a safe cracker, her concentration intense.

"Hello? Come in…" she felt a knot growing in her stomach. She switched it off and back on, waited a second or two, and then began to move the dial again.

Please, oh please. Cate exhaled, leaned her head back and closed her eyes. Once again she switched it off and back on,

"Come in, *please*, come in."

"What is it?" Greg asked, kneeling beside her. "Isn't anyone there?"

Cate removed the head set and handed it to him. "You try." She didn't want to tell him, and hoped it was just something she was or wasn't doing.

Greg snatched it from her, and placed the set over his head, fiddling with the dial, switching it on and off. "Hello base, *hello*, is anyone there?" He swiveled the dial, his movements becoming faster and more agitated.

"*Fuck it!*" He gritted his teeth. "Come-in – we're trapped down here. You were supposed to fucking… hello… *HELLO!*" His voice boomed in the cave, pounding away into the darkness.

Behind Cate something splashed, and she spun her head, but could see nothing but dark.

Greg dropped his head, dragging off the earphones. He started to shake, and Cate thought the young man was sobbing. But when his head came up he was laughing.

"Well that's just great." He got to his feet. "Maybe we should call a technician." His laugh became a manic roar. "Why don't we put in a fucking support call?"

He stomped away, but spun and came back, fast. *"Now... fucking... what?"* He glared down at her.

Her usually mild-mannered and nerdy colleague momentarily struck Cate mute. She held up a hand. "Greg, calm down."

"Is problem maybe?" Dmitry's question came from the top of the submersible. Cate heard him repeat the words, softer, probably back down into the hold.

Greg placed his hands on his hips, leering. "Yes, comrade, if you call being stuck miles under the earth with the local help-line being as dead as a fucking dodo a problem, then hell yeah, I guess you can say we've got *'is problem maybe'.*"

Cate pushed to her feet. "Can you please cool it?"

Greg spun to her, his teeth bared. One of his fists was up. Cate stepped back.

Dmitry slid down the ladder. "Captain Monroe, I think we have problem outside."

Jack looked from the Russian to lean forward trying to see the pair on the dark ledge, but due to the angle, they were just out of sight.

Dmitry hopped from foot to foot. "You better get out there; talk to your friends – calm them down."

"Huh?" Jack leapt to his feet, and headed for the steel ladder.

Abby rose as well.

"Stay here." Jack held up a hand flat. "I don't want everyone running around out there. I'll be back in a minute."

"But..." Abby stared, open-mouthed.

"Is okay, little sparrow. You wait here." Yegor waved her down into her seat, and then turned to Jack nodding. "Go; is important."

Jack was up the ladder in a few seconds, and gone.

Greg's fists were balled as he stood before Cate. In the glow of her flashlight his face looked beet-red. But in a moment or two, he sucked in a few deep breaths and shook his head. It was if he had opened an escape valve, letting all the pressure escape.

He sunk to his knees. "I'm sorry; I'm just..." He covered his face for a moment before pushing strands of long hair up off his forehead.

"I know; it's okay. Hey, I'm scared as well." Cate laid a hand on his shoulder. "But you've got to hold it together."

"Hey." Jack jogged towards them. "What's happening? Did you make contact?" He stared hard at where the cliff wall met the shelf, momentarily transfixed.

Greg scoffed, and simply gazed off into the darkness.

Cate sighed. "No, no we didn't." She pointed. "We couldn't; it's dead."

"What?" Jack pulled up frowning. "Dead? Not working?" A dawning realization broke over his expression. "What if..." He turned to the pair. "What if those who sabotaged the crane...?"

Cate nodded. "Got here too."

Jack tilted his head back, putting his hands on his hips and looking up at the dark ceiling hundreds of feet above them. "Well that's just god-damn great." He rubbed his face. "Greg... *Greg!*"

"What?" The young scientist's head whipped around at Jack's raised voice.

"Go check out the other buoys and see if there's anything else there we can use... or is still working."

Greg's mouth worked for a moment before he nodded, and stepped in amongst the coils of cable and other pods.

Jack turned back to Cate. "That's it; show's over." He panned his light around, stopping at the cliff wall, his eyes narrowing.

She nodded, knowing there was only one priority now – escape.

The sudden noise from the submersible confused her at first, and also caused Jack to frown and turn as well. The thumping stopped, and then the next sound was monstrously out of place, but recognizable as hell.

Valery Mironov gripped his armrests, curiosity now burning inside him. "What's happening?"

Yegor grunted. "I think there is trouble." The big Russian leant forward onto the u-shaped wheel, trying to see around the edge of the curved glass at the trio on the rock ledge.

"I should go out there," Mironov said evenly.

"What are they doing?" Abby said, standing and then trying to see over Yegor's shoulder.

"Talking; they're fine... busy." Dmitry spun in his seat. "We should all sit down, and wait."

Yegor turned slowly. "Is okay, you can come up here, little sparrow."

Mironov also got to his feet. "I'm going to offer my assistance. After all, the silos were prepared by my people."

"No, you stay. *Both* of you stay," Dmitry said quickly.

Yegor's frown deepened, and he quickly glanced at Abby before turning back to Dmitry; he switched to Russian.

"What are you doing?"

Mironov stayed on his feet and also spoke rapidly in his home tongue. "You work for me, Dmitry Torshin. You will stand down immed—"

"*Shut up, fool!*"

The billionaire froze, confused.

"Your authority has now expired. We will be taking this submersible... in a different direction." His eyes slid to the huge Yegor. "Want to be rich?"

Yegor's brows went up, and his look went from surprise to horror. *"Nyet!"*

The single word was more a shout, and carried a hint of anxiety that also seemed to bunch his huge shoulders. He locked eyes with Dmitry, the smaller man returning his fierce stare.

"What's, going, on?" Abby's voice was small and she shrank back into her seat. Mironov tapped her shoulder, and then quietly motioned her to her feet.

Yegor began to rise, and the huge man filled the entire front of the small craft. His hands flexed, and he continued to shake his bear-like head.

Dmitry's grin returned, and spoke a soft word or two as the big man continued to advance on him.

Like magic, a small gun appeared in Dmitry's hand.

Yegor froze, and his face went a deep, dark red. The huge man lowered his head, his muscles bunched and then he charged. For a big man, he covered the few feet in the blink of an eye.

Gunshots. Two of them.

Jack stared at the *Prusalka*, his mouth open, but then snapping shut. He began to run, sliding on the moss-covered rocks, falling, gathering himself back up and running again. Greg and Cate sprinted after him.

The Priz Class submersible began to ease away from the rocky ledge. A small figure came out, fast, sliding down the side of the vessel and landing hard on the rocks and stayed down. The *Prusalka* continued to pull back, and was already ten feet from the ledge when Jack began to accelerate.

"Don't!" Cate's scream pulled him up at the very edge of the shelf.

Jack knelt by the fallen figure. "It's Abby."

Greg and Cate also came and crowded around the groggy woman. Jack stood, and as they watched, it looked like someone else was climbing out.

"Hey, I think that's Yegor." Jack cupped his mouth. "Hey, what the hell is happening? Get back here!"

The big man came up jerkily, his head first, then shoulders, and then when he neared waist level, his body slumped forward.

"Wha...?" Jack frowned.

In the next moment, Yegor jerked again, and his huge body came up to the thighs, and then he slid forward over the side of the hull, to splash in the water. The large Russian bobbed for a moment, and then sank.

"Shit." Jack dived in.

"Jack..." Cate dropped her flashlight and followed him in, stretching out far as she dived. She swam to where Jack had followed Yegor down. The water tasted of salt and machine oil where the submersible had been. It was also the warmest water Cate had ever felt in her life. She had swum down, perhaps twenty feet, until the pressure on her ears started to become painful. She waved her arms around, but there was nothing – it was an impossible task, as the water was blacker than hell.

A light current brushed her face, and she immediately jerked back, remembering the things they had seen, and realizing she might not be alone in the water. She pulled back, and then stroked hard for the surface.

Cate breached and sucked in a huge breath, a light's glare immediately in her eyes.

"Cate..." Greg was holding his flashlight up at her, the beam only just illuminating the water around her. She felt something strike her legs and she screamed. Jack burst from the depth beside her.

He spluttered for a moment, and sucked in more air, once, twice, and Cate realized he was getting ready to dive again. She grabbed him.

"Forget it, he's gone."

Jack face was screwed in torment. "Goddamn it."

She pushed him towards the ledge. "We've got to get out."

They swam fast, and clambered up on the slick rocks, Greg hauling them up like fresh caught fish onto a boat's deck.

She and Jack knelt, coughing, and Greg helped Abby sit up when she groaned, still lifting from her stupor. They stared, still in shock and confusion – the submersible was now fifty feet from the ledge, and the hatch on top closed with a deep and final clang. The *Prusalka* then began to ease around to face them.

Cate could just make out the red glow of the interior, and Dmitry, the sole pilot at the controls. He grinned, and lifted a single hand, the fingers just curling in a comical wave of goodbye. Then the craft slowly began to submerge.

"No!" Jack yelled, the shout bouncing back at them inside the huge cavern.

Behind them Greg hugged Abby, who was sobbing softly.

"I don't understand – where's he going?" Greg brushed the slick hair back off her face. "Is he going for help? Was there a fight… with Yegor?"

Jack exhaled long and slow. "I don't think so."

"Is he coming back?" Greg blinked several times. "Maybe he saw something, and needed to keep the *Prusalka* safe."

Jack scoffed. "Yeah, and Yegor just decided to go for a swim… after he shot himself."

Greg shook his head. "We don't know—"

"Dmitry… he shot Yegor." Abby groaned, reaching up to feel a lump on her forehead. "He ordered me out, but made Mr Mironov stay."

Cate's heart sunk as she watched the retreating submarine. "Going, going…."

The water finally closed over the top of the submersible. There was a tiny whirlpool spinning on the dark surface, and just below it a soft red glow that soon also vanished.

"Gone." Cate slumped.

Jack went and crouched in front of Abby. "What happened in there? Why did Dmitry go crazy?"

Abby shook her head. "He wasn't crazy. They spoke in Russian, argued, and then Yegor tried to stop him. Dmitry shot him dead, and then made me get out." she looked up. "But he made Valery stay."

"He wanted the submersible? Why?" Greg was still wide eyed.

"No, I don't think so. I think he wanted Valery." Abby wiped her nose.

Jack rubbed his face, hard. He looked up at Cate. "The explosions, this…" he waved an arm at the communication silo. "It's probably all sabotage. I think they've been after Mironov all along." He gave her a tight smile. "I think he had some powerful enemies, and we saps are just friendly fire."

Cate groaned and lay down on the slick rock.

Greg started to laugh. "*Friendly fire*; I like that."

"Be thankful we're not dead," Jack said getting to his feet.

"Not yet, but it's still early," Greg shot back.

"Shut up, Greg. Jack's right." Cate sat back up. "You could have been shot and dumped into the water as well."

"Might have been more humane…" He walked away continuing to mutter.

Jack walked to the edge of the rock shelf, and stared down into the stygian water. He shined his flashlight over its top that was once again as smooth as glass. There were wisps of vapor dancing on its warm surface.

Cate joined him, her voice low. "It's bad isn't it?"

He turned and gave her a tight smile. "It certainly could be better. But, for now we have water, oxygen, we're dry, and that'll do for a few days. After that, then we can start to worry. So…" he turned, and looked over her shoulder, back towards the cliff face. "Two things – Greg, Abby, go see what else they dropped down for us." He turned back to the cliff wall. "And you and I need to check something out."

Greg and Abby crossed to the pods, and Jack led Cate back along the ledge to where the impossibly-high wall rose up before them.

"I knew it." He lifted his light. "This is a good sign… seems the Nantouk, or someone like them, were here as well."

Cate stepped forward, seeing the same cave drawings they had seen high up above when they had first flown the miniature drone copter into the rock crevice.

"Older, much older," she said as she walked sideways along the wall, lifting her light to the images. "These almost look Neanderthal, if that's even possible." There were warriors in canoe-like boats, some standing on rock edges, perhaps this very one, and either hauling on nets or throwing spears.

"Why fish in a freezing ocean, when you can come down here to your own private tropical sea."

"Friend of yours?" Jack stepped back, holding his light on a particular group of images.

Cate came closer. It was an image of a shark, crudely drawn, but the dorsal fin, curved tail, and massive jaws were unmistakable. There looked to be spears sticking from it, and underneath it were drawn dozens and dozens of images of warriors. All of them lying down with their eyes closed.

"They tried to catch it, or kill it," she said, following the images along the wall.

"Or at least they tried." He pointed. "Look at the size – the figures are about one tenth of the shark; that would be fairly accurate for a Megalodon." He moved his light-beam. "See the warrior's eyes – all shut. I don't think all of these warriors below it are sleeping. More like these guys were eaten trying to capture it." Jack turned to her. "Maybe their own private tropical sea had a drawback or two."

She snorted in wonder, and focused her beam on the giant shark. "They were always here – the Megalodons – right under our noses. We just didn't know where to look." She turned and gave him a crooked smile. "I don't know whether I should be thrilled, or even more shit-scared, right now."

Jack put his arm around her shoulder. She let it stay. "Right now? Right now, we go and see what else Valery's team sent us."

Jack and Cate joined Greg and Abby and chose another of the buoys to investigate. The three-foot pods each had an indented locking mechanism that when turned and slid across caused a door to pop open. Inside his, Greg found some luxury foods, meant as a treat and perhaps a surprise for Valery Mironov from his support team – tinned caviar and pate, biscuits and salmon – nibbles for a fun afternoon, and far from the life-sustaining supplies they now desperately needed. There was even a well-packed half-bottle of champagne.

The other two pod contents were more practical: water bottles, first aid materials, a pair of new hunting knives and a small compass. The final one was the real score – a four-person raft, and the best of all, a dozen spare flashlight batteries.

"God love you, Valery," Cate said holding them up. "I can take hungry, and I can deal with thirsty until it kills me, but being trapped in darkness, now that's a nightmare I don't want to live through."

Jack was strapping on one of the hunting knives. "My

guess is that each of the communication stations might have similar items, but..."

"But, we're not going to be seeing those anytime soon," Greg snorted. "Unless Dmitry has a change of mind." He picked up one of the small flat tins of caviar. "Golly, why didn't he drop us down something useful... like trucker's hats." He tossed a small flat tin of caviar out over the water making it skip half a dozen times along the glassine surface.

"Hey!" Cate sprang to her feet, and crossed to him. She pushed him in the chest. "I should make you go and get that."

Jack growled. "That's your rations you're tossing away, son."

Greg held up his hands in surrender. Cate scowled a moment longer and then turned to Jack.

"Anyway, why not get to the other stations? We've got a raft." Cate began to fashion a small pack out of the lining of the communication buoy, stacking all its items inside.

Jack took the compass, reading from it, and then holding it up to angle the small dial for a second or two. "I like the idea, but what's the point of paddling twenty more miles to the next communication buoy? The odds are it will have been sabotaged by whoever destroyed this one."

"*Shit*, you're probably right." Cate straightened quickly. "Well, I'm not just sitting down and waiting for the lights to go out."

"Me either." Jack looked up from the compass. "There might be another way." Jack held out an arm, pointing southward. "Heceta Island."

"I remember, in Viva Silva Cave, you mentioned it on the surface – one of the deepest caves in the continent." Cate lifted her chin.

Greg edged closer, and Abby sat forward.

"That's it – on Heceta Island." Jack's jaw set. "Pronounced *HECK–ah–Ta* a long way – around fifty miles to the south. But it has something that no other island in this area has… or for that matter, most islands, anywhere. The Viva Silva Cave is eight hundred feet deep, and I know it, because I've been in it."

"Does it go all the way down to here?" Greg's eyes were wide and round.

"Unlikely, and anyway, we're much deeper than that. But I know the cave ends at a depth of eight hundred feet with a few small cracks. There could have been further honeycombing pockets that take it even deeper." He shrugged. "Bottom line is, there's a chance it may end close enough for us to break through."

Greg nodded, grinning. "I'll dig with my bare hands if that's what it takes."

"I'll help." Abby held up a hand for Greg. He took it and lifted her to her feet.

"Me too," Cate said, eyebrows raised. "And we now have a way to get there – our raft."

Jack turned away to the dark sea. "And fifty miles of dark ocean to cover. It's going to take days." He exhaled through compressed lips then shone his light out over the oil-dark water.

Cate let her gaze follow the beam. The black water seemed like an endless sheet of dark, fathomless glass.

Jack turned back, smiling. "But at least we've got champagne."

Valery Mironov worked at the plastic cable around each of his wrists. It was tight, cut deep, and was making his hands throb. He'd never cry out, ask for help, or even acknowledge the pain to the man in front.

Dmitry turned, and Mironov relaxed his face into an expressionless mask. "There was no reason to kill, Yegor."

Dmitry grinned and shrugged. "He killed himself. You heard me ask him to join me, but he said no. He left me no choice." He turned back to his console. "If he said yes, he would be alive. So, in a way, he killed himself." He shrugged again, and made a little farting noise with his lips.

"I see." Mironov went back to his bonds. "And what of the others that you have left stranded? You've certainly killed them, just as if you put a bullet in their heads too."

Dmitry waved the question away. "They'll be safe." He turned to him, his mouth twisted. "Would you prefer I had dropped them off in deep water?"

"No, no, I'm sure in your own way, you think you did the right thing." Mironov was determined to keep the man talking. There seemed to be a flavor of unbalance to the submersible pilot that worried him. Sane men he could deal with, but often insanity had no market price.

"They must have paid you a fortune to undertake this mission, comrade. As I expect they'll be seeking a thousand king's ransoms for me. Maybe I could cut out the middlemen – give the king's ransom all directly to you. Make you rich beyond Croesus's dreams. I could even spirit you away to a tropical island so you could live out your life like an emperor; no questions asked." Mironov watched Dmitry closely, looking for any sign he could move the man.

"Money?" Dmitry turned to him, his eyes narrowed. "What I want, only Brogidan Yusoff, can give me."

On hearing the name of the Head of the Russian Ministry of Resources and Agriculture, Mironov's hopes sank. It was personal then, and perhaps there was to be no ransom after all.

"So then, I can assume it was you and him, that organised the destruction of the crane, and contamination of the entire site."

"Yes, yes, of course – blew up the crane, blew up the communication silos, and sealed you in." Dmitry turned away, his expression bored.

"And how will you get out, then?" Mironov waited, as the silence stretched for several seconds.

"We have a plan." Dmitry turned in his seat. "You're worth much more alive than dead. But the dead never misbehave." He laughed softly, but there was no humor in the sound. He turned away. "So behave."

Mironov worked harder at his bonds – they were a thin plastic type of cable-rope that was used for repairs. He'd been swiveling his wrists, and had made them bleed a while back now. The pain was excruciating, but he kept his face expressionless as he cut his flesh, his eyes on Dmitry the entire time.

The blood was impossible to feel against his skin, as it must have been close to the same temperature as the inside of the *Prusalka*. But the fluid had a purpose and there was design to his self-mutilation. The blood flowed, and the blood was slippery.

CHAPTER 16

Sheslay, British Columbia, Canada
58°16′00″N 131°48′00″W

The two black-clad agents waited in a shadowy twilight that was cemetery still. They were ex-Spetsnaz and recruited by Uli Stroyev himself. He had been pleased with their progress, but urged greater speed. He had reminded them their success bonus only came at the end of the job.

One tugged his collar higher, breathing out slowly so as not to create plumes of vapor.

"I thought Russia was cold."

The other pulled field glasses from his eyes and turned. "You've been to Siberia?" He went back to scanning the cleared area of the forest. "This is tropical compared to there."

Like Hobart Bay, Sheslay was a small settlement with just a few houses and some hunting cabins set in amongst forested mountains and situated at the convergence of the Hackett and Sheslay Rivers. Once again their target was a small building set apart from all the others. They knew that just like at Hobart Bay, inside the nondescript-looking shack, the metal communication silo that reached all the way down to the subterranean sea sat waiting patiently for its potential travelers below ground.

The agent lowered his field glasses again, and tucked them away. Once again there was no guard, and just a blind reliance on their technological sentinels. Like at the previous silo, they deployed the electromagnetic pulse and then waited a few seconds to ensure there was no other response.

"Remind me how westerners actually get anything done," the man sneered. "They make our job so easy." He nodded forward. "Let's go."

They sprinted again, staying low and zigzagging between trees and then pushing hard over the last hundred feet to the cabin door. One of the men grabbed the handle and turned to his partner, holding up three fingers. He counted them down – three-two-one – then both went in fast.

He shut the door and spun. Years of experience immediately told him they were not alone. The first shot, little more than a muffled spit, slammed his fellow agent's head back against the door, the bullet passing through the skull and wood, letting in a beam of muted moonlight. The dead man slid to the ground.

The remaining agent then went for his gun. He was lightening quick, but still no match for someone with theirs already drawn. The next shot took him in the shoulder of his gun arm, shattering the clavicle, acromion and scapula, and making the arm hang useless at his side.

A small light came on then. It was on the shooter's forehead, making them invisible in the dark behind it.

"Let us be clear, you are a dead man. But how you spend the last few minutes of your miserable life is now up to you."

The voice was female, but there was no hint of uncertainty or compassion; this was the voice of a stone-cold killer. The agent quickly sorted through his options: charge the light, stall for time, beg for mercy.

He still had one good arm – *it is enough*. He got ready to run at the light. "Well now…"

The next shot, took him in the kneecap. The pain of the obliterated patella was excruciating, and immediately made the option of charging redundant.

"I have plenty more shots, and plenty more time. My next will be in your testicles."

The agent groaned, now knowing the promise of death was no warning or bluff, but an absolute certainty. If he had a cyanide pill, this would have been the time to take it.

Fuck it. He owed no one anything.

"What do you want?" he hissed through pain-gritted teeth.

"Tell me, who?"

The gun hand came up, and in the light he saw the barrel lower towards his groin. He told her everything he knew.

Sonya Borashev checked her watch as she ran to her snow sled. The Russian agent had been very informative. As she expected, the hit had been ordered by Brogidan Yusoff, head of the Russian Ministry of Resources and Agriculture, and his henchman, Uli Stroyev.

These two agents were simply ensuring there was no back door, while the real killer was already onboard the submersible. Sonya stopped for a moment, concentrating on easing the shaking in her arms and legs. The tremors weren't from fear or the cold, but instead from pure rage. That Valery could already be dead made her fury volcanic, and her vision misted red for a few seconds.

For now, she had to assume they were all alive. The team comprised of Valery, marine biologists, and a geologist – all smart people. If she was there, she'd be looking for another way out – so would Valery.

By now, the team would know the Hobart Bay silo was destroyed, and must undoubtedly assume all the other silos were in the same state. So, what would they do? Where would they go?

They'd look for another escape hatch. She threw a leg over her snow mobile. She needed to speak to a local geologist, *now*.

The machine roared to a start, and she sped away through the twilight snowdrifts.

CHAPTER 17

Jack, Cate, Greg and Abby stood around the inflated raft. It was twelve-feet long with a raised bow and three inbuilt seats. There were also two telescopic paddles now lying in its bottom.

Jack bobbed his head. "We could have done a lot worse; it's a Whitewater, they're often used for rough-river rafting. Polyurethane alloy with a reinforced floor – pretty damn tough."

"Plenty of room," Greg said, nodding as he felt along one gunwale.

Cate, hands on her hips, tilted her head at Jack. "We have fifty miles to cover, all under paddle power. How long do you think?"

Jack rubbed his chin. "Couple of days, at least... and that's if we only take short breaks. For paddling it'll be two on, two off, right around the clock."

"And *ah*, what happens if something from below takes an interest in us?" Greg straightened, but kept his eyes on the raft.

Cate nudged the raft with her toe. "You think those oars are just for paddling? We beat the shit out of anything that even looks sideways at us. Deal?"

Greg held up one of the lightweight, plastic oars. "*Ooookay.*"

Jack smiled. "That's the spirit."

Abby hugged herself, her voice tiny. "Maybe someone might rescue us." She looked out over the dark water.

"Some of those things down there were a lot bigger than the raft."

Jack's smile faded. "Yes, they were. But the bottom line is, right now, we've got plenty of bad options. We can certainly stay here and wait to be rescued. But how? The entry site is contaminated, and no one even knows where we are." Jack went and placed a hand on Abby's shoulder, and looked into her eyes. "We'd just end up dying slowly in the dark. We could paddle to the next buoy, which is probably sabotaged as well. Or we risk it all trying to find a way out... and that could also be a dead-end – back to square one." He sighed. "But the way I see it, the worst thing we can do is become paralysed by indecision." He gave her a grim smile. "Because doing nothing, will lead to certain death."

Abby continued to look out over the water. "Maybe Valery will overpower Dmitry, and come back for us..." Her voice trailed away, and she turned and walked off along the rock ledge.

Jack watched her go for a moment. "We pack the raft with everything we need or even might need... and break the doors off the pod; they'll be our extra oars."

Cate turned her head slowly, looking from Abby, to the huge cliff wall. The cave drawings were lost in the darkness now, but she remembered all the bodies that seemed to float beneath the monstrous shark.

She then looked out over the steaming sea. There was nothing here for them now. "The least bad option it is then. Ready when you are."

"Let's do this," said Greg, reaching down to grab one side of the raft. He turned to the lone figure of Abby. "Abby, c'mon babe. All a-*boooard*."

CHAPTER 18

The Bering Sea,
Ten miles west of the Baker-Shevardnadze Line
168° 58'37"

The Russian drill ship, the *Viktor Dubynin*, groaned and tugged against its sea anchors. The six wrist-thick cables whipped tight in the air, flicking spray and causing even their best seamen to grab railings, table tops, anything, as the powerful vessel jerked sharply in the rough water.

Captain Boris Gorkin exhaled blue smoke into the bridge room, as chief engineer Olaf Kozlov bent over a computer screen that showed a graphic representation of the seabed below them.

"We are through the shell and into the source liquid. As we expected, it is sea water." He lifted his radio to speak furiously to his rig team for a few seconds. "Okay, capping now…"

Kozlov gritted his teeth, leaning in at the screen as the numbers spiked. "*Ach*, we have instability in the crust."

Gorkin turned, his eyes half lidded. From Brogidan Yusoff's perspective, it was his responsibility for breaching the crustal coating over the subterranean liquid bed, attaching the extraction pipes, and then waiting for the package to be in place. His success bonus would be six figures. But only if everything went to plan. If anything went wrong, he'd damn well make sure it wasn't his head that was on the block – literally.

He watched closely as Kozlov grunted at the screen, his teeth still bared, and veins now popping at his temples. "Easing." He started to nod, his face relaxing. "Stabilizing..." He straightened. "...and capped." He plonked down in his seat and grinned. "Ready and awaiting object extraction."

"Everything okay now?" Gorkin lumbered over, looking over the man's shoulder at the screen.

Kozlov shrugged. "Sometimes the skin over the bed is weaker in some places more than others. You can't know until you start drilling. This area's crust layer must be particularly shallow... and brittle. Not ideal." He cracked his knuckles. "But all good now, we have a cap, and a firm seal. Ready to start pumping when they're in place."

"Will it hold?" Gorkin watched the man closely.

"Of course it will hold." He grinned, his brows up.

Gorkin continued to stare at the man. Senchov's smile looked fragile, and he knew why. There was no such thing as a guarantee in his business. He'd been out on dozens of seabed drilling projects, and most times the caps held. Only one in a hundred didn't. But he knew deep liquid was always under pressure, and the ocean was quite shallow here, so less corresponding pressure on the crust.

But the deep liquid beds were always trying to escape. Like living things they wanted their freedom. If there *was* a seabed collapse, then whatever was in that subterranean place would end up right underneath them.

They rowed slowly, Jack and Greg taking first shift. Their paddles dipped in, swept back along the side of the raft to pull them across the water, and then being slid out from the dark liquid. There was very little sound, as both men automatically knew to make as little noise as possible.

By now, Jack guessed they had passed well over the underwater cliff they had seen in the submersible, and below them now was nothing but the pitiless void, where it dropped away thousands of feet into the abyss. There would be movement down there, and he hoped that was exactly where it would stay.

To conserve power, they travelled in the dark, just the glow of the compass to guide them.

Something splashed out in the darkness.

Jack slowed his paddling as the splash came again, and this time it was accompanied by a smell of age-old barnacles and ocean bottoms.

"Stop," Jack whispered, switched on one of the flashlights and trained its beam in the direction of the commotion.

His breath caught in his throat as at the far edge of his light, something huge lumped the water's surface, rolled once and then slid beneath the oily sheen of the dark water.

The ripples bumped at the raft, and the small group all sat frozen, watching the water. Jack felt his heartbeat racing in his chest. No one moved a muscle.

Jack trained the beam down into the water, but it was impossible to see anything, and the beam might have stopped at a few feet or dozens. He continued to stare for several more seconds.

He had been in predator's water before – tagging Great White Sharks down at Hell's Teeth in South Africa where the monsters grew to twenty foot and as wide around as a hippo. He had also been near orca packs when they rounded up seal pods, herding them in towards an ice wall and then picking them off one by one, playing with the carcasses like vollyballers at the beach. He'd swum with giant saltwater crocodiles, and moray eels as thick as your waist. But those times he had known what was down there, had known what to expect, so when the animal finally appeared, it was thrilling and frightening, but expected.

He remained gazing down into the darkness, knowing this was different; he had no real idea what was down there. Or even what *could* be down there. His gut told him the armored Placoderm was just one of the denizens of this strange place. There would be others, and he just hoped they stayed down deep, ignoring the twelve-foot long flat thing that glided near silently on the surface, thousands of feet above them.

"Let's go," he whispered, unlocking their muscles once again.

They paddled on, maintaining a speed of three miles per hour, or around walking pace. They could have gone faster, but that would mean making more noise. Jack estimated at the rate they moved they'd be paddling for around thirty-two more hours. Cate and Abby would take over soon, but even then, it wasn't possible to continue around the clock, and they hadn't slept since they left the surface.

Jack watched Greg for a moment, checking for fatigue. The young scientist paddled smoothly. "All okay there?"

Greg nodded.

They'd push on for another few hours, Cate and Abby for a few more on top of that, but then would need to find somewhere dry to rest. Jack didn't like the idea of sleeping in the raft. It was bad enough being in a near pitch-dark environment, but closing your eyes meant not being able to avoid even the most obvious danger.

Cate sniffed, and then leaned towards the water and inhaled. "Sulphur." She narrowed her eyes and looked around, flicking on her light and playing it across the water's surface. "The mist lifting off the water has a sulphurous tinge. I'm guessing this is the result of geological activity."

Abby quickly dipped a hand over the side, cupped some water, and then bought it to her lips. "No real taste, other than salt, but I'm betting there might be some smoker vents down deep."

Greg also cupped some water, sipped from his hand, and then spat a long stream back over the side.

"Keep paddling," Jack said.

"Yes, master." Greg grinned at Abby, and then turned to Cate. "Hey, shouldn't one of you be beating a drum so us slaves can keep in rhythm?"

Cate half smiled. "I don't know about a drum, but I know what does need a beating."

Greg put on a shocked expression. "Easy now..." he laughed.

The sound of a heavy body moving through water shocked them to silence. It grew louder, and then stopped.

"*What. The fuck. Was that?*" Greg whispered, cringing.

"Keep paddling, easy and slow," Jack said looking over his shoulder. "*Uh* Cate, while we're doing this, can you please shine your light over the stern. Just for a little look-see?"

She nodded, swung around, and then held the flashlight in both hands, as she tilted it downwards.

"Oh god."

She lifted the light.

"Stop paddling."

Valery Mironov's wrists were shredded and his hands now slick with blood. He drew in a deep breath, absorbing the pain, and kept his gaze fixed on the back of Dmitry's head. He didn't flinch as he slowly drew one hand from the binding, tearing away more of the skin.

"We're nearly there," Dmitry said over his shoulder.

Mironov's hand came free, and he quickly reached across to untie the other. When complete he sat still, watching Dmitry pilot the submersible ever deeper.

Dmitry had switched off all Mironov's screens, perhaps not wanting him to know where they were. He continued to watch, and hoped when it came time to seize the craft, he could successfully subdue the man. If he had to kill him, then he would. He would rescue Cate and her friends or die trying.

Though Mironov wasn't a pilot, he had watched enough to get an understanding of the basics. He looked along the banks of controls, dials, and screens – he needed little of the analytical technology, and only the maneuvering capabilities. It could be done.

"I know you are free."

Dmitry's words brought his head around. Mironov waited, but the pilot's hands stayed at the controls and didn't reach for the gun.

"Where are we going?" Mironov had no option now but to play for time.

Dmitry half turned, his grin now gone, and his eyes dead level. He was no longer the jovial clown, but now the killer he probably always was.

"Valhalla maybe?" He gave Mironov a sneering grin. "You are a rich and powerful man, Valery Konstantin Mironov. But I am afraid you also have rich and powerful enemies. Enemies who are patient, and far more ruthless than you."

"You mean to kill me?" Mironov waited.

"That all depends on you." Dmitry continued to smile.

"But then how will you escape?" Mironov tilted his head a fraction, studying the man.

Dmitry studied him for a moment. "Why not?" He shrugged. "We have a rendezvous out under the Bering Sea, and then we will be going for a little trip in the pod." Dmitry's eyes lost their focus, and he turned away. Mironov saw something behind the expression – doubt, regret perhaps; he wasn't sure what it was exactly, but there was something there – a sliver of hope, perhaps.

"I don't believe you're doing this for money."

Dmitry shook his head. "What good is money without health, security, or a future?"

"But not yours." Mironov sat forward.

Dmitry just sat and stared out through the toughened glass window.

Mironov angled himself so he could see the side of the Russian pilot's face. "I know Yusoff is blackmailing you, or he's promised you something." He continued to study the man, a picture forming. "No, perhaps not you, but he's promised to do something for a friend, or maybe for your family."

Mironov sat back. "Dmitry, I know this man, a thousand, thousand times better than you do. You have served your purpose, played your role, and I can tell you, that he has already forgotten about you. And he will certainly have forgotten about your family, or whoever it is you think you are saving."

Dmitry shrugged. "It is a chance I have to take."

"No, it isn't." Mironov sat forward again. "I can guarantee your family's safety. I have many contacts around the world. I can get your family out, and get them somewhere safe within an hour. And there's something far more important you should heed – I always keep my word."

Dmitry stared for a moment or two before his mouth began to curve into a smile again. "They said you would be clever, and they were right." He lifted the gun.

Mironov sighed and sat back, his gaze unwavering. "I think you are not a bad man. If you were, I'd be dead already, and you would never have let the others go. You are torn." He knew Dmitry was listening now. "If we make it to the surface again, your reward will be a bullet in the head. Not safety."

Mironov sat forward. "*Listen to me*. I give you my word that I will see to it personally you are never found by Yusoff. You would be safe; *they* would be safe, and happy, forever. Dmitry, you owe it to your family to at least think about it."

The scream of the proximity alarm made both men cringe, and Dmitry cursed. "The roof of the cavern is dropping down again. We'll need to dive, deep." He growled under his breath. "Sonar should have picked this up."

"You need more hands, and eyes," Mironov responded.

Dmitry eased the submersible down to just a few knots, and then swiveled in his seat to stare for a moment. "Yes, I do." He turned back to his own panel, and returned Mironov's access to his screens. He pointed. "That screen opening for you is the peripheral sonar. I need you to keep watch. Look out for hanging crags."

"Understood." Mironov switched on his other bank of screens. Leaving the thermal gradient, ppi pressure, battery life, fuel, and oxygen level stats to the side, he enlarged the single sonar matrix. He saw the problem immediately.

"A new lip of the ceiling; drops down another thousand feet – you will need to take us to twenty-two hundred."

"Okay, then down we go – hard dive." Dmitry pushed the u-shaped wheel forward and the *Prusalka* angled downwards into the inky depths.

The minutes ticked over, seeming ever slower as they maintained their downward descent. Mironov's computer analyzed the terrain, advising him to maintain their current trajectory to undershoot the huge stone lip, and move ever deeper in amongst the canyons of the abyss.

Dmitry started to hum, and then whistle as if out on a Sunday drive. Mironov lifted his gaze from the sonar, watching the man for a few moments.

"Dmitry, have you given anymore thought to my proposal?"

Dmitry breathed deeply for a few seconds. "It is impossible. Yusoff would still find me, and then kill all of us."

"No he won't. Do not overestimate him; he is not as well connected as you think. Yusoff has crossed the line now. One word in the ear of President Volkov about one of his ministers attempting an unauthorized assassination, and what do you think would happen to him? I'll tell you, he'd be fed feet-first into a wood-chipper."

Dmitry turned, his eyebrows raised. "My family." His lips compressed for a moment or two as his mind worked.

"How would I get them out?" Mironov smiled. "I own a global transportation business. I could have them in a car, and taken to an airport within an hour. They could meet you here, in America, where I can guarantee you all permanent residency, and completely new identities."

"A lot to think about." Dmitry turned back to the curved window then eased back on the engines, and just let the *Prusalka* drift. "It's true that I do not trust Yusoff." He sighed. "I want to trust you, but..."

Outside, lights twinkled in the distance – bioluminescent fish, squid, or some other sort of deep-sea creature trying to attract prey, a mate, or mark out its territory. There were so many, it reminded Mironov of diamonds scattered on a dark blanket.

"You *can* trust me," Mironov said softly. He closed his eyes, feeling like he might have finally broken Yusoff's hold on the man. When he opened them, he looked back out of the curved window, and frowned. He leant forward – the lights were suddenly going out as quickly and completely as if someone had just thrown a switch. He knew what that meant and quickly turned to his sonar.

"I have contact."

Dmitry's head snapped around momentarily, his brows drawn together. He then looked down at his depth gauge.

"We're deep. I thought you said we'd be below the hard-head fish."

"We are," Mironov responded. "We're well below the usual zone for anything other than the deepest-diving cetaceans and giant squid." He knew that was true in the world's oceans, but this sea was different, this one was populated by creatures not of the normal oceans, and who lived by primordial rules he had no hope of understanding.

"What does it look like?" Dmitry threw the words over his shoulder.

Mironov quickly read the scrolling data under the image. "It's no Placoderm." He read some more of the incoming data. "Computer approximates its length at sixty to seventy feet – torpedo shape, and moving at thirty knots. Coming up from directly below us. It's still at forty-three hundred feet, but coming up fast."

"Thirty knots?" Dmitry shook his head and licked dry lips.

The proximity alarm began to sound again inside the *Prusalka*, and Dmitry quickly reached down to switch it off.

"Eight hundred feet; still coming up at speed." Mironov sat transfixed. He felt fear, but also eager anticipation. He would see it soon. This was what he lived for.

Dmitry turned the u-shaped wheel and angled the submersible away, but even he must have known he had no hope of outrunning whatever was coming up. "Maybe another squid." He nodded, as if trying to convince himself. "They are jet-propelled, and move fast if they want to... and can be that big, easy."

Mironov read more figures from the sonar, and looked at the computer representation of the mass of the thing – it was no squid. "Now at four hundred feet out, three hundred, two-fifty, two hundred... wait, wait... it seems to be changing course." Mironov couldn't suppress a smile. "Moving away."

"Good, good." Dmitry's smile split his face. "Maybe I will take your offer. Who else is ever going to believe I lived through this if you're not around to tell them."

Both men felt the *Prusalka* tilt in the water, and then yaw first to port and then to starboard.

"Dammit, it's going around us – circling." Mironov felt his heart sink. *So close,* he thought. He knew what was happening. Of course the thing hadn't really changed course. Instead it was just taking a look at them. Most predators circle their prey before making a killing run.

"Where *is* it?" Dmitry's words hissed from his mouth like steam.

"Still circling. Increasing speed now." Mironov couldn't

help a feeling of excitement building in his gut. "Its circle is getting tighter."

Dmitry reached forward to switch on all the external lights. He paused for a moment, and then included the powerful spot light.

"Good idea," Mironov breathed. "Hopefully the corona of light will make us seem bigger – at least too big to eat or attack."

The Russian billionaire sat back sharply. Out at the far reaches of the spot light, he saw something huge sail past – a gray-black torpedo shape – fast and impossibly powerful.

"Big fish," Dmitry muttered. "Maybe a killer whale," he said hopefully.

"No. This creature has a side-to-side tail motion, and whales are up and down. And we're far too deep for those type of cetaceans." Mironov's gaze was riveted on the curved window. "I believe we are about to meet the true ruler of this world."

Dmitry leaned forward, staring out front as the thing made another circuit. This time, any hope it was a whale was immediately dispelled. In the glare of the lights, the full shape of the thing was imprinted into their minds.

The mouth, hanging open, reminded Mironov of bear-trap lined with hand-length triangular teeth, each serrated and designed for tearing and cutting flesh. The long powerful body was gray-black with a pale belly. And then there was the fist-sized eye, cold and darker than the surrounding water. The creature seemed to slow momentarily, and Mironov knew it saw them then. It looked in through the glass, saw them, and wanted them.

A single flick of a two-story tall, scythe-like tail, and it vanished again in the stygian darkness.

"Shark." Was all Dmitry said.

"It's much worse than that," Mironov said softly. "It is the father of all sharks – the *Carcharodon Megalodon*."

Time seemed to freeze, and Mironov knew he was holding his breath. Through the window there was nothing now but an impenetrable darkness. He strained every sense he had, waiting, and then the *Prusalka* rang like a bell and half rolled in the water. Both men were jolted in their seats.

"We're hit." Dmitry looked everywhere at once.

Mironov quickly checked his screens. His thinking was scrambled and his head ached as it seemed every proximity and warning alarm they had was screaming at them in unison.

Dmitry moved from screen to screen. "No sign. Maybe we are not to its taste." He shut down the alarms and checked the sonar again, putting it on speaker. There was no sound, no telltale pings that heralded the return of their attacker.

Dmitry nodded. "Time to go." He powered the vessel away and upwards, heading back the way they had come.

"Where are we going?" Mironov kept his eyes on his screens.

"Anywhere but here," the Russian declared.

Mironov wiped his brow. "When I was much younger, we sailed through the seal colonies in South Australia. They congregate on rocky outcrops, but when they entered the water to fish, they had to first pass over some deep underwater trenches. They usually learned to stay at its edges, and not venture out over the dark water." He looked across to Dmitry. "Because that mistake was only ever made once – the deep water was where the big sharks waited. Circling down in the dark, they would come up from the depths so fast the seals never had a chance."

Dmitry nodded, his face white. "Just keep watch on the sonar – I'm putting it on speaker."

There was silence for several seconds.

Ping…

The two men froze.

Ping…

Mironov's hands gripped his armrests.

Ping… ping… ping…

"Chyort voz'mi!" Dmitry's teeth showed in a frightened rictus. "Coming from below – like for seals." His arms strained on the wheel, and his lips remained pulled back. He seemed to be willing the submersible to go faster, adding every ounce of his own strength into the engines.

The second impact threw them from their seats again, even though they had braced themselves. Their world turned upside down. Alarms screamed again, and this time something hissed. Metal groaned beneath them.

The *Prusalka* still listed at an angle as Dmitry scrambled to his feet and pulled himself back into his seat. He wiped his face, and took the wheel again. "Check for fires."

Mironov felt his temple and his hand came away wet and red. He looked towards the front and saw something that scared him more than the leviathan outside – there was now a thin line running down the center of the curved glass window.

He blinked and pointed. Dmitry seeing him, snapped his head around, and also saw the hairline crack. He leapt forward to reach up and lay fingers on it.

"Impossible," he hissed.

The next impact jolted them again, and Dmitry's voice was high and shrill as he scrabbled backwards along the floor. The submersible was being pushed backwards, but what had frightened the Russian pilot was what covered the impossibly strong viewing glass. The Megalodon had them in its mouth, lips pulled back exposing the hyper-extended jaws, and huge triangular-shaped teeth. And behind them, a cavernous void of internal ribbing and ventral flaps, down a train-tunnel sized gullet.

Mironov rose to his feet. Statistics ran through his head: the jaws of an average Great White Shark can exert a bite pressure of up to one-point-eight tons, but this thing with its pure mass would be able to exceed that by at least a dozen times. He remembered what Yegor had told them about the *Prusalka*'s ability to withstand crush depth pressure – no problem, as long as it was exerted al over the craft at once. He suddenly wished Jack Monroe were here so he could ask the expert's advice.

There was a smell of smoke in the cabin, and the engines droned on, but were useless as something much bigger and more powerful was now in control of their fate. The submersible's angle changed – downward – Mironov began to slide.

Dmitry wrestled with the wheel. "It's trying to take us down." He grimaced and then yelled over his shoulder. "I'm going to deploy electric charge." He flicked up the clear cover over the array of switches which he set on, and then calibrated a dial. "Priming for full charge this time." He didn't bother to count, but instead hammered down on the large flat button. The cabin lights flickered but unlike with the squid, the Megalodon either didn't feel it, or didn't care.

Dmitry kept his hand down hard on the button until the internal lights dimmed and the smell of smoke now pervaded the cabin. The submersible suddenly kicked backwards in the water, but began to list to starboard.

"We're free." Dmitry spun, grinning madly.

"Free, but dead in the water," Mironov observed as he sat slowly.

Dmitry tried the controls but nothing responded. The red internal lighting was down to a few ruby jewels along the cabin ceiling, and only some of the screens still shone.

"We need to recharge." Dmitry sighed and sat back. "We need *time*."

"Time, yes, but I'm afraid that's something that might be in short supply for the *Prusalka*." Mironov continued to gaze out through the curved glass. He had paid a fortune to perhaps catch a glimpse of a legendary and fantastic creature. *Don't wish too hard for what you want, or then you might get it.* He smiled, dreamily at the thought. He looked down at the depth gauge. They were still descending.

Perhaps the Megalodon had been taking them to its home in the pitiless void of the cave depths. Perhaps it still would; if it attacked again their defenses were now exhausted. It didn't matter now. They were still safely within the crush tolerance of the submersible, except for one thing. He looked up towards Dmitry and the front window – sure enough, with a plinking and popping sound, the crack in the curved glass was growing longer. When its two ends touched, top to bottom, it would fail.

Dmitry gave up trying to draw some sort of response from the flattened batteries. He turned slowly. "I'm so sorry, Mr Mironov."

"Valery." Mironov nodded. "And I forgive you."

The Megalodon passed by the window once again.

CHAPTER 19

Chief Engineer Olaf Kozlov aboard the *Viktor Dubynin* grimaced at the computer screen. The new seismic numbers coming from the seabed stability sensors were telling him the sea floor, or rather the skin over the huge bed of liquid, was shuddering and complaining as if it had growing pains. And it rose like a blister.

He'd told Captain Gorkin he had successfully capped it, but for how long he had no real idea. If the seawater he detected was only a few million gallons and could be siphoned off easily and allow the pressure to ease, then all would be good. But if not, and there was a lot more water under pressure than he expected, then the entire capping seal could give way. And as the subterranean bed was under colossal force, the seabed would not collapse down, but explode upwards.

Kozlov glanced surreptitiously over his shoulder before looking back at the continuous data feed. He knew he certainly did not have the necessary equipment he needed to cap hundreds of feet of sea bottom if that occurred.

"Please hold, please hold," he whispered. At least until I'm a long way away… and paid.

"Nobody… move," Jack whispered.

The raft glided now, all four of its occupants sitting stone still and eyes wide. Cate and Abby had their flashlights trained on the open water behind them, and the cold gray mountain that rose from the misted surface, fell back again into its inky depths.

The thing came up again, this time closer, and rolled. One huge, almost human-like eye swiveled to stare up from the water. A geyser spouted in the air, and the drops rained back down on them.

"Oh god, a whale." Greg exhaled, almost giggling. "*It's just a freaking whale.*"

"Nearly no dorsal fin, and a blow hole, so definitely a cetacean." Cate leaned forward. "But not sure what type; maybe of the baleen family, but can't really see..." She turned to Abby. "...means no teeth, just a feeding comb. Not a big one, smaller even than a humpback." She sat back, feeling a huge lift of relief in her chest. "What do you think, Greg?"

"Certainly has some baleen characteristics of a longer skull, but there are features there I don't recognize." Greg pointed at the huge mammal now hanging stationary in the water. It returned the scrutiny. "It seems to have an extended snout, just like some of the first toothless baleen whales. Going out on a limb here and saying, maybe it's a Eomysticetus or even a Micromysticetus." He grinned. "They were around in the late Oligocene, about thirty million years ago."

"Very good, Greg. Impossible to verify, but can't fault your analysis." Cate lifted her light.

"I'm hoping it's just checking us out," Jack said. "They're intelligent and inquisitive. We're the ones who are the strangers down here." The whale floated a little closer, it's eye turned to them seeming to move across each of their faces. It turned a little more onto its side and a flipper rose momentarily.

"Holy shit, look! See that? It's still got a bit of a forearm, and thumb." Greg pointed, an excited smile plastered on his face.

"You're right." Cate rose from her seat.

"Sit down, please," Jack warned.

"It's far more primitive than we thought. They were land creatures once, whose limbs evolved for water living. This creature might even be some sort of transitional form." She grinned. "Now what do you say, Greg?"

He nodded, enjoying the game. "Okay, what about a Rodhocetus?" He shook his head. "Nah, they were only about eight feet long; this guy is easily twice that. Okay, something more our pal's size…" He rubbed his chin, and then clicked his fingers. "Durodon." His smile suddenly dropped. "*Oh shit.* Those guys ate meat."

"Yikes." Abby pulled her arm in.

The ancient cetacean continued to glide closer, its huge intelligent eye still watching them. "Hey big guy, don't suppose you can give us a lift to Heceta Island." Greg pointed, his arm out over the water. "It's thatta way."

Jack used the oar to paddle backwards, keeping some distance between the raft and the creature.

"Be careful. I've dived with humpbacks, and seen orcas from a cage. They're usually pretty sociable, but they have a habit of breaching and landing in your boat."

Greg pulled his arm in. "Easy there, jumbo. We're mammals, just like you."

He waved, and the huge beast rolled and sank. It rose again another forty feet from the raft, and then went down for good.

The group paddled on, minutes turned to hours, and then many hours. They swapped paddle duties back and forth, with the sessions growing shorter. The warmth meant they perspired heavily, and Cate worried their water would soon be gone.

"Jack, any idea on how far now?" Cate wiped her forehead, and felt her eyes sting from tiredness.

He shook his head. "No, but can't be many more miles." He pointed upward. "The roof is lowering, so fingers crossed there's a chute we can climb." He turned. "And pray its entrance is at this level, and doesn't open in the ceiling where we can't get at it."

"Great. What do we do then?" Greg asked, lifting his oar, and leaning it across his knees.

Jack shook his head slowly. "Grow gills."

"Hey, our friend is back." Abby brought her hands together.

Cate thought she was going to clap like a child, but understood her feelings – it was kinda nice to have something like a fellow traveler in the darkness.

Greg turned back to the water and the primitive whale keeping a silent vigil beside them. "Hi there, buddy." He turned to Abby. "You know what he needs? A name." He rubbed his chin. "*Um*, how does 'Thumbs' strike you? You know coz he's got a pair."

Abby wrinkled her nose. "That's a dumb name. I bet you've got a dog named, Spot." She looked back at the gliding creature. "Jonah."

"Jonah?" Jack grimaced.

"Yes, why not?" Abby raised her chin.

Greg shrugged. "Fine with me… if I can't have Thumbs, that is."

Jack continued to paddle. "I'm just saying, that *a Jonah* is an expression for something or someone that brings bad luck, that's all."

"Maybe he'll bring us good luck." Greg leaned forward. "Your name is Jonah, do you like that buddy?"

"Greg, maybe he's hoping for a hot meal, rather than a few new water-friends," Cate said, grinning.

"*Nah*, he's friendly, I can tell." Greg looked briefly from Cate to Abby. "Jonah it is. I like it."

The eruption of water made all four of them fall back in the raft. The dark sea exploded from directly under the drifting cetacean, lifting it several dozen feet in the air. Cate would have screamed, but the breath was locked in her chest as she saw the whale suspended in the air, its huge body, hanging either side of a massive column of muscled flesh.

The whale made a sound like a scream that carried with it all the pain and anguish a being could feel as it knew it was about to die. Huge jaws came together with bone crushing force as massive teeth sank deeply into the blubbered flesh.

The whale was then dragged under; leaving nothing but a sucking whirlpool on a surface that swirled with red froth. Waves slapped at their raft, spinning it round.

Jack was first to break the spell of horror that gripped them all. *"Paddle! Paddle!"* He began digging his oar in deep and sweeping water back along the side of the raft.

Cate, Greg and Abby started to do the same. Cate momentarily used one arm to pull her pod-door oar, and lifted her flashlight shining it down into the water – it was stained wine-red from the blood of the whale.

"Move it," Jack hissed. His head moved left and right, as if to get his bearings. "Veer right, we need to get out of the kill zone."

"You guide, we'll paddle," Cate yelled back. They all dug their oars in deeper, causing the nose of the raft to come around.

The muscles in Cate's shoulders and back began to rebel, but she focused on the drips of perspiration running down her nose, and her rhythm, and nothing else.

Greg's breathing rasped as he pulled the oar back hard through the water. "That… was it, wasn't it?"

"Don't know; happened too fast… couldn't really see it in the dark." Cate grimaced as she dragged her own oar. She knew she was stonewalling herself as well.

Jack wasn't hazy. "Yes." He said over his shoulder. "No use pretending it wasn't."

"Shit, I knew it." Greg looked out over the dark water. "We're fucked."

"Shut up and keep paddling." Cate dragged hard on her oar.

"Do you think the whale might have filled it up?" Abby asked, her voice little more than a squeak.

"Maybe, *uh*, I mean, sure," Cate said, but was concerned to see that Jack briefly turned to shoot her a look that had implied he thought anything but.

Cate kept her head down. She had lied to Greg; she had seen the size and shape of the creature that had grabbed the whale. It was the Megalodon she had expected – the dinosaur shark – alive, and now, perhaps circling somewhere below them. The portion of the creature that had launched itself out of the water had dwarfed the twenty-foot mammal, and from what she knew about sharks, they could consume enormous amounts of meat. Like Abby, she just hoped it was full for now.

They rowed, hard, for many more minutes, probably moving another half mile from where they had seen the attack, when Cate felt her shoulders, back and arms turning to jelly. She and Greg paddled on one side, and Jack on the other. Abby was already in the bottom of the raft, vomiting from fatigue.

"Jack... *Jack*," Greg rasped. "I can't..."

Cate lifted her pod door to poke him. "*Keep, going, Greg.*"

More minutes passed, and then finally Jack turned, his face slick and pale. He looked from Cate to Abby, and then nodded. He straightened, pulling his oar from the dark water.

"Let's take a minute. Grab some water, but just a few sips."

"Thank god." Greg slumped forward.

Cate also flopped back for a moment, breathing in the humid air. The perspiration on her face refused to dry, and it stung her eyes. Laying down, her light beam became a pipe of light up toward a ceiling that was lost in an impenetrable darkness, a hundred or maybe a thousand feet above them. She lifted an arm to read her wristwatch. They had been paddling now for just over twenty-four hours. She did the math – at about two miles per hour, that meant they had covered around forty-eight miles – *not bad*, she thought.

She pulled in a deep breath and eased upright. Spots of light popped in her eyes, and she knew it was fatigue dizziness. She saw that Abby and Greg were lying down, and Jack had bent forward, his forehead resting on his knees. The raft continued to glide on the oil-dark sea, and she lifted her light, panning it over its surface. She wondered what they looked like from out there – she imagined them as a small dot of light on a fathomless sea, a speck, like a single, tiny star in a massive universe of darkness.

Cate carefully looked over the side – *nothing*, not even her reflection. Except down there, she knew there wasn't *nothing*. She crushed her eyes shut, and rested her hands on her knees for a moment, feeling a gurgle of hunger gnaw away in her stomach. The warm smell of salt lifted from the tropical water, and the low mist smelled of seaweed and slick rocks. She lifted her flashlight again, this time higher – out to their side, she could just make out an enormous cave wall, with a small shelf of stone that formed tiny islands at its base. Ahead, and to her right, or starboard, there was nothing but infinite dark water for as far as her light beam extended.

In the bow of the small raft, Jack consulted his compass. He looked up, and seeing her watching him, smiled.

"Not far now, by my reckoning." He lifted an arm out toward the front and slightly to their right. "Just a few more miles, and then we'll be directly underneath the caves. Let's hope there's something there."

"An elevator would be nice," Greg said, groaning as he raised himself up to sit. He rubbed his face, hard.

Abby smacked dry lips. "You said the caves were eight hundred or so feet deep, but down here we're at least double that. What happens if…" Her voice trailed off.

Jack nodded. "Yup. So we're hoping there is some lower hole we can punch through. It only needs to be a few feet wide." He sighed. "I'm not going to lie to you, there needs to be a lot of cave, heading upwards, before we even get to the basement level of the Heceta Island cave system."

Greg blew air between his lips, and then shrugged. "I don't care. Not even if there's another two thousand feet of climbing to do. If we're off the water, and can maybe get out of here, then I'll be happy."

"That's the spirit," Cate said. She felt her stomach growl and gurgle. "Anyone else hungry?"

"Oh god yes, I thought no one would ask. I'm famished." Abby grinned tiredly.

"Oh yeah; time to refuel – we need it." Jack looked up. "Break it out."

"There's somewhere we can land over there…" Cate pointed out to the side.

"Not yet," Jack said, giving her an apologetic smile. "We're making good time. Best to keep on – we'll snack as we go."

"I'm good with that." Like a conjuror, Greg was already laying out the tins. "Caviar, duck pate, dry cheddar, Camembert – *yech* – and crackers."

"I'll have one with the lot." Jack grinned, and leant back against the inflated gunwale.

There were small plastic spoons and knives in the pack, and Cate set about using them to spread the fragrant ingredients on the crackers until the small tins were all empty.

"So much for portion control." She rested them carefully on the top of the pack. They each looked fit for a dinner party, rather than something to be hastily consumed by the remains of a submarine crew who'd been abandoned on an underground sea.

Each of them took turns lifting them to the mouths. They nibbled at them, chewing slowly, and savouring each bite.

Greg licked each of his fingers. "Bit rich for my liking, but... delicious." He lifted one of the empty tins to his face and stuck his tongue in. He then spun it over the side where it flew for a good twenty feet, before landing upright, and then bobbing like a small round boat.

Cate sipped at her water, still famished. The small amount of food had only just knocked the edge off her hunger. She sighed. "When we get out, I think I'm going to pretend it's thanksgiving and have turkey and stuffing."

"And potatoes, fried and covered in salt and pepper." Greg closed his eyes. "And a pitcher of beer big enough to bathe in." He turned to Abby. "Join me?"

"Only if you're also having pie – pecan, with cream." She smiled dreamily, but then her face screwed into a grimace. "God, I'm still starving."

Jack snorted. "That makes two of us. I think Valery should have packed some fishing rods."

Cate looked out over the water. "I wonder where they are now." She turned back to Jack. "Do you think he's still alive... Valery?"

Jack shrugged, looking away. "You saw what happened to Yegor."

Cate nodded slowly.

Jack sipped some water, and then dabbed at his mouth, ensuring any remaining drops were smeared on his lips and not wiped away. "Okay everyone, here's where we row again – do I need to beat the drums so we all stay in rhythm?" He grinned.

"Sure, as long as you avoid ramming speed; I'm beat already," Greg said, lifting an oar but then jerking his hand away to look at his palm. "Shit. Blisters."

"Welcome to the club." Cate held up her hand showing Greg the dime sized holes in the skin, before going back to putting the remaining empty tins into the plastic bag they came from. She spotted the one Greg had flung over the side. It still bobbed lazily, now just half a dozen feet from the boat. She reached out with her paddle.

Greg scoffed. "Seriously?"

"Yes, seriously. This is pristine water, and suddenly one of the first people to explore it decides to throw his trash in it."

Greg gave her a lopsided grin. "*Ah*, you did see that crane wreckage a few miles back, *huh*?"

Cate ignored him, and dipped the paddle in the water, pulling it back towards her, and causing the can to spin and bob closer. She reached out again, extending her arm, just able to hold the oar straight as it suddenly dropped to tip the edge of the tin, filling it, and causing it to sink.

"*Damn.*" She leant over, holding her flashlight up and watching the silver tin sink, its inside reflecting her light back as it got smaller and less distinct the lower it went. It surprised her, as even though the water was oil dark, it must have been clear as glass, as she could still see the glinting dot of the tin, now a good fifty feet down.

The huge shadow torpedoed past underneath them, causing her to jerk back so fast she fell into the bottom of the raft, with her heart hammering.

"Easy back there, you'll tip us over," Jack said from over his shoulder.

Cate tried to speak, but she felt light-headed from the shock, and all she could do is point.

Abby rose slightly, staring at her. "*Ja... Jack...*"

Jack turned just as the raft gently lifted from the surge beneath them. His lips were pressed tight as his gaze went from Cate to the dark water. He sat higher, spinning left and right, and then pointed with his paddle.

"To the shoreline, there, quickly now."

"What is it?" Greg started to paddle slowly, but then looked back to see Cate's waxen face.

Cate jumped to her knees and began to paddle furiously. "Down there... big."

Greg looked over the side, and frowned. "There's noth..."

As Cate watched, his mouth dropped open and he pointed. She followed his arm. A dorsal fin rose from the water. Higher and higher, until it topped out at about ten feet.

"Shit – there's two of them." Greg's voice was high.

The four rafters pulled hard, but all of their heads were turned as they watched the things glide in tandem through the water.

Cate felt her gorge rise from fear. But knew sharks were solitary hunters. If there were two of the things then maybe, just maybe, it meant they were something else entirely.

Jack stopped paddling to watch the water for a few seconds. He grimaced and shook his head. "Bad news – that's not a second fin – it's all part of the same creature, and a goddamned big one."

Cate immediately knew he was right. "Shit. Tail fluke." She didn't bother looking, but instead dug her oar in deep, as they headed to the rock shelf more than five hundred feet in the distance.

The fin circled them and then tilted, angling away slightly. Cate imagined the huge, black soulless eye now staring up at them. She knew it saw them a lot better than they saw it. Its closest living relative, the Great White, could see in near complete darkness *and* in light. It was also one of the few aquatic animals that saw perfectly well above water.

Then twin fins started to sink, finishing with a flick of the tail as it dived.

"It's gone," Greg said, and then giggled a little manically. "We don't look that interesting – too small."

"No, it's just gone deep," Jack said. "Keep paddling."

"Shit – shit – shit." Cate cursed in time with her paddle digging into the water. Her muscles screamed but nothing else mattered.

Greg's paddling was getting erratic. "My hands are bleeding."

"Just, paddle, you *sonofabitch,*" Cate rasped back at the young man. "Don't think about anything else."

The four dug and pulled, dug and pulled, eating up the yards between them and the island-like outcrop of rock in the distance.

Jack started muttering. "*Keep... going.*" He suddenly reached for one of the flashlights in the bottom of the raft, flicked it on, and then flung it a few feet out to the side of them. It sank quickly, the dot of yellow light falling away into the depths... and then, it simply vanished as if it had been switched off, or swallowed.

"Coming up!" Jack yelled without turning.

Cate felt her scalp tingle, and had an urgent need to urinate. She knew she was going into prey-shock – the state some creatures enter as they are about to be attacked by a large predator. She gritted her teeth, hard, and prayed.

The explosion was like being on top of a bomb. They were lifted in the air, and Cate's stomach flipped as they rose higher and higher. Each of them was slammed back into the bottom of the raft, as the colossal Carcharodon Megalodon erupted from the water beneath them. Its huge jaws were opened and extended forward, but perhaps as Jack had hoped, the light descending had distracted it just enough, to throw off its aim by a few feet.

They were suddenly thirty feet in the air, balancing on the snout. The open maw was just to the rear of them, with their tiny raft threatening to fall in. Cate smelled the age old stink of the massive sea creature as they balanced momentarily at the apogee – it was probably only for a few slices of a second, but time seemed to have slowed as they teetered in space, just inches separating life and a bloody gruesome death.

The massive creature fell back to the sea. The raft, being light, hung in the air for another second before it, too, began to drop.

Unfortunately, it didn't stay upright, and flipped on the way down. The turning raft allowed the occupants to see the titanic beast below them as it splashed back into the dark water – it was massively powerful, with jaws big enough to swallow a horse, and though they could only see the front half, this alone was a good thirty feet, meaning the beast was easily double that.

It is death itself, Cate thought morbidly. The dinner plate sized eyes had rolled back for the attack, but now they rolled down exposing the dark orbs. The shark thumped back into the water, creating a massive depression that quickly crashed closed, and geysered back up to meet them.

Cate struck the warm water, went under, and immediately panicked, clawing back to the surface, and only just managing to stop herself from sucking in a deep breath to scream her fear while under the water.

She breached, gasped and spluttered, and immediately heard Jack screaming for them to swim and swim hard. He pointed to the cliffs and the small jutting island that stuck out about three hundred feet from them.

Jack was a strong swimmer, and was moving fast, even though he pushed Abby before him. Cate followed, and she heard Greg coming up beside her, and already thrashing like the devil was on his tail – which in a way, it was.

The raft was now back on the water, and amazingly still afloat. It was a few dozen feet out to the front and side of them, and she was tempted to divert to it, as it was nearer.

Suicide, she thought. The raft had already proved to be no safe haven. She put her head down and swam. She opened her eyes in the water but could see nothing, so shut them tight. She concentrated on maintaining her stroke, slicing through the water, even though her legs wanted to blur and thrash.

Little more than a couple of laps in an Olympic swimming pool, she kept telling herself over and over, so as to leave no room to think about the leviathan she knew was undoubtedly circling beneath them.

Stroke-stroke-stroke, breathe, repeat. Swimming in clothing and shoes was hard, and she felt she was simply staying in the same spot. She lifted her head to suck in a deeper breath and saw from the corner of her eye, their raft explode – really explode, as the Megalodon rose up, and its jaws extended forward and over it, and then dragged it back down to vanish completely.

Two hundred feet, *just two hundred more feet*, that's all. How many strokes? She concentrated on the math, counting them off, guessing how far each one took her. Maybe sixty, maybe seventy, tops – I can do this.

Jack and Abby were just ahead of her, but keeping pace. Cate knew Jack could have been on the rock ledge by now, but instead, he swam-pushed Abby, thinking of others before himself. She wanted to tell him to move away, as all together they presented a much bigger target, and therefore a more attractive meal.

Cate heard Greg splutter behind her, and she quickly switched to backstroke for a few seconds to check on him. Greg was a few dozen feet back, and falling behind. In the weaker light of the beam from her forehead light, she saw him look up and cough-grin at her.

He swam with his head up. "I'm – *cough* – coming."

Her light cast a shimmering path back towards him, but coming into the range of the light was a lump in the water. Further back, something cut the surface, rising higher and higher – the tip of a dorsal fin.

"Swim!" Her voice echoed back at them, as she knew that even though the fin was forty or so feet from him, that would mean the head was...

A black mountain rose up behind her friend, and then surged forward, a cavernous maw already open that was edged in the cruelest teeth she had ever seen in her life. It closed and sank. One minute Greg had been there, and the next he was simply... *gone.*

"Greg!" She screamed his name. "Greg!" She was treading water, and had stopped swimming and without even realizing it, stopped thinking. Insanely, she took a few strokes back to where he had been. "Oh god, no."

"Move! For god's sake swim, Cate!" Jack's voice cut through to her.

"*Wha...*" She thrashed, panicking, feeling like her body was short-circuiting as she tried to move, anywhere. She was grabbed then. An arm wrapped around her shoulders and neck. She shrieked involuntarily, until she realized Jack had come back to get her. He started to swim, lifeguard style, towards the lip of the island ledge. Cate felt herself go loose. She couldn't take her eyes from the water, even if she wanted to.

I'm in shock.

In what seemed another few seconds, he and Abby, were roughly hauling her up onto the slick rocks, and then kept dragging her until she was twenty feet back from the water's edge.

She felt sick, and couldn't control the racking sobs that started in her gut and welled up to make her back and head throb. "*Oh god no.*" She pounded the slick stone beneath her. "*Fucking, fuck, fuck...*" She sobbed and looked back out over the oil-dark water. As she watched, something rose, huge, and only a few feet from the edge of the rock.

"Jesus Christ." Jack grabbed her shoulders and even though they were twenty feet from the water, he hauled her backwards as the thing loomed over them.

The Megalodon shark sank slowly, but it had wanted to see them, perhaps even count them, if that mechanism was possible within its crude brain.

"It's still there," Abby said softly.

"We're trapped." Cate watched the monster slide back into the water with barely a ripple.

"We're alive," Jack said crouching, and wiping hair back off her face.

"No we're not." She lay down trembling. She knew what Jack said wasn't true for all of them. Cate stared up into the darkness. Her body felt like it wanted to shut down.

Cate lay there on the slick stone for ages, just staring up into a black sky that wasn't a sky at all. It ended only several hundred feet somewhere up there in the dark. From the corner of her eye she could see Jack, squatting with his elbows on his knees, just staring out over the stygian water. He still had the compass, one of the small items he had in his pockets. Everything else was gone.

She sat forward; every muscle in her body ached, and her shoulders and back actually felt like something might be damaged inside. She held her head in her hands.

"Hey there." Jack had turned to her. "You okay?"

"No. I feel like shit. We're lost, shipwrecked, and Greg's dead." She knew she sounded bitter, and hated it. "Do you know the last thing I said to him?" She laughed sourly. "I called him a sonofabitch."

He nodded. "Yep, I heard." He sucked in a deep breath. "So what?"

"I made him come down here. I killed him." She felt it coming then, rising up within her. A sense of blackness so heavy it overwhelmed her. Cate threw herself forward to vomit what little contents she had in her stomach. She couldn't stop the tears.

"I'm an asshole." She pressed her forehead against the stone. Jack grabbed her then, holding her close. She felt his strength, smelled his sweat, and clung to him. She knew she needed him. Probably always had, but now more than ever.

"You're the bravest, smartest, most beautiful woman in the world. You had nothing to do with that." He hugged her tighter for a moment, and then eased her back, staring into her face. "Take a breath. You're here, and I'm here. For me, it's my lucky day."

She closed her eyes and sucked in a deep breath. "I'm okay." She used both hands to push the wet hair back off her face, and looked at him, managing a weak smile. "See? I'm good to go again."

"Good." Jack looked back out at the water. "Because we can't stay here."

Her eyes widened. "Oh yes we can. I'd rather die here than go back into that fucking water."

Abby came and sat with them. She hugged her knees. "I'm not either."

"I know, I know. I don't really want to either. But guys, we aren't that far away from Heceta Island." Jack lifted an arm, pointing out to the left of them. "The cliffs along here seem to curve in the right direction, we try and follow them, staying out of the water where we can – rock hopping." He looked down at his hands for a moment, before turning back to her with his head tilted. "But I'm not going to bullshit you; where we can't, we'll need to wade, and maybe, we'll have to swim some."

Cate flicked her hand at him. "No fucking way, Jack. I'm not going back in that water, end of story." She turned away from him, her beam illuminating the slick rock next to her. At the shelf edge something like a foot-long cross between a crab and a lobster, all spiky legs and eyes on stalks was levering itself from the water to sit staring and waving long feelers in their direction.

"That's dinner sorted," Jack said.

"Great." Abby's nose wrinkled.

Cate just shook her head, determined not to allow him to placate her. She kept staring at the large crustacean as it moved past a round rock – *too round*. Cate frowned, squinting. She got to her feet, carefully moving around the spiny creature.

"Piss off."

The thing's eyestalks just seemed to prick higher as it watched her. She carefully crouched at the object, dug her fingers under it, and lifted – it was light, not solid. She turned it over in her hands, and then quickly started to rip away some of the weed and mollusks that had built up on its surface. Remnants of yellow paint began to show through.

"What is it?" Jack asked.

"I think, it's…" She grabbed and flicked away more weed and shells. The engraved letters were still there: *Jim Granger, Foreman.*

She sat down heavily, shaking, feeling like she wanted to laugh hysterically.

"It's a helmet." Cate held it up briefly. "Jim Granger's."

"Your grandfather's?" Jack came and sat beside her, and threw an arm over her shoulder.

"This place…" She stared down at the ancient hard hat in her hands. "No one gets away." She sniffed at her runny nose. *Sorry Granma Violet, maybe he did meet the devil this time after all,* she thought as she screwed her eyes shut, feeling the tears squeeze out again.

"I can't go back in the water, Jack."

Beside her, Jack sighed. "Cate… *Cate.*"

She looked up at him, her eyes still burning.

He smiled sadly. "Turn your light off."

She looked at him for a few seconds, but then shrugged and did as he asked.

"Abby, yours too." Abby's went out, and then Jack did the same with his.

The darkness was absolute. "See this?" There was nothing but Jack's disembodied voice.

"Our batteries will last another six to eight hours… and we've lost all our spares." He left the comment hanging.

Cate turned her light back on, and sighed. She began to chuckle, shaking her head, not wanting to fully let the implications sink in.

Jack went on. "I've done cave diving many times. But there was this one time, when we were diving into a newly-discovered sinkhole in the Amazon. There were three of us. We were eight hundred feet in when our batteries began to fade, and then die. They must have soaked up some moisture on trip way down; corrosion ate them from the inside out. Anyway, the thing was, when you're in a cave and the lights go out, it's not pretty." He snorted softly. "You can't see the hand in front of your face." He looked at Cate, his mouth momentarily set in a hard line. "Then you start to see things."

Cate groaned, and let her head drop so her forehead rested on her knees, the helmet still in her hands. She could smell it then – the weed and shells and odors of ancient oceans. It was near tropical warmth in the cave, but she began to shiver. She lifted her head.

"Fuck it." She turned to the spiny lobster thing that had advanced another few feet towards them. "And you can fuck off!" She ripped more weed from the helmet and tossed it at the thing, whose stalks retracted for a moment, but it held its ground.

Cate looked back out at the now calm water. There wasn't a movement or sound from its oil-slick-like stillness. She didn't know what frightened her more – the thought of being back in that water, or of sitting here when the lights went out, and perhaps having something even worse than the lobster-thing climb out of the water to investigate the strange warm-bodied bipeds sitting alone in the dark.

She turned to him. "Which way?"

Jack gripped her shoulders. "Good on you." He let her go and turned to Abby, raising his eyebrows.

Abby nodded. "Well, I'm not sitting here alone in the dark." She gave him a sheepish smile. "But dry is better."

"Good girl, and I promise, if we can stay dry, we stay dry." Jack pointed. "This small outcrop we're on is joined to the cliff wall. I can just see there are boulders and outcroppings for quite a way. We can walk and stay back from the water… at least for a while."

Cate held out a hand for him. "Then what are we waiting for?" He hauled her up, and she turned briefly, spying the spindly crustacean that had advanced on them once again. She had an evil desire to take a running punt at it, except it looked solid and heavy and would more than likely shred her boot.

Jack led them off. "We only need to cross a few more miles. Maybe this will get us close enough to the island so we can see what we have to deal with."

She unzipped her suit, and jammed the helmet inside and then rezipped it. It was damned uncomfortable, but she wasn't leaving without it.

Cate nodded to Jack, and together they hopped across rocks, heading towards the cliff wall. Some of the boulders marched out into the water, and on either side of them the dark water was impenetrable ink. Unless she shone her light directly down into it, it could have been inches deep or the edge of an undersea cliff that dropped away to Hades itself.

There came a splash from somewhere further out on the dark water. They froze, listening for several moments.

Jack half turned. "Don't worry about it, I don't think anything can reach us here." He continued on, keeping his arms out like a tightrope walker.

Cate noticed he didn't sound confident. How could he be? Even though he was an expert in sharks and marine biology, what they had entered down here was so alien and primordial no one living today could possibly be an expert. Everything they encountered or experienced here was best guess only.

Better than nothing, she knew. The corners of her mouth twitched up, as she watched him leap from rock to rock. After all, that was why he was here. She blushed. *The only reason?* A sly voice asked. She shook it away. Now was not the time for self-analysis.

They walked, hopped and skipped in silence for another half hour, Cate brought up the rear, sometimes they strung out for fifty feet, and sometimes they all ended up on the same large flat rock together. But as she moved, she noticed Abby, like her, let her eyes wander to the dark sea.

"Do you think it's following us?" Abby asked.

Jack looked out over the water. "Possibly. Sharks are certainly territorial, and something that size will have a territory that ranges for many miles – hundreds." He shrugged. "The upside is, from what we've seen so far, there is no shortage of food, so…" he shrugged.

"So probably no, huh?" Abby brightened.

"No, is my guess." He didn't turn.

In another few minutes he held up a hand as they came to where their rocky path suddenly ended. It resumed again about fifty feet from where they stood. He looked up at the cliff wall – there was a huge gouge out of the stone, creating a sort of little bay. He then turned the light back out to the water, shining it over the still surface.

"Can't see the bottom. Maybe a rock slide or and entire section of the cliff wall slid into the sea." He turned, grimacing. "We're going to have to swim it, sorry."

Cate knew it would come sooner or later. But now it had, she still felt her stomach roil. She set her jaw. "We gotta do what we gotta do. Abby, you okay?"

"No." She flashed them a fake smile.

Jack hiked his shoulders. "I wish there was another wa…"

Cate walked past him, and waded straight in. The bottom immediately vanished and she found herself in deep water. She started to breaststroke, hearing Jack and Abby hurriedly following her in.

As she swam she refused to look out at the open sea. If there was something rising there, a fin, tail, or even just a ripple, she knew she would have frozen then.

"Nearly there, Cate. Can you feel bottom?" Jack asked.

"No… yes." Her fingertips struck something hard, rock, and then she was scrabbling from the water. It was at that moment fear crushed down on her. She scrambled from the water, leaping the last few feet. Jack pushed Abby up and out, and came up behind her, and then together they threw themselves down on the new rock shelf, panting as though they had just swim the English Channel, rather than a few dozen feet of black water.

Cate rolled towards him. "Well, that was intense." She grinned through her heavy breathing.

"Walk in the park." He sat up.

Cate did the same and looked back out over the water. "Can't help feeling its still there, just below the surface, watching and waiting."

Jack bent to pick up a fist-sized rock and flung it a hundred feet out over the dark water where it splashed loudly, sending ripples in all directions. They waited. The surface returned to its oil-slick stillness. There was nothing, and after a moment he shrugged and turned to her.

"Maybe made no difference, but, I'm not sure we'd keep its interest now that we're out of the water. Come on."

They continued for another twenty minutes, sometimes wading, sometimes scaling huge rocks, and sometimes hopping from stone to stone, until Cate stumbled, not seeing a small depression in the rocks at her feet.

"Shit." She fell to her hands and knees. "Goddamnit." She got to her feet and checked her right palm, now scraped, and suddenly realized why she missed the hole – her light was dim, dimmer than Jack's and Abby's. "Oh no, we're losing them."

Jack had been checking the compass, and then exhaled slowly through his nose. "*Dammit*," he whispered, causing Cate to frown. His head went from the compass to the water again, and once again he cursed.

Something was wrong. *What a surprise*, Cate thought.

Jack went to sit down, but then paused, craning forward. He ran to the water line, and stood there, pointing.

"Look... *look there*."

Cate and Abby joined him.

"Is that our raft?" Abby asked.

"Yep, what's left of it," Jack said, unable to contain his grin.

"Thought it got eaten," Cate said, and flinched as a sudden image of a dark mountain rising behind Greg welled up in her mind. She felt gorge surge to the back of her throat, and she painfully swallowed it down. Her empty stomach rebelled.

"Maybe it did, and got spat out." Jack squinted out at it. "There's still some air in the cells." He turned, hands on hips. "That'll still float us." He shrugged. "Water line, sure, but the cells will retain some buoyancy."

"You mean we have to carry that just in case?" She scoffed. "Maybe I would if we could eat it. I'm starving."

He straightened, his jaw set. "Well, I've got good news and bad."

"Unless you tell me the good news is that this is all a dream, then..." She waved her hand. "Okay, give me the good news; I need it."

"We're very close; about a mile or so from Heceta Island."

His mouth was a flat line, and she felt her heart sink. "And..."

He lifted one arm pointing. "And the bad news is, the mile we need to travel is that way..." His finger was pointing out over the dark water. "We need that raft."

Cate sank down to sit. "Great... just, freaking great."

Abby plonked down beside her. "We won't even be above the water... much."

"She's right. We'll be barely above the water line." Cate wiped her eyes. "We might as well be in the water."

"But the thing is, we won't be. And I can't tell you how important that is." He squatted in front of them. "It'll keep our scent out of the water. I know sharks, and it damn well matters. Just having that layer of raft underneath us will make a hellova difference. I promise you both."

"Didn't make a difference before, when it attacked us." Abby wouldn't look at him.

"We were making more noise than the circus. We won't this time." The corners of his mouth quirked up. "Bottom line is, we only need to travel about a mile out over the water. We can swim, or we can paddle." He turned to nod at the raft. "This is a gift."

"A gift?" Cate couldn't help her mouth twisting on the word.

"Yep." He waited.

She nodded, and reached out to lay a hand on Abby's shoulder. "I guess I'll take a half sunken raft over swimming any day."

"Good. I'll go get it." He turned started to wade in.

"Hey, wait." She crossed to him, grabbing his arm, staring up into his face for a moment. "And if anything happens to you, I'm stuck here by myself…"

"Thanks," Abby said, her mouth turned down.

"That's not what I meant." She turned back to him. "I'm coming."

"Forget it." Jack turned back to the water, but she lunged and grabbed his arm. "I'll fucking come anyway, Jack, and you know I will."

Abby stood. "And then *I'll* be here all by myself." She pointed a finger at Cate's chest. "You stay, or we all go."

"This is madness."

Cate shook her head. "No, it makes perfect sense. If you went by yourself, you'd be making multiple trips – retrieving the raft, bringing it back, and then we all travel back out. This way, it's just one trip." She tilted her head, one eyebrow raised.

He started to laugh. "Stubbornness and logic, two things I love and hate in a woman." He threw an arm around her shoulder and pulled her close. "Thank you." He kissed her, and she returned it, hard.

"We'll be fine." She said as they broke away, a flippy feeling in her stomach.

Jack turned back to the water. The raft was about a hundred feet out, not moving at all. "Well, no use waiting for it to drift in on the tide, so…" he started to wade in. "We take it slow, no splashing, no talking, no urinating."

"Yeah right," Cate scoffed. "Something pops up in the water beside me, I'll be doing more than urinating."

Together they waded into the dark water. Even though Cate knew it was about seventy-eight degrees, it still chilled her to the bone. Beside her, Jack was breathing heavily as he worked up some courage. To her other side, Abby looked as white as a sheet.

"You okay?" she whispered. Abby nodded, but didn't look at her.

"Turn your lights off," Jack said softly.

"*Huh*... why?" Abby frowned.

"We need to save the batteries, and besides, the light just might attract... something," he whispered.

They flicked their lights off.

"What about yours?" Cate said too quickly.

"We need to see, but we don't need to be a carnival." He smiled, put a finger to his lips, turned, and pushed out.

Abby went next, and then Cate.

She could barely see a thing, definitely not the raft, and just concentrated on following Jack's light. She stroked, keeping her arms beneath the surface, and movements even and slow. In front of her, one of Abby's boots broke the surface, a small splash, but it made her heart thump in her chest, and her anger flare. She bit down the curse to stop it moving past her teeth.

Jack's light bobbed, but now and then she caught a glimpse of the raft edge. They glided towards it – forty feet, thirty, twenty, ten... and then they had it.

Jack held the edge, and brought them all in close so he could whisper to them. "I'm going to lift you in first, Abby. Then you help Cate in, okay?"

Abby nodded, and turned to place her hands on the edge of the floating pancake. "Nice and easy." He sunk beside her, and must have put his hands underneath her boot or butt as she was lifted up and onto the flat surface without dipping the raft further under the water.

Cate grinned. "It works." Abby didn't sink, but stayed just above water level.

"You now, and then you help me up." Jack went down again, and she felt his hands on the sole of her boot. It lifted and she used it like a step to propel herself up, kicking something as she came up. She rolled into the raft, once again not sinking it.

"Yes." She said, rolling back to the side. She looked down, and saw Jack's light down deep, too deep, and then it went out. Her mouth fell open, and she stared. She placed her face in the water, and reached up quickly to switch on her yellowing light.

Jack's face was right there, coming up. He rubbed his forehead. "Nice kick in the head, girl. Lost my light."

She grabbed his face. "Get in here." She switched her grip to his shoulders and with Abby's help managed to carefully lift Jack over the side. The raft sank a little then.

"Spread out, everyone lie flat," Jack hissed.

She looked at him and he her. Together they all sat in a warm bathtub, full of water in a dark sea beneath the earth.

"This'll work," he said, pushing the hair back of his face. He checked his compass, but had to hold it a few inches from his face to see. "We need to travel about a mile, that way." He pointed out to the front, starboard, or about two o'clock.

Cate took the yellowing light band from her forehead and held it out. "Here, you need to direct us."

"Thanks." He took it, slipped it on, and rechecked the compass once again.

"Paddles?" Cate asked.

"Home-made." Jack turned and held up his hand, fingers together. He pointed. "You two on that side, me this one. Once again, just ease the water back, nice and slow. Going to take us a while, but we'll get there."

Laying down, he reached over and dug an arm in and dragged the water back. The raft, like a giant lily pad, barely inched forward.

Cate and Abby dug in and pulled. She turned her head; behind them there was nothing but a wall of dark. For all she knew there was a monstrous fin gliding up behind them. She dug her hand in again; it tingled, probably from fear, knowing what could be down there.

She looked up to the comfort of the light. Only to the front could she see anything, and even now, Jack's light range was shrinking. When that went out, they had Abby's in reserve, and then...

Cate shut her eyes, and stroked. *There's nothing there, there's nothing there,* she kept repeating with each drag of water.

Minutes passed, then more minutes. They were surprisingly quiet, with just the odd gentle lap of water against one of their prone bodies that came over the side. There came a splash from out behind them. And Jack's head whipped around.

There *was* something out there.

"Jack." She hissed his name, pulling her arm up from the water. Cate suddenly felt her stomach flutter as she realized how vulnerable it was laying on the raft.

"Stay still, and be quiet." Jack's light played over the water.

The huge body glided closer, and a pressure wave pushed at the raft. Abby whimpered, and turned away. Cate was transfixed and Jack's light stayed hard on the massive thing.

It rolled then, and the whale's far too-human eye regarded them with curiosity. Another one, smaller, surfaced beside it, blowing spray into the air. Then another came up, and another.

"Whales..." She laughed, feeling relief wash over her. "Thank god. Abby, it's okay, look."

Jack commenced to paddle again, as one of the huge bodies came beside them, and nudged the raft, lifting it momentarily. They all felt the solid bulk beneath them, like they'd been beached.

"Easy, big guy." He looked back. "They might not attack us, but they can still swamp us."

The raft tilted again as a smaller whale lifted them up onto its back and carried them twenty feet. "Shit."

It submerged, leaving them still scudding along the surface. "Thanks," he said, looking down. "At least if there's a Megalodon down there, it'll see these big guys long before it sees us. Keep paddling, harder, and we'll try and stay with them."

The whales accompanied them for another ten minutes, the huge cow-like creatures taking turns to either glide closer to examine the strange beings floating above them, or one of the younger ones would lift and carry them again, giving them a free ride for a few dozen feet.

Cate allowed herself a small smile of comfort as the leviathans took turns coming within a few feet of the side. She reached over once, to lay a hand on the slick surface, and noticed the scars and rents in its flesh.

"Hard life, *huh*?" she whispered to the large dark eye that seemed to hold the wisdom of the world in its gentle orb.

In an instant the water swirled and lumped and they were gone.

"What just happened?" she pulled her hands from the water again. "Did something just scare them away?"

"Forget it; paddle... *there*." Jack pointed. There was a cliff face, and one section looked slightly smoothed or melted. "Water erosion; means there's been some sort of drainage from above. Good news, I hope."

"We made it?" Abby said, suddenly brightening.

"That's our destination. Pray there's somewhere in there we can climb up," Jack said, stroking hard now.

Cate turned back to where the pod of primitive whales had just been. There was nothing, not a swirl, lump or ripple on the dark surface. Jack turned briefly, his light now down to a dim burnt orange color, and she took the opportunity to look over the side. She squinted; did she just see something pass underneath them?

"*Jaack.*" She continued to stare over the side.

Jack was breathing hard, pulling the water back furiously now. "*Keep – paddling – almost – there.*"

She gritted her teeth, and hesitated, not wanting to put her hands back in, Abby watched her, eyes wide in the dark.

"Damn it." Her heart hammered, and every part of her body and mind screamed not to do it, but she still dug her arm in deep, looking over the side again. Something else passed underneath them, and something else, and she was about to call again, when more of the objects appeared – rocks, weed, and darting fish as the water became shallower.

Looking up, she saw they were only a few dozen feet from a rocky shore line, this one unlike the last, did not start as a cliff face, but a gradual shallowing like a normal beach.

In another moment, her fingers struck gravel and the raft grounded. Jack immediately jumped free, dragging the raft and them with it, up onto the dark beach.

The three of them crawled free, and lay on their backs, breathing hard. He turned to her, and grinned. "Next time you've got a job, please lose my number."

She looked back, sharing the joke. "And I forgot to mention; you don't get paid until you get us out."

"There's pay?" Jack laughed then, and in the next moment all three of them were laughing uncontrollably, relief bursting from them in waves. The sound bouncing away to repeat countless times in the monstrous cavern.

Cate sat up first, and smacked dry lips, for the first time feeling a thirst that made her throat rasp and head pound. She bet Jack and Abby were the same; they'd need to drink soon, or be in trouble. She grinned again. In trouble? In *more* trouble, she adjusted.

She picked up a pebble and tossed it at an army of small blue crabs that marched like a wave along the shoreline, stopping now and then to pick at small mosses and feeding them into their constantly moving mouths.

Jack got to his feet with a groan, and walked up the beach. He stopped and stood with his hands on his hips, looking around. "This is as close as we're going to get." He lifted a single finger, pointing upwards. "Heceta Island – thatta way."

He turned back to the cliff face, but then stopped and stared. "Well, well, looks like this *is* the place." He turned back to them. "Cate, Abby, look here…"

They crowded closer.

"Abby, switch your light on."

Instead she took the light band from her head and held it out. "You guys are getting me out of here, so you lead – take it."

Cate shrugged, took it from her and switched it on, the brighter beam illuminating the cave wall for dozens of feet in either direction.

The cave drawings were the same as the last they'd encountered, but showed more of the story and struggle the people had endured down on this dark sea. Many figures rowed to the shores, this time dragging a giant shark by the tail, dozens of spears sticking from its body. There were also more peoples coming out of a crack in the wall, and at first, Cate thought they were greeting them, until she saw the next tableau of arrows being fired at the newly arrived party.

"Turf war," Cate said softly.

"Looks like it, but more importantly, what it says is, this is where the fishermen came ashore with their prize. Unfortunately, the Heceta Island natives weren't exactly welcoming." He shined his own rapidly-diminishing light over the scenes. "Many tribes worshipped sharks. And the Megalodon would have been the ultimate shark god."

"And the Nantouk killed one," Abby said.

Jack lifted his light to the depiction of the place the new figures had emerged – the cave opening. He moved the light from the drawing to the cave opening on the cliff wall – the shape was exactly the same. "I feel good about this."

"But there are no natives on Heceta Island," Abby said. "I don't think there's ever been."

"Not now. But what about twenty, thirty, fifty thousand years ago?" He stepped closer. "I'm no expert, but these are very old – stone age, maybe?"

"Yes, late Pleistocene, I think," Abby said. "We see a lot of cave art in geological excavations. And you're right, this could be anything between thirty and fifty thousand years old."

"That's a lot of time to have passed," Cate said.

"Not geologically," Abby said. "That's like yesterday on the geo-clock."

Cate nodded. "I'd agree, if this area wasn't prone to earthquakes."

Abby sighed. "Yeah, there is that."

Jack turned back to the beach, his eyes on the crabs. "Well, if those peoples were able to come down and go back up, then *goddamn* so will we. But first, we need something in our bellies."

They all turned to the wave of crabs. Cate hated the thought of trying to make a meal of the tiny living creatures, but her stomach growled loudly, and she knew she'd eat as many as she could catch.

Cate spat more crab shell onto the ground. It reminded her of when you had a fried egg, and managed to score the shard of eggshell between your teeth – except this was twice as hard and unyielding. In the end, she gave up trying to remove the minuscule amounts of meat, and swallowed everything down.

She spat again and looked up, and then across at the cave wall. There was a vast rent in the cave wall, disgorging tumbled boulders to the shoreline. Some were rounded, almost looking melted together as if the cliff face had vomited the stone down into the water.

The cave looked to only extend in about fifty feet. "Doesn't go in very far," Cate said, feeling her optimism dip.

"No, but that's not the direction we want to go," Jack said. "We see where it leads."

She nodded, and looked back over her shoulder at the sea. It was still as glass, just some vapor rising from the bath-warm water. She couldn't shake the feeling something was gliding past, frustrated now that they had escaped.

"Yes, we see where it leads." She continued to watch the water. "I'm finished with sea travel for a while," she added softly.

"Let's do this." Jack started off, followed by Abby.

Cate gave the water one last look. Anger flared, as she tried to see beneath its surface. "Fuck you." She turned away and followed Abby and Jack into the cave.

CHAPTER 20

Alaskan Department of Natural Resources
Geological Resources Division

Sonya's stomach knotted from impatience as David Meltzer, their chief geologist, pulled yet another map up on his screen showing colored images of Alaskan geological striations. She paced.

"Thank you, Dr Meltzer, that's all very interesting, but if I needed to reach a destination below ground quickly, how and where would you recommend I do it?"

He clasped his fingers together as he watched her move around his office. "As I said at the beginning of our meeting, you could excavate, which by traditional means would take between a few weeks to months. This all depends on the geology of course, which is why I was showing you the different morphological blends along the western coast." He looked at her over his glasses. "Was this too much detail for your movie?"

"A little, it's a balance thing; we need accuracy, but it doesn't have to be so granular." Sonya forced a smile. "The script calls for us being able to get down there quickly."

"How quickly?" he tilted his head.

"Days, hours would be better?"

He snorted. "If you really wanted to accelerate that process, then I would suggest a targeted explosive charge." He raised his eyebrows. "The military has significant ground-penetrating capabilities – take you down a thousand feet in a single blow, I understand." He smiled.

Sonya's gaze was flat. "And what would that do to someone a thousand *and one* feet below that detonation?"

He smoothed his tie. "Yes, I see, give them a bit of a headache, I would imagine. But this is fiction you'll be shooting, right?"

"Of course. It's that balance thing again. I'm looking for something fast, but a little less… lethal." She paced again.

"You could halve the job, I suppose. You could travel down via one of the many caves. Alaska is famous for them. Meet them half way, so to speak."

Sonya paused and turned. "Go on."

"Well, you suggested your area of interest was the western coast. We have numerous caves along that geo-ridge; in fact hundreds."

"I like it; narrow it down to deep ones only, please." Sonya sat again.

He nodded. "There are over fifty that drop below two hundred feet."

"Now we're getting somewhere." She stared. "But deeper."

Meltzer closed his eyes and steepled his fingers over his belly as he spoke. "Well, there is the Mossy Abyss under Dell Island that runs to four hundred. Then there is the Snowhold and also the El Capitan Pit that both fall to around six hundred and fifty feet – that's deep." He peeked at her, as though checking she was still listening. Satisfied, he leant back, closing his eyes once again.

"And not forgetting the real biggie, the Viva Silva Cave on Heceta Island. Now that goes all the way down to eight hundred feet, and is fully accessible all the way. That'd be my choice."

She put her hand on his leg, and his eyes popped open. "Dr Meltzer, where exactly is the Viva Silva in relation to Baranof Island?"

His eyes bulged slightly, as he looked from her hand to her face. "Very close actually, only about fifty miles. It's closed now, but—"

"Thank you." Sonya was up and out of his office before he could say another word.

CHAPTER 21

The booming thump made everyone freeze on the drill ship. Captain Boris Gorkin's round eyes jumped to his Chief Engineer, Olaf Kozlov, and saw that the man's face was drained of color. Both men knew what the sound could mean, but still they waited, perhaps hoping it was anything but what they feared most.

The next sound was like the tearing of a titan's sailcloth, and its vibrations passed through the ocean, the ship, and then tickled the soles of their feet. It was immediately drowned out by the seismic alarms competing with the drill-shaft stability warnings from the control room.

Kozlov shook his head. "It is breaking apart."

"It has to hold; *it has to.*" Gorkin spoke through hard-gritted teeth. He moved to grab Kozlov in one huge hand and shake him. "Fix it... do something." The man was supposed to be his expert, and was paid a fortune. Now he wanted to freeze up when he was needed the most. Gorkin shook him again.

Kozlov grabbed at Gorkin's hand, twisting. "Drop the shaft rods; we need to get out of here." He looked about to scream and his eyes were round and wet. "The seabed is collapsing for miles; there is nothing we can do. We'll be swamped."

Gorkin erupted, shaking the man until his eyes rolled in his head. "Bastard! I'll lose everything." His turned left then right, indecision wracking him. He held onto to his engineer's shirtfront. "No, we're staying, we're miles from the penetration site." He grimaced. "We drop those shafts and we're finished."

Senchov's mouth worked and then twitched up into an insane grin. "Concrete... we can pump concrete down to plug it; create a seal."

The next sound was like a thousand thunderstorms just over the horizon. But both men knew the storm was coming from somewhere much closer – beneath them. The *Viktor Dubynin* was tugged hard in the water as if its wrist-thick anchor cables were like fishing lines that had each hooked a massive fish.

The drill shaft snapped then, like a cannon shot, making every alarm, horn and bell scream, ring and roar in warning and compete for the honor of splitting the eardrums of the entire crew.

Kozlov broke free and raced up to the deck. Gorkin followed. The ocean boiled, sizzled and popped like hot oil in a pan as if there was a fire lit below the deep, dark, cold water of the Bering Sea. Then an almighty thump followed by a shock wave travelled over the surface, which was immediately followed by the horizon becoming ragged and indistinct.

Kozlov let his arms drop to his sides. "The subterranean body of water has broken through."

Gorkin turned, screaming orders. "Drop the cables, hard to starboard, full speed ahead." He raced to the bridge room.

Kozlov gripped the railing, his teeth showing, and his fingers so tight on the cold steel they would have ached if he could feel anything. The engineer couldn't drag his eyes from the thing that rose in the distance. It continued to climb, blotting out the sun, and then the sky itself. This monster was not a wall, but a cold mountain peak, rising hundreds of feet into the air and moving out in every direction like a mushroom, widening, and gathering speed. For now, it looked like it was coming at them in horrifying slow motion. But in reality, it was devastatingly fast and would soon be travelling at around two hundred miles per hour.

The *Viktor Dubynin* turned hard, the side of the ship dipping as it tried to flee the impossible show of nature's power. Kozlov grinned, and then began to giggle. That fool Gorkin; didn't he know? They didn't need a ship, they needed a damn helicopter.

A breeze blew up, a pressure front being pushed before the spreading mountain that was rapidly becoming a range of mountains. The ship started to rise up its face, higher, and higher, the angle of the deck going from horizontal, to near vertical in a few moments.

Kozlov wrapped arms and legs around the cold steel railing as the ship was turned sideways. With the sunlight blotted out, darkness fell over him and he looked down to the ocean far below. Impossibly, beneath him, there were seagulls flying for their life to try and beat the wall of water bearing down on them.

Finally, when the ship was at the crest, they began to tumble down the face of the wall of water. Kozlov let go then.

The Megalodon had cruised along the edge of the rock shelf where the small creatures had fled. It had tasted them, and found them to its liking. But its huge bulk made it ever hungry and it wanted many more.

The water in this area shallowed too quickly for it to get closer and it remained farther out in the dark water. Moments ago it had lifted its head above the surface, its cold dark eyes scanning the rocks for any movement – there was nothing – it had lost sight of them for now. However, above its cavernous maw, the lateral pores in its sensitive snout still detected their tiny footfalls on the rocks that sent the vibrations out into the water.

The Megalodon's lifespan was long, much longer than that of its closest cousin the Great White Shark, and it could be patient. It could wait hours, days, or even weeks for the creatures to return. But moving into this area of the subterranean sea it had detected something else in the water. Far away it sensed miniscule movements – strange, constant, but getting louder as if something was approaching. It could be food, or it could be a threat.

With a few flicks of its huge tail it accelerated towards the new sensation. The more it travelled, the more the vibration increased in intensity. It was driven now by instinct – the strange sound might have been some creature in distress, and for the monstrous shark, that was impossible to ignore.

The Megalodon increased its speed, swimming hard now, and moving its massive torpedo-shaped bulk through the water at thirty-five knots, or just on forty miles per hour. Other creatures, some huge themselves, sped from its path, and were perhaps relieved it was not hunting them that day.

It caught up to the strange, bulbous creature that gave off a distinctive hum, and came up from the deep fast. It circled first, using all its senses to see, hear and taste the slow moving beast. There was little sign that the thing was edible, but its presence was a challenge that could not be ignored – it attacked.

The shell was too hard to crack, and then the thing defended itself inflicting pain and causing the Megalodon to spit it out. The shark circled as the thing sank slowly, motionless but not dead. Inside the shell it could detect the flutter of tiny heartbeats.

It prepared for another charge, when above it there came another maddening sound that seemed to come from within the stone roof itself. The Megalodon's movements became ever more frenzied as something ground its way from the rock to poke down into the water. The massive eighty-ton, territorial beast accelerated to attack the new enemy.

It struck the end of the drill, further cracking the already weakened ceiling. Veins ran from the impact site in all directions, and then like some sort of colossal lid, it lifted away. It didn't collapse and rain rocks down upon it, but instead the sheets of granite and silt were blown upwards by the subterranean pressure of the hidden sea.

The warm water rushed to the cold, rising rapidly and taking everything with it. The current created was irresistible, even for the sixty-five-foot giant. The Megalodon and everything around it, was caught in the torrent and dragged upwards. It was drawn higher and higher, and its home of tropical darkness, suddenly became freezing cold and strangely light.

Most of the other creatures sucked up with it died immediately, not able to deal with the rapid change in pressure, temperature and even light waves. But the Megalodon was a creature that had come from a line that had existed for four hundred million years, and could tolerate all manner of extremes.

When the rushing maelstrom had subsided, and then collapsed behind it, the monstrous shark found it wasn't in its own world anymore.

CHAPTER 22

Cate sat for a moment and squeezed her hands into fists to quell the throbbing. Her fingers ached, her palms were raw, and even though she had short nails, she was sure every single one of them was broken and ripped. She leaned back, letting her head rest against the cool stone and sucked in humid air. The climbing had been difficult, and there were no easy tunnels with nice flat cave floors leading upwards. Instead, there had been a torturous climb up one narrow chute after the other.

Jack climbed up to sit beside her. She looked across to his face, sweat slicked and dusty, and she could see his eyes were red-rimmed.

"I've just about had it," she puffed, trying to smile, but failing miserably.

He nodded, looking up into the chute momentarily. "I know how you feel – we've come a long way. But I promise you this is a good thing. As long as we continue towards the surface, then every damn inch *up*, means one less inch *down* someone needs to dig."

"Yep." She tried to spit out cave dust, but there was nothing but sticky dryness in her mouth. She just swallowed it, where the grit travelled a little to then lodge painfully in her throat. She coughed, and spat again.

"Yeah, I get it, think positive thoughts."

Abby climbed back down. "All clear ahead."

"Good." Cate took off her light band and handed it back to the young geologist. "Here, you're the one who's blazing the trail; your turn to take it."

She looked like she was going to refuse, but Jack nodded to her, and she relented. They all knew she was the only one young and limber enough to scamper ahead and scout for all three of them.

Abby turned, leapt up onto the next ledge, and was gone. The darkness quickly crowded in. Jack helped her up.

She stood back. "You go next, I'll be along in a minute."

He looked into her face. "Promise?" He stepped forward to hold her chin up for a moment; she thought he was going to kiss her, but she pulled away before he could see the heavy fatigue in her eyes.

"Yeah, I promise. Go."

He exhaled through compressed lips, chose his next handholds, and then lifted himself up. She watched him ascend for a moment.

"C'mon girl, you can do it." She reached up, barely feeling the stone under shredded fingertips. There was nothing but pain and fatigue now. She looked back to the cool stone. It would be so easy just to stay, rest, and maybe sleep. Cate shook her head to clear it, and looked up.

"I promised." She stepped up.

In another thirty minutes she climbed onto a ledge to find Jack and Abby waiting for her. She lay down and turned her head to them.

"Walk in the park," she grinned, panting.

"You're doing great," Abby said. "This is a tough climb. We're just lucky there looks to have been a tumble in here within the last few thousand years… means the rocks are jagged with a lot of handholds." She shone her light around, and rested it on one section of darker rock that was near smooth as glass. "That's what it all looked like before the rockslide – water smoothed. Climbing that would be impossible without professional gear."

Abby sprang to her feet and walked to the edge of the ledge, shining her light straight up. "Yep, lucky."

Cate propped herself up on one elbow and turned to look up at Jack. "We're lucky."

"My middle name." He winked.

"How high do you think we've come?" Cate eased herself to a sitting position.

Jack turned, and wiped a forearm up over his face. "Long way. Eight hundred feet, maybe a thousand." He shrugged, and then leaned in closer, the corners of his mouth lifting. "But I'm guessing what you're really asking is, how much further to go?"

She pointed one bleeding finger, gun-like, at his chest. "Bingo."

He looked up for a moment. "I think at least another five hundred feet until we get to the absolute bottom of the Heceta Island caves. And then..." He sighed. "Then, if that lucky streak is still with us, we can find a way into them. Or we can contact someone on the other side." He looked away.

"If not?" she smiled weakly, but knew it was a dumb question to ask.

He turned back to her. "If not, then we just sit a while and work out what we do next." He nudged her. "We always think of something, don't we? By the way, did I thank you for inviting me?"

Cate laughed, and then coughed. "Yes, I think you already did. But if you're after an apology, then sure, I'm sorry about all this, but who knew, *huh?*"

"Who knew indeed." He shook his head. "You know what? Even if I lived to be a thousand years old, I can honestly say that I will never, *ever* see things like this again." He reached out to her. "It has been a privilege."

She took his hand. "Thank you."

He placed a hand over hers, and she noticed his fingers were just as shredded as her own. He continued to watch her. "You know, I didn't come for the adventure, or the money, or even the chance to see a prehistoric shark... you do know that don't you?"

She held his gaze, and nodded. "And I didn't need you for your expertise. Lord knows there're a hundred specialists who know more than you do."

He threw his head back and laughed for a moment, before she tugged on his arm, pulling him closer. He leaned into her, and she kissed his dry lips. Even in this dark, dismal place she felt desire well up, and his hands quickly found her body.

She pushed him back. "Save your fluids, Romeo."

He laughed softly into her cheek. "Rain check then?"

"*Sheesh*, take a guy below the earth once, and he thinks you're easy. At least buy me dinner first." She squeezed his arm and leant back, feeling her heart beat fast. She didn't think it was from the climb this time.

She lay out flat and closed her eyes. *Bad Water*, the Nantouk had called the underground sea. Now, she could think of no better name for the place.

She was suddenly on a tropical beach, and looking down saw her long, tanned legs glistening with suntan oil. Jack was crossing the sand towards her in swim trunks, his muscles working fluidly. In both his hands he held long tall glasses of fruit juice. She smiled, holding out her hand. *Perfect timing, handsome*, she said around her smile. He handed it towards her.

Cate felt someone tugging hard on her arm, and her eyes flicked open in and instant. The beautiful dream vanished.

"*Huh*?" She sprang forward.

"Easy." It was Jack, and also Abby squatting close by. "I let you sleep. You've been out for about twenty minutes. How do you feel?"

"Oh god, my throat," she croaked. "So thirsty." She sucked in a deep breath. It hurt. "Glad we're not still on the water, or this is about where the sailors would start drinking seawater, or something worse."

Jack stood, and helped her to her feet. "Okay to go?"

Cate stood. "Sure, onward and upward." She tried to smile, but felt her lips crack in the center.

Abby walked to one wall. "This way. It starts to narrow in a few dozen feet, but its still passable." She stepped up.

Jack put his hand on the back of Cate's neck. "You're up next, beautiful."

She looked upwards, sucked in a deep breath, and then reached up to grab a handhold. She continued her climb, chasing the dying glow of Abby's light. She wondered whether they would reach the top before the light went out; didn't matter – they'd climb in the dark if need be. They'd climb until they hit a wall, and then they'd just sit down, and rest awhile. Climbing back down in the dark would be near impossible, she imagined.

She switched to auto, climbing on, not thinking, following the light, just mechanically lifting one foot, one hand after the other, grabbing the next stone or handhold, and so on. Sometimes the chute narrowed to a few feet, and they had to slither through. Sometimes she became stuck, and Jack would climb up behind her and push.

'You need to dump the helmet,' Jack had said when she got stuck yet again.

'Never,' was all she replied, and then *made* herself fit through the narrow gaps.

In another hour, the pipe opened up to a shelf of stone and a total blockage – it was the end of the chute, and her worst fear. There was a wall, ribboned with cracks and fissures, and seeping water. Abby felt along it, tapping her wristwatch against the stone and listening. Jack turned left and right, looking for another way – there was none.

Cate sat, her stomach filling with bitterness. "Looks like we've just hit our peak."

"There's always another way." Jack also searched the entire length of the wall, tapping with his compass. It sounded as solid and final as death. Eventually, he and Abby sat next to her.

"Let's take five." He rested with his elbows on his knees. "We'll find another way."

Cate snorted softly. "Of course we will."

Jack picked up a rock, hefting it, and then turning it around in his hands to examine it closer. He picked off a chunk of matrix, turned it over, and then banged it on the ground, dislodging more of the loose outer material. "Abby, shine your light over here."

Abby took it off her head, and handed it to him. He angled it down at the stone and began to laugh softly. He showed it to them; inside was a perfectly preserved tooth, as big as his hand.

"Ugh, get rid of it." Abby pushed his hand away.

"Carcharodon Megalodon." Cate stared. "Seems these guys have been here for a long time. Maybe they swam in twenty million years ago, like everything else, when it was somehow open to the ocean, and then some sort of rockslide or earthquake sealed this part of the sea off, covered it over or sunk it." She sighed. "There was so much I wanted to see here, to study."

"Yeah…" He nodded. "Yeah, me too." He broke the tooth from the matrix, and held it in one hand. In the other, he hefted the remaining rock and exhaled loudly through pressed lips. "I just wish…" His jaws tightened. "I wish we…" He looked at the large tooth for another moment before his teeth bared and he swung the stone back behind them. "Fuck it." The rock pounded into the wall with a deep thump, and then ricocheted off the ledge to then bounce down the chute.

The echo thumped back in the alcove they had wedged themselves in, fading away, until there was nothing, but their own breathing.

"Feel better?" Cate asked.

"A little," Jack said. "You should try—"

The thump came back again, twice.

Jack lifted his head, and half turned. Cate looked up at him, while Abby jumped to her feet. Two more thumps, followed by a soft tapping.

Cate frowned. "Is it... a rockslide?" She waited, listening. "Maybe we should..."

Jack also got to his feet, and turned to *shush* her.

She rose slowly. Both Jack and Abby stood with eyes round, heads tilted. Jack licked paper-dry lips.

The tapping came again: *dot-dot-dot-dash.*

Dot-dash.

Dot-dash-dot-dot.

Dot.

Dot-dash-dot.

Dash-dot-dash-dash.

"That sounds like..." she began.

Jack waved her to silence again, his eyes closed tight in concentration.

Dot-dot-dot-dot.

Dot.

Dot-dash-dot-dot.

Dot-dash-dot-dot.

Dash-dash-dash.

He turned and clapped once. "Yes, *it is*, Morse code... goddamn-Morse-fucking-code." He concentrated. "And it says: Valery, hello, Valery, hello."

He rushed to the wall, still holding the massive tooth, and used its hard edge to bang against the stone.

Dot-dot-dot

Dash-dash-dash

Dot-dot-dot

He waited, and sure enough the dots and dashes repeated. Jack listened, his grin widening. "Okay, we need to stand well back, they're going to come through."

"Who is?" Cate asked.

Jack grinned. "One of Valery's teams, I'm guessing. But frankly, I don't care if it's Satan himself."

Jack herded Cate back behind him at the far end of the ledge as there came the pneumatic staccato of a small jackhammer behind the wall. Abby was beside them, and pointed.

"Be careful; if the rocks fall this way, they'll bounce right at us." She looked over the edge. "And knock us over like tenpins."

The hammering stopped, and was then replaced with the whine of a saw, then something unidentifiable that was even softer, until finally a single spike appeared in the center of the wall. It was quickly withdrawn, and then in the dimming glow of their remaining light, they could just make out the tip of a snaking cable that poked in.

"Camera," Jack said.

Cate held up her hand to wave, and the cord pointed towards her, and then moved all about, as if searching. It vanished as quickly as it had appeared.

More giant needle holes were punched through, and then came the blade of a saw, crossing between each of the holes. After another few seconds of silence, a small section of stone was eased out, revealing a glaring light. More blocks were pulled away, carefully at first, but then quicker.

"I think these guys are in a hurry," Abby said backing up.

The rocks began to be pulled out faster and faster, the last few almost manically. The rest of the wall began to collapse.

Jack swept an arm in front of Cate. "*Get back.*"

The rest of the wall collapsed.

Sonya began to scrabble against the last few rocks, and would have continued to drag them out, even as they fell, except she was grabbed and pulled away. As soon as the collapse finished, she shrugged free, and lunged forward into the swirling rock dust.

"Valery, are you there?" She spoke in rapid-fire Russian. "Valery, *Valery*..." She strained to hear.

"English only." A male figure stepped forward. "It's Jack Monroe, Cate Granger and Abigail Burke."

The dust began to clear. She changed to English. "Valery... where is *Valery Mironov?*"

"Sonya?" Cate coughed and waved away dust. "Sonya Borashev, is that you?"

"Yes... are there, any more survivors?" Sonya shone her powerful light at their faces, and then along the ledge. "Who else is with you?"

"Only us three, " Cate said. "I'm afraid Valery, was... taken."

"Taken?" She felt a coil of nausea writhe in her gut. "And where is the crew of the submersible? Dmitry... where is the one named Dmitry?"

"Gone or dead. He was the one who took Valery." Cate came closer. "He also killed Yegor. I'm sorry."

"Taken by a killer." Sonya leant forward onto the broken stone, gripping it hard. She couldn't stop her hands from vibrating as she gripped the stone ever tighter. Like boiling water under pressure, the scream that erupted from deep within her, smashed around the chamber. She stood, with her head back, and fists balled, and screamed a Russian death curse.

In another second it was over, and she lowered her head. Her team behind her remained in respectful silence, and the three survivors also stood mute. *Yusoff has won... for now,* she thought.

Sonya stood straighter, and dimmed her light. "Sorry." She wiped her mouth. "Cate Granger, I'm glad you made it. We have a chopper waiting to take you all to a hospital."

She reached in a hand and Cate stepped forward to take it. Sonya was momentarily shocked by the woman's appearance. The attractive, strong-looking woman she had met just a few months ago now looked ten years older. Her hands were bloody, as were her lips where they had cracked and split. But it was her eyes that betrayed the horrors she must have had endured – they were sunken, dark and haunted.

Sonya turned. "Water, quickly."

Jack Monroe came next, and then the girl, Abby. They too had that similar look; the same tormented expressions of people who had survived a terrible disaster. But they were lucky; they lived, unlike her Valery.

"I am very happy for you." Sonya shook hands, hugged them, and tried to make her face create a smile, but found it impossible. "My team is here to assist you. Hurry now; there's a helicopter waiting."

She almost pushed them up into the higher cave.

Cate let herself be hauled through the opening in the stone, and then be wrapped in a silver thermal blanket. Jack and Abby got the same treatment. Sonya walked just ahead of them, her shoulders rounded. It was obvious she took Valery Mironov's death badly. Even though Cate felt bone tired, she hurried forward to catch her up. Jack followed.

"Sonya, thank you."

The young woman looked at her briefly, and then nodded.

"Hey, how did you know?" Jack asked. "Heceta Island, this cave; how did you guess we'd be here?"

Sonya spoke over her shoulder. "No guess; it's what Valery and I would have done. You too. Survivors never give up, they just look for other ways to survive."

"We're sorry about Valery," Cate blurted.

Sonya stopped then, turning to stare into Cate's face. "Yes, I'm sorry too." After another moment, she turned away. "Hurry now; we must not attract attention. Already there are too many questions following the explosion."

Cate let the woman get ahead of them. Her eyes had seemed almost resentful. *Of what?* Cate wondered. That they survived, and Valery didn't?

Jack placed a hand on her shoulder. "You okay?"

"Yeah, I guess." Cate reached up to rub his hand. "I guess we all lost something down in that dark sea."

"In that *bad water*," Jack said softly.

The two huge helicopters were perched like giant insects at the entrance to their nest, and their rotors were already turning as the group approached. Sonya was in amongst a group of men, and she seemed to be issuing instructions. She turned briefly to point at one of the helicopters, and then waved – *goodbye*, Cate expected.

Cate pulled her blanket a little tighter around her shoulders. She looked back at the cave entrance. It was only about twenty feet wide, and oval shaped, and reminded her of an open mouth. There were lights set up on tripods outside, but deeper inside it was impenetrably dark.

"Like Jonah and the whale, we've just been spat out by the monster," she said softly. "Let's get the hell out of here."

"I heard that," Jack said, and then he, Cate and Abby ran towards the chopper.

The huge machine lifted off immediately. Cate lent back in her seat, and found Jack's hand. She squeezed it and looked up at his ruggedly handsome face, now streaked with dirt, the eyes blood-shot, and his lips split and flaking. She felt the tears well up, and she gave him a brief watery smile, before looking away.

"I should have known better," she said, too softly for them to hear over the engine noise. "I followed a legend, and also my grandfather, down into a dark hidden sea and met a monster."

She rested her head on the seat. An old Shakespeare quote jumped into her head: 'Fishes live in the sea, as men on land; the great ones eat up the little ones.' She, Jack and Abby just came face to face with one of the great ones.

The pilot turned in his seat, lifting an ear cup, and yelling back at them, "First stop, Vancouver, Professor Granger, and then on home?"

Cate nodded. "Just got one stop on the way. Someone's been waiting three quarters of a century for this." She closed her eyes then, her hands resting on the crusted helmet of her grandfather.

Sonya Borashev watched Cate Granger's helicopter leave. She felt happy for the woman, but inside Sonya was dead.

She turned to yell more instructions to clean the site, and then reseal the bottom of the Heceta Island cave. She tried to calm her breathing, but could not ease the surge of blood that rushed past her ears like the drums of war.

They thought they'd won, killed Valery, and condemned his body to the dark depths. She opened her eyes to slits. *There is no action without an equal and opposite reaction.*

She turned away to her waiting helicopter, pulling her phone to speak careful instructions to a waiting team she had hand picked. In another few hours she would be on route to Russia.

CHAPTER 23

Cate hugged her mother, and hung on tight – partly due to love and relief, but also because her legs were still weak. She had seen her mom's face when she'd opened the door. Cate knew how bad she looked, and now was not the time for a parental scolding.

"I'm fine, Mom, *really*, just very tired." She kissed her and stepped back. "Is Granma Violet awake?"

"She was before. I told her you were coming." Rebecca Granger smiled sadly. "But be patient, she... forgets things. And don't be alarmed if she doesn't recognize you at first."

"Are we losing her?" Cate asked.

Rebecca shrugged. "They've been saying she could go any day for the last ten years. But she's a strong old bird. They certainly don't make them like that anymore."

"Not for years." Cate turned to the stairs. "Okay to go up?"

Her mother nodded, and Cate headed up, walking almost reverentially, for some reason feeling the need to stay silent.

She approached the door and hesitated.

"Catherine; is that you?"

Cate smiled at the familiar voice. It was thinner now, and a little dry, but still held the recognizable Irish lilt in the vowels. She pushed inside.

It was twilight dark, and she smelled the usual lavender scent of her favorite perfume. But there was also an odor of medicine and antiseptic. The figure on the bed was even smaller than Cate remembered, child-like, with a halo of silver curls spread on the pillow. *We all return to whence we came*, she thought, as she sat carefully on the edge of the bed.

"Help me up a bit, dear." Violet lifted a hand for Cate to take. The stick-thin fingers held no strength, but when Cate pulled her forward, the woman smiled and her eyes still shone with the intellect and energy that was always there.

Cate stuck another pillow behind her gran's back, and the old woman eased into it, partially sitting now. She continued to watch Cate with love and interest.

Cate took her hand again. "We found something." She reached down to open a small bag, and drew forth the helmet, now cleaned of much of its debris. Violet's mouth dropped open and she held out her hands. Cate laid the metal hat in them.

The old woman turned it around and around, and then stopped when she came to the name. Cate waited for her to say something, but Violet just continued to stare at the engraved name, almost trance-like.

"Gran? Violet? Are you okay?" Cate reached across to touch her arm.

"I remember this – *his*." She traced the letters with her fingers. "You found it in a cave, didn't you? *Deep* in a cave?"

"Yes we did. In a hidden place all the way up in the Gulf of Alaska."

She nodded. "My beautiful husband; I loved his hobby and his passion, but hated him doing it." She turned watery eyes on Cate. "Why would a man of such light and warmth want to spend his time in dark caves?" Violet sighed, the air seeming to escape from her, making her shrink even more. She slumped in bed.

"He was very brave, a true pioneer explorer. And someone who was searching for answers." Cate shrugged. "Some go looking for them."

Violet had turned away. "I told him, if you go looking

for the devil, one day you'll find him." She seemed to vanish into the folds of the blankets, the helmet still clasped to her chest. "Thank you for finding him for me, Catherine." She turned to stare deep into Cate's eyes, holding them for several more seconds, until finally her eyes closed. "I'm tired now. Goodbye, my dear."

Cate waited for several minutes and then pulled the blanket up around her chin. *Don't worry, Violet*, she thought. *We've got that devil trapped.*

She leant forward to kiss her grandmother's cheek. Violet wasn't breathing.

CHAPTER 24

Khamovniki District, Moscow

Brogidan Yusoff, head of the Russian Ministry of Resources and Agriculture, poured two large glasses of Kors vodka. At one thousand Euros a bottle, the vodka was one of the country's most luxurious brands. Its pure liquid was filtered through a blend of crushed charcoal and diamond powder; drinking it was like imbibing water from one of heaven's lakes that when swallowed, turned to fire as it went down the throat.

He turned away to gaze out over the Moskva River. His apartment traversed the top floor of the building that sat just on the bend of the river that overlooked the Bolshoi Kamenny Bridge. It was known as the Golden Mile, and one of Moscow's most expensive housing areas.

It was early evening and the lights were just going on – golden-white gems popping on all over the cityscape. There were leafy trees, high-end shops, and tonight, a darkening blue velvet sky that all added to his glorious mood.

His doorbell rang, and he crossed to admit Uli Stroyev into the downstairs foyer, where his expected official would take the lift to his front door. He unlocked it, ready for him, and walked back to the small antique table with the glasses waiting. His lifted one and saluted the winding river.

"To you, Valery; may your bones never find peace." He grinned. "Wherever they lay scattered."

Behind him the door squeaked open and then closed

softly. He reached down for the second crystal glass of perfectly clear liquid, and lifted it, turning to his friend.

"A job well done, my friend…"

He froze, tiny crystal glass suspended in the air. Stroyev was being held by two large figures, all in black with balaclavas pulled down, and just showing merciless eyes. His colleague was pale as milk, and his eyes were so round they threatened to pop right from his head.

Two more figures stepped closer, dressed exactly the same as the others. Both held guns, pointed at his chest. One motioned towards his outstretched hand.

"Drink it." The voice was feminine.

Yusoff began to smirk. "Do you know who I…"

The gun lowered to point at his groin. "Drink it, or lose your balls… comrade."

He licked his lips. What the hell, he needed the drink, and he would play for time. He downed the expensive liquid in a gulp.

"Delicious. Can I offer you—"

"Pour another. Drink it."

The voice was far too cold for his liking. He tried to think who it could be, and what they wanted. He poured slowly, lifted the glass again, his mind working.

"Keep going. Faster. Finish the bottle." She motioned with the gun.

"You have no idea, what you're getting yourself into. Who are you?"

The woman ignored him, turning to one of her partners, and speaking quietly to him. The man nodded, and raced away to one of Yusoff's back rooms. One of the other two men holding onto Stroyev began to unbuckle the man's trouser belt, and then roughly pulled down Stroyev's pants, then the same with his underwear.

Yusoff saw that Stroyev's genitals were so shrunken from fear they were almost completely lost in amongst his graying pubic hair. Stroyev whimpered, the sound reminding Yusoff of a fox with its paw caught in a trap. *Coward*, he thought.

"I demand to know what's happening." They ignored him, and Yusoff ground his teeth, standing straighter, but couldn't stop the sick feeling in his gut, from both the vodka and an ice-cold fear.

The figure that had entered his rear rooms now reappeared holding Yusoff's laptop, that was open, and his codes obviously broken into. He set it on the table, typing furiously, and then finding the pages he wanted, turned to nod to the woman before standing back.

Yusoff looked down to see the page that had been saved to his favorites held horrifying graphic images of child pornography. He looked up again. "What is this? Blackmail. When I find who you are, I'll—"

"Finish the bottle." The words cold as ice.

Yusoff downed the final glass, his hand shaking now, and the woman strode forward, taking the empty bottle from the table. She turned, took two steps and swung the heavy crystal decanter-style bottle in an arc that finished up against Stroyev's temple. The man fell like a sack, his forehead massively dented. He twitched on the ground for a moment before she reached down to feel his neck, grunted approval, and then straightened.

"Anything... whatever you want. Whatever they're paying you, I'll double... *triple it*." Yusoff babbled, but the woman's demeanor was rock solid. She looked down and shrugged.

"A lover's tiff, perhaps." She tilted her head. "At least that's what the press will say."

"*Who – fucking – sent you?*" Yusoff's voice sounded shrill, even to himself.

The woman stepped closer to him. "Valery sends his regards... from the grave." She shot him in the chest, once, twice. The big man fell heavily, and she then emptied the entire magazine into his jerking body.

Sonya Borashev then bent to place the gun in the dead hands of Uli Stroyev, and angle his body slightly. She wanted to spit on their corpses, but knew the evidence would corrupt their staged crime scene.

She clicked her fingers, and the team turned on their heels. In an hour, they were already in the air.

RETURN OF THE MONSTER

CHAPTER 25

The fishing trawler, **Omaru**
West of Vancouver Island
Two months later

The rain machine-gunned the deck from every direction at once. Even though the *Omaru* was a decent sized ship at a hundred and twenty-two feet, it still bucked up and down with each growing swell.

"Storm'll be right over us in an hour, boss." Brendan Cooper, his deck foreman, had to yell the words even though only standing a few feet away as the scream of the wind made everything seem like a whisper.

Still, Captain Will Harper's trained ears heard every word. His stained slicker's hood was pulled far down to keep the stinging rain from a face that was the texture of weathered teak, and he grabbed at its rim, looked up, and then nodded.

"Yup, get 'em in, son. We'll head in closer until it blows through."

The *Omaru* was after the demeral fish – the bottom dwellers – like the Pacific cod and haddock. Ever since the ban on net fishing was lifted in 2015, the government had granted just a few precious licenses. Harper's family had fished the area for two hundred years, and also had impeccable government connections, and so managed to secure one of the rare pieces of paper.

Right now they were on the edge of the continental shelf, eighty miles out from the Canadian-US border, with two nets still out. They'd need to be reeled in from deep water – fifteen hundred feet. They'd be partially full by now, so they could expect to take an hour to get them up and in.

Harper had no choice. Even though he knew they could ride out the storm, if the ship floundered and caused any sort of spill, he'd have a devil of a time trying to regain a license a hundred other boat owners would kill for. Better to play it safe and lose a few days, than lose the family business.

He checked his wristwatch, and then looked to the east. Though dawn was coming on, it was still as black as Hades out on the water. The bastard, boiling clouds above refused to let a dot of morning sunlight down for them.

The winches started up, and Harper felt the drag on the boat. They had two thousand horse power to call on and could get the high-powered vessel up to eight knots if need be, but for now, he'd keep the nose to the swell, and hold her steady while the bags were brought up from the deep.

He looked back down along the railing to the stern where the arc-spots threw huge pools of light down on the deck and surrounding water. The ship still rose and dipped, but his crew was experienced, sure-footed, and worked like the machines whining all around them. Looking briefly over the gunwale, he saw the water was a frothing iron-gray, and the super bright lights created a ball of illumination all around the *Omaru*.

As Harper watched, his hands snapped tight on the railing as a giant torpedo-shaped shadow passed underneath the boat. The reptilian part of his brain screamed a warning, automatically recognizing the primordial danger of a giant predator close by, and it formed a single thought: *shark*. But the logical part of his brain refuted it as being too fast and too big; it was something else entirely – had to be.

He shook his head to clear it. During storms at sea, men had been seeing things for hundreds of years. It must have been a shoal of fish, wave-shadow, or a whale, or anything but what his gut told him it was. He shook it away; if he had the time or inclination, he'd have his team check the fish-finding sonar, if it didn't mean he had to recalibrate it from looking down at the depths.

Harper licked salty wet lips, and turned back to the winches, urging them on. They'd been running for a good thirty minutes, the nets must be close by now, and—

The ship jerked and then sagged in the water as it was dragged hard to starboard. One of the cranes bent and screamed, and the sound of metal under enormous stress overshadowed that of his men frantically yelling to each other. There was a sound like singing, and it took the captain a few seconds to work out it was actually a cable attached to one of the nets that was now piano-wire tight, and was strummed like a guitar as spray was flicked away from it.

The *Omaru* groaned and turned sideways in the crashing surf. Harper exploded into action, racing back to the cabin where his crew was fighting controls, yelling and shaking their heads. As soon as he entered, he brought calm, but only for a few seconds before questions and guesses were flung around the small room.

"We're snagged on something! The starboard net's not budging. Brakes are now on." Ethan Minnez looked from screen to screen, his face now sweat-slicked, even though the room was like an icebox.

"Well, fuck it then." Harper wasn't worried about the ship. To avoid the boat capsizing if the trawl snagged on the sea floor, the *Omaru* had winch brakes and auto-safety-release systems built into its boom stays. He was more pissed off about the potential of losing his catch. They were already heading in early; it'd be a goddamn sorry assed trip if they came in even more tons light.

"We're not going anywhere, Captain." Minnez turned to him, waiting.

Harper tore off his slicker and flung it to the corner. "Fucking wrecks, bottom is littered with too many of these bastard sunken shit buckets."

Minnez grimaced, shaking his head. "We're at five hundred feet; bottom is another thousand below that. This is no wreck."

The ship jerked again, and the stability alarms sounded. "Gonna lose it, Captain."

Harper looked from the now flaring-red warning screens, and then to the faces of his control room crew; he saw fear. He knew there was only one order he could give – to release it. A sense of calm settled over him, and just as he opened his mouth, the *Omaru* leapt forward, and immediately straightened in the water.

"What just happened?" Harper's legs were planted.

"We're free." Minnez beamed. "The bag musta come lose." He bent over a screen, but his expression immediately clouded. "Coming up too fast; must be empty, or gone."

"Like I didn't see that coming." Harper began to turn. He'd check on the deck crew and also see what damage they had sustained.

Just then the ship jerked so hard that even Harper, with more than half a century sea-leg experience, was thrown from his feet. They were tilting at an angle he knew would mean water would come over the gunwale. He then heard the sound he feared the most: men screaming.

"Men overboard! *Three men out!*"

The deck foreman's shout over the emergency comm was the worst thing you ever wanted to hear in a heavy storm swell – *men overboard* – even in life jackets, with personal signal beacons, a bobbing head was near impossible to find.

And then there was that big shadow, a small dark voice whispered in his mind.

"The damn second net's now snagged." Minnez's voice was high and his face was screwed in both disbelief and fear.

The boat jerked again, and Harper knew that was no snag – they were now being tugged backwards. Ever since he was a small boy, fishing on a dock, he had known what a hooked fish felt like – it jerked a few times and then it ran as it tried to escape with its prize. And if whatever now had them was trying to make a run, it might just roll them over.

"Emergency drop, now!"

Minnez banged his hand down hard on the release button. And the sound of whipping cable reverberated inside the cabin. The *Omaru* rolled hard the other way, then righted and straightened. It still bucked and rode high on the heavy sea, but at least now they were back in control.

He grabbed some field glasses, and through the rain-battered window, Harper saw the first beacon light of one of his men. Then the second and third. He exhaled with relief – *god bless for small miracles* – they were close together, and hadn't been washed far.

"Loop around them, and we'll get them in the lee of the wind." He lowered his glasses. "I'll be down supervising the rescue. Keep her steady, Ethan, and…"

His brows came together, and he quickly lifted the field glasses again. The first beacon light went out, and moments later, so did the second.

"What the fuck?" Harper's mouth hung open.

As he watched, the third light vanished in the darkness. The beacon lights were all gone; his men were gone.

Remember the shadow, his mind whispered again.

CHAPTER 26

Nick's Cove, Marin County, California
Sixty-five days later

Jack Monroe hummed as he sanded the flaking deck; nice smooth circles, lightly does it, respect the wood, as his father used to say. He stood, admiring his work for a moment, with a grin beginning to split his face. He turned, sanding block still in hand, and now pointed at his Australian terrier, Ozzy.

"There is nothin' like a dame – c'mon, join in, buddy." Ozzy cocked his head. *"– there is nothin' you can name – that is anything, like, a, da-aaame!"*

Jack lowered the sanding block, brows up. "How was that, Oz?"

Ozzy turned in a circle, his mouth open, and tongue out, in the doggy equivalent of manic applause.

"That's what I thought." He looked back at the deck – *magnificent.* He sighed, *The Heceta* – named in honor of the island cave that saved them – was all his. The sixty-two-foot motor yacht, designed and built in 1938 by the great pair of Alden and Jacob, was a beautiful mix of original teak planking over a white oak frame, and with enough modern equipment and power in its engine room to fight the most ferocious swells. Old world charm combined with new world tech.

Jack sat on a single small stool, coffee mug resting on an

unread newspaper. Ozzy came and lay at his feet, having found an old dry paintbrush to work on.

Jack lifted his mug to sip at the lukewarm liquid. He grinned again; he still couldn't believe he owned it. Right now, *The Heceta* was up in dry dock on Miller's Boat ramp, and he had given himself the entire long weekend to do nothing but sand back the peeling paint on the deck, the last real job needing to be done. By tomorrow evening he hoped to begin the varnish and paintwork – the fun stuff. Then he'd polish the brass fittings, and she was ready for inspection and duty, and also visitors... or at least just one special visitor.

He looked up at the pilothouse. There was a saloon inside, a chart table, fully stocked bar, and two cabin bedrooms. He smiled and nodded; the Mironov Foundation had been generous; he could never have afforded a boat such as this on his salary – not in a dozen lifetimes.

"To Valery." He toasted the lost Russian billionaire, and then sipped as he read the headlines. His eyes were always drawn to any articles about the sea, sea-life, or boats. He stopped at one.

'Dolphin visitors moved in for good?' The headline asked.

He flipped pages until he found the body of the article and began to read: swimming beaches all along the coast from Laguna in Orange County, on down to Coronado, Venice, Hermosa and even La Jolla, were all reporting pods of dolphins in close to the shoreline. Not actually beaching, but simply refusing to be herded back out to sea, or even to deeper water.

"What's with you guys?" Jack read on, sipping slowly. They weren't even the same type of dolphin; there were hundreds of Common dolphins, little guys that were fast and normally friendly. But also their bigger cousins, the Bottlenose – ten-footers who weren't afraid to take on predators who invaded their patch.

He frowned. "And Rissos, too?" The Risso dolphin

looked more whale-like than a dolphin with its round, blunt head. They were also pretty damn big, growing up to twelve feet. And they were shy, usually staying well away from humans.

Jack rubbed his chin. He'd followed dolphin pods before. An earthquake could throw them off and drive them into the shallows, so could a pod of hungry orcas, or a big a fishing party, like the slaughter fests in the outer Japanese islands.

Weird. He read the last paragraph where a meteorologist was blaming climate change. Jack snorted. Was anything not climate change's fault these days?

He dropped the paper and stood, looking back at the last bits of work to do. He was on schedule, and wanted to be ready to receive guests by Tuesday. Jack looked out over the calm, blue water, daydreaming for a moment. There was just one guest – Cate Granger, and she was coming down from Redwood to spend a week with him. They'd been dating again, and things were going great. But he knew if she was coming all the way over to finally set foot back out on the water, he'd see to it that it was done in utmost luxury.

He was a man of the sea. It was going to be awkward having a potential wife who couldn't even look at saltwater. The boat had to be in tiptop shape, champagne in the icebox, the weather calm, and himself on his charming best behavior – everything all safe and secure. *What's not to like?*

He lifted his sanding block. "Ready, Ozzy?"

The small dog dropped the brush and spun again, grinning madly.

"Then let's do this." Jack knelt, rubbed, and hummed.

CHAPTER 27

Cate held a half eaten apple in her hand as she and Abby sat on the Stanford lawn close to the main building. Neither spoke, and there was an awkwardness between them. She looked up at the small, brass plaque once again.

'Dedicated to Greg Nathan Jamison – missed but never forgotten – From his family, friends, and faculty.'

That's all that's left of him, she thought, sighing and turning away. Abby had her face turned to the sunshine. Cate studied the young woman. She looked... *better*.

"So, how's the geology department treating you?" Cate asked.

Abby shrugged. "It's okay, I guess." She turned to look at Cate with ancient eyes. Her smile seemed forced. "What good is a geologist who can't stand to go below ground?"

Cate nodded her understanding. "Yeah, it takes time."

Abby tilted her head back to the sun. "I think they're going to downsize us."

"It's happening all over. But you're welcome to join me in the biology department. We can always use good people." Cate chuckled. "After all, ever since the Mironov Foundation set up an annuity donation of one million dollars a year to our department, and in my name, for now at least I'm a highly protected species."

Abby wrinkled her nose. "I'm a geologist, not a biologist. Thanks anyway, but I'll be fine." She stood, brushed her dress down, and turned to Greg's plaque. "We care, but no one else does." She turned to Cate. "I'm not even sure they believe us." She snorted. "Not that we can tell anyone."

Cate hiked her shoulders. "Does it matter? As long as no one else goes down there." She, Abby and Jack had been interviewed too many times to count, by everyone from the Environmental Protection Authority through to Homeland Security. Bottom line was, they barely listened about the underground sea, or the Megalodon, or even Greg's death. What they wanted to know was more about the tactical nuclear explosion, the connection to the billionaire, Valery Mironov, and also the Russian citizens, Dmitry Torshin and Yegor Gryzlov. *Things they could understand and deal with.*

Cate looked across the verdant lawns. While the authorities continued their investigation, the trio was instructed to talk to no one, any time, any place and any where. It was just fine by her.

Abby sighed. "You know, up here in the sunshine, it feels like it was all just a dream." She looked down at Cate. "A bad dream."

Cate nodded. "It was just a nightmare. That's what I keep telling myself."

Abby knelt to hug her, and then stood again. "Brings back bad memories." Her smile faded. "Sorry, but even seeing you does it to me. Good luck, Cate. Give my love to Jack." She turned and strode away.

Cate groaned, sitting cross-legged. *Wish I could just walk away from it all,* she thought, watching the young woman vanish across the perfectly manicured lawns. She took another bite of her apple and chewed slowly, but the flesh was cotton-wool tasteless to her.

Yech. She dropped it onto the grass. She looked up at Greg's plaque again – it accused her, damned her for pushing him, and there was that tiny voice that continued to whisper to her that he only went because she asked him. She sat back, her vision turned inwards. Even if she had been told of the dangers, she still would have gone, and so would Greg. How could any evolutionary biologist worth their salt have said *no* to the opportunity to witness the primordial past first hand? They were both just slaves to their professional curiosity.

"It wasn't my fault, Greg," she whispered. She tore her eyes away, and looking for a diversion switched on her slim computer. She placed it on her lap, signed in and then opened up her favorite link to a paleontological news site that listed global events, and read with passing interest about the latest discoveries unearthed from as far away as the Himalayas and Greenland, to the Australian outback – like the new raptor-like dinosaur discovered in the north-west Queensland in an abandoned opal mine, with claws the size of kitchen knives – it was a big guy, termed a megaraptorid, and showed just how far these things had spread, or perhaps was an indicator of concurrent evolution of the species.

She scrolled some more, to a story on how the Chinese were going to try and clone a gigantopithecus, the ten-foot tall, prehistoric hominid. They believed they had extracted viable DNA from a hundred and fifty thousand year old canine tooth – she'd love to see that one, she thought, smiling.

She scrolled again. Even though the site was supposedly run by academics, sometimes the articles tended to cross the line into cryptozoology, which was as much wishful thinking as it was science. She flicked to the next page, feeling slightly better, when she froze. Cate sprang in closer and enlarged the image to full-screen mode.

It was a fish, a dozen feet long and powerfully shaped. But it was the now rotting head that got her attention – it was armor plated. The Russian fishermen had claimed they pulled the creature from waters near Bering Island, a barren, desolate piece of land that was two hundred miles from the Russian mainland. The creature was already dead, and the freezing waters had preserved it intact for however long it had been floating out there.

She quickly read down the page – Russian scientists

were awaiting final verification, but believed it was a hypercarnivorous apex predator species of Placoderm that had supposedly vanished during the late Devonian period. They were calling it the biggest find since the rediscovery of the Coelacanth in 1938.

Cate enlarged the image further, and then sat back. "Oh no, no, no." Her stomach turned. Even though the thing was little more than a pipe of gray meat, the shape of the head, the heavy armor plating and mechanized looking jaws were unmistakable – after all, she'd seen one up close and personal.

Impossible. It couldn't possibly be that much of a coincidence. *Could it?*

She wished Greg were here, her ever-present colleague, friend and scientific sounding board. She folded her arms, her mind working. She should take a look at it, up close, just to satisfy her curiosity. She distantly remembered an earthquake followed by a tsunami a few months back in the northern hemisphere. She thought nothing of it at the time, but now wondered, was there a relationship?

Time to talk to the experts. But, let your fingers do the walking. She entered her browser and typed in a request for a contact number for a west coast earthquake center. The closest link returned was a seismic activity center in Colorado. She punched in the number, and let her Voice-over-Internet connect her.

"National Seismic Activity Information Center, Colorado; Frank Hennie speaking."

The voice was laid back, but she smiled at her luck. In their website's *Who's Who* section, Frank was one of their chief scientists.

"Hi there Dr Hennie, it's Professor Cate Granger of Stanford University calling. How are you today?"

"I'm okay. What can I do for you?"

Cate bristled; the man sounded like he had zero enthusiasm for speaking to the public. She decided to be brief and cut to the chase.

"Dr Hennie, I'm doing some research down here and wondered about a recent seismic event I believe occurred in or around the Bering Sea a few months ago. Did you guys have any more information you can share with me?"

"Not really." There was a long sigh.

"Anything, *please.*" Cate ground her teeth.

Next came a pause, a grunt, and then the sound of some liquid being sipped. "It was a bit of an anomaly. Out of nowhere we got an ellipse-pattern of a seismic shock moving out from an epicenter that was some place in the middle of the Bering Sea." Another sip. "There's an area up there called the Denali Fault; it's a major intracontinental strike-slip fault in western North America, extending from northwestern British Columbia, Canada, to the central region of Alaska. It's a big one, and prone to shifting. But where this new movement came from was nowhere near that. It was weird."

Cate smiled; Frank seemed to be warming as he remembered the scientific data. "Weird? I like weird. Tell me more."

Frank chortled. "Well, there was no prewarning shocks and no aftershocks – a single event, pinpoint, and then our ocean-based surge buoys detected tsunami movement. We put out a standard alert to all the coastal communities of Alaska, Canada and even Russia. But the surge dissipated pretty quickly, with no damage."

"Interesting," Cate said. "Anything since?"

"Nada. Been quiet as a tomb since."

Cate's mind worked. "Doctor Hennie, was there anything out of the ordinary that you can remember?"

Frank exhaled and then sipped again. "There was one thing. We have surge buoys dotted throughout the oceans. They monitor everything from wave surge to climate conditions. At the time of the seismic event, the buoys in the Bering Sea all registered a temperature spike of over twenty degrees." He snorted. "It was as if someone had emptied a jug of hot water into a cold bathtub."

"Shit," Cate breathed.

"Like I said; weird. Well, that's all I got Professor Granger. Was there anything else?" Frank was moving back into bored mode now that he'd finished talking.

"No, no, thank you. You've been very helpful." Cate cut him off and looked again at the picture of the rotting fish. She tapped her chin; she was going down to see Jack again in a few days, and she'd love to get his opinion. She hit the print button on her computer, sending the data to the printer. She felt a little better knowing she'd have her sounding board after all, and also just the thought of spending time with her Captain Jack lifted her spirits. She missed him all the time now, bad, and sometimes thinking of him made everything else seem unimportant.

Get a grip, girl; you're not a teenager anymore, she tried to tell herself. She sighed. Love makes everyone a dumb kid, she knew. She remembered an old saying that went something along the lines of: the human brain works twenty-four hours a day, from the time you are born until the day you die… and only ever stops working when you're in love.

"Just a pair of old dummies in love then." She grinned, and picked up the printed pages.

CHAPTER 28

Let's bring her round for another coastal sweep. We'll start the next run from Big Sur and round it out up at Santa Cruz." Senior Chief Petty Officer, Vincent Kelly, lowered the field glasses and felt his breast pocket to assure himself he had his sunglasses ready to pull on. The horizon was just beginning to glow as the sun was about to poke its head up. Once it came over the rim, then the glare would reduce surface visibility to near zero without polarizing lenses.

"Okay, got a slight onshore breeze picking up now, so any floating debris should be pushed towards the shore."

Pilot First Class, Regina 'Ginny' Boxer, eased the wheel around. The HH-3F Pelican helicopter responded smoothly, and turned in the air. The massive machine was seventy-three-feet long from cabin to tail, and with a rotor diameter of sixty-two feet. It was invaluable to the Coast Guard, as it was one of the few craft that was air-amphibious – being able to land and take off from water.

The Pelican was a fast and tactical search and rescue tool. The downside was that the big baby was thirsty as hell, and in an hour they'd have chewed through nearly seven hundred gallons of gas. This was their third time out that night, and this trip they'd already been out for thirty minutes and still hadn't found any trace of the latest boat to disappear, a small pleasure craft called the *Bella Donna* out of Monterey, with two onboard – Brad and Cindy Levinson. It was in this search quadrant the boat had called for help; either the owner, Brad Levinson, had activated the distress beacon himself, or it was auto-activated by an EPIRB – Emergency Position-Indicating Radio Beacon – a tracking transmitter that was triggered upon immersion, when a boat got into trouble.

So far, Vince and Regina had seen nothing up top, and their worry was that if the *Bella Donna* drifted, and then sunk over the edge of the shelf, then the beacon would be compromised as the pleasure cruiser models weren't designed for depths – after about a thousand feet, they simply stopped working.

Vincent lifted the field glasses again; last night at about twenty hundred hours *Bella*'s beacon had lit up and pinged them, and then gone dark. He didn't have a good feeling about their chances. So far this month there had been five boat disappearances, none had been located, and not a single body recovered. Something weird was happening, and he was pretty sure they hadn't found themselves in some sort of new Devil's Triangle.

"We'll have better light in the next twenty minutes," Regina said, confidently.

"Yup, but by then we'll have burned through most of our tank. We'll have to head back in and refuel," Vincent responded.

"Then we'll have to… *whoa*." Regina slowed the craft in the air. "Hey Vince, check that out. I have never, ever seen one of those big boys – a blue whale."

Vincent's mouth curved into a smile and he leaned forward, raising the glasses. "Hold the phone; you're close, but no cigar, Ginny. That's a fin whale; they're darker and see the prominent fin on its back? Still big though, grow to eighty feet, and this guy must be near that." He lowered the glasses. "Way off course, and shouldn't be here this time of year. Take her down lower, there looks to be something wrong with it, and it's not moving. If it's a floating corpse, the last thing we want is ninety tons of whale meat rotting on some Californian shoreline somewhere."

"No problem." Regina's voice held a note of excitement, and Vince knew she wanted to take a closer look, the missing Brad and Cindy momentarily forgotten.

She took the helicopter down to hover about fifty feet above the stricken cetacean. It lolled in the water, its long snout gently opening and closing. Vince knew an immobile whale might not be a sign of trouble, as the huge mammals sometimes slept on the surface. It only became a problem when they decided to do it in popular shipping routes. Running into one of these giants could sink a boat.

"This could have been what happened to the *Bella Donna*," Vincent observed.

"See there, I think its been speared," Regina said. "There's something sticking out of its back." She moved the helicopter a little closer and tilted it forward so the cockpit was angled downwards. She flicked on the spot light, and in the pre-dawn light, the massive creature was lit up like on a stage.

"Holy shit, that's no spear. That's its backbone, busted clean through its skin. That big guy has been broken in two." Vince leaned forward, frowning. "Maybe it was hit by a boat – a big one."

The huge creature bobbed on the downward surge from the chopper blades, and rolled slightly in the water. Regina recoiled. "Where the hell is the rest of it?"

The giant whale's entire gut section was missing, and it looked as though someone had buzz-sawed it cleanly from the body.

"Got to be five tons of meat missing." Vincent eased back, feeling troubled.

"Shark attack?" Regina asked.

"To take that much meat, I'd say a pack of orcas more like it." He lifted the glasses, scanning the dark water. "And where are they?"

"Looks like a single bite to me," Regina said, and shrugged. "All quiet. Seems the party's over for now."

"Take her down a bit; I want to get some photos." Vincent turned to her. "While I'm doing it, radio base and let them know what we've found. They might want to come out and drag it back over the shelf and detonate it."

Vincent switched on the undercarriage camera, loading two types of film to capture standard images, and also some hydrological film to give them some depth in the water for an almost 3D image of the mutilated creature.

Regina first hovered at fifty feet, and Vincent swiveled the undercarriage camera from tail to snout. He spoke while keeping his eyes on the small view screen. "Take her lower, so I can get a shot of the wound."

"You got it." Regina dropped them to within a dozen feet of the water, and then skillfully hovered just over the floating island of blubber and flesh.

Vincent magnified the image and then frowned. He stopped shooting, and lifted his head from the viewfinder to stare down at the massive creature. His brows came together and he squinted, before reaching up to swivel the spot light. "Okay, Ginny, keep her tight, I'm going to step out."

"Seriously?" Regina stared hard at him.

"Sure am; the thing will be like a floating island. I just want to check something out, so take me in as close as you can get." He grinned at her scowling face. "Don't sweat it, Mommy, I'll harness up first."

Vincent threw off his seatbelt, climbed into the back, pulled a harness from a compartment, and then threw it over his shoulders to begin buckling it from under and between his legs. He then grabbed a tool belt, wrapping it around his waist and finally attached himself to the cable, taking a control pad and hooking it to his chest.

The Coast Guard officer eased himself towards the door, grabbed the solid handle and yanked the door back. Immediately the sound and fury of the churned spray and wind from the rotors rushed in at him. He held an arm up over his face, and waited as Regina maneuvered them down another dozen feet to hover directly over the carcass.

He leapt out, swung in space for a moment and then used the controls to lower himself onto the huge body. It was like setting foot on slippery rubber, as the surface had both give and rigidity in its texture. It was still a fresh kill, he guessed, as there was no smell of rot, or the sensation of either slimy putrefaction, or stiffness.

"Take it easy down there." Regina's voice came in over his helmet's headset and he turned briefly to give her the thumbs up.

"Just keep her steady, Gin; I'll be done in a minute."

He used the controls to release more slack and moved to the edge of whale's gut to investigate the enormous wound. Vincent crouched, and ran one hand along the edge of the flesh – fairly clean cut, as though someone had taken a very sharp knife to it. A portion of rib was showing, the gleaming white bone was a massive plank thicker than his waist. It, too, was cleanly sheared off, but at its edge what he hadn't seen from the helicopter's cabin, something that didn't belong was wedged in the edge of the bone.

Vincent drew forth a pair of pliers from his tool belt, and leaned out. He grunted; short a few inches. He leaned out farther, his boots beginning to slip towards the dark water, and just got the tip of the thing in the pliers. He gripped the object, tugging, twisting, and straining.

"Come *o-oon*, let fucking go." He braced and tugged again. The object popped free, and he fell back on his ass. Beneath him he felt the rumble of a deep moan, and he looked back alarmed. *"Jesus Christ."*

"You okay down there, boss?" Regina's voice held a degree of concern.

"Yeah, yeah, I'm okay. It's just… this guy, he's still alive." Vincent knew the damage the huge leviathan had sustained meant it was doomed to die slowly, and there was nothing he could do for it. If he had dynamite, he would have rigged a charge against its head, and put it out of its misery.

He looked down at the object in his hand, lit up by the helicopter's spotlight. "Is this what did it to you, big guy?" He held a fragment of a tooth, broken off some-ways, but still several inches long. He had no idea how big it might have been if fully intact.

"So, looks like shark attack it is then." Vincent looked down again at the wound. He could see clearly now that the cutting he imagined was actually sawing done by something serrated – exactly like the razor-sharp serrations he felt on the shard of tooth. It would have been perfect for making the cut. But the wound size... it was way too big for a single animal to make.

He remained crouched, his forearms resting on his knees, and let his eyes travel to the dark water. It was impenetrable, and about two hundred feet deep in this area. But he also knew that just a few miles away, the edge of the continental shelf dropped away to cold, dark fathomless depths of an abyssal plain. He suddenly felt the hairs on his neck stand on end. He looked around at the whale, and then back to the water. The helicopter's spotlight made him and the whale glare brightly, a glowing beacon for miles in every direction, above and below the water. But his ability to see anything ended at a few feet below the surface.

Down there, he could not see, but something could sure as hell could see him. Vincent Kelly slowly got to his feet, and backed up, feeling a sensation of impending danger he hadn't felt in years.

Vincent kept backing away, keeping his eyes on the water. He'd known this area all his life, and had seen sharks, moray eels as thick as your waist, and even giant pacific octopus that had attacked and drowned divers. Nothing scared him, and pretty much nothing surprised him anymore. But today, there was a feeling in his gut, a trembling and horrible anticipation that made him suddenly want to be off the whale and up in the air – way up.

He punched to the controls and lifted off. It was only twenty feet to the helicopter, its wide bottom hovering over the water – it felt too close.

"Take her up, Regina, *now.*"

"*Huh?* Vince, you're not in yet." Regina sounded confused.

"Take her up, fast; I'll climb in as you go. That's an order." He never pulled rank on her, but today, he wanted no hesitation from his pilot.

Vincent felt the drag on his body as the huge helicopter climbed and added additional G-force to his own ascent from the winch. At the door, he grabbed on, gritted his teeth and struggled to pull himself back in. Once finally done, he quickly spun to look back down at the water.

The whale was gone.

Vincent sat slowly at his desk, his long shift finally over for the day. They'd made six trips overall, and had seen no sign of the *Bella Donna*, or for that matter, any trace of the whale. He guessed it sunk, and had noted it in his report – a potential biological hazard just waiting to resurface.

He flicked on his computer, still troubled by the feeling he'd had when standing on the floating giant's back. His gut told him danger was imminent – he'd only ever had that sort of feeling once before, and that was a few years back when he was on the deck of a ship minutes before it exploded under their feet. He was in hospital for a week, where they had to rebuild his leg, and pull a three-foot section of cedar railing from his gut. He swore he'd never ignore that type of warning again.

Vincent shook it away, and held up the fragment of tooth. It was big – three inches long, but broken, maybe at the dental matrix end, maybe in half, or just maybe they only got the tip. *Impossible.*

He recognized it, sort of. It was a big shark, and by the shape and serrations he thought probably a Great White. Not something they wanted in these waters, but it was exactly the sort of predators that would be attracted by the dying whale, and would undoubtedly have come in from the open ocean. After all, they had that big girl down of Guadalupe Island, called Big Blue or Big Betty, or some cutesy name that tried to make you forget it would tear you to bits if it got the chance. And that big bitch was over twenty feet long with several inch-long teeth.

Regina came over to his desk and plonked herself down next to him. "Long night." Her mouth curved into a smile and she pushed a fresh coffee towards him.

"Bless you." He took the cup, lifted it and toasted her. "*Salud*... and you got that right, girl. A *veeery* long night. My back needs to stretched out, or walked on by one of those qualified foot masseuses."

She grinned. "Just say the word, and I'll walk all over you." She sat back sipping her coffee, her eyes still on him.

He laughed softly, but knew one word from him, and she'd be his. He liked her, a lot, but reckoned the twelve-year age difference would probably kill him. Still, he looked back at her, returning the smile.

She nodded to the tooth on his desk. "So, anything from that, or on the pictures we took?" she asked.

"Carcharodon Carcharias, also known as the Great White, White Pointer, or White Death, and a damned big one by the look of that. But I don't know if this was one of its largest teeth, or we only got the tip of one of its smallest." He shrugged. "I'm no expert."

"Holy shit," Regina said, picking up the tooth. She held it against her chest. "Make a cool pendant." She looked at the broken end. "Can't you tell how big it is from its growth rings or something?"

He took it back, grinning. "What, it's a redwood tree now?" he turned in his chair to his computer. "Forgot all about the pictures; let's have a look."

He'd sent the pictures back to the Coast Guard image database, where they'd be cleaned up and forwarded on back to him. No sending things out to be processed and wait hours or even days anymore. "I love modern technology," Vince said as he opened the directory.

He'd taken dozens of shots, and Regina had kept shooting when he was down on the whale. He flicked through the first tranche. There was nothing conclusive on them other than some damned interesting size-difference pictures of him on the huge floating cetacean. The hydrological film was in a separate library and he opened that next. Once again, good pictures of the wound that'd he'd get checked out, and he was about to shut them down when the next to last made him sit upright.

"Jesus Christ, Vince." Regina put her cup down on his desk with a bang. "How big did you say that whale was?"

"*What?*" He spoke without being able to drag his eyes away from the picture. "About, eighty feet, I guess."

"Well that fucking thing underneath it is nearly as big." Regina crowded in beside him.

Vincent sat back, licking lips that had suddenly gone dry. No wonder his gut had told him to get the hell off that whale. The almost 3D hydrological image showed the whale, with him crouching at its edge, as it had with the previous shots. But this one showed something passing underneath, a shadow that was nearly as big as the whale itself.

"I hope that's another damned whale," Regina said.

Vincent couldn't speak; only stare. He felt the hair on his neck prickle, and he had that funny feeling inside, the one his old granma used to say was death walking over your grave. He knew the shape was all wrong for a whale, and he looked back at the tooth. He suddenly had the feeling it was just the tip after all.

"I think we just found out what happened to those missing boats." He rubbed a hand over his mouth and stubbled chin. "You know what? I think I need to speak to an expert." He turned to her. "We may have a bigger problem than a hundred tons of rotting whale meat washing up somewhere."

"An expert? Your friend?" Regina looked into his face.

He lifted his coffee cup, his hand shaking slightly. "Yeah, my old sparring partner, Jack Monroe." He looked up at her. "Feel like taking a little trip?"

CHAPTER 29

Cate took the 101 north, and exited at Washington Street, Petaluma. Her GPS applauded her choice, and encouraged even more twists and turns on her way to Nick's Cove in Marin County.

Jack had rented a cabin there for so long the landlord let him have it now for peppercorn rent, provided that was, he maintained the place, and stayed out of it over spring break so it could be rented to the high-value tourists. Whenever Jack had a boat to work on, which was most days of the year, he could be found on Miller's Wharf, sanding, painting, or elbow deep in a marine engine.

She turned into Shoreline Drive and saw the cluster of beautifully painted cottages crowded around a long wharf. She slowed, taking it all in – the Cove settlement was one of the last remaining historic places on the Tomales Bay coastland. The few sailing boats anchored on the silky-smooth blue water, the green of the forest crowding in behind it, and the wheeling gulls made it seem a million miles away from the city or from modern life at all. She could see why Jack liked it.

She drove slowly past the famous restaurant – Nick's Cove – named after one of the original owners, and had been here in some form since the 1930s. Out front, the little sea captain statue in his rain-slicker gave her a cheery grin with one arm raised and fist closed. Jack told her the story went he either used to hold a storm lantern, or he was carved punching a drunken local who'd got a bit too rowdy in the bar.

Lights were strung along the eaves and also the railing of the wharf. At night they would be lit in different colors, and gave the whole place a carnival feel. It all made her want to go in, sit down, and eat. Come to think of it, she was starving, but would first see what Jack had planned.

Cate stopped and looked towards the end of the wharf and saw the boat bobbing gently on the water. It was the only one tied in close, and its deck, fittings, and double masts gleamed in the afternoon sunshine. Jack had done a magnificent job. The sails were furled at the moment, but they were wrapped and ready to go. She pushed open the car door, stood, and immediately placed both hands on the center of her back to stretch it out.

She inhaled the smells of low tide, warm sea water, pine trees and a hint of old wood – it smelled like heaven.

"Hi ho, there!"

The voice drifting from the end of the wharf made her smile. That, and the accompanying manic bark of his dog, Ozzy.

Jack stood out on his deck in shorts, t-shirt and she bet, bare feet. He waved once, and then lifted the small dog to toss it up onto the wharf, and immediately leapt to follow. Ozzy didn't wait and his tiny legs were a blur as excitement overtook the terrier as it motored down the wooden planks towards her.

Ozzy was first to her, and leapt, coming at her like a furred missile. She had to act quickly – drop her bag, brace her legs and then catch him. Once in her arms, he was a blur of cycling legs, wriggling body and tongue flicking madly for her chin and lips.

"*Blerk.*" She shut her mouth tight after the terrier scored a direct hit with his tongue to her lips and teeth.

"Hey, save those kisses for me." Jack jogged towards her, and took the dog from her arms, lowering him to the ground where he circled them both yapping madly.

He hugged her, and then held her out. "I'd kiss you, but you know – your mouth – dog germs."

She punched him in the stomach, and he relented, kissing her long and deep.

"That's more like it." She tilted her head. "But Ozzy is the better kisser."

Jack bent to pick up her bag. "How was the drive?"

"Easy." She looked around. "I can see why you love it here – so peaceful."

Jack shushed his dog. "It would be if not for some people's maniac pets." He started down the wharf, and motioned towards his boat. "So, what do you think?"

She nodded appreciatively. "Looks beautiful. *The Heceta*, huh? Yeah, good choice."

He came to the wharf edge, and put a leg onto his boat. Jack held out a hand. She took it stepping up and onto the gunwale and then jumping in. Jack leapt in behind her, followed by Ozzy.

"Want to freshen up? The cabin downstairs has everything you need. Come up on deck when you're ready."

"Sure." She took her bag. "But after driving for an hour, priority one is a washroom." Cate went down the stairs, taking in the fresh varnish, and wood scents. *The Heceta* bobbed on a few slight swells, and below deck there was the pleasant sound of lapping water against the hull.

Cate stood with her hands on her hips. The cabin was immaculate – there was a double bed, with fresh linen, and flowers everywhere. Sunlight streamed in through old-style portholes, and there was an ensuite washroom. She grabbed her makeup case, and pushed in. Upstairs she could hear Jack lurching around, and the skitter of Ozzy's claws on the polished wood.

She changed into shorts, deck shoes, and a t-shirt, and emerged into the afternoon sun to the sound of cicadas somewhere off in the trees behind the cabins, as well as a few gulls squabbling on the railing of the wharf.

"Drink?" Jack asked, pointing to a fully stocked bar.

"Just water for now; I'm still a bit parched after the drive down." She sat in one of the seats on the rear upper deck; the breeze from the water felt great against her skin.

"No wonder you never come into the city." She took the offered glass.

Jack continued to stand and looked out over the water. "No need to now; most of my work is on the water, and this baby, has WiFi connectivity for phone, fax, and Internet. I'm free of your mortal city constraints."

She gave him a crooked smile. "Why do I get the feeling you're running away from something?"

"Who me?" He looked shocked, but then grinned. "Not at all. You know, most people work all their life and then hope to retire to something like this..." He placed one hand on the polished railing beside him, and rubbed. "I get to continue working at something I enjoy, and now thanks to the Mironov Foundation, I have my retirement dream here and now." He sat down, one eyebrow up. "Some might say I'd be a good catch."

She raised her glass. "Here's to never-ending fishing quips."

He raised his beer bottle. "Aye aye."

Jack's phone rang in his pocket, and he grimaced. "Sorry." He pulled it out quickly, and looked down at the small screen. "Hey, an old friend." He held it up. "You mind?"

"Go ahead, but I'll be looking for one of those beers in a minute." She eased back in her chair, looking towards the shoreline; she still wasn't comfortable looking over open water, even after half a year.

Jack got to his feet, turning away. "Vince, how you doin'?" He frowned. "Speak up, buddy, what're you in the chopper?" He turned back to Cate, his mouth open. "You're where?"

The sound of a helicopter could be heard in the distance, and Jack turned to face it.

"I've got company…" he stopped to listen some more, his frown deepening.

Cate watched closely now.

"Yeah, yeah, sure. See you in…" He looked up at the huge helicopter as it came around the bend in the coastline. "Probably five minutes I'd say. I'm at the end of Miller's Wharf; you can't miss me."

"Friends of yours?" Cate asked, eyes on the approaching chopper.

"Yeah, Vincent Kelly, we go way back. He's a senior officer in the Coast Guard. We've worked together numerous times over the years." He put his beer down. "Says he's got something for me to look at." He shrugged as he got Cate a cold beer.

Cate took it and turned to the settling chopper. "Something that was important enough for him to fly all the way up here to show you personally."

The huge helicopter settled gently on a grassy picnic area. A few residents stuck their heads out of cabin doors, shielded their eyes and stared as the craft powered down. Jack knew he'd have some explaining to do after this was over. The last thing he wanted was for one of them to tell his landlord he was disturbing the peace – he might find his rent suddenly going up… *waaay* up.

The chopper's rotor brakes slowed the sixty-two-foot blades until they finally stopped. Jack could see two figures inside pull off their helmets, and then they jumped out, and immediately headed towards the wharf.

Jack saw the familiar gait of his friend, and with him a slimmer female figure, dressed in a near identical Coast Guard uniform.

"Looks like he brought a date," Cate said. "Better get me another beer before the party starts."

"*Huh*?" he turned to her and grinned. "Good idea." He went to the small icebox and grabbed another cold bottle and handed it to her. "Somehow, I don't think he's here for the booze."

Vincent Kelly stopped at the wharf edge, looking down. "Captain Monroe, permission to come aboard." He saluted, grinning.

"Only if you brought rum." Jack held the boat and wharf to steady them, as Vincent jumped onto the deck. He didn't turn to help the woman, who jumped down beside him, landing lightly. She had short-cropped red-blond hair, a snub nose and a dimpled chin. Her green eyes glinted with fierce intelligence.

Vincent turned to her. "Pilot First Class, Regina Boxer." He turned back to Jack. "Regina, Jack Monroe, the guy I told you about."

Jack shook her hand, and stood aside. "And this is Cate Granger, a good friend." Cate nodded and shook hands with both of them

"Beer?" Jack asked, already reaching towards the box.

"We're working, but..." He shrugged. "Sure." He looked briefly to Regina who nodded. "Make that two."

Jack grinned up at Regina. "And two for you as well?"

Vincent nudged her. "I told you, he's got old jokes."

Regina laughed. "Just the one; I'm the sap who has to do all the flying."

Jack led them under the canopy, and motioned to the storage benches that had cushions on them. He and Cate sat back in their chairs.

"So, Vince, long way to come for a beer, buddy. What's up?" Jack could see something in his friend's eyes – impatience, worry... something.

Vincent's eyes shot to Cate for a moment. "Please tell me you don't work for the *LA Times*."

Cate scoffed and Jack waved the question away. "Don't worry, she's an evolutionary biologist, so may have some insights into whatever it is you want to chat about." He leaned forward. "Which is?"

Vincent reached under his jacket and pulled out a folder and opened it. There were several pictures in it, and he quickly sorted through them. He began to hand them one after the other to Jack.

Cate leaned closer. Jack looked at the first – an image of nighttime scene on the water. A person, Vincent, he assumed, was standing on the body of a floating whale.

"Big whale." He looked up "Blue or fin?"

"Fin, about eighty feet we think." He handed Jack another photo. "Now look at the bite mark. Please tell me that's multiple bites and not a single one."

Jack turned to the next shot. The huge chunk of missing flesh showed the white blubber cut all the way down to pinkish meat of muscle that continued on down below the water-line. The sheared off rib was also visible.

Jack pursed his lips to whistle, but no sound came. He felt his gut give a little kick. "Yeah, maybe."

Vincent sat forward. "Could a prop do that? A big freighter, with a twenty-five foot screw on full rotation?"

Jack knew it couldn't make a wound that clean, no matter how sharp, or how fast the propeller was turning. "Maybe." He handed the picture to Cate, whose brows were drawn together.

"Two maybes." Vincent sighed and handed Jack his last photo. "Then there's this, Mr Maybe."

The image showed Vincent once again on the whale carcass. The picture was taken with some sort of 3D illuminating film that made much of the whale seem to float in space. But it was the huge torpedo-shaped shadow passing underneath the carcass that sent a jolt through Jack's body.

He swallowed dryly. He knew exactly what it was. He went to hand it back, but Cate caught his arm, dragging the picture towards her.

Cate squinted hard at the image, and then straightened, her eyes dead as she handed it over. Jack felt her turn to him, but he wouldn't look at her for fear of betraying his own thoughts.

"Well, Jack, you're the expert. But tell me that doesn't look like a shark." Vincent sat back. "And yes, I know water can magnify some objects just below the surface, but the refraction and distortion rate is only in the order of about ten per cent." He exhaled. "That damn thing looks to be sixty feet."

"I also took some thermal shots. It was no whale, but it flared hot." Regina's green eyes were like gun barrels.

Jack nodded. "The Great White is warm-blooded, so it can regulate its own body temperature. That's why it can adapt to different water temperatures. It'd be as hot as a whale."

"A Great White; that's what I originally thought." Vincent reached into his pocket and pulled out the tooth fragment. He held it out. "From the bite wound."

Jack took it in his palm, feeling its weight. It was a glossy white, around two and half inches long. He knew the largest Great White tooth ever found, measured out at about three inches. That was estimated to be from a shark around twenty-five feet in length. He looked at the blunt end – broken off – it had been bigger.

"Now that's a goddamned big shark," Vincent said.

Jack held it up. "Carcharodo…"

"*Carcharodon Carcharias* – yeah, that's it… the Great White. Now I remember." Vincent turned to Regina. "Thought so."

Jack stared. "No, it's something else."

"Shit." Cate stood up too quickly, knocking her chair over, and walking away.

Jack turned to her, reaching out to grab her forearm. She looked pale. He held on, looking up at her. "It can't possibly be…"

"Yes it can." She gently pulled her arm free and disappeared down into the cabin. Jack thought she had panicked, and went to follow her when she reappeared, holding a plastic sleeve with some papers in it. She sat back down, and held it out to him.

He took it from her, turned it around, and looked at the pages. They were from a web site and showed an image of something on the deck of a fishing boat. He frowned and then angled it to get better light.

"Russian?"

Cate nodded.

Jack scanned the printed story underneath the images, and then his eyes went back to the long fish-like thing. "The Southern Bering Sea." He looked up. "Not that far from Baranof."

Cate just stared back at him. "There's something else; remember that small earthquake in the papers a few months back? Well I spoke to the Colorado seismic event facilities. They recorded a huge warm-water temperature spike in the Bering Sea."

Jack held her gaze. "Upwelling?"

Cate hiked her shoulders. Vincent watched them and reached out to take some of the pages from Jack. Regina leaned in closer to look over his shoulder. The Coast Guard officer looked up.

"Is this related?"

"Maybe," Jack said.

"Will you stop saying that, Jack?" Vincent shoved the pictures back at him. "Listen buddy, we've got a dozen boats and a total of thirty people now missing off the Californian Coast. That's in the last few weeks, and just the ones we know about. There could be more still unreported. There've been no storms, no tidal surges, no boat hijackers in the area." He rubbed the back of his neck. "And then I see the shape of something that might or might not be a freakin' nightmare, and I'm betting you guys know more than you're letting on." He sprang forward. "Jack, don't bullshit me, please. Have we got a problem or not?"

Jack sat back, lifted his beer, and sipped. The liquid wet his dry mouth, but was tasteless. Cate continued to stare at the ground, but nodded almost imperceptibly.

"Okay." Jack put down his beer and clasped his hands in front of him. "This is confidential, okay?"

Vincent shrugged.

Jack sighed. "There was an expedition a few months back – an exploratory excursion to a newly discovered environment buried below the north-western Alaskan coastline." He looked up at his friend. "It was a body of water – huge, and been locked away for millions of years. It contained life forms, *big* life forms."

Jack held up Cate's picture of the armor-plated fish. "Like this thing; a Placoderm, been extinct for a hundred million years – same amount of time as the coelacanth."

Vincent took the picture back, and held it next to his image of the shape under the whale. "This is not what I saw. This thing only looks to be about a dozen feet long. What I saw—"

Jack held up his hand. "Let me finish. There were other life forms down there. It was no lake, but a damn subterranean sea. We lost good people. Only Cate, myself, and one other walked out of there." He sighed, feeling the heaviness in his chest. "We encountered a massive predator; a Megalodon – a *Carcharodon Megalodon*." He nodded towards the pictures in Vincent's hands. "The Placoderms were just its food source. But that thing passing under your whale – it was like that."

Vincent sat back, just watching Jack for a moment. "And it got out... how?"

Jack shrugged. "Don't know. The site was sealed, and our reporting was also classified as not for public dissemination under the EPA's environmental hazards act. Homeland Security has said we're not supposed to even talk about it anymore. They've shut down any reporting of the site, and may do further analysis and exploratory later – when they can work out how to do it safely."

He sucked in a deep breath. "That body of water underneath the western coast of both Alaska and Canada also stretched many miles out into the Bering Sea." He looked to Cate, and raised his eyebrows. "Whether it was an earthquake or somehow, someone managed to breach the partitioning sea walls, and broke into it. If that occurred, there might have been some biological transference – the Megalodon could have gotten out. Anything else that came with it, like the Placoderm there, should have been killed instantly by the temperature or pressure differential."

"Well, no maybe this time, mister. And why the hell is it here... and for that matter, staying here?" Regina's jaw jutted.

"Makes sense," Cate said. "This is its home... or was, around fifteen million years ago. Many creatures retain primordial base memories. Sharks are one of evolutions enduring success stories, and can live in all sorts of temperatures. But they prefer to hunt in warm water." She laughed with little humor. "You might say it's come home."

Vincent gritted his teeth, looking from Cate to Jack. "And you've been sitting on this for how long?"

"Hey..." Jack held Vincent's fierce gaze. "We didn't even know about the shark until about five minutes ago. So don't come onto my boat pointing fingers, okay?"

"You should have told someone, Jack. Now I got people missing all over, and I'm betting they aren't going to be turning up any time soon." Vincent got to his feet. "That's on you."

Jack also got to his feet, stepping in close to the Coast Guard officer. Jack was taller and well muscled. But Vincent looked like he was made from iron and teak. Both men stared hard at each other.

"Sit down," Vincent said, holding his eyes.

Jack's jaws worked for a moment. "I know what this thing can do, and if I had any idea it was in these waters, I'd be first in line to do something about it. But there's no proof."

Vincent snatched up the picture of the Placoderm. "There's your proof."

"Calm down." Cate got in between the two men, and pushed them apart. "This isn't helping."

Jack folded his arms. "Vince, you came here for help. No use trying to beat me up, because that isn't the way to get it." He sat down heavily.

Vincent Kelly paced for a moment but then plonked down in his seat. "We need get back out there, and we need to go public – issue a general alert."

"Go public?" Cate snorted. "You'd have every recreational fisherman on the coast, no, *worldwide*, out on the water in everything from a destroyer to a dinghy. This is no ordinary shark, and what you need right now, is education. Jack…?"

Jack nodded. "She's right, Vince. This is a hyper-predator of unprecedented magnitude. It is the biggest, meanest killer that has ever lived on land or sea. If it's taking boats, it's learned that's where the food is. So, a lot more small boats on the water will be nothing more than a smorgasbord."

Vincent sat forward "We restrict it to boats over fifty feet, sixty… I dunno, a hundred feet."

"And made of pig iron?" Jack's eyebrows went up. "An oversized Great White has a bite force of around thirty-eight hundred pounds per square inch. Your picture tells me that this thing is around sixty-five feet, and will have a comparative bite force of up to forty thousand pounds. Let me give you some context: the T-Rex could only bite down at around seven thousand pounds. Unless your fishermen are in a destroyer they'll just be sailing on out to their deaths. Plus its territory will be hundreds of miles – it could be anywhere along the west coast."

Cate looked over the side at the still, blue water. "I'm suddenly thinking I'm not going to go for that little sail around the bays after all."

Jack reached out and grabbed her hand. He rubbed it.

Vincent's eyes narrowed, as his vision had turned inward. "Fine, then we take the *Bertholf* out – she's a National Security Cutter – four hundred and eighteen feet, two by 7.400 kilowatt diesel engines, plus one pumped up 22.000 kilowatt gas turbine engine, that can fire us up to twenty-eight knots." He smiled grimly. "Plus, she's got a fifty-seven millimeter deck cannon, and four fifty-cal machine guns – we'll blow that fucking fish back to hell."

"*Yeah.*" Regina turned to bump knuckles with him.

Vincent got to his feet. "Jack, sorry, but you're gonna need to file another report so I can get this project underway. With your input, we can keep a lid on it for public safety perspectives. But we need the *Bertholf* on the water."

Jack shook his head slowly. "You'd be wasting your time. Your boat is fast, but the Megalodon will move at twice that speed. Added to that, how are you going to shoot something that won't come to the surface? It's probably down in the trenches, and only comes up to feed at night." He grimaced, seeing the blood rising in his friends face. "Look, Vince, just issue a stay-clear order for the waterways. Just for a week while we check some things out. It might move out to open waters, and then we can—"

"A stay-clear order. For the entire Californian coast? And how do we police that?" Vincent scoffed. "And what do I say – steer clear of jellyfish? Come on, man, help me here. Have you got any serious suggestions?"

"I *am* trying to help." Jack felt his own frustration rising.

"Time's up; people are dead." Vincent spun to the wharf and leapt up in a single bound. Regina jumped up beside him, standing with her hands on her hips. Her green eyes flashed for a moment, and then they were both gone.

Jack rubbed his forehead as he watched them head back to their helicopter.

Cate came and put her arm around his waist. "So, that was a friend of yours? Hate to meet an enemy."

Jack laughed softly. "Yeah, Vince can get a little... *spirited*." He looked at her. "I was about ten seconds away from sicking my dog on him."

Cate looked down at Ozzy. The dog's brown button eyes lit up at the sound of his name and he cocked his head to the side, listening intently now.

Cate laughed, but Jack's expression quickly clouded. "But... he's right. I think we've got work to do."

Cate nodded, looking out at the setting sun. "Yeah, but can we please do it in there?" She nodded towards the restaurant. "Always wanted to try it, and I think I'd like to be off a small boat right now."

CHAPTER 30

On the edge of the shelf
Fifty miles out from Mendocino

The yacht glided over the dark blue water with barely a ripple. The gentle breeze was enough to just tilt the magnificent boat and push it along at about five knots. William Harris had the wheel of *Sulacco*, and by now could have put it on autopilot if he chose, but there was something about standing, legs braced, holding the wheel, and in total control that he really loved.

Maggie, his wife, was below. It was her turn at kitchen duty, and hopefully something close to edible would be served soon. He looked over his shoulder; his two sons were out in the dingy being dragged a few dozen feet behind. Though they were around fifty miles out from Mendocino, the kids still managed to pick up enough reception to keep their noses buried in their phones or iboxes, or whatever they called them.

Even now in the dinghy, he saw they were crowded around a small flat screen, faces lit by the blue glow of something or other that was riveting them. He hated to think what.

Maggie had demanded the boys be in by six, and he'd tried to talk them into coming back onboard with the setting sun. But the looks they had thrown him bordered on disbelief and downright disdain. *Gotta love teenagers.*

Anyway, the tether line was inch-thick marine rope, and he guessed they could tow Neptune himself before it would break. Besides, there was barely a ripple right now, and he didn't really want the grief.

"Ten more minutes, boys," he yelled over his shoulder. He decided he didn't want grief from Maggie either. He turned back to the wheel. They had miles yet before they reached San Francisco Harbor, but he guessed they'd be in before midnight. Waking up in San Fran would be the real start of their holidays.

The sun was now a huge orange, wavering ball on the horizon. Harris leant down to towards the galley. "How's that dinner going, Maggie? Something sure smells good."

He straightened, grinning. No it didn't, not at all. But he'd do his bit for solidarity, and eat whatever she managed to put together for them.

"Nearly done... I think." Her voice sounded frustrated – not a good sign. He grimaced and smacked his lips. He'd love a beer, but he wouldn't dare ask her for one.

The sun went down and the dark settled over them as suddenly as if someone flicked a switch. Almost immediately, his fish finder started to ping at him.

"*Huh?*" Harris looked down at the small screen. It was supposed to show him a rough approximation of the sea bottom, and anything that moved above it – schools of fish showed up as green smudges, the bottom black, and snags as red blobs, or at least that what he was told. He had never used it before, as he'd never been fishing in his life, let alone on the boat.

Regardless, there was a big school of something down there. "Mackerel, I bet," he said, naming the first fish that came to mind.

He watched as the big green blip moved quick, staying deep and shooting past them. The hair on his scalp prickled. He looked in at the coastline, now showing as pinpoints of light on a dark landmass. On instinct he eased the wheel around, heading them in closer.

"Jimmy, Daniel," he yelled. "Time to come in, boys... *now."*

He turned to where their small dingy was being dragged on the end of the fifty feet of rope, and instead of just seeing the glow from their screen, he could also make out what he thought looked like a dark mountain rising up. Immediately the rope went insanely tight, and the *Sulacco* stopped dead in the water.

Harris was thrown forward into the wheel, and below deck Maggie screamed, worryingly, it was the howl of someone in pain – burned, he bet. He guessed whatever she was cooking she was now wearing.

"Fucking snagged." Harris climbed to his feet. The boat was dead in the water, with only the sound of stretching rope fibers. He dragged open a hatch and pulled out one of the large spotlights and spun to shine it behind them. There was no dingy anymore, the tether rope was still there, but so tight it looked solid, and the worst thing was, it vanished into the dark sea.

"Fuck!" he raced to the stern, holding the light high. *"Jimmy, Daniel!"* He moved the light one way then the other. There were no bobbing heads or spluttering curses, or cries for help. There was nothing but the wire-tight rope, angled back into the black water.

The *Sulacco* groaned like a living thing, and then began to move backwards, but only for a second or two. The rope's tension suddenly eased, and Harris stood, eyes wide and mouth open, and heard Maggie sobbing then. Before he could even think what to do next, the rope snapped tight against the stern gunwale. This time, the angle was down, hard.

"No, please, no." The boat started to tip as the rope was being pulled by something that far outweighed the buoyancy of the yacht.

Maggie came up, unsteadily with a towel wrapped around her arm. "Did you run into something?"

He turned to her, his mouth working, but no words coming. The boat tilted some more, and equipment started to slide towards the rear of the deck.

"William, where's Jimmy and Daniel?" She grabbed at him, with eyes wider than he had ever seen.

Harris held onto a railing with one arm, and pulled Maggie close to him. The rope started to make its way around the boat, popping off brass fixtures as the thick cord came towards them. The toughened mix of natural and synthetic fibers made short work of anything in its way.

It reached the cabin wall, and stopped its forward movement. It was then they began to be pulled over. Maggie started to scream, and whatever she had been cooking, was now on fire as an orange glow appeared from the galley doors. Harris smelled oily smoke.

"We're going to be sunk." William Harris held his wife tight as water poured over the gunwale and began to flood the deck.

"Cut it," Maggie screamed.

He felt shocked at the blinding obvious suggestion and that he had never even thought of it. He dived for the tackle cabinet and fiddled with the catch. Inside there was a new knife, silver sharp, and serrated on one side. He grabbed it and leapt to the rope sawing and hacking, the tight fibers resisting every slice.

The *Sulacco* moaned again as she was pulled onto her side, and the gunwale went level with the water. A waterfall commenced pouring over the side. He wrapped his hand around the rope, and realized it had gone slack. He drew it in a few feet, and saw his spotlight bobbing beside him. Harris snatched at it, and shone it down into the water.

The devil himself stared back.

The thing rose from the black water, and his light shook in his hand as it followed the mountain higher. The rope was still trailing from its mouth that was lined with teeth as big as his head. There looked to be ragged portions of meat and what could have been shreds of clothing caught between them. The monster then surged towards him.

William Harris was still alive when the massive jaws extended to take him and a good portion of *Sulacco*'s wooden railing. He was alive for mere seconds more as they closed on his soft body, the ten-inch serrated blades cutting all the way through him, before it took him down to the darkness below.

He wasn't alive when the fire in the galley made it to the fuel tank, and blew Maggie and the ship to smithereens.

CHAPTER 31

Vincent Kelly stood in the bridge room of the National Security Cutter. Being aboard the huge Coast Guard vessel never failed to inspire him – modern, well maintained, and with enough firepower to keep the country's borders secure from any attempt at crime or intrusion.

He looked down at a screen showing an image of the rear deck and saw Reggie there securing their chopper – this time, it was a smaller HH-65 Dolphin, built more for speed and maneuverability than sea air rescue.

Vincent straightened. He could feel Captain Loche's eyes slide to him again as they had several times before. Every time he felt the man's gaze fall on him, he wished he had of somehow forced Jack Monroe to come along. He could tell the senior officer wasn't okay with a major chunk of their fleet hardware being used on a shark hunt – even if it was one supposedly to be sixty-five feet long and responsible for sinking a dozen boats.

Allegedly, sinking a dozen boats. Vincent sighed. He'd had to call in so many markers to make this happen, but even after only a day, he was starting to doubt the logic of his own story. *Jesus Christ*, he should have just said, a *big* shark. But a Megalodon, an extinct dinosaur shark, a freaking monster that had somehow busted out of a cave in the freezing Bering Sea, and then swam a few a thousand miles down the coast to sink boats and kill some two-dozen people.

Damn, he wished he'd made Monroe come with him to impart some of that scientific jargon and expert logic.

Vince groaned as he felt the cold steel glance from the captain alight on him once again. He kept his eyes on the water, praying for something to show up on the surface, the sonar, the depth finders or anything, anywhere would do. At the moment, they were burning through twenty grand a day using the *Bertholf,* looking for something that was a shadow under the water, and he had nothing more conclusive than a shard of tooth.

"We've got debris, sir."

"All stop." Loche lifted some field glasses. "Get a dinghy out."

Vincent cleared his throat. "Sir, I strongly recommend you keep a small craft out of the water."

The senior officer held up a hand. "It's all right, Senior Officer Kelly. I think we got this." He smiled, a little too patronizingly, Vincent thought.

"Boat One away, sir."

Loche lowered the glasses. "There's nothing on sonar, radar, or hydrophone. Not even an inquisitive dolphin down there."

"Yes, sir." Vincent gritted his teeth. "Permission to leave the bridge."

"Permission granted." Loche didn't bother to turn.

Vincent jogged across the deck to where Reggie had her hands deep into the engine of the chopper. She saw him approach, and leaned on one elbow. "Hey boss, how's it going in there with the brass?"

"About as I expected – *bad.*" He nodded to the dinghy shooting away. "They've spotted a debris pattern on the water." He walked to the railing, watching as the small inflatable boat's powerful engine made it skip across the surface until it reached a darker patch of water, where it began to circle, before slowing.

Vincent gripped the railing, his eyes now unblinking. He saw one of the men lean far out over the side – "*stay clear of the water,*" he whispered.

The man grabbed a pike and reached out again. Vincent grimaced, imagining the dark water below him. *Come on, son, hurry it up,* he thought, barely able to watch.

"They've found something." Reggie's voice made him jump. She was just behind him, a small pair of field glasses to her eyes. She lowered them, and reached out to grasp his forearm. "Hey, calm down, okay?"

Vince felt her thigh against his. He nodded, but couldn't settle until he saw the small boat speeding back to the *Bertholf*. They'd hook it back up and haul it aboard in a few seconds, and he jogged back towards the bridge to get an update.

He saluted at the door and entered. Captain Loche graced him with a flat smile, and his 2IC, Lieutenant Mitch Andrews, also nodded to him.

Andrews handed Loche a steaming mug of coffee from a tray held by a junior officer, and Loche sat in his chair, and folded one leg over the other.

"Boat debris," he said.

A man came to the door, still wet from salt spray and quickly saluted. He entered and stood rod-straight with his arms folded behind his back, and legs spread. He stared straight ahead.

"At ease; report." Loche blew on his coffee.

"Thank you, sir." The man relaxed, but his body remained straight. "After an examination of the area we sighted an engine-oil slick, and floating motor yacht debris – name and registration unknown. Most of the debris has signs of charring and explosive force. Looks like a fire and then explosion, sir."

"Bodies, or any sign of life jackets?" Loche asked slowly.

"Nothing sir, no trace of any sea survival kit on the water. Everything else must have gone to the bottom."

"Thank you, Sergeant. Dismissed." Loche turned in his chair towards Vincent. "Explosion." He nodded slowly, his eyes on the senior chopper pilot. "Lieutenant Andrews…"

"Sir." Andrews stopped and listened.

"One more sweep of the area to search for survivors, or bodies… and then we head in." Loche looked away at last.

"Yes, sir." Andrews relayed the orders.

Vincent began to protest, but knew he had nothing, and his mouth snapped shut.

Andrews leaned closer as he passed by. "Hey, maybe your monster used an RPG." He winked and continued on.

"*Asshole,*" Vince whispered to his back, before heading for the door. There was no more he could do.

CHAPTER 32

Off the western coast of Mexico's Baja California, near Guadalupe Island

Two of the three men stood in full wetsuits with goggles pushed up on foreheads, and tanks over their backs. The third, Jackson Biggs, moved around behind them, checking their equipment and making sure everything was hooked, strapped, and in tight to their bodies.

Jackson was the dive captain, and his job was to ensure everything that went into the water came back out again – that was doubly true for his charges.

His cameraman, Philippe, held the streamlined Nexus model camera loosely in one hand. He would take streaming video and stills from the moment they entered the water, and then continually from when Big Betty came up from the depths.

Finishing with Philippe, Jackson went to check Arthur 'Big Arty' Freeman. The man, shivering in the pre-dawn coolness despite his bulk, was here for his wallet alone. Jackson groaned, imagining how uncomfortable he must have felt in the wetsuit. It was the largest they had, but his stomach was still threatening to explode from within the black neoprene. Extra weights were added to keep him down, as his natural buoyancy would be extremely high.

Big Arty had paid twenty-five thousand dollars to dive with them, but the condition was, they get him and the shark together in at least two photographs. Considering

Big Betty was as regular as clockwork these days, it was money for old rope.

Seeing Big Betty up close was a rare and privileged event, and normal tourists were discouraged from the area. Jackson, a marine biologist, was one of the few allowed to dive and monitor the huge shark's wellbeing. The fees they collected from the likes of Arty, paid for their research.

Betty was a pregnant Great White, twenty-one feet from nose to tail, and the largest specimen ever captured on film in the wild. She had moved into the area a few months back, where she had been tagged with a small receiver just behind her dorsal fin. They could track her every movement, and they were excited by the prospect of witnessing her giving birth any day now.

"Ready?" Jackson waited for his dive companions to nod. He then quickly ran through some dive hand-signals. Philippe knew them by heart, but still paid more attention than Arty, who looked disinterested and a little bored.

Jackson guessed he just wanted his pictures, and then hoped to be back home, showing the girls in the office how fearless he was by midday. Jackson wondered how much the creep would have paid to take the shark's head home as well.

The forty-foot cruiser bobbed on the dark swells, and Jackson leaned over to flip open the cage door. Dawn wasn't far away, and though his signal locater told him Big Betty was close, she only ever made an appearance near the surface around dawn. She'd grab her snack, and then vanish back down to the depths. She was becoming so accustomed to the tiny creatures in the dive cage; they even devised a way to call her, using a child's party clicker.

"Okay, Philippe you're up." His cameraman nodded, threw a leg over the side, and expertly slid in through the cage's trap door. For now the cage was suspended at the water line, but once all in, Jackson would take control and winch them down to meet their giant friend.

"Arthur, now you." Jackson helped Arty get one trunk-like leg up on the gunwale, and between he and Philippe they managed to get him wedged into the cage.

Jackson sat astride the gunwale, and one of the deck hands handed him a three-foot fish – it was a fresh tuna, sliced open and starting to drip deep red blood onto the deck. Jackson groaned under its weight. A natural fiber rope was tied around its tail, and he lowered into the cage, for Philippe. Jackson then opened a dive pocket on his vest, and felt for the waterproof tracker. In a moment he saw the orange blip – a mile out and three hundred feet down, but closing – good.

He pulled his facemask down and turned to give his crew a wave, before sliding in through the cage door. He closed it, and went to the cage's winch controls and pressed the red button to take them down – they immediately began to be lowered into even darker water. Time was racing them now, and Betty had been known to rise up, not see them, and then turn tail, as if worried about the coming sunlight. The last thing Jackson wanted was to have to suffer their rich fool passenger one minute longer than necessary.

The cage gently lowered. The deck spotlights that were angled down into the water created a giant halo around the boat, but as they sank below the hull it quickly became dark with just a blush of light coming from above. Philippe's camera was loaded with light-sensitive film, and the lenses could be relied on to provide excellent depth, but still, they needed Betty to be as close as they could get her.

At twenty feet, Jackson stopped their descent and floated closer to Arty, and gently took hold of him, pulling him close so he could look into his eyes. They were wide, and he could immediately tell he was sucking oxygen too fast. *Good grief,* Jackson thought, what was he going to be like when a twenty-plus foot behemoth came out of the shadowy depths? He'd fill his damn wetsuit. He tapped the man on the head and gave him a thumbs-up. Arty nodded and returned the gesture.

He supposed it didn't master if he chewed through his oxygen in half the time; after all they had enough air for an hour, and they should only be down for twenty minutes if Betty was on time. Jackson floated back to the controls and started them down again, the electronic whine of the winches a background hum as they were lowered to their destination depth of forty feet below the keel.

Once they settled, Philippe positioned his lights and switched them all on. Spots at each corner of the cage illuminated a massive halo around them for a good fifty feet in all directions. Jackson took the tuna and lashed it to the bars of the cage. When Betty came in for her breakfast, he'd cut it loose. Though the inch-thick titanium bars could stop a freight train, he didn't fancy the idea of having five thousand pounds of shark getting tangled in their overhead cabling.

Jackson breathed slowly. The sound of his escaping bubbles, and the occasional bump or knock from the boat above, and there was nothing else. Philippe was ready on the camera and Arty was gripping the bars with both hands and looked frozen with fear.

Jackson grinned around his mouthpiece, not believing he actually got paid to do this. He loved this moment – the anticipation, the utter darkness beyond their halo of light, and the unknown depths below them. The three of them were small alien creatures that had descended to another planet to observe the weird and wonderful life forms. He brought out the tracker. Betty was around but seemed to be keeping her distance.

He pulled out his clicker, and began to snap it, making a popping sound under the water. It usually brought her up fast, but today she seemed a little skittish. Rising up, but then darting off, or heading back down.

Come on, my big darling. Jackson clicked it again, and was relived to see the blip on his tracker begin to change direction and rise. She was coming up from the south, and he tapped Arty on the shoulder and pointed out into the blue-black water.

She usually came in slow, her massive body seeming to glide or float from the depths. The shark would circle them, passing by several times before judging all was in order, and then come in fast to take her prize.

Beside him Arty started to jostle Philippe who was trying to hike his camera a little higher. And then, from out of the deepest shadows the familiar torpedo shape appeared.

He grinned, feeling the thrill pass through his entire body. She never failed to instill awe, and a little primal fear. Her girth was astronomical, as wide around as a draft horse, and everyone knew she had to be pregnant. It must have been why she would accept easy meals from cumbersome little human beings in a cage, and not have to try and chase anything down. But today, strangely, instead of gliding in, she moved fast, shooting by them so quickly, they all felt the current rock the cage.

Jackson pulled back, spinning to watch her go by. He turned to Philippe who shrugged and shook his head – *no shot*. At least Arty seemed happy, and he tapped Jackson on the shoulder and gave him a double thumbs-up.

Betty came back, once again, travelling at speed. She came a little closer this time, and he could see the recognizable scars from either netting or fights with other denizens of the deep. On her back, just behind her massive dorsal fin there was a small pad with two exposed wires affixed that looked like some sort of shrimp had attached itself to the huge shark's body. It was this that transmitted Betty's every move to Jackson and marine biologists everywhere in the world.

Betty came back fast, her tail flicking now. The creature was obviously agitated by something, and Jackson looked up briefly at the boat to make sure someone wasn't doing something out of the ordinary.

Philippe tried to follow her with his camera, but soon lowered it, and turned to him shrugging and shaking his head. *Shit* – it'd be impossible to get anything meaningful in the frame if she was going to move so quickly. And no picture, meant no twenty-five grand from Arty-Farty.

Jackson pulled out his dive knife and made a few more slits in the tuna's body before letting it out another dozen feet, hoping that seeing the solitary fish further out might at least slow her down. *Come on*, he urged. The scent trail from the bleeding fish should have created a floating highway a mega predator should have found impossible to ignore.

He hit the red button, and lowered them another ten feet to hold at a depth of fifty. Then, as he hoped, Betty swam through the cloud and blood particles, and found it irresistible. Hunger and instinct overriding any other sensations she was feeling. She turned and slowed. Jackson saw Philippe was already rolling, and he grabbed and pushed Arty close to the bars so he was in the shot.

The big shark approached the tuna, and its massive mouth opened. The maw was big enough to nearly take in the three-foot tuna in one bite. He always wondered what it would be like for those teeth to clamp down on you – he guessed, like several dozen blades attached to an industrial press closing over you.

Betty's jaws extended and she gripped the fish, and tugged at it, but immediately spat it out. Jackson's brow furrowed behind his mask.

What the fuck is wrong with y...

The behemoth rose from the darkness, and grabbed Betty in exactly the same manner he had expected her to grip the tuna. The massive head, with possibly ten-foot wide jaws now extended forward, snapped down on Betty's torso and first crushed and then sawed at her body as it shook its head like a massive hound.

Jackson screamed into his mouthpiece. Beside him Philippe had dropped his camera and had moved to the back of the cage. In front, Arty seemed to be doing a little dance like he was receiving an electric shock.

The water was suddenly full of blood. Just visible, was Betty's head, little more than the jaws and gill slits, now tumbling free. Betty's mouth gaped wide like she was trying to draw a breath, and as the damage had occurred so quickly, he wondered whether she even knew what had happened.

Jackson's mind refused to process what he had seen. Something, maybe a shark, some sort of whale, or some other sea monster had erupted from below, and cleaved his twenty-one-foot shark in two with a single bite.

A fist punched down hard on his shoulder, and he screamed again, spinning to see Arty's red face behind his goggles. He looked like he was screaming something – Jackson didn't need to know what it was. He pushed himself to the cage controls, and immediately punched the green button to lift the cage.

Jackson looked up and saw that his boat seemed to be miles above him, and he wished now he hadn't dropped them that extra few feet lower. The lights of the boat were obscured and they lifted through a dark red haze. Impossibly, a scream and rush of bubbles dragged his head around. Philippe had climbed to the top of the cage, drawing his legs up, and facing down. His eyes almost filled his facemask. Jackson's head snapped down.

Rising into the range of the lights was a vision straight from hell. He knew what it was now, a shark, but of such monstrous proportions it defied belief. The monster came with its jaws already open, and the gullet behind those long daggers seemed bottomless. It came for its next meal. *Them.*

The shark exploded into the titanium cage, ripping it from its cables, and launching it and itself from the water. In the air now, Jackson had a brief image of his boat, and the deck hands, the captain, and behind them, the morning sun. It was if time moved at one-quarter speed. The men on deck were frozen in place with their eyes wide and mouths hung open, as the monster from the deep hung in the air, metal cage in its mouth, and three men still trapped inside, before falling back into the dark water to create a wave that nearly swamped the boat.

It took them down rapidly, and as it travelled, its jaws began to compress, and the titanium bars, formidable against most anything under the ocean began to crumple. There were furious bubbles and movements from his two colleagues, and a feeling of intense pain in their heads as they began to move into very deep water.

Jackson found himself crushed to the top of one side of the cage, with Philippe and Arty on the other. Ten-inch shovel-sized teeth gripped them, and behind it there was nothing but blackness and, Jackson knew, death.

Without thinking, Jackson's self-preservation instincts kicked in. He pushed upwards, the cage trapdoor flipping open, and he slipped through. Jackson dropped his weight belt and in a single motion looked back. In the glare of Philippe's shrinking camera light he saw his friend, arm out through the bars and behind him, the fatter silhouette of Arty, just before they and the monster vanished into the fathomless depths.

CHAPTER 33

Cate watched Jack pace, phone to his ear and a face like thunder. He grunted occasionally as he listened.

"Cate's here," he said. "I'm opening this up on speaker for her to listen as well. You can repeat what you told me." He set the phone down on the table setting it to speaker mode. "It's Vince." He straightened, folding his arms.

Cate heard an exasperated sigh.

"Cate, how you doing?"

"Vincent, we're okay here; what news have you got?" she said, as Jack sat beside her.

"You guys were right; the Coast Guard don't regard it as their problem. Fact is, I don't think they even see it as a problem at all." He sighed again. "This thing is such an efficient killer it's leaving no bodies, no residue, no... proof."

"We've got eyewitnesses. Have you heard about Big Betty down in Baja? Took out a dive team, and the thing breached – everyone on deck saw it." Cate leant forward on her knees.

"Yes, just saw the reports. But that's at the other end of the coastline, and in Mexican waters – well out of our jurisdiction. Once again, we got an eyewitness, and guess what? He went in the water with a camera, and came out with a heart condition and no camera. We still got nothing." There was the sound of a squeaking chair as if Vincent was sitting back. "Sorry guys, but Coast Guard has handballed it to the FWS."

"Seriously?" Cate scoffed. "The Fish and Wildlife Services?" She felt her face go hot. "To do what? Try for a tag and release?"

Jack held up an open hand waving her down a few degrees. "The thing is, Vince, I'm as supportive of sharks and sea life as any other Ichthyologist. But this thing is an abnormality in these waters, or any modern waters. It'll make shipping impossible for however long it lives, and by the way that could be many more decades, or even centuries, for all we know. And I haven't even mentioned the cost to human lives."

"I know, I know. I needed you with me, and I should have goddamn made sure you came. Thought I could handle it..." There came a sound like a fist coming down on a desk. "I fucked it up."

Jack shook his head. "Don't be too hard on yourself, buddy. Even if you managed to locate the Megalodon, you still had the odds stacked against you. It might never have surfaced, or when it did, it might have been a hundred miles away."

Vince groaned. "So, now what?"

Jack looked to Cate. "We still need to go after it. This thing is only just staking out its territory. Once it does, sea travel in anything under a hundred feet will be at an end."

"I agree; but I've seen the size of the thing, Jack. If you go out in *The Heceta*, I'll be scooping up its kindling in a week." Vincent voice lowered. "What you'll need is some sort of submarine, right?"

"No goddamn way." Cate was on her feet. "I agree we need to go after the thing, but there is no way I, and for that matter you, Mr Jack Monroe, are ever going below the surface while that thing is down there."

Jack exhaled. "We need help." He frowned and then sat forward, to start tapping keys on his computer tablet.

"That's it, Jack; I'm out of ideas. The Coast Guard has dropped this one onto the pubic servants, and not for a

New York second is there a chance the Navy is going to pick up any slack."

Cate sat forward. "Vincent, what *does* Fish and Wildlife have?"

"Hardware?" Vincent snorted. "A few small cruisers, open topped boats, plenty of dinghies, and a truckload of goodwill to man and beast. Just enough to get themselves all killed. Bottom line; we won't find *it*, until it decides it wants to find *us*."

"Good grief." Cate sat back. "We've got nothing."

"No," Jack said, finishing his typing. "We've got more than we could ever hope to have." He grinned, as he let the silence stretch. Cate frowned but her lips began to curve into a smile.

"Well?" She tilted her head.

"C'mon buddy, we need some good news," Vincent said. "Don't leave me hanging."

"I think I've got some – the report from Jackson Biggs, the marine biologist. He said the Megalodon came out of very deep water just off Guadalupe Island and took Big Betty whole." Jack still grinned.

"That's right." Vincent's voice exuded impatience. "So it proves the old maxim – what do big predators fear? Even bigger predators. How is that good news?"

"But that's a good thing, you see, because Big Betty was tagged. Its tracking frequency was available online for you to follow her movements via the Sharkwatch App. No one has thought to check whether it was still active."

"Oh my god." Cate's mouth dropped open. "But you did, didn't you?"

Jack grinned. "Oh yeah, just then, and guess what? Surprise, surprise, the beacon is still active, and it's moving. Last I checked it was over the edge of continental shelf. Our Megalodon is patrolling its new turf."

"You clever sonofabitch, Monroe." Vincent sounded like he rocked back in his chair. "Holy fucking hell – sorry Cate – we can find and track that big bastard." He whooped.

Cate's phone rang, and she looked briefly at it, frowned, and walked away.

Jack's watched her go for a moment, before Vincent dragged his attention back.

"So what next, Jack?"

Jack's forehead creased. "Well, I'm afraid tracking it is only part of our problem. Sure, we can track it, but then what?" He stood. "We can't make something two thousand feet down come to the surface, and believe me, *no one* should go down there after it."

Cate rejoined him a puzzled expression on her face.

"What's up?" he asked.

She held up her phone. "That was Sonya Borashev. She's invited us to a meeting. Says we seem to have a problem she might be able to help with."

Jack held the phone back to his ear. "Vince, like I said, this is where we'll need help." He grinned at Cate. "And I think we have just the party in mind."

CHAPTER 34

Cate and Jack sat in deep leather chairs in the foyer of the gleaming silver spire of the Mironov Tower. Cate occasionally pointed out different objects of art to Jack who stared in wonder at all the gleaming marble, chrome, and glass.

"I feel underdressed," he whispered. "In fact, I feel like a country bumpkin who's just stumbled into the big smoke."

Cate reached across to squeeze his forearm. "It's fine, darling. Just don't sip your moonshine or try and speak, and no one will know you're a little slow." She grinned and sat back.

Jack made his eyes go cross-eyed and leaned towards her. "I'll try not to scare the purdy lady, Miss Granger, ma'am." He sat back, his face becoming serious. "So, Sonya, she took Valery being killed, badly, huh?"

"Yeah." Cate leaned closer to him, and lowered her voice. "I have a feeling she and Valery had something going on. She was deeply affected by his death."

Jack nodded. "Good to know." He looked around. "I'm guessing she got over it pretty quickly, after she learned he left her everything."

Cate shrugged. "Would have helped."

"Ms Granger?"

Cate turned to the receptionist, who smiled benignly. "Someone is coming down for you now."

"Thank you." Cate got to her feet, straightening her

dress. Jack also rose beside her. She turned and looked him over briefly. "And you behave."

"I'll be my normal charming self." He half bowed.

She rolled her eyes, and turned to the elevator doors just as they opened. It wasn't Sonya Borashev, as she expected, but instead a tall man, with a face that looked carved from stone, and a jaw she could have cracked walnuts on.

"Jesus," Jack breathed as the hulking man came towards them.

He stopped and nodded to each of them. "Good morning, Ms Granger and Mr Monroe. I'm Drago Andovich, Head of Security for Mironov Enterprises. Please follow me."

Jack went to hold out his hand, but the man had already turned away. Cate nudged him in the ribs.

Once again she found herself in the small wood-paneled elevator speeding to the 110th floor. Cate inhaled the scent of lavender, and this time, an aftershave that was strong enough to repel insects.

They both stood behind the huge shoulders of Drago, and Cate turned to Jack, and held her nose, sticking out her tongue in case he didn't get it. Jack grinned, raised his eyebrows and motioned with his eyes to above the elevator doors. She followed his gaze to a small slide of silver metal, and she could just make out Drago's eyes, watching them in the reflection. She lowered her head, groaning softly.

Jack leaned in close to her ear. "Do you need a sip of my moonshine?"

In another few seconds the elevator slowed, stopped and the doors slid soundlessly open. Drago led them to the familiar set of double doors, with 'AKM' in calligraphic style crest on a band of gold across the panels.

He knocked and stood aside. If he had seen Cate making fun of him, he gave no sign.

Jack pushed the door and held it open for Cate to go through. Once again she was knocked out by the size of the room. It was still as dimly lit as she remembered – it seemed Sonya had changed nothing. There were the sparse decorations, huge antique desk, and dark burgundy leather couch, now hidden in shadows.

"Wow." Jack held up his arms toward the wall of glass holding a shimmering blue Olympic pool size fish tank. He rushed to it and crouched; Cate could tell he was trying to take it all in at once – the swaying sea grass, weed-covered boulders, and the two ancient fish that sinuously approached him.

He grinned, pointing at the strange fish. "What the hell are they?"

"Some of Valery's pets – *Polypterus Senegalus,* dinosaur eels – very rare, very ancient transitional species." The last time she had seen the prehistoric-looking creatures she had been mesmerized. This time, she was strangely revolted.

The click of heels drew their heads around, and Sonya powered towards them smiling broadly. "Cate, Jack, welcome." She stuck out a hand.

The first thing that struck Cate as odd was the way Sonya beamed. No more the sullen woman who had rescued them. *Could she have gotten over her grief so quickly?*

They each shook her hand, and then let her lead them to the couch. A figure rose to meet them.

Cate stopped dead and Jack bumped into her back.

"Valery? *Valery?* What the hell?" Cate walked forward slowly, her mouth hanging open.

Jack grinned, but his brow was furrowed. "But you… we saw… *how?*"

Cate managed to close her mouth. "What happened to you? How did you escape? Where's Dmitry?" She went to him and embraced his slim figure, but he quickly disengaged himself and pointed to the couch.

Cate sank into the soft leather, Jack beside her. "I have so many questions that I feel my head is going to explode."

Mironov sat back down, but Sonya remained standing. He nodded to her.

"Dmitry Anatol Kuchina was an agent working for Brogidan Yusoff, one of Valery's business and political adversaries," she said, her eyes unblinking.

"Bastard," Jack said. "Will he ever be brought to justice?"

"The rubbish has already been taken out, so to speak." Mironov looked up at Sonya, whose mouth lifted slightly at the corners. "Sorry for the cloak and dagger pantomime, but until we knew the full extent of the parties involved, it was best for me to remain... dead." He turned back to them. "As for Dmitry, he and his family are now living safely in Albuquerque, with different names."

"What? He killed Yegor, and stranded us; we could have all been killed! As it was, we lost our friend, Greg Jamison, because of him." Jack said, his brows snapping together. "He should be in jail, or worse."

Mironov watched them for a moment, and eased back into the chair. "Perhaps. But he was being blackmailed. I know he did what he thought was necessary to save his family." He looked from Cate to Jack. "What would you do for the ones you love? Lie, cheat, kill?" He shrugged. "I know I would."

"It's not right," Cate said.

Mironov tilted his head as he regarded them. "Nothing ever is."

Cate licked lips that had suddenly gone dry. "But what happened? How did you escape? The last we saw of you, Dmitry submerged, and then you were both gone."

"Dmitry piloted the submersible to a location under the Bering Sea. Somehow, they planned to extract us. But the roof of the cavern collapsed, but not down. It blew upwards, sucking us up and out."

Jack slapped a hand on his thigh. "The warm water surge in the freezing Bering Sea."

"Yes, we were thrown out, rising from the ancient sea to the modern one. We floated for miles, resting on the bottom that was thankfully only a few hundred feet deep, as our hull had been compromised. It took days for the *Prusalka*'s batteries to recharge. We came to shore at Port Hardy, north of Vancouver. We sank the submersible, and Sonya came and picked us up." He smiled. "And now here I am."

Valery Mironov sat forward, his face growing serious. "But I don't think we alone were drawn from that primordial world. I have been following events along the west coast. I think we have a problem, and that's why I called for you."

Jack nodded. "Yes, we believe one of the Megalodon sharks was released into our seas. It's made its way down to the coast of California, guided by some sort of genetically stored memory, and is now hunting... *us*. So far, over a dozen boats have been lost, with men, women, and children taken. We need to do something about it."

Mironov sat stone still, watching them. Sonya looked briefly at an expensive gold watch on her wrist. "And you would like Valery to donate some money to assist in catching this big fish?"

"Catch it?" Cate's mind took her back to a presentation she gave her students; it felt, a lifetime ago. She remembered telling them that there were some creatures that don't deserve to exist – they're aliens, deadly invaders, she had told them. And if they can't be moved on, then eradication was the only solution. "No, not catch it..." Cate's eyes welled up as she saw Greg Jamison's face as he swam for his life, just before he was eaten alive. "I want it dead."

Mironov looked towards his huge fish tank. "It is a species unlike any other."

Cate launched herself forward. "It's a fucking monster."

Sonya stepped in front of Valery Mironov, her eyes suddenly going flint hard.

Jack pulled Cate back onto the couch. She grimaced, and continued to lean towards Mironov, who still watched the dinosaur eels snake around the blue tank.

"Valery, when I first met you, right here in this room,

you said something that now rings true more than ever. You said sometimes evolution tries things out. Sometimes they don't work out, and then even God himself realizes he has made a mistake."

Valery turned to her then, and Cate went on. "And you said, when a mistake is realized, then these things get cancelled out. Well, this Megalodon monster was cancelled out over one and a half million years ago, for a damned good reason. It's a killer, and it will either keep on killing until they day it dies, or we retreat from the waterways."

Valery's eyes were unblinking, and Cate wondered whether he was even listening now. After another moment, he sighed. "In the submersible, Dmitry and I were attacked. We only just survived. But in that few minutes, I looked into the maw of the devil himself." He began to nod slowly. "I agree, this creature was cancelled to make way for others. It has no right to be here now."

Cate reached out and placed a hand on his forearm. "I want it dead. If not for my friend, Greg, then for all the others it has already killed, and those it certainly will in the future."

Valery placed a hand over hers. "Yes." He stared into her eyes. "What is it you want? Another submarine?"

Jack shook his head. "Unless we have an Ohio Class, then I wouldn't recommend going below the surface with that thing down there." His eyebrows flicked up. "But there might be something we can use. Modern whaling ships are fast and equipped with enough technology to bring it to the surface. They also have harpoon cannon with explosive tip projectiles. We need the best there is."

Sonya frowned. "A whaling ship?"

"That's not all. We need it within a few days. There's a tracking device in the Megalodon's gut that will be excreted in a week."

"Now I'm interested." Mironov began to smile and he stood. "Leave it to me. And be ready to leave immediately."

CHAPTER 35

Cate and Jack sat next to Regina on one side of the cavernous helicopter. Valery Mironov, the statuesque Sonya, and a besotted Vincent on the other. Regina shot Vince hard glances from time to time, but for the most part, everyone sat in silence – or as much silence as you could conjure inside the yawning interior of the Russian built Mi-8T Helicopter.

The massive and powerful helicopter could fit twenty-four people inside. And with a sixty-nine-foot rotor being whipped madly by two Klimov TV3-117Mt turbo shafts, it was like sitting inside a combination of flying tank and metal tornado.

They travelled at the maximum speed of one hundred and fifty miles per hour, and their destination was somewhere in the Northern Pacific. Mironov had obtained their whaling ship – a Russian-built whaler, whose designation was research, but had a ninety millimeter harpoon cannon built by Kongsberg Våpenfabrikk mounted on its foredeck. Plus it had a full armament of whale grenades in a variety of flavors – explosive tip, tranq-dart, and percussion heads.

The ship, the *Slava*, was rented for the year at a fee that made Jack's eyes water. There was no crew required as Drago and four of his team had already left to take over the controls. As there was no actual whaling work to be done, they only needed a pilot, engineers, and deck hands. Vincent would take over the ship when they arrived.

There was only one Russian crewmember that Mironov

negotiated into the transaction – and that was Alexi, the harpooner.

Jack nudged Cate, and motioned to one of the tiny windows in the helicopter. Below them the boat was moving at full speed. And the chopper circled it, coming up from behind. The *Slava* wasn't a huge ship, at only one hundred and seventy-one feet, and with a displacement of eight hundred tons. But it had a three thousand horse-power diesel engine and could crank itself up to eighteen knots, which it seemed to be doing now.

The powerful chopper hovered over the deck, and each of them was harnessed in, and then lowered, usually in twos – Jack and Cate, Vincent and Regina and then Valery and Sonya. Drago and some of his men were there to receive them, and also take another cable the chopper had dropped. This they then attached to the bow of the ship. The Mi8T helicopter slowly lifted away, adding its forward lift power, and an extra kick of speed. Together, boat and chopper, now cut the cold sea at around twenty-five knots – unbelievable for a ship of its size.

In the control room, Vincent immediately set about familiarizing himself with bridge room, with Drago assisting with the key controls he would need and their Russian-English translations. Jack and Cate did their best to stay out of the way.

"Got it." Vincent turned to Sonya. "It'll be two days until we're in warmer water. That is, as long as we don't run into any weather."

"Good." She seemed in no mood for conversation, and left to speak to Mironov and Drago.

Jack and Cate joined Vincent at the wheel. Vincent raised his eyebrows. "Two days to get there, and we have two or maybe three max after that until your shark will shit out the tracker. We're cutting it fine."

"And then what happens if we get there, and find its about three thousand feet down, and we can't get it to come to the surface?" Cate leant her hands on the sill and looked from the window. "This is where we pray for luck."

She lifted a hand from the sill edge, looking at her greasy fingers and grimacing. "*Ugh*, Jack, this place is an abomination."

Regina slid the heavy door open, and entered, rubbing one of Vincent's shoulders.

Jack grinned. "I hear you. I guess a few decades of fletching and butchering whales hasn't exactly left this place a bed of roses."

"You can say that again," Regina said. "Below, it stinks to high heaven. Oh yeah, and the mattresses look like a cat peed on them."

Vincent grinned at her. "Jezuz, and we took a week's leave for this?"

"Paradise," she responded, smiling.

Mironov rejoined the group, and introduced them to Alexi, their gunner. The stocky, young man shook hands all-round, and Cate noticed the incongruity of youthful eyes in a weathered face, and palms that were as tough and calloused as old leather.

Mironov put a fatherly hand on his shoulder. "Alexi is not very good with English, but he came with the ship… at great expense."

He said something in rapid Russian, and the young man nodded. "I not cheap."

Mironov grinned. "And let's hope we get our money's worth. He tells me he can hit a bullseye every time."

"Good," Jack said, his eyes on Alexi. "Because I'm not sure we'll get that many shots. This is no whale that needs to come to the surface. If we fire and miss, it's liable to dive deep and stay deep, and then stay down for days. And once that tracker is out, it'll be damned near impossible to find again… unless it wants to find us."

Mironov translated, and Alexi nodded his understanding.

"If it comes to the surface, it will be dead," Alexi said, his chin out. "Speak slow please."

"Have you ever shot a shark before?" Cate asked. "And for that matter, we think this thing is around sixty or more feet long, and can move at about thirty knots. Oh yeah, you'll need to make it a head-shot, as there is no blubber, just a skin like rough armor plating, and under that, several feet of solid muscle."

Alexi shrugged. "I don't care how big. If it comes to surface, I have enough explosive harpoons to turn it to cat food."

Cate's lips compressed into a flat smile. "Well, that's the trick isn't it; getting it to come to the surface." She turned away, to lean on the sill and look out over the iron-gray swells parting before the *Slava's* bow. There was a small part of her that hoped the Megalodon didn't rise up, and vanished to the dark depths never to be seen again. She still had nightmares of the monster shark emerging like a black mountain behind Greg. She imagined the monstrous jaws closing over him. God, she hoped it was quick. She lifted her arm, and grimaced at the streak of black grease she'd picked up from the sill. *Fuck it*; she ignored it.

Sonya strode in to the center of the group. "Confidence is a good thing. And now we can add competence." She looked at each of them. "We have the best skills and equipment available. This ship is old, but it has everything we need to do the job."

Regina nodded, and her eyes found Vincent again. "And it's built like a freakin' tank. Do whales ram them or something?"

One corner of Vincent's mouth hiked up. "No, but enviro-activists do. The whalers these days tend to have extra armor plating at the bow, and shielding over the prop-shafts to cut through cables dropped by protestors." He tapped the iron of the wheel mounting. "These babies are the Mack trucks of the seas. Frankly, if you have to be on the water with a giant shark, then this thing is probably the safest place to be. Long as it comes to the surface, we have a chance."

Sonya grunted her agreement. "It will come." She turned to Regina. "And that magnificent odor you can smell is a twenty-foot minke whale carcass ripening down in the hold. Once we get into the waters we want, we'll drop and drag it."

Mironov raised an eyebrow. "What shark can resist a dead whale, *hmm*?"

Regina's brow furrowed. "Is that legal?"

"I doubt it." The Russian billionaire turned away.

CHAPTER 36

Annabel Van Horten bounced into the control room, computer table held aloft. "Oh my god. This is *so* unbelievable." She slapped the tablet down, and used thumb and forefinger to enlarge the image. "*Look,* there's a Russian whaler, the *Slava,* heading into our waters. It's now just two hundred miles to our north."

Captain Olander Blomgren's brows went up, and he looked down over Annabel's shoulder. Other young crewmembers crowded around, all wearing the matching red hooded jackets with the Earthpeace muscled penguin logo on its breast.

"What the hell is a fucking Russian whaler doing this far south, man?" A young man, barely old enough to shave, shouted while looking agitated.

Olander patted his shoulder. "Easy there, Nathanial. Maybe they're illegally tracking a pod. These guys have a habit of not following anyone's rules but their own. I think I know the *Slava;* it's responsible for the murder of nearly a thousand cetacean beings. These guys are criminals, and now they're trying to sneak into our jurisdiction."

Olander stroked a perfectly manicured white beard, and turned away for a moment. From the bridge window the azure blue ocean stretched before him. On the foredeck a few of his crew sunbathed. They'd just come from the coast of Mexico and were heading back to Californian waters to engage net fishers who were competing with the native seal colonies for food. The *Slava's* intrusion might be a useful diversion, and very newsworthy.

He smiled; his ship, the *Gaia Warrior*, was Earthpeace's largest purpose-built electric sailing yacht on the water, and was a marvel of engineering. She was a one hundred and fifty-foot trimaran motor sail yacht with an A-frame mast and sails, and a full electric drive system that was silent as it was near emission free. Everything about her was kind to the planet. Her superstructure was made from recycled timber beams, and the hull was old PET plastic bottles pressed into shape. They even had biological treatment of sewage and an environmentally-friendly paint job. It made Olander and his young crew feel good just sitting inside it.

An appropriate chariot for the saviors of the planet, he thought. And if some knuckle-dragging types objected or got in their way, well, no matter what action they took, he was confident history would be on their side.

Olander composed himself and straightened, knowing image was everything to his impressionable, young crew. He turned, a smile spreading against his round cheeks. "Well then, if a band of pirates comes onto our turf, then I say we meet with cutlass, cannon, and hearts of lions. Who's with me?"

The cheer was near deafening in the bridge room, and Olander leant down towards Annabel. "Alert our friends in the media. This is going to look great on the news." He straightened. "Plot an intercept course and full speed ahead. We've got a date with destiny."

Olander tapped a knuckle against his chin as his mind worked. Annabel still hovered close by, absolute adoration in her wide-eyed gaze. "Annie, get Jupiter and Milo to take 'Tweety' up. Let's have a little look at these guys up close."

She scampered away and Olander took control of the wheel. The *Slava* was only a day away if they powered towards each other at full speed. He had plenty of time. Tweety would give him an idea of how he could craft a physical response that would maximize his media grab, and cause her the most benign damage. He only cursed the good weather. Idyllic calm, blue seas didn't ramp up the tension like the cold iron-gray swells of the Antarctic.

Olander leaned forward to look at his sunbathers. Still, the warm weather had its advantages. He could only pray the ships would meet each other closer to dusk – darkness and dark water was perfect new's optics.

He saw the small yellow chopper's blades begin to turn. Tweety was a bubble-cockpit Hughes 500. It was a small, but maneuverable helicopter. But its key strengths were it could travel a long way on little gas, and was as fast as a hornet.

"Go get em, Tweet," he whispered.

The Russian Mi-8T helicopter pulling the *Slava* had been released and had headed off into the sky. Its work was done, fuel low, and the ship was now benefiting from entering the strong Californian current.

They were still around five hundred miles out from Seattle, but the powerful currents formed a huge tornado shape circulating the ocean from the bottom of the Bering Sea, to all the way down along the Californian coastline.

They were making good time, and though Vincent looked pained, he agreed with Drago that now was the time to hang the whale carcass out. It would take a few hours to fully thaw in the warmer waters, but the scent trail laid down in the Pacific current would be ten miles wide, and a huge fast-moving funnel out in front and below them – exactly what they needed to bring the huge predator to the surface.

"How long?" Cate asked, her arms wrapped around herself.

Vincent looked from the controls, to his wristwatch. "We'll be at the start of our run in about eight hours."

Cate exhaled through compressed lips. "Don't know whether I want it to be sooner or later."

"Sooner it's over the better," Jack said. He checked the signal tracker. "The Megalodon is deep, and still heading our way. But it's coming up out of the trench." He frowned. "That's strange. It's too soon for it to have picked up the scent trail."

Cate turned to him, and then Vincent. "Vince, I thought most of the attacks occurred at night, or at least at dusk or dawn."

Vincent nodded. "That's right. Our predator doesn't seem to like strong light. We'll arrive right smack bang at the center of the Californian coast just in time for it to surface and hunt... hopefully."

"Then why is it coming up out of the abyss now?" Regina asked.

Jack shrugged, frowning down at the tracker. "No idea; maybe something's got its attention." He looked up. "But Vince is right; far too soon for it to be us."

Tweety sped overhead, reaching the *Slava* quickly and circling them several times. Milo took multiple aerial shots, and sent them straight back to the *Gaia Warrior* via sat-link to their onboard server.

He nudged Jupiter, eliciting a curse. "Hey man, you're not going to believe this. But those fuckers are dragging a full grown minke behind them."

Jupiter snorted. "I'd believe it. Those Russian cocksuckers are invading Europe, and running down people in tanks all over. So what's a little extra whale torture?" He gritted his teeth. "I feel like fucking crashing us into those commie bastards."

"Commie bastards?" Milo guffawed. "You sound like my old Uncle Frank. Anyway, easy bro, we're in a Hughes 500, not a Jap Zero. All we'd do is crumple on their deck, and leave a skid mark."

Jupiter grinned. "Hey, I want that on my headstone – he was nothing but a skid mark on a Russian asshole."

Milo snorted and put down his camera. "Let's head back to the *Gaia*. These guys just declared war on decency, and worst luck for them, *us*."

CHAPTER 37

Annabel already had the pictures up when Jupiter walked back into the Bridge room. They made a space for the pilot.

"Definitely a Russian whaler, old, but moving fast. Strange, it looks like it's riding very high in the water; only be a twenty-foot draft at best. Maybe it hasn't commenced its whale-take yet." She enlarged a section of the bow. "Oh… that's a Kongsberg Våpenfabrikk harpoon cannon – a big one."

Olander stroked his beard again, knowing this made him look contemplative, and fatherly. "Russians have learned to use propeller guards, and sharpen their bow." He nodded slowly. "So, we'll need to weight the cables, and use the new elastic fibers – won't cut, and we can still wrap around the screws – stop 'em dead. Might even come along myself this time."

He lifted his chin. "In two hours, they'll be in range of the dinghies. Prepare stink bombs for the deck, get the white paint, rollers and brushes, and also throw the new elastic cable in Flying Bird-1. I want to stop the *Slava* in its tracks." He checked his wristwatch. "If we hurry, we should all make good viewing on tonight's news."

"Let's do some good." Jupiter raised a fist.

Olander almost laughed out loud. *Was I as naïve and dumb when I was his age?* "Well said." He leaned towards Annabel. "I'll be in Flying Bird-2."

Her eyes were almost luminous. "Me too."

Cate and Jack stood out on *Slava's* deck, the air warm and sultry now. She had a pair of field glasses to her eyes.

"Did you see who they were?" Jack squinted into the distance before going back to his tracker.

"No, had some sort of sign on the chopper's side, but couldn't make it out. Vince thought he recognized it, but said they refused to be hailed." She lowered the glasses, nodding to the tracker. "Anything on our big friend?"

"Fifty miles to the south; still staying deep for now. But we're definitely heading towards each other." He lifted his head in time to see Alexi blow thick blue smoke following a long pull on his stubby cigarette. The short Russian waved with two fingers, and then went back to chatting with Valery Mironov who sat beside him in a deck chair, legs crossed.

"Those two look relaxed."

Cate followed his gaze. "Wish I could. My stomach is doing cartwheels." She looked past the pair. "Harpoon looks ready."

The harpoon cannon was a squat and powerful-looking device, and the tip of the dart that extended from the muzzle was two feet long, bullet-pointed, and with four wings just behind its nose. Cate had been told those weren't just for improving aerodynamics, but also created the arrowhead effect of once being embedded in the whale's flesh, they made it impossible for the leviathan to pull back out.

Even though Alexi had said he would hit the shark first attempt, beside him on the deck three more harpoons waited to be loaded. She hoped they wouldn't be needed, as the one he had ready was red-tipped, meaning it was an explosive charge. Once the thing impacted with hard flesh, a split second later it would explode forward, detonating inside the animal. It was meant for a quick death and a more humane way to kill. A bit like getting shot in the head by a hollow-point slug – it went in, blew up, and turned the brain into scrambled eggs.

Good, she thought, grimly.

Regina jogged out onto the bridge deck. "Cate, Jack, better come see this." She then yelled to Mironov, waving him in.

Jack quickly checked his tracker – the Megalodon was still miles away. "What now?" He grabbed Cate's arm and they headed up to the bridge.

Once inside, there came the smell of coffee, but the Californian warmth was causing all manner of new fish and oil odors to be released to compete with it.

Sonya paced, her arms folded. Mironov entered, and she addressed him first in Russian. The billionaire half smiled and nodded.

"English, please," Cate said sharply.

Sonya then turned to them. Her teeth were grit. "Seems we are about to have a welcoming committee. They'll be here within the hour."

"What? Who?" Jack looked to Vince who was grimacing.

"One guess – who else harasses whaling ships on the seas?" Sonya asked.

Jack put a hand to his forehead. "You gotta be shitting me."

"Who is it?" Cate grabbed at Jack's arm.

Jack leaned his head back, closing his eyes. "They think we're actually whaling… and probably Russian." He looked at her. "Earthpeace."

Cate's mouth dropped open. "Earthpeace." She put a hand over her mouth, her eyes crinkling. "You're joking?"

Jack nodded. "Great damn timing."

"Well, we need to make contact." Cate folded her arms. "Vincent."

He shook his head. "Not taking my calls." He shrugged. "But think about it. We tell a boatload of penguin-huggers we're about to put a harpoon into a giant prehistoric shark

– the only one in the world – yeah, that'll get them onside."

Jack nodded. "He's right. I've had to deal with these guys before. Uncompromising ignorance is a badge they wear with pride."

"Jesus Christ." Regina threw up her hands. "They start to buzz us, and they'll make it impossible to take a shot."

"That cannot be allowed to happen." Mironov straightened. "Shoot their boats."

Cate scowled. "The hell we will."

"Just to scare them off." Mironov waved her away.

"Oh shit." Jack's face looked agonized. "They're going to arrive about the same time as the Megalodon."

Sonya turned slowly to Mironov, a cruel smile twisting her lips. "Maybe we didn't need the whale after all. Maybe there will be something else in the water to attract our fish." She checked her watch. "I suggest we make sure the boarding nets are in place so those fools can't set foot on deck and sabotage the cannon."

Regina stood beside Vincent. "They'll try and snag us – I hope that prop shield does what it's supposed to."

Drago took his jacket off. He wore a green shirt, plastered to him with perspiration. Cate noticed that as well as having bulging muscles, in the small of his back the guy had a holstered gun on his belt. She saw that Vincent noticed it as well.

"Hey, big guy, I hope you don't expect to use that?" Vincent was a half a head smaller, but lowered his brow at the huge Russian.

Drago put a hand on the weapon, as though he had forgotten it was there. Mironov stepped forward, putting a hand on Drago's forearm.

"Not on people." Mironov smiled. "Self defense only, I assure you."

Sonya folded her arms. "Don't worry, there will be no laws broken today. But..." Her eyes became steely hard. "...these fanatics better not interrupt what we are doing here. It is for their benefit as well." She nodded to Cate. "Ms Granger, you are the nice one. Hail their ship one more time, and try and talk them down, or at least get them to stay clear."

"Too late," Regina said, looking down at the *Slava*'s active sonar. "We've got two rapid bogies in the water." She grimaced. "I'm betting dinghies, coming at us hard and fast."

Sonya's teeth showed, and Cate could have sworn she heard the woman growl. "Then it is game on." She and Mironov headed for the deck.

Cate then noticed there was also a gun tucked into the back of the tall woman's waistband.

CHAPTER 38

Olander stood in the bow of Flying Bird-2, holding tight to a rope tied to its nose. Behind him, a cameraman kept him in frame, while the late afternoon sun made his silver hair and beard seem to glow. He pointed, his arm outstretched. They knew which way to go, but he guessed it would look fabulously heroic, almost like Leutze's depiction of George Washington crossing the Delaware.

The ocean was glass smooth, with any vestige of a breeze dying away hours back. Olander inhaled deeply – he loved this – the smell of brine, humid salty water, and fresh clean air. They were well out over the continental shelf, and too far out for sea birds, but he bet if he dived over the side he'd see all manner of sea life, from dolphins, tuna, and maybe even a small mako shark or two.

He inhaled deeply again, this time leaving his chest out, and chin pointed. There was nothing more satisfying than giving a voice, and a strong arm, to creatures of the sea who could not defend themselves. Doing right, never felt so good. From the corner of his eye Olander saw the camera lift, following his every move. And doing right never *looked* so good. He fixed his expression. Annabel's head also came up this time.

"Sir, we're only a few miles out from the *Slava*."

Olander nodded. "Signal Flying Bird-1, and we'll commence our tandem approach."

He looked down at the coils of the wrist-thick elasticized polymer rope. Whalers today had developed sharpened and armored propellers and bows to cut standard cables. But not this one. This one would bend and slide under the prow, and then find the props, wind around them and hang on, getting ever tighter.

He reached a hand out behind him. "Glasses."

An expensive pair of polarized field glasses was handed to him, and he lifted them to his face. A warm smile spread there as he caught sight of his quarry – there she was, coming right at them out of the sinking sun – the *Slava*, a big, fat Russian whaler.

He turned, handing the glasses back. "Get ready people." He put two fingers to his lips and whistled, loud and sharp. Flying Bird-1 veered in towards them, and one of his four crew handed across one end of the elasticized rope.

"Stay tight – on my word." Olander's mouth set in a firm line. In each of his dinghies, he had a crew of six: two would hold the rope, one would steer, one would film, and the others would be ready with stink bombs, paint and grappling hooks.

Olander grinned; today would be a good day. They were now within three hundred feet of the bow of the *Slava*.

"Now!"

The two craft split apart, and the rope stretched out between them. It was a colossal tripwire designed to hamstring ocean-going vessels. Flying Bird 1 and 2 dragged it, allowing more of the rope to feed out so it moved just below the water line. More bodies were called on to help, as the weight became a monstrous burden.

"Hold it, hold *iiit!*" Everything counted now on precision timing. They needed to maintain their grip and tension just long enough to ensure it went under the bow evenly, but not hold on long enough that one of their people could get dragged out.

Both dinghies passed each side of the whaler, losing sight of each other behind the huge steel hull. Olander had one arm raised in the air, and Annabel waited, walkie-talkie pressed to her lips and eyes round with excitement. He suddenly waved it down.

"Drop, drop!" Annabel yelled.

The rope was released, and Olander hoped his opposite boat did the same. At the end of the rope there was a round, red buoy, just large enough to keep the end above water, ensuring a nice belly for the prop to run across. He spun, watching it, his teeth gritted in anticipation, until he saw the rope begin to get sucked down like a giant strand of spaghetti.

Just as they began to pass by the rear of the *Slava*, Olander heard the satisfying fluttering thump of fouled machinery, and knew they'd succeeded.

"Victory!" He fist pumped, turning to beam down at Annabel. The girl clasped her hands to her breast.

As the dinghy peeled away, he looked up to see figures leaning over the gunwale, gesticulating and yelling down at him. Strangely, it didn't sound like Russian, and some words could have been in English – *out of the water*, they seemed to yell, and then something that sounded like *megalomaniac*, or *dark* something. He gave them the finger.

Olander looked to the burnt orange glow on the horizon. The sun was fast going down, and they had perhaps thirty more minutes to accomplish their work, get it all on film, and then package and send it to the media.

He picked up his front rope again, and placed one leg on the bow, in his favorite Delaware pose. They sped out in front of the slowing boat to meet with their partner dinghy. Together they skidded in the water to face the crippled whaler.

Olander waved the exuberant whoops down for a moment, and once silence was returned, they could hear the *Slava*'s crew still yelling – abuse now, no doubt. He blanked it out until gunshots sounded.

He cringed. "*Fuck!* Those Russian assholes are firing at

us. Get down!" He flattened to the rubber floor and turned crablike. "Keep filming, keep filming."

His cameraman, also lying flat, lifted the lens above the inflated gunwale.

There were more gunshots – three in fast succession, and he saw Flying Bird-1 speed out to the left of them, heading momentarily into the setting sun. They obviously hoped to make it difficult for them to be seen, or move out of range. He should do the same.

Annabel was down low, but had field glasses to her eyes, and had the twin lenses perched gunwale.

"I think they're firing in the air."

Olander spun. "Bullshit." He turned to the cameraman. "Edit those last remarks out; Russians don't give warning shots."

He snatched the field glasses from her hand and after quickly refocusing for a few seconds; he saw she was probably right. Olander got to his knees. He lowered the glasses and whistled again, waving his second boat in closer.

They waved back, and did a huge loop in the water, beginning to speed back towards him.

"Will we paint them now?" Annabel asked.

He watched Flying Bird-1 come back in; the half disc of a huge setting sun silhouetted the small boat as it threw up a rooster tail of white spray behind it.

"I think..." Oleander's words froze in his mouth. Flying Bird-1 was rising in the air, a mountain of dark flesh coming up beneath it that was wider than the entire boat.

There were no screams, as most of the dinghy seemed to fall back into a massive hole that extended forward before a prison of jagged white bars closed over the small boat. The thing fell back into the water, creating a massive wave.

"What...?" Olander gulped, his brain feeling like it was short-circuiting from confusion.

There was little debris, except for a solitary figure, swimming furiously towards them.

"What just happened?" His brain was still locked.

"We need to pick them up," Annabel screamed.

Once again the huge lump rose in the water, coming up behind the single swimmer. This time a recognizable triangular shaped fin also lifted. Big. Bigger than anything Olander had ever witnessed in his life. Whether the figure saw or realized what was behind him, he never knew – *he hoped not*. In the next second, the lump surged, a massive maw opened, lined with huge jagged teeth, and then it crashed down on top of the poor soul. Just as quickly as it appeared, the behemoth submerged.

Olander stood in the bow, eyes wide and mouth hanging open. He looked down in time to see the huge shape surge past just below the clear water. The thing was momentarily turned sideways. Time seemed to slow as his brain fired into overdrive and adrenaline surged through him. He saw it all – the dead black eye as large as a dinner plate that he was sure was fixed upon him. A single arm, hanging only by the tattered red material of its sleeve, extended from the side of massive jaws now clamped shut, and a gray-black torpedo shaped body that seemed to go on forever.

He sunk to his knees; his legs wouldn't hold him upright anymore. "Fu... fu... fucking, get us out of *heeere!*"

The dinghy started up with a roar, and spun in the water, heading back to their mother ship. He suddenly realized what the *Slava* crew were yelling at them – not *dark*, but fucking *shark* – they had been trying to warn them.

All of Olander's teeth showed in a grimace that was like a frightened chimpanzee. It was miles to the *Gaia Warrior*, an impossible distance with this creature in the water.

Olander spun. "We'll never make it." He pointed. "To the *Slava*."

He fell back as the boat turned sharply. The *Slava* was only five hundred feet away – they could make that. He sat up, spinning one way then the next. It was going on full dark now, and there was only a half moon rising. The water was still glass-smooth, and there was nothing on the surface to break its glimmering sheen.

He waited, his stomach roiling. The moon made the water a sea of mercury, and he bit his lip as they cut through it. Maybe it had gone, eaten enough and dived deep. As if in answer to his question, the tip of a fin rose in the water, then more and more of it, until the nine-foot triangle of dark flesh resembled a small sail, cutting the water, keeping pace and not a thousand feet out from them.

"*Faster.*" His command was high and shrill, though he knew they were already travelling as fast as the dinghy could go.

"Where?" Was all he heard his pilot could yell to him.

Olander squinted, seeing the rope mesh strung at the sides of the boat. "To the nets."

They could make it. He turned, snatching a peek, and saw the monster shark had closed the gap and was coming impossibly fast. Now a wake had formed more than a dozen feet in front of it, as the ten-foot wide spade-shaped head was rising in the water, perhaps getting ready to lunge as it had with the Flying Bird-1, and take them the same way.

Olander felt a small whine escape his throat and hunched. Even though they skimmed across the flat-water at around thirty knots, the shark seemed to be toying with them, closing with little difficulty. He stepped a little closer to the bow, preparing to leap for the net the moment they were close enough.

"Easy, *eeeas-ssssy.*" He wouldn't look back at it, he couldn't.

The dinghy came in hard and fast, and though the pilot tried to swerve it in sideways, he still managed to come in at an angle of about sixty degrees, making the small craft hit and bounce.

"Abandon ship." Olander was already leaping, his fingers hooking like claws to the net. He struggled, a long life of good food created a sagging belly that made his climb difficult. Beside him bodies thumped and scrabbled, the more youthful and lithe going up the nets like Capuchin monkeys.

There was some splashing and yelling from behind and below, and it told him not everyone had made a successful leap. The dinghy, now free of people began to float away. Olander was ten feet up, and hearing his name yelled, chanced a look back.

Annabel was flailing in the water, and she spluttered and thrashed as she struggled to get her hands wrapped around the rope netting. Above, people yelled encouragement, and helped the others over the side.

"Hurry, hurry," he yelled back at her.

"I *caan't*..." Her voice was a long scream.

Olander turned away and continued to climb, just as the side of the boat clanged deeply, and was rocked as something struck it hard. Looking back, he saw the massive jaws of the beast scraping the ship where Annabel had been seconds before. He thought he saw her face screaming even under water, but knew it was probably only his imagination.

The monster shark pulled back, and with it started to go the netting that had snagged on its shovel-sized teeth.

Olander whimpered and climbed; the shaking net became impossible to hold onto as its angle moved outwards. He started to hear rope strands popping and separating, and to his horror saw that the tears were occurring above not below him.

He wailed as gunfire sounded just over his head. The shark momentarily released and then re-gripped the ropes a little higher, as if it was trying to climb after him. He scrambled up a few more of the rope squares, but actually felt he was lower towards the waterline than before, and he knew his boots must only be feet above that cavernous mouth.

Olander refused to look back, but he could smell something now – the deep sea, old and new meat, and a sense of ancient waters lost in some dark primordial time. He knew he was smelling the insides of thing as it opened its jaws trying to get to him.

Olander realized he was crying when he was finally pulled up and over the gunwale. The nets tore then, and as he fell to the deck, they were whipped away and below the now pitch dark water.

He stayed down. Fear had rolled him into a tight ball, shivering uncontrollably. Olander felt a soft hand on his shoulder, one of his crewmembers, and he swung an arm.

"Get away, you little prick."

It was not supposed to happen like this, and he quickly wiped his face with a soaking arm. He stood, and saw his crew staring at him, confused and frightned as hell.

He straightened, hating the monster, but hating them more for fucking up. He quickly wiped his eyes and face again, and then met their eyes. "I weep for our lost brothers and sisters. You should too."

Jack caught Cate as she slid to the deck. Her face was bleached of color and her eyes had momentarily rolled back. "It's okay, I've got you."

She moaned, and then sat forward. He rubbed her neck, and after another few seconds she nodded, but he still felt her shaking beneath his hands.

"So scared."

"Me too." He turned. "Get me some water, quick."

Regina rushed back with a plastic bottle, and knelt to look into her face as Cate drank. "She's in shock."

"I'm fine, I'm fine." She drank deeply, waving Sonya and Drago away.

Jack leant closer to her "We're okay, darling; it can't get us here."

"I thought I could handle seeing it again," Cate

whispered. She wiped her mouth and nose, but continued to stare at the deck.

Regina stood. "We're fucked," she yelled. Her jaw jutted as she stared at the remaining Earthpeace crewmembers that sat huddled together, hugging their knees or each other.

"Ease up, Ginny," Vincent said. "We're safe here. We can call in one of the long-range Coast Guard choppers and lift us all off. Then tow this big lug into harbor."

Mironov turned to click his fingers at Drago. "Get the whale carcass in. No use just feeding the Megalodon." He looked over the side. "Not while we're dead in the water."

"Thanks a fucking lot!" Regina yelled at the crew, then stormed to the railing.

Cate exhaled with a judder. "We just need to get out of here."

One of the dinghy crew got to his feet, and cleared his throat. "Excuse me, who's in charge here?"

Eyes turned towards the silver haired, bedraggled looking figure. He smoothed his soaking pullover.

"My name is Olander Blomgren, *Captain* Olander Blomgren, and it seems you have put us, and yourselves in danger. That whale you killed and dragged here has obviously attracted some sort of massive shark-like predator. I can't tell you of the trouble you'll be in when we get back home."

Mironov stood smiling with arms folded. He looked like he was enjoying the show.

"Piss off." Regina took a few steps towards him, but Vincent grabbed her and hauled her back to talk quietly with her.

Olander's teeth were grit, and he took several quick steps towards Vincent and grabbed his shoulder. "Do you have any idea—"

Vincent spun and took him by his collar, pulled him close for a moment so their noses almost touched, and then pushed him back hard. "Get away from me, asshole."

Olander was a big man, but he staggered back, now looking a little wild-eyed. He balled his fists, spluttering. "That's, that's assault. You're an American and I'll fucking sue you back to the Stone Age."

There was a small click, and Olander's mouth snapped shut.

Sonya had a small, dark pistol pointed dead center at the man's temple, her eyes calm and unblinking.

"*Sonya,*" Jack warned.

"Little man, you – *just you* – have stranded us. Just you with your stupid little protest. You have managed to get your own people killed, and now, *just you*, dare to make demands on our boat?" She stepped in closer; her gun now pressed to his skin. "Please tell me why I shouldn't have you put back over the side?"

Olander gulped, eyes darting. "I'm an American citizen, and you can't."

Jack helped Cate to her feet. "I'm okay," she said and swiveled her head on her neck for a few seconds. "Let him go, Sonya. He's guilty of being an asshole, that's all."

Sonya's eyes bored into Olander. She continued to hold the gun to his temple and didn't move a muscle.

Valery Mironov came and stood in front of Olander. "Dear sir, you're aboard *my* ship, and you're endangering *my* crew. I'm well within my rights to neutralize any threat to life or limb. And besides, you're now starting to annoy me. So listen, you overblown, stupid little man, sit down and shut up, so we can try and get us all out of here."

Valery Mironov glared, his eyes going from indifferent to suddenly blazing with animosity. It was the first time Cate had seen the man step out of his calm and congenial guise. He was terrifying.

Olander shrunk back, holding up his hands. "Okay, okay, no need to get heavy. Let me just radio my mother ship, and they can come and take us all off."

"We should just lock them up below deck. They've

vandalized private property." Regina folded her arms, and stuck her chin out. "And here's the news, we weren't even fucking hunting whales, you pack of assholes."

"I just want him off the ship. But he also needs to tell his people to stay clear for now, as I doubt they're in the type of armored tank we are." Sonya reholstered her gun. "But, we're here, the Megalodon is here, and we need to take the shot."

Jack looked at the signal tracker. "It's still right below us, circling." He raised his eyebrows. "Sonya's right; we might not get another chance."

"Then let's do what we came for," Cate said.

Regina ran a hand up through her short, damp hair. "Gonna be tough without maneuverability; we're dead in the water."

"Looks like no more whale hunts for this death ship." Olander turned to smile confidently at his crew who seemed to perk up at the news.

Jack put his hands to his head. "You *idiot*. That thing we were hunting will kill more whales than this boat ever could. It's killed people, other sharks and I can't imagine how much other marine life."

"That's nature's way," one of Olander's crewmembers added.

"Not anymore," Cate fired back. "It might have been nature's way a few millions years back, but this thing does not belong here, in these waters, in this time. End of story."

"You shouldn't be in these waters either." Olander narrowed his eyes.

"*Uh*, maybe they've got a point, skipper." Another of Olander's crewmembers still hugged himself tight. "We're a little over our heads on this one. Let's just call it a day; get the fuck out of here."

"Annabel is dead." Olander shot back. "Because *they* are here, *it* is here. And because *it* is here, our sisters and brothers are now dead."

"Wrong, it's attracted by sound and movement, buddy. And you gave it plenty." Jack's jaw jutted.

Olander kept facing his crew. "You drew it here to kill it, because it's the only thing you know how to do. And now good people are dead. The world needs to know what you're all doing." He held out an arm back towards Jack and Cate. "These are the ones who are over their heads. You all know the only thing that will really keep us, and the ocean's life safe, is the eyes and ears of the world. And they'll be here soon."

"Oh for god's sake." Cate threw her hands up.

Sonya growled, and Mironov went and placed a hand on her shoulder. "Best we get him out of our sight. But first make sure he warns his people away. I don't want anymore lambs slaughtered today."

"Yes, let me speak to them." Olander nostrils flared.

Drago walked him up to the bridge room, followed by Cate, Jack, Sonya and Valery Mironov. They quickly found Olander's correct frequency, and handed him the microphone. He cleared his throat.

Cate leaned towards him. "Just tell them to wait where they are until the Coast Guard gets here. Or better yet, retreat to an even safer distance."

Mironov watched the man with narrowed eyes, one corner of his mouth turned up.

Olander's lips twisted into a sneer. "You really have no idea who we are, do you?" He pressed the open button on the hand set. "Captain Olander to the *Gaia Warrior*, over."

"Captain! Welcome back – what happened – both dinghies went off the screen. We thought the Russians had sunk you."

He smiled thinly. "In a roundabout way they did. They seem to have attracted an oversized ocean predator to themselves, using the corpse of a murdered cetacean." He sucked in a deep breath. "And our sister, Annabel, is dead."

Cate screwed her eyes shut and pressed a hand to her forehead.

"Those fucking bastards," came the seething response over the line.

"Yes, they are." Olander turned to Cate and Sonya, his eyes flat. "But there will be justice." Olander turned his back. "Take no calls from anyone, but me. Please proceed to our position at maximum speed. I want off this floating pirate ship now."

Jack lunged. "You idiot!"

Olander signed off and tossed the mic in the air.

Drago caught it, and stood with it clasped in his huge fist, looking like he was going to crush it.

"Get him out of here." Sonya's yell bounced around the small room, and Drago grabbed Olander's collar and jerked him off his feet.

Mironov smiled from under lowered brows. "So foolish, and so predictable. Take him out."

Olander held his hands up over his head, batting at the Russian, but Drago just dragged him to his feet, and pushed him towards the lower deck door. "Come on; you and your crew get to sit this one out."

They followed him down to the deck, and Olander's crew got to their feet. Some stood pale and docile, while others began cursing and throwing threats, but none dared to actually intervene. Drago and a few of his crewmembers rounded them up, and led them to rooms below. Vincent watched them go for a moment more.

"Guy's an asshole, but the law might be on his side. If we detain him, there'll be repercussions."

"Happy to help push him and his hipster crew over the side," Regina said.

"We rescued him and his friends. We aren't detaining him, but are concerned by his erratic behavior." Mironov's smile was without humor. "And I have a legal team that'll tear him to shreds if he wants to go anywhere near a courtroom." He turned away to walk to one of the windows. "So, here we are." He spun back to Jack. "Do we try and take this thing down, or do we baton down the hatches and wait until we are rescued... by Olander's crew."

Drago reappeared in another minute, and nodded to Mironov. He opened his mouth, but before he could say a word, the massive collision threw them all to the bridge room floor.

Only Vincent remained on his feet, his experienced sea legs braced. "Jesus Christ. Was that what I think it was?"

Jack leapt to his feet and rushed to the railing. "Drago, get the spot lights on." He gripped the gunwale railing and leaned over.

Down at the waterline, he saw that one of the thick plates was dented, and worse, a join in the panels was showing.

"Ah, shit. The damned thing torpedoed us."

Cate came and leaned out, just as the spotlights came on. The second collision hammered the *Slava* from further down the side of the ship, and it turned the large craft in the water. Jack had to grab at Cate to stop her going over the side.

Jack lifted her back to her feet. "We've got a problem."

"Can it smell the whale carcass?" Cate asked.

"Maybe, but I don't think that's it. The Megalodon is like the Great White in that it's highly territorial – this patch is its own. It simply thinks its defending it against a bigger adversary."

"This whaling ship is nearly as armor plated as a frigate. It'll end up knocking itself out – might be our opportunity to put an exploding harpoon into it after all." Vincent clapped and then rubbed his hands together.

"Knock itself out?" Jack shook his head. "Unlikely; these guys have a head that's all cartilage and muscle mass. In humans, we're about forty per cent muscle; but in sharks it's typically eighty-five per cent. It's a living torpedo, with its own armor plating." He looked over the side as another titanic blow came from directly below them, lifting them in the water.

"Committed," was all Valery Mironov said, as he looked from one of the windows.

"It's denting the plates. If it hits twice in the same area, we might get a breach."

"*Ah*, Jesus Christ." Vincent threw his hands up, and looked skyward. "Can we get a break here?"

Cate looked panicked. "That's it; we're outta here." She spun to Sonya and then Jack. "Sorry, but this is over. If this thing starts to sink, I am not going in that water. We need to be off, now."

Jack grabbed her and hugged her in close to his chest. He looked over her head to Vincent. "Get that chopper in Vince – *fast*. Let's at least get some of us back on dry land."

"Yes, now might be a good time for a mayday." Mironov turned back to them.

"Yep." Vincent raced up the steps to the bridge.

Jack held Cate back a step. "You okay?"

She nodded and paced away, her arms wrapped around herself.

Jack watched her for a moment and then he, Sonya and Mironov went and looked over the side. Even though the lights only seemed to reflect the black water below, they were actually seeing down quite a few fathoms. The huge torpedo shape glided underneath them, barely moving its body at all.

"Shit," Jack whispered. It was even bigger than he remembered. He knew sharks, and he knew their territorial instincts meant it would never give up until the *Slava* was gone, or laying on the sea bottom.

It finished its pass, having rolled in the water slightly, and he had seen the absence of claspers underneath the torso – female then. But there was something else in its shape that worried him.

"*Can't be*," he whispered. Jack exhaled and leant back. He still remembered Greg Jamison, and he damn well wasn't going to allow Cate or himself to end up the same way. At the very periphery of the spotlight's illumination he saw a huge lump rise from the water, to hang there, motionless.

"Can you see that?" Jack asked, feeling his heart race in his chest. He'd spent his entire life dealing with sharks of all shapes and sizes, but at that moment, he knew fear – the Megalodon shark was looking at them – it had lifted its head from the water, and those soulless black orbs were fixed on the people, not the boat.

"Oh yes," Mironov responded softly. "I think it's counting us."

"*Shit*," Sonya breathed.

Vincent jogged back towards them, and Cate followed. "Good and bad news; they'll get a chopper up ASAP – that's the good news. Bad news is we're fifty miles out, and that again from the nearest base." He winced. "It'll take them at least three hours even if they hustle." He hiked his shoulders. "I've given them our location; that's all we can do."

"We just wait?" Cate snorted softly. "Well then, I guess we need Olander's boat after all."

Jack sighed. "Better get Captain Nemo back up here. He can at least tell his people to be on guard."

CHAPTER 39

On the southern horizon, a ball of rainbow light was appearing. Olander folded his arms and widened his stance. He smiled and nodded to his shipmates who whooped and glared at the crew of the *Slava*.

Olander turned to tilt his head towards Cate and Jack. "By the time you're next allowed out on the water, you'll all be in wheelchairs."

A young bearded man stuck up a finger. "Planet rapists."

"Oh, for fuck's sake." Regina walked away muttering.

Jack looked from the approaching trimaran to Olander. "Do your people have any weapons? Anything at all?"

"Weapons?" Olander's lip curled in derision. "The *Gaia Warrior* is the fastest, cleanest thing on the water, and represents a near invisible silhouette to the environment." He pointed down at the stained deck of the Slava. "This thing is like a brass band falling down a flight of steps... where my boat is a violin in a garden."

Jack grimaced as he watched the locater. "The Megalodon is leaving us." He looked up. "Heading your people's way – you have to warn them. How many are onboard?"

"*Uh.*" Olander's brow creased. "A dozen, *no*, eleven now."

Valery Mironov lowered his field glasses and handed them to Sonya. "The poor fools." His eyes slid to Olander. "They have no idea of what you have just invited them into."

"*Think* man, do they have any weapons, or anything to defend the ship with?" Regina yelled now.

Panic edged into Olander eyes as he searched the deck. He put a knuckle in his mouth and chewed on it as he moved away.

"Well?" Jack asked, reaching out to stop his pacing.

"Boat hooks." Olander stood a little straighter. "Why would we need anything else? We have moral justice on our side."

"God help them then," Jack said. He looked back down at the tracker. "It's moving fast – intercept course." He looked up slowly. "They can't outrun it. But *you* can damn well get on the radio and warn them, you sonofabitch."

"I, *ah*, well I suppose I can tell them to ensure they have all loose objects secured." He licked his lips. "It's a triple-hull design, based on an ellipse – strongest structure in nature, you know."

Drago jammed the portable receiver into the front of his chest. Olander cleared his throat again. Behind him, his small group of youthful crewmembers now looked a little subdued.

He clicked open the mic. "Captain Olander to the *Gaia Warrior*, over." He held the microphone away for a moment, listening. "Olander to the *Gaia Warrior*, over."

"Hiya, captain; we have you in sight. But we also have something else on the sonar. Has the *Slava* sent out a boat or something to meet us? Coming at us real quick – thirty knots."

"I, *ah*, have a change of plans for you. I want you to engage the engines, and head back into the shore for a bit. Seems this large shark is a little more aggressive and dangerous than first thought. Made more so by the *Slava's* crew no doubt, but..."

"You idiot." Jack snatched the microphone from his hand. "This is Jack Monroe, marine biologist, who am I talking to?"

"Who is this? Where's Olander?" the voice was heavy with confusion.

"This is urgent. Turn your ship around and head in now. There is a massive marine predator headed your way." Jack clicked off waiting for a response.

"Too late," Sonya said, holding the huge field glasses to her eyes. "It's there." She handed the glasses to Jack, glared at Olander for a moment, and then headed back up to the bridge.

Jack pressed the glasses to his eyes and walked to the railing. He could see the fairy-lit boat clearly. It was a magnificent looking trimaran, and he could make out tiny figures on the deck, probably all waiting to catch sight of their heroic captain, or maybe rain abuse down on the *Slava*. But then he saw what Sonya had – the monstrous fin circling them for a few seconds before submerging.

"*Jesus*." He leant forward.

Suddenly, the *Gaia Warrior* looked like it had struck a reef as the ship's three hulls lifted in the air. The larger center hull had something that looked like a giant fist wrapped around the front of it, and when it pulled away, it took a large portion of the ship with it.

Jack wondered what the boat was made of, as it seemed thin and brittle, and was probably feather-light on the water. *So much for Olander's expensive high-tech ellipse design.* It might have been able to withstand the pounding of huge swells, but it was just matchsticks against something with a jaw compression force of over forty thousand pounds.

The beautiful boat rapidly filled with water, and immediately sat lower on the surface. Jack was riveted as he saw people now running madly over the deck. At the rear of the trimaran, he could just make out small helicopter blades beginning to turn. He spoke from the side of his mouth.

"They've got a chopper – it's taking off."

"That'll be Milo," one of Olander's crew said, as he squinted into the dark. "What's happening over there?"

Jack jammed the glasses back to his eyes. The Megalodon rose from the water again, this time it came up on the stern, as if trying to attack the small helicopter before it could get away. It attacked anything it could get in its mouth. It seemed to be working itself into frenzy, and Jack saw the recognizable shaking as it sawed through the wood and synthetic materials. Once this was pulled away, the ship was sitting right down at the water line. The tiny helicopter buzzed away, and Jack could swear he saw a figure hanging onto to one of the landing struts for a few dozen feet, before falling back to the water.

Small boats were being pushed out as the Megalodon shark surged fully up onto the deck; its massive tail flicking as it pursued the running bodies. The few remaining people not in small rafts, leapt into the water. The shark then followed.

Jack saw the recognizable surface feeding patterns – the head thrashing, the circling, the surge waves, as it took the swimmers first, and then found the crowded rafts. He thanked god he couldn't hear the sounds of their screams.

The magnificent boat began to fall below the surface. He finally lowered the glasses then.

"What… happened?" Olander's eyes were round and confused.

"What do you think happened?" Regina grabbed at his shoulder. "Your boat, your people… they're all gone."

"They just got what *you* deserved." Mironov's mouth was turned down in disgust.

"We have rafts. What about survivors?" Olander asked.

Jack rubbed the back of his neck, before looking up at the man. "If there are any in the water, then they won't be alive for long. And even if they were, we couldn't get to them anyway – you've seen to that."

The sound of a helicopter could be heard buzzing overhead. "Clear the deck; he's going to try and put it down," shouted Vincent.

Regina pushed people back and then dragged some rope coils out of the way. "Gonna be tight."

"Nowhere else," Jack shouted above the din. "We're fifty miles from shore, so it's here or ditch it in the sea." And he knew that would be the end for the pilot.

People scrambled now, trying to clear enough room for the helicopter to land. "Heads up." Vincent dragged a few more of the *Gaia Warrior* crew out of the way. The small helicopter only needed a small pad, but the rotors were going to find it difficult to come down without striking the gunwale, bridge deck or bow cannon. If it struck anything at all, the rotor blades would most likely shatter, sending high-velocity shards all over the deck

"Hope they know how to fly." Regina took cover.

The brilliant-yellow Hughes 500 chopper circled once, and then stopped to hover over the flattest portion of the deck. The only one to stay standing at his post was Alexi, holding a flashlight and waving it over his deck mounted harpoon cannon. He was determined to keep the chopper as far from his gun as he could.

The chopper came down hard, as if the pilot was in a hurry and cut the power from six feet. It skidded for a moment, bounced towards one of the railings, and then gravity took over, holding it in place as the rotors rapidly slowed. Only one man leapt out.

"Hey, Milo." Jupiter stood away from the group and waved at him. "I knew it'd be you!"

"Did you see that?" The youth put his hands to his head. "It was a fucking monster, man."

Olander was first out to him. "Was there anyone else? You had a spare seat on board."

Milo shrugged. "No one else wanted to come, Captain." He shook his head. "We all thought it was a whale at first, so…"

"Big mistake, bro. It ate Annabel too," Jupiter said.

Milo opened his arms. "But I made it."

"Yeah, you made it, straight from the frying pan into our fire," Regina growled.

Jupiter hunched. "Yeah man, we kinda fouled the prop, and we're stuck here. We really fucked everything up this time."

"Guess you did your job a little too well, huh?" Milo snorted and then turned to give Sonya an apprising once over. "Never thought I'd be saved by a whaler."

"Saved?" Sonya's eyes bored into him. "You put us in this mess, and one way or another, you're going to get us out."

CHAPTER 40

The next impact made Jack's teeth clack together. This time, it was followed by a slightly different sound from deep in the bowels of the ship. Somewhere else, an alarm went off.

"Look's like our friend is back," Regina said, gripping a railing.

"What's that alarm?" Cate's hands tightened into fists.

Vincent spun to race up the stairs to the bridge. "Not sure, but I'd hazard a guess and say we just sprung a leak somewhere." He called to Drago and together they armed themselves with large flashlights and headed below decks.

Cate looked down at her feet for a moment. She laughed with little humor in it. "We're not going to make three hours, are we?" She looked up unto Jack's eyes.

He smiled, trying to radiate calm and confidence. "Of course we will. You just wait and see. This old hulk will stay afloat for many hours yet. And don't worry, when the Coast Guard chopper gets here, I'll make sure you're first out."

"Not without you." She hugged him tight.

"I'll be there." He lifted her chin.

She looked up into his face. "Jack, but then what? We just leave this thing in the waters?"

He shook his head. "We can't do that. Based on fossil records, this one looks to be a good-sized animal. But it could potentially grow much larger."

She smiled weakly. "Well, I guess that'll make it easier to spot then. Thank god there's only one them."

Jack let her go and turned slightly. Cate must have seen something in his face, because she grabbed at him, turning him around. "What? *What is it?*"

He grimaced. "There's only one way to tell a female from a male Carcharodon, and that's on their underside. This one had no male claspers. When it passed underneath us, I saw it just... it just looked to have a very round shape. I think it's a pregnant female."

"Oh, Jesus Christ." Cate put a hand to her head.

"So we could end up with two of these things in a few months," Regina said, overhearing.

Cate straightened. "To start with." She turned to Regina. "Sharks are able to mate with their offspring. If it has a male pup, within a few years, they'll be a breeding pair. They dominated the global seas for twenty million years. If they return, it'll finish shipping worldwide for anything other than a supertanker."

Mironov turned to Sonya. "Take a note, my dear; must invest in international airlines when we return."

Sonya grinned.

"That's a big help, Valery." Cate glared.

He shrugged. "A little graveyard humor, Cate."

"Bottom line, we still need to kill it, somehow, some way," Jack said. "Just maybe not this day."

The boat took another hit. Cate fell backwards and Jack went to his knees. When he scrambled back to his feet, he skidded sideways a few inches. "*Shit*, we're tilting."

The hold's door banged open, and Vincent jogged towards them, while Drago headed for Sonya and Mironov. "I don't need to tell you this, but were taking in water. The *Slava*'s pumps are working at capacity, but they're old..." Vincent wiped his slick face, and took a few steps towards the railing. The Coast Guard officer stared out over the black water for a few seconds before drawing in a deep breath. He spoke without turning. "I think we've got about an hour. And that's only if we don't split any more plates."

Drago was covered in perspiration as he talked animatedly to Mironov and Sonya. The woman looked like she wanted to murder something or someone. The big Russian pointed, and Valery Mironov threw his head back to laugh. They came and joined the group.

"It seems there's only inflatable dinghies – two of them – just enough, *hmm*?" Mironov half smiled. "Lucky for us, they each have oars."

Regina started to laugh cruelly. "That's a fucking death sentence."

Jack shook his head. "We're not there yet." He kissed Cate's forehead. "Check on the Coast Guard chopper; see how far out they are."

She nodded and headed up to the Bridge, taking Regina with her. Mironov looked out over the dark surface as the *Slava* settled another inch into the water. He turned to Sonya and Drago. "We best speak to our crew. When the time comes, we'll all need to move quickly."

Vincent watched them go for a moment and then came and stood in front of Jack, legs planted. "So, I'm guessing this is how every shark specialist in the world wants to end it."

Jack grinned. "Not in a million years, my friend." His smile fell away, and he held Vincent's gaze. "Vince, we need to move this clunker closer to the oncoming chopper if we're going to have any chance of surviving. That means, the propeller needs to be untangled."

Vincent stared, waiting. Jack held his gaze. "Whalers always have diving gear; it's standard kit."

Vincent's mouth slowly dropped open, and then he began to laugh. "That, sir, is a gold-plated suicide mission for anyone that goes over the side."

"Maybe a fifty per cent chance of survival, but that's better than what we have right now," Jack said. "I'm going to risk it."

Vincent shook his head. "More like a ten per cent

chance… *for you*." He started to grin. "Look, I can ask Sonya or Drago to shoot you right now if you're in a hurry to get yourself killed."

"Vince, when the boat's deck drops low enough, it'll surge right up onto us, just like it did to Olander's boat. The alternatives are to go below deck in a sinking ship, and hope an air pocket will sustain us. Or we take to the life rafts." Jack's mouth turned down. "We might as well swim for it." He smiled, trying to look more confident than he felt. "And by the way, I don't intend to die today."

"But you will die, Jack. Then we *all* will." Vincent was slightly smaller than Jack, but he seemed to be made of something more durable than flesh and blood. He gripped Jack's forearm in a vice-like grip. "You're a good diver, Jack, but do you know how to work equipment under the water?"

Jack hadn't thought about it, and stood thinking for a moment. He shook his head.

"I didn't think so. You'd waste your life. All you would achieve would be to give that big bastard below us a heads up, and make it impossible for us to try it again… after you've been torn to shreds or eaten whole. How would Cate feel about that?" Vincent walked to the edge of the boat, and looked over the side. Jack joined him, and together they saw at the far periphery of their lights, the huge fin cutting the water.

Vincent snorted. "Yeah, sure, the propeller shaft needs to be defouled." He looked at his friend. "But not by you."

"I can't let you do that," Jack said. "Besides it was my idea."

"Fight you for it?" Vincent grinned.

Regina quick walked in between them. "Make Drago do it."

Olander and his crew started to talk loudly on deck, and Regina turned towards them. "Better yet; make that fat asshole do it. Or at least use him as a diversion – send him out on one of the rafts."

Jack and Vincent laughed grimly, but Regina's face remained clouded – he guessed she meant it. Cate and Sonya joined them, and Olander seeing them all grouped, also barged in.

He folded thick arms. "I have some very scared people here. We need to get them off, and into special care, fast."

"Funny, we were just talking about options to get you off this boat, *fast*." Vincent eyeballed the Earthpeace captain. "Listen up, captain to captain; if *we* survive, then maybe *you* survive. So do us a favor, and stay out of our way."

"Fuck you for putting us all in danger," Olander stormed off.

Jack watched him go for a moment. "We need to talk, make a decision, right now… *all* of us." He pulled in a cheek. "Yeah, even him."

In the bridge room, Cate, Jack, Vincent, Regina, Valery Mironov and Sonya formed a ring in front. Behind them to one side, were Drago and Alexi, and loitering at the rear was Olander and his youthful crewmembers.

Drago's other men were below deck trying to work miracles with the pumps. All of them tried hard to ignore the obvious tilting deck and the occasional thump of the behemoth battering them from below.

Inside the room, the quiet murmurs were broken by a sharp metallic clanging sound.

"Sorry, sorry," Jupiter picked up an old-style alarm clock he had knocked to the ground. It was large, and one of the type that had two copper bells on top and a small hammer in-between. "My bad." He waved it around, his other hand also held up in surrender.

They turned back to the map table, where Jack had spread a schematic of the *Slava* out in front of them. He stood with his hands on his hips, looking down at the bow.

The alarm clock went off, ringing loudly, and making the entire room of already tense people jump.

"*Shut that fucking thing off,*" Jack yelled.

A red-faced Jupiter carefully set the clock back on the shelf. "Oops."

"You asshole." His pilot friend, Milo, smacked the back of his head.

Cate sighed. "The vibrations alone will attract the Megalodon... not that I think it needs any more incentive."

Jack glared again at the young bearded man, before turning back to the schematics. "Let me say at the outset, there are no easy options left." He looked up at each of them. "The Coast Guard chopper is still around two hours out. Olander's boat is gone, and their tiny helicopter only seats two. Plus it doesn't have the fuel to get even half way to shore." He exhaled slowly through his nose, staring down at the table for a moment longer. "We have two small dinghies... that will be the final option for when, not if, the *Slava* sinks to waterline level."

"We'll sink? *Really* sink?" Jupiter straightened.

"Bullshit." Milo shook his head, one corner of his mouth lifting. "I know for a fact that even whalers like this old clunker can use their empty barrels for extra buoyancy. Don't worry, this thing aint sinking anytime soon."

"What barrels?" Vincent raised silver eyebrows. "Didn't need those, as we're not whaling."

"There're no barrels, no second chances. Understand now?" Jack paused and noticed no one met his eyes, bar Vincent – only the tough Coast Guard officer returned his gaze. The man nodded to him. Jack went on.

"We need to be out of here. We need to at least head towards the approaching Coast Guard chopper to try and shorten the distance. The boat will still sink, but at least it'll be sinking while we're being lifted off." He folded his arms. "So, we need to try and defoul the propeller... from below."

"Yeah, right," Jupiter gave them a bitter laugh, but his face was ashen. "Good luck untangling that elasto-fiber material. You'd need to pull this hunk-a-junk up into dry-dock."

Regina spun, launching a straight right that caught him flush on the chin. He dropped like a sack. Vincent pulled her back, but she pointed down at him. "I vote this sack of shit to be last off."

Jupiter held up his hands. "Just stating the facts, Eva Braun."

"Son, just keep your mouth shut... or I'll let her finish you off." Vincent 's eyes blazed with cold fury and Jupiter quickly made a mouth zipping gesture.

Vincent turned back to the table. "I'm going into the water."

Regina made a small sound in her throat and turned away. Vincent followed her with his eyes. "Unfortunately, it's the only option that might work."

She turned back, and he looked apologetic. "Please don't think for a minute I want to do this. But if we don't, we'll all end up like..." He wouldn't or couldn't finish.

"It's a bad plan," Mironov said, lifting his head. He met Regina's eyes. "But it's the only plan we have."

There was silence for several moments, before Jack sighed, breaking it. "We'll have Alexi manning the harpoon cannon. But we'll also need a diversion." He turned to Olander. "And that, mister, is where you can help. Your pilot will use his helicopter to drag the whale corpse we have in the hold. Hopefully, it'll lure the Megalodon shark away long enough for Vincent to untangle the ropes."

Milo snorted. "No fucking way."

Vincent stared from under lowered brows. Everyone turned to the young pilot.

He licked his lips. "*Um*, I, I'm not dragging any whale corpse." His words came out in a rush. "I'm not desecrating the dead."

"Listen, I know you're scared..." Vincent growled. "... but if you *don't* drag that whale, then the next dead things you see being dragged will be your friends right there, by the shark." Vincent pointed gun-like to the huddled youths behind him. He turned to Olander. "Talk to him."

Olander shook his head slowly. "We can't make him do anything he's opposed to."

"Oh, good grief." Cate placed her hands to her head. "This is an insane asylum."

Olander turned momentarily to look at the faces of his crewmembers. He eased back, smiling sadly. "Sorry, but actually, we don't condone murdering this animal." He ignored the widening eyes of his crew. "Maybe if your man just tries to scare it off, we can agree to all work together."

Jack chuckled. "Yeah, scare it off." He looked to Alexi, who grinned. "Just scare it off, right?"

Alexi saluted and winked.

"You may mock, but when this is all over and the eyes of public opinion are upon us, then you'll be sorry." Olander folded his arms.

Sonya whispered something to Drago, who nodded, and edged quietly around behind the group. He pulled Milo aside, and spoke into his ear, holding him by the arm so tight; the skin bunched either side of his huge fist. Drago motioned to the water, and the color drained from the young man's face. He gulped and nodded, his head jerking rapidly. The huge Russian let him go, but remained at his shoulder.

"I've had a rethink – I should at least try," Milo said. He licked his lips, looking from Jupiter to Olander. "I mean, for Annabel, right?"

"Good man," Jack said. "Any questions?" He waited for only a few seconds. "Then let's do this."

CHAPTER 41

Vincent stood on deck, tugging into place an oversized and old-fashioned rubber wetsuit. Even though the water here was around seventy degrees, he even pulled on a hood, boots and gloves. Swim fins lay beside him, ready.

Cate and Jack dipped their hands into a bucket filled with thick viscous oil and smeared it all over his suit.

"Jesus, that stuff is making my eyes water." He turned away as Jack layered some over his head and neck. "It stinks."

"Sure does, but not of human being," Cate said, smearing more on his cheeks. "This should mask your scent. Even though the whale carcass Milo will be dragging away should overpower anything else for miles, let's take no chances."

"No argument here," he said. Vincent turned, arms out to a sullen looking Regina. "Hug for luck?"

Her eyes narrowed. "If you survive this, I'm still gonna kill you." She turned and stormed away.

Cate gave him a crooked smile. "She'll get over it. And you *are* mad, but... thank you." She leaned forward to kiss him.

They walked him to the stern, and stopped at the gunwale. New netting had been lowered, creating another rope ladder to the water line that was now only a dozen feet from the surface.

"Not far to the water, that's the good news..." Jack said. "...and also the bad news. It means the propeller is now an extra ten feet down. And you don't have air tanks."

"I know." Vince went to spit inside his facemask, but just a little sticky foam came out of his mouth. He still rubbed it onto the glass. "I can swim a lap of an Olympic pool underwater." He swallowed dryly, and patted a makeshift toolkit around his waist that held two sharp knives, wire snips and iron bolt cutters. "If it can be cut, then I'll damn well cut it."

He looked over the side into the dark water. Cate knew the man was nervous, and at that moment, realized how glad she was that Jack wasn't attempting it.

Vincent turned back. "Jack, just... just try and keep that freaking big thing away from me, okay?" He sucked in a deep breath and then swung a leg over the rail. He paused for a moment to give a small mirthless laugh. "For some reason, I feel cold all over."

Above them the small yellow chopper rose, and went to the rear of the ship. The down-lights made it impossible to see much of its shape as it edged closer to the open back of the whaler. Some of Drago's men leaned out to grab the trailing cable, and quickly attached it to the Minke whale's tail, and then gave a thumb's up. The chopper moved backwards and the stinking whale slid free.

The small chopper wasn't powerful enough to lift the twenty-foot whale above the water, and all the chopper could hope to do was drag it. It swung away, and Cate saw Jack quickly check the signal tracker for a few moments. He began to nod and then grin. "It's working – the Megalodon is following."

"The whale or the chopper's vibrations?" Cate asked.

"Does it matter?" Vincent asked.

"No." Jack straightened, and looked into his friend's eyes.

Vincent reached out to shake his and then Cate's hands. "Well guys, I'm on the clock." With one hand holding his swim fins, he climbed quickly down the rope netting.

Jack walked back a few paces, his head bent over the tracker. "It's still heading away."

"Hey, what the hell are you doing here?" Cate felt a shock go through her body. She quick marched towards Milo, who was edging along the deck.

"*She made me.*" Milo threw his hands up as Cate grabbed his collar, and led him out of the shadows.

Jack's brows knitted. "Then who…"

Milo shrugged out of Cate's grip. "She said if I fucked up, she'd kill me. So I said, you do it… and she said fine." He saw the look on Jack's face, and he opened his arms wide. "She's a fucking navy pilot or something, man."

Jack smacked his forehead. "Regina, you fool." He began to run to the bridge room.

"No," Cate yelled.

Jack pulled up. "We've got to get her back."

Cate slumped. "We can't. She'd drag the whale back towards us. Not that she'd listen anyway."

Jack threw his head back. "Shit!"

Cate walked to the railing, and looked down into the oil-black water. "Let's just hope that by the time Vince finishes, she can ditch the whale, and head back."

Jack looked back down at the tracker. "Then the best we can do is stay in touch; let her know what were seeing. C'mon."

CHAPTER 42

Y ou can do it, baby." Regina urged the small Hughes 500 helicopter to give her every ounce of lift it could squeeze from its compact Allison turboshaft. She had let out all the cable available, but was still only thirty feet above the dark water surface. It was pushing the craft to its limits, as the whale, coupled with the drag from the water, was a monstrously heavy combination.

Regina was glad she had forced the huge Drago from the cockpit before taking off. With his added weight, she was sure they'd be belly-dragging the whole way. She looked out of the cockpit, and shivered. The water was so dark, and except for a strip of moonlight on its surface it was an impenetrable and foreboding place. She had no idea where the monster was. That's what she thought of it as now – *a monster* – what else could it be, but something from some fuck's twisted nightmare.

The radio blinked in front of her, and she snatched up the handset, thankful for the chance of speaking to another person. "Regina here, over."

"Regina, you mad crazy bitch," Cate said.

"Nice to hear your voice too, Cate." She grinned around the mic. "And hey, if Jack went over the side, what would you do?"

There was silence for a moment, and then Jack came on the air. "She'd be down there too, handing me the tools under the water, that's what."

"That's what I thought, Jack." She laughed then.

"Regina, you're doing a great job. You've got the Megalodon well away from us... from Vincent. But be aware, it's tracking you, about a hundred and fifty feet back, and probably that again below the surface.

"Good; long as its eyes are on me, then they aren't on you guys." She swallowed dryly.

"Okay, but be ready to drop the cable when we say. You're out there to lure it away not do a spot of night fishing."

Regina smiled. "Now wouldn't that get me few hits on YouTube? A chick in a helicopter flying home with a sixty-five-foot shark hanging off a line." She briefly looked down at her controls, seeing the winch button release. "And don't worry, my finger is ready to go."

"How's the fuel?" Jack asked.

She tapped a dial and grimaced. "Not great, but enough to keep me in the air, lugging this big bag of meat for another fifteen minutes, easy – longer, once I drop it."

"That's good. Hopefully fifteen is more than we need." Jack exhaled. "Okay Regina, good luck, over and—"

"Wait, wait. *Uh*, can you guys stay on the line? Let me know what that thing is doing?" Regina licked her lips. For some reason, just hearing their voices made her feel a little safer.

"You got it, babe," said Cate. "We're right here for you, and not going anywhere."

Minutes ticked by, and Regina grimaced as she looked out of the bubble-shaped cockpit window. There was nothing but an oil-flat dark ocean below her. She turned back and forth, looking over her shoulder – the cable stretched away behind and below, ending at the whale's fluke.

"Jesus." The radio crackling to life made her jump and whip her head back around.

"Regina, don't want to worry you, but its closing on your position. Can you pump the gas a little?" Jack's voice was calm, but she sensed a new the note of urgency.

Regina looked down at the controls – she was at maximum power now – the small chopper had no more to give.

"No can do, Jack. I'm giving this baby a whoopin' as it is." She looked back over her shoulder again, feeling her stomach do a little flip, and the hair prickle all over her scalp.

"*Ah*, guys, I can't see a thing down there." Looking up, she saw the *Slava* was now just a dot of light on the horizon – it made her feel a long way from home. "Jack, how's my Vince doing with the prop?"

There was silence and then muffled speaking for a while as a she assumed he and Cate conferred. Jack came back on, calm as ever.

"Still working on it, but we think he's getting there. Guess he wants another few minutes – can you stretch it for another five?"

She looked down at her fuel gauge. She still had a few gallons left, and knew once she let the whale go, the loss of weight meant she'd make it back to the *Slava* with gas to spare. She swallowed dryly – the problem was, it wasn't the fuel that she felt leaking away, it was her nerve.

"*Um*, yeah sure… I guess I can do that."

Regina kept the throttle pushed forward, hard, but there was nothing extra to give. Her mouth half twitched into a smile. She'd just do the equivalent of counting sheep, she told herself. After all, five minutes is only three hundred seconds, so: two hundred and ninety – breathe, two-eighty-five – breathe, two-eighty…

Regina's eyes stung as drops of perspiration ran from her forehead into her eyes. She reached up a forearm to rub it across her face, when the tiny yellow helicopter suddenly jerked to a stop in the air. Regina was strapped in, but was still thrown painfully forward. The whiplash effect, catapulted her at the bubble-window and then back into her seat like she was on elastic. She would have been paste on the cockpit glass if not for her seatbelt.

In a matter of seconds she had gone from being in the air, to being smashed into the water. She was groggy, but if she thought it was over, she was immediately reminded her nightmare had only just begun. Regina felt the chopper begin to be dragged backwards, and then under.

The sudden rush of water jolted her back to full consciousness. The monster had come up and taken the fucking whale, she knew, as she went deeper.

Everything went dark, but she was an experienced pilot, and a Coast Guard expert. She'd trained for water ditching, and worked to stay calm, work through the motions – unbuckle the belt, grab any survival kit, and find the exit. And then, importantly, get to the damned surface.

She was under now, and the pressure at her ears told her she was heading into deep water. She couldn't help it; panic started to set in. No matter how much she had trained, no one had ever prepared her for being in the water with a Megalodon that was longer than a school bus.

She fumbled with the clasp at her chest, as the pressure on her eardrums started to cause her pain. She came free of her belt, and propelled herself from the cockpit. The worrying thing was, the helicopter had now stopped being dragged down into the depths.

Regina crawled back to the surface. She knew the helicopter not being dragged anymore meant one of two things – either the shark had ripped the whale free. Or, the other scenario she tried to push from her mind – the monster was coming back up.

"Regina, come in." Jack paced. "Regina, come back, girl." He shook his head, feeling a coiling in his gut. He looked up at Cate, and shook his head again. He felt sick.

Cate was hugging herself, and looked over the side. The ocean's surface was now only about six feet from the rear deck as the *Slava* settled deeper in the water. She stepped back.

"We need to get to the bridge, somewhere higher." She grabbed at Jack's arm. "Remember Olander's boat – the Megalodon – it came up."

"I know." Jack stopped, looking into her eyes. "But Vincent will be surfacing again soon. I need to be here."

The ship lurched again, settling to one side. The lights sputtered, and the deep throbbing stopped. Thankfully, the lights remained on. "Sounds like we just lost the pumps, but I think engine room is okay for now," he said, wearily.

Jack turned away, not wanting her to see his face. He now knew that even if Vincent managed to free the propeller, it might be too late if the engines became submerged. At the front of the ship, Alexi and Mironov stood together. The harpooner saw them watching him and gave a casual salute. He still waited by his harpoon cannon, as cool as if this was all in a day's work for him.

The stern sunk a little lower in the water, and the bow rose. They'd slide below the surface rear first.

"Cate, get to the bridge room; find out where the Coast Guard chopper is. Tell them… Just tell them to get here." He looked back over his shoulder. "As soon as Vincent comes up, we'll join you."

"You got it." Cate headed for the metal steps.

Jack looked down at the signal tracker. The Megalodon was a few miles out, probably occupied with the whale carcass… or Regina, he thought darkly.

"*Come on, Vince,*" he whispered, once again looking down into the oil-dark water.

CHAPTER 43

Cate entered the bridge room. Sonya stood near the wall, staring out at Mironov who was talking to Alexi at the bow. She straightened when she saw Cate.

"What is it?"

Cate shook her head. "It was Regina in the chopper. We lost her."

"She crashed our chopper?" Jupiter's mouth twisted.

Cate glared, unable to form words for a moment. "No." She spoke through gritted teeth. "We lost Regina, *our friend*, who was doing the job Milo should have been doing."

"We needed that chopper." Jupiter grabbed his head and turned away.

Cate's eyes blazed. "*You fuc—*"

Olander held a finger up in front of her. "Please, I'm sure we all haven't surrendered our manners just yet, have we, my dear?"

"My dear?" Cate held her breath as she looked at the man, and then to his crewmembers. Some were scared shitless, but many still looked defensive, disdainful, as if they were occupying an executive's office during some sort of protest. She let the breath out and turned away, feeling for the first time in her life she could actually murder someone. Above her the lights flickered.

She looked up at them, feeling her stomach sink. "See that?" Cate looked from the light back to Olander. "That's the engine room flooding. Soon well lose our lights. We've already lost our ability to pump water. Once the power goes, then even if we manage to defoul the propeller, we won't be able to restart the engines."

She placed a hand against one of the windows, keeping her eyes on the group. "Now take a look out there." She waited. "See where the waterline is? It's nearly at deck level. Not long after that, we'll either be in it, or on it, in a few tiny dinghies." She pointed her arm out to where Regina had gone down. "Regina, our friend, and the helicopter have gone into the ocean. That was the decoy leading the Megalodon shark away from us. So now, it'll have no reason to keep heading away."

"But if it ate the whale, then maybe it won't be interested," Milo said, his voice small.

Cate walked to the opposite window, and saw Jack holding a flashlight down into water that was far too close to him. She sighed. "It's not about food anymore." She turned back to the group. "This is no big doe-eyed whale. This is a Megalodon shark, like the Great White but about sixty-five feet long and a hundred times more aggressive. It's territorial, meaning it will attack and kill anything in its domain." She found and held Olander's eyes. "And right now, thanks to *you*, that's us."

🦈 🐧 🦈

Vincent went down for what he hoped was the last time. He had to go deep this time – twenty-five feet, as the *Slava* props were now at the lowest point on the sinking ship. His single waterproof flashlight didn't give him much illumination, but he was grateful for it for keeping the stygian dark back just a dozen feet.

The elasticized rope, was woven through with steel fibers – this allowed it to stretch, but gave it a tensile strength well beyond normal rope. It also stopped it being sliced by the propeller blades, and doubly so by a puny human's attempts to hack at it.

He swam back to his work area and picked up the coil of rope he was working on. It had been wrapped tight around the shaft. If he could just cut through this section then the others should be unwound fairly easily.

Vincent could hold his breath for many minutes, but each time he went down, he became a little more fatigued, and a little less able to hold on. At least the work kept him focused, and allowed him to avoid the nagging temptation to look around. He had before, but there was nothing to see but walls of sheer blackness. He just prayed the kid in the chopper could entice the monster well away and *keep* it away from him.

He hacked and sawed, using the bolt cutters for a few seconds, and then going back to the blade. He hoped this would be the last time.

The back of his neck tingled, and the urge to turn around came over him again.

Jack felt like he needed to pace, but the angle of the deck made it impossible now. He had to hang onto the railing with one hand, and in the other he held his tracker. The blip was increasing speed and heading straight for them. He found it easier to think of it as nothing more than a small green pulse on a screen, rather than a monstrous super predator that would inevitably drag them down into the pitch black water, and then...

He turned away and looked up to the bridge room. The weak orange glow from the dying bulbs showed several dark silhouettes, the few figures standing motionless. There was only one he recognized – Cate waved down to him, and he smiled and gave her an all-okay sign in return.

Stay cool, we'll be fine, he tried to project to her. The Coast Guard must have been only about thirty to forty minutes out, maybe just over the horizon now. He tried to cheer himself with the thought, but his logic whispered that their helicopter still wouldn't make it before the boat was underwater. And even then, it would still take them a good ten minutes to hoist everyone up into the cabin. The Megalodon would be here long before that.

Jack screwed his eyes shut, not wanting to imagine what it would be like to be in the water, waiting his turn, while the massive Megalodon was down in the darkness. He opened his eyes; what would he do? He had no idea, and felt ill all over again.

Jack turned back to the bow; Valery Mironov was using a lighter on a cigarette that Alexi had clamped between his lips. The young man leant towards the billionaire but continued to forensically scan the water. The harpoon cannon had its own backup battery and would retain a charge for a short time after the engine died. But it too, would soon lose power.

He exhaled long and slow, and turned back to the stern. The dark water was just about at the deck line now. He saw it lapping gently just over the side, waiting to crawl forward like a living thing… to create a ramp for its master.

That's where it will come. And that was the only place the harpoon cannon couldn't be turned to. After all, what whaling captain is going to want some lunatic letting loose an explosive harpoon into his deck or the bridge room.

Valery Mironov leaned against the railing and Alexi waved again, and Jack felt like laughing out loud. How did those two do it? How do you stay so goddamn cool? *Must be a Russian thing.* Jack snorted and looked briefly back to his tracker – *shit* – he felt a jolt go right through his body. His head jerked up, and he looked first to the dark water, and then to Alexi.

"It's here."

Mironov spun to the water, and the young man nodded, flicked his cigarette away, and placed two hands on the cannon. His eyes were rock steady as they cut the darkness.

Cate grabbed at Sonya's arm as the ship lurched. The lights above them blinked a few times, and then finally died. A few flashlights came on, but immediately the room seemed smaller.

Cate heard some of Olander's crew whimper, and Sonya leaned close to her.

"We need to make a choice. We either stay here and go down with the ship, or we take to the rafts."

Cate looked out the window, trying to find Jack, but without the deck lights the ship was in utter darkness. "We drown or get eaten alive," she whispered, feeling a creeping nausea rise within her.

"No, we choose between certain death, or a chance at life." Sonya's hand on her arm tightened. "Yes, some of us will die. But if we split up, then maybe, *just maybe*, some of us will live until the Coast Guard gets here."

Cate's galloping heart made it hard for her to think. "I don't know what to do anymore." She looked up at the woman's face. "Help me decide."

Sonya put an arm around her shoulders. "Easy; we will decide to live, *together*." She turned to Drago. "Ready the life rafts."

"No, no, no." Olander barged closer, waving a hand in their faces. "We are not getting into life rafts. That thing destroyed the *Gaia Warrior* as if it was a toy boat, and you saw what it did to my high-tech dinghies. I've seen your life rafts; they're no better than toy pool floats."

Cate held a hand up flat to stop the man from coming any closer. "The last thing I want to do is be out on that black water in a tiny raft. But the cold hard fact is, this boat is sinking. You can try your luck in a raft with us, or you stay inside this room and get dragged to the bottom, or maybe you'll float free when it goes under – that'll mean you'll be *in* the water instead of on it." She smiled flatly.

"You can make up your own mind, but we're getting into one of the rafts. You have to decide what you and your crew are doing for yourselves."

"Then we need another decoy, or, *ah*, something." Olander backed up, his eyes round. For the first time the man seemed genuinely frightened.

"Yeah, *now* you get it." Cate said.

A flare popped and rose into the sky. Drago stood out on deck; his arm raised and still holding the flare gun. The red ball of fire rose hundreds of feet in the air, before flaring even brighter, and then slowly dropped back down. It would be seen for many miles over the horizon.

Sonya grabbed her arm again. "Ready?"

Cate shook her head. "No."

The Russian woman grinned. "Me neither; so let's go."

CHAPTER 44

Vincent had a few strands left to cut, and allowed a speck of hope to enter his mind. He might just be able to finish the job before he needed to surface. He pinched his nose and blew, popping and repressurizing his eardrums once again as the stern sunk even deeper. He didn't know how much lower it would be before the water rose above the stern gunwale, or the engine room became inaccessible. But the hull was silent now, meaning the pumps had ceased – it was a bad sign. He began to furiously saw again, and then rested for a few seconds to ease the burning fatigue in his arms and shoulders.

In that few seconds of nothingness, he felt it, the pressure wave, the push of water from something moving past him in the darkness. He'd been a navy frogman in an earlier life, and he knew what it felt like when one huge body moved past another.

He didn't want to turn, but found it impossible to resist. Fear was making the hair prickle on his scalp under the wetsuit head covering. He turned his flashlight into the darkness behind him. There was nothing. He brought it around in a slow arc, finishing with it pointing through the propeller shaft to the other side of the boat – the huge creature came at him so fast he had no time to react. It struck the ship, its huge mouth open and jaws extended forward intent on swallowing him whole.

Instead it struck the ship, missing him, but bending the steel propeller shaft, and smashing it into his chest, jolting the flashlight from his hands.

The propeller may have been cut enough to begin turning, but even if it wasn't, his time, breath, and luck had been used up. Never in Vincent's life had he propelled himself so fast to the surface.

"It's here." Vincent threw Jack his facemask as he scrambled up the rear deck that was now edging into the water.

Jack went to meet his friend, while above him, Cate yelled for them to get the hell away. Drago and Sonya stood with legs braced and guns held in two handed grips, and pointed at the dark water.

The *Slava* juddered, and then it came – the huge Megalodon shark surged up from the water. The massive maw was already open, and to Jack, it seemed a train tunnel-sized cave lined with horrible teeth. Gravity alone slowed its monstrous bulk, but combined with the force of its slide the ship angled even lower.

Jack fell, slid, catching hold of the metal steps. Vincent managed to catch Jack's foot, and also held on. Drago and Sonya were not so lucky. Sonya just caught a railing with her fingertips and hung on. Drago had managed to fire a few rounds, but the heavier Russian slid the fastest, and with nothing to hang onto, he had nowhere else to go.

The ten-foot wide head, swung back and forth like a dog, crushing the big Russian's body against the gunwale, and then turning just enough to lift the still conscious man into its mouth. Drago screamed once as the serrated teeth came together, his gun hand must have clamped down on his revolver as bullets fired nonstop into the air, sounding like celebratory fireworks.

Sonya lost her grip and also began to slide. Jack was too far away and could only watch as the tall woman skidded down the deck. She never made a sound as she headed towards the monstrous head. Instead, she just tried to keep her gun hand steady so she could aim and fire at its eyes. The jaws opened once again, and Jack didn't want to watch, but couldn't turn away now.

Mironov leapt then, sliding fast and catching Sonya by the collar. His momentum took them both to the railing, just below Jack. The Russian billionaire grabbed on and swung Sonya onto the metal beside him. He wrapped an arm around her.

The Megalodon slid back into the water with Drago its only prize, and once gone, the ship bobbed and settled a few feet. The small group immediately scrambled up the deck

"Gotta get to the rafts," Jack screamed. He heard the sound of the dinghies inflating – two of them – each accommodating ten people. There was more than enough room, but no one worried about that being their problem.

Debris littered the water around the stricken ship that continued to edge into the sea. The occasional huff of air came from below, and huge bubbles now began to roil on the surface near the railings.

"We're out of time – she's going under." Vincent helped Sonya and Mironov to their feet.

Olander was first to Jack when he made it back to the huddled group. He snatched at his jacket. "This is madness! You said yourself this thing will swamp us. We're just committing suicide."

"I don't know what to tell you." Jack disengaged his hand. "But there's a lot of debris in the water now – this thing is like most Carcharodon sharks in that it tracks by vibration, sound and sight; if we're quiet, and real lucky, it might not find us."

"So your plan is we just row like hell and hope for the best?" Olander's voice was becoming shrill.

"No, it isn't. We just float... and pray. We stay down low, and quiet, and maybe it'll think we're just another piece of floating trash."

"So, if we're quiet, it won't hear us?" Olander's brows rose as his eyes shifted away.

"Hey." Vincent spotted Milo amongst Olander's crew. "Is the chopper back?"

Not one met his eyes. Jack's lips pressed tight and he turned away. Vincent's head came up, and his eyes went wide. "Where the fuck is Regina?"

His head snapped to Milo. Vincent's teeth now bared, his large hands came up, the blunt fingers curling into hammer-like fists.

The young man held up his hands. "Hey, don't look at me. Xena *wanted* to do it, so…" he backed away his hands waving in front of him. He looked like he was ready to bolt.

Vincent turned to Jack, furious, grabbing his shirt and tugging him closer. "You let her go? You fucking let her go, *by herself?*"

Jack grabbed his wrist, but Cate got between them.

"No, Vince, she did it herself. If we'd known what she planned, we would have stopped her," she said.

Vincent made a small sound in his throat and his shoulders slumped. Jack put a hand on his shoulder. "She gave us a chance."

"Stupid woman," Vincent whispered.

"Stupidly brave." Jack shook him. "But we need to get everyone off now. This is all going bad here, buddy."

"I don't care." Vincent wouldn't look up at them.

"*Yes you do,*" Cate said into his face. "You're Coast Guard, help save these people. *Do your job, mister.*"

Vincent groaned.

"If Regina was here, she'd do the same," Cate said, softer now.

After another moment, he nodded.

"Okay?" Jack asked Cate.

"No, but I'm ready," she said, giving Vincent's shoulder a last rub.

Jack then looked to Mironov and Sonya who also nodded.

The boat groaned as it settled a little lower in the water. It was flooding the deck now, one third of the *Slava* was more a boat ramp than a ship.

"Time to leave," Cate said, sharing a fragile smile. Jack noticed that in the remaining flashlight's glow her face looked almost totally bleached of color.

"Olander." Jack called the captain over. "You and your crew take one of the rafts. Stay low and quiet. Let the current float you away, and hopefully the chopper can pick us up." He pointed. "Push out that way... we'll go the other. No use being both together, in case..."

"I get it," Olander said quietly.

"Valery, your remaining team, and the three of us will take the other one." Jack gave Cate a crooked smile. "Added bonus – we go first."

They all dragged the rafts to the side. Jack tossed Vincent's facemask into the bottom then placed a flashlight in each, and also a few stick flares. He jammed one in his back pocket. Olander also gave them some clothing he'd rolled up tight.

"Just in case, we're out here for a while." He shrugged.

"Thanks," Cate said. "And good luck to everyone."

Mironov joined them. "Alexi will not come."

"I'll go get him." Jack straightened.

"Forget it. For him it is about *vypolnyat* – honor." Mironov lifted his chin. "This is his ship, and he will stay with it."

"Is he mad?" Jack asked.

"Probably." Mironov's mouth twisted into a half smile. "But maybe he thinks we are the mad ones – the Megalodon is in the water, and soon, so will we be."

Jack quickly got everyone to push as much floating debris out into the water. He prayed it created a lot of sensory white noise, to buy them some time. He straightened, and sucked in a huge breath. He laughed a little then, feeling his own heart hammering. He realized he couldn't ever remember being this scared in his life.

He was last in and he felt their eyes on him. "Let's do it." He heaved the raft out and stepped in, and they glided away from the sinking ship.

They all stayed low. In the moonlight, they saw Olander do the same, but in the opposite direction. Jack could see there was only about thirty feet of the *Slava* still above water. At the bow, there stood Alexi, hanging onto the cannon. Jack wondered what would happen when the boat sank – either the man would go under with it, or finally be forced to swim.

Jack lay down in the raft. Cate was cradled under his arm, and he had his ear pressed to the bottom. He had placed the facemask on his forehead, maybe expecting the worst. From below, he could hear the soft sounds of water passing underneath them, but thankfully, little else.

He looked up at the stars, seeing a particularly bright one, and wishing it was the searchlight of the Coast Guard. A held-breath type of calm settled over them as they drifted. Then a brassy, clanging alarm shattered the silence.

"What the fuck is that?" Vincent sat bolt upright. Everyone scrambled, looking firstly at each other, and then searching for the din. Cate snatched up the clothing bundle Olander had given them, quickly unwrapping it. The still ringing alarm clock fell to the bottom of the raft.

Jack snatched it up, and tossed it as far from the raft as he could manage. It hit the water, but he was sure he could still hear the damned thing ringing as it sank.

"That sonofabitch." Cate's eyes were wild, with fury. "He set it to go off, and then gave it to us."

The shark exploded up from underneath them, throwing the raft in the air and scattering bodies in every direction. They hit the water, dozens of feet apart, and when they surfaced, not all of Sonya's men came back up.

"Stay still," Jack yelled. He didn't know now if this would work, as the Megalodon would see them clearly in the low-light water, much better than they could see it. But one thing he was sure of; if they began to thrash or even swim, they'd be dead.

Off in the darkness there was a Russian voice, yelling, and Sonya hissed something back at the man. He ignored her, continuing to curse and yell, until they heard the sound of surging water, like a wave breaking, and then the screaming was gone.

In the distance Jack could make out the bow of the *Slava*, now angling at about forty degrees. The intermittent, soft red glow of a cigarette told him Alexi was still at his post. Further out on the glass-like surface, he could see another floating shape that might have been the other raft.

Valery Mironov was off somewhere in the darkness, and Vincent bobbed up beside him. Sonya and Cate had linked up. Even though this created a bigger mass that might be sensed by the shark, he knew the need for human contact now was always going to override logic.

Jack's mind raced – sooner or later the Megalodon would find them. They needed more options. He tried to think, but fear shut down any good ideas that tried to enter his chaotic mind. There would be few options anyway – after all, what else was there?

He looked up at the sky, and then to the luminous dots on his wristwatch. He knew it all came down to one thing, one magic ingredient they all desperately needed now – *time*.

Jack could just make out the bobbing head of Cate. He had promised her everything would be all right. *Fuck it.* There was only one thing he could think to do.

"I got a plan," he whispered to Vincent.

"Thank god, Jack. What can I do?" The man bobbed closer, listening.

"One thing – take care of Cate." He pulled Vincent's facemask down over his eyes.

"What?" Vincent snatched at him, but Jack had already started swimming – hard – back to the *Slava*.

One chance, one chance only. Jack stopped swimming for a moment, to roll on his back, and try and calm his racing heart. He could hear Cate screaming his name, and he shut it out.

"Hello Jack." Mironov floated close to him.

"Jesus!" He spluttered coming upright. "Valery, get back to the group," Jack said as he snatched out the stick flare.

"Will that make me safer?" Mironov asked.

Jack could swear the man was smiling. "No, but it'll stop you giving me a freaking heart attack."

He saw what Jack had in his hand. "A flare... yes, *do it.*"

"Like you said; a bad plan... but the only one we've got." Jack ripped the end off and punched it against his fist, immediately igniting it, and throwing a massive ball of red illumination around them.

Jack waved it back and forth, and slapped an arm on the water. As if in response, a huge sail-like fin appeared a hundred feet away and then turned sharply and submerged.

"It'll come now," he said, noticing his voice seemed strangled.

"The devil rises to meet us," Mironov said. "It's been a pleasure knowing you, Jack."

"Here goes nothing." Jack waved the flare again. "Alexi!"

The flare was so bright; he could barely see anything beyond its glow as his night vision had been temporarily ruined. He held up the flare, and thought just maybe he could see the *Slava*'s silhouette in the weak glow of the moon. But as he concentrated, something rose up, fully blocking it from his view.

"Oh god," he whispered, and felt his balls shrivel. Jack knew what it was, and he knew the cavernous jaws would already be open, extending forward, to then slam those vicious blade-teeth down on him. The ten-inch triangles shearing him in half... if he was lucky. He shut his eyes.

The *thump*, and hot concussive blast blew flesh in every direction. His eyes flew open as chunks of meat splashed heavily in the water around him. The massive shark listed sideways, and then began to slide away.

Jack pushed the flare down below him, lighting up the ocean, and used the facemask to illuminate the beast on its way. He lifted his head to quickly gulp in a deep breath, and then dived to follow it down.

The Megalodon shark wasn't moving, but a thick blood trail billowed from its massive head. The angle made it impossible to make out the damage, and soon, Jack's lungs began to rebel and pressure in his ears was becoming punishing. He stopped swimming and just let himself hang in the water.

Jack released the flare, letting it sink after the Megalodon. They were over the edge of the trench here, so the monster would fall deep. The red of the flare made it seem like it was a hellish beast on its way back to Hades – *appropriate*, he thought, as he watched the tip of the massive tail vanish in the gloom.

He turned, crawling his way back to the surface, only the easing pressure in his ears letting him know when he was going to break free. When he did, he threw his head back to suck in a huge breath. Vincent was already there to grab him by the collar to keep him afloat and Cate wrapped him in her arms.

"You asshole!" Vincent yelled.

"Double asshole," Cate said through a wide grin.

"I think we got it," Jack gasped.

Vincent whooped, and lay on his back then whooped again for good measure.

Sonya swam over and rubbed his head, but then stroked out after Valery, wrapping herself around him. Mironov kissed her and then pulled himself from her attentions for a moment.

"Now, if one of you can get me out of here, the drinks are on me."

Vincent swam back in close, his grin having fallen away. His cold eyes were on Olander's raft.

"Yeah, but I think I want to be in *that* raft first."

CHAPTER 45

Cate leaned against one wall of the raft, eyes open and watching the stars. Jack was slumped beside her, and next along was Sonya, who had an arm behind her head, and looked to be dozing. Vincent sat forward, his hands clasped and resting on his knees. His eyes were haunted. His right fist had a cut across the knuckles.

The only survivor of Mironov's crew was Alexi, who had finally given up his post at the harpoon cannon and now lay dozing on the bottom of the raft. His snores sounding like a small rusty motor grinding its gears.

Jammed at the other end of the inflatable were Olander and his youthful crew. The big man still had a hand to his face where he sported a mouth full of broken teeth and split lip, with a pattern that perfectly matched the scarring on Vincent's fist. The environmentalist captain was lucky – Vincent had only wanted to hurt him, but Sonya looked like she wanted to kill him.

"*Hey!*" Jack said, rousing Vincent. Cate jerked upright. The splashing had started a while back, and grew stronger. The light of a crescent moon wasn't enough to illuminate much, and Olander's last flashlight couldn't yet pick anything up.

They had no weapons, and all they could do was sit and stare in the direction of the churning water.

"*Ahoy, there.*"

"What the...?" Vincent got to his feet.

"*Ahoy there, the Slava.*"

Vincent threw himself over the side. Cate stood, followed by Jack.

Sonya knelt, her gaze fixed. "What is it?"

In a moment there was more splashing, but also laughter and cursing. Vincent swam back to the side of the raft, with another person under his arm – Regina.

"I found a mermaid. Can I keep her?" He pushed the tired woman over the side, where she flopped down and lay panting, but grinning madly. After a moment, she lifted her head.

"I saw the flare – I'm assuming you won?"

Jack hugged her and Cate knelt to push the wet hair back off the woman's face.

"Damn right we did," Cate said. "We killed it." She knelt back, and thumbed over her shoulder. "Well, Alexi did."

The young harpooner shrugged. "My job, but Mr Monroe made it come to surface. Use himself as bait – crazy man."

Jack opened his arms wide. "Yeah, don't mess with Jack Monroe." He high-fived Alexi.

Valery Mironov leant forward to rub the harpooner shoulder. "That job just earned you a million dollars and a new home in America if you want it."

Alexi turned and grinned. "Yes, I would like it, very much, Mr Mironov."

"*Shush*, listen," Cate said.

The group quietened, and a tiny thumping could be heard in the distance. Vincent lifted Regina into his arms. "That's our ride. See? You've just brought us luck."

She threw an arm around his neck. "What a dream date you turned out to be."

Jack held out his hand to Olander. "The flashlight." He stood, beginning to wave it back and forth. He looked down, grinning. "Am I the only one looking forward to a cold beer and some ribs on dry land?"

"You just described my heaven, buddy." Vincent held onto Jack's leg as the downdraft from the huge chopper passed over them, shaking the raft. "They've seen us."

Jack eased down beside Cate as the Coast Guard helicopter did a quick circuit over the area. Cate felt her body finally begin to relax, but there was still a niggling worm of doubt crawling in her mind. She turned and tugged on Jack's shirt, leaning close to his ear. "Did we? Did we really kill it?"

Jack nodded. "Yeah, I think so. It was badly wounded, most likely mortally so." He leaned back and opened his mouth as if about to say more, but then let it snap shut.

"I hope so," she said. "But the thing about sharks is, they are such great survivors. They're one of the few creatures in the world to never get cancer."

"I know," he said softly.

She looked up at his face, but he continued to stare out over the water. "And there's this other damn thing about them; they've evolved an almost miraculous biology for wound repair. Even if it's a serious trauma, within two weeks the wound secretes mucus, then the epidermis regenerates and expands to close over the site. And then they're as good as new."

He turned to smile at her. "Stop worrying; we got it this time." He kissed her forehead.

"Good," she said. "I didn't want to just scare it off to someplace else. I just wish we could see the carcass." She sighed. "I should be sad, or angry, or something – such a unique creature."

Mironov sat forward. "Do you remember, Cate? Sometimes evolution, or maybe God himself, makes mistakes. And that abomination was certainly one of them. We can live without it."

She nodded as the huge helicopter began to settle in the water. "Amen to that; let's all go home."

EPILOGUE

An Australian film and science team in southern Australia is dismayed and confused about the fate of their ten-foot Great White Shark they had been tracking for their research.

According to the tracking data, the shark started to behave erratically, and then vanished just over the edge of the Australian continental shelf. Strangely, the electronic tag that had been implanted in its skin was found washed up on shore, several miles from where the shark disappeared.

When scientists were able to retrieve the data from the tracking chip it led to even more confusion, as an analysis of the shark's last movements showed that the animal turned to head closer to the shore at high speed, but then was stopped dead. Inexplicably, it then took a rapid dive down the side of the shelf to a depth of fifteen hundred feet.

Strangely, the data indicated a large temperature change from thirty-five degrees, the ambient water temperature, to then jump to seventy-six degrees, the gut temperature of a large Carcharodon species shark, where it remained for eight days.

The researchers refused to state their conclusions on the record, but later said there was really only one observation they could make – their Great White had been eaten by a mega-predator that had risen from the depths – at this time, type unknown.

Channel 29 Technology News - 3:40pm June 8

AUTHORS NOTES:

Many readers ask me about the science in my novels – is it real or fiction? Where do I get the situations, equipment, characters or their expertise from, and just how much of any legend has a basis in fact? In the case of the Carcharodon Megalodon, it is all fact. The only disputed area is whether the creature may still exist in the deep, dark depths of our oceans.

CARCHARODON MEGALODON

Our oceans are vast, and the massive sea reptiles were long gone, the sea serpents of old, now all died out. The Alpha predators were missing, the oceans were still warm, and nature abhors an unfilled niche. It was soon filled.

About twenty million years ago a creature evolved that was more fearsome than anything that ever stalked the land or ever would; something that was reputed to have been between fifty and seventy feet in length (with some oversized at one hundred feet), and perhaps weighing in at eighty to one hundred tons. The Megalodon Carcharodon – the dinosaur shark – was the apex predator of apex predators. Not only was it the biggest prehistoric shark that ever lived; it was the largest predatory marine creature in the history of the planet. It vastly outweighed the ancient sea reptiles like Liopleurodon and even the Kronosaurus.

Its hunting grounds were the warm shallows seas of the Cenozoic Era, and its only rivals were bigger Megalodons than itself. Records indicate it last existed a little over one-point-five million years ago, so when early man walked the land, Megalodon swam just off the coast.

Would they have seen each other? Probably. Man was an observant, intelligent species, and Megalodon would have been just as watchful. After all, it had probably developed the same vision as its smaller cousin, the Great White shark – an ability to raise its head above water and use eyes that saw above and below the surface.

The flooded estuaries would have provided plenty of opportunities for the massive hunter. There it could circle, just offshore, waiting patiently for something to wash in, stumble in or venture out into the depths. Because once in its domain, then all belonged to it.

But the world that bred the Megalodon was changing. In fact from the moment it had evolved, the seas were already cooling. Between thirty-five and two million years ago, the continents were still sliding around the Earth's surface. This titanic movement had significant effects on both land and sea – while the Indian subcontinent crashed into Asia, throwing up the Himalayas, more tectonic impacts pushed up the Rockies and Andes mountains. These colossal alterations to the geography affected worldwide weather patterns. As well, these land-based events changed the ocean's topography – newly formed mountains changed rainfall patterns, creating rain shadows, and therefore, the water run off redistribution meant shallow inland seas dried up.

Below the mighty Atlantic Ocean, a colossal tear opened up in the seabed, caused by the continental spread that extruded magma from the deep earth and distorted abyssal currents. In addition, this seafloor spreading caused the Gulf Stream to become sluggish, and so reduced the surfacing of cold, nutrient-rich water near North America's southeast. Such upwellings were critical to supporting the diverse marine life that provided a food source for

Megalodon. It is also important to note that the cetotheriids (primitive baleen whales), undoubtedly one of the dinosaur shark's food sources, became extinct at the same time as Megalodon.

Then the cooling climate began to lock up water in glaciers. This caused the global sea levels to drop by nearly seven hundred feet. Estuaries that were the breeding habitat for the Megalodon vanished.

But for all these assaults on the giant predator's environment, it also benefitted from its success. The Megalodon shark was found worldwide – from Europe to Africa, North and South America, throughout Asia, Indonesia, and Australia. And it is well known that broadly distributed species were much better able to weather periods of significant change. Even under such altered conditions, a few populations could have (should have) adapted and survived.

Could it have? Let's look at the evidence:

The case AGAINST:

Their habitat is now too different to support a mega-predator. For all of their great size they were shallow warm-water hunters, preferring depths of only about fifty to two hundred feet deep. Unlike their cousins the Great Whites, who liked deep and colder water.

Like the Great White they have row upon row of serrated teeth, designed to be discarded when damaged. We find Great White teeth embedded in whale carcasses all the time – why not Megs? The Megalodon's bite power enabled it to shear through the heaviest bones and heads of its colossal prey. In the process it lost teeth that were quickly replaced. Where are the new ones? None, other than fossils exist. And where are the whale carcasses washing up with a ten-foot bite radius?

Great Whites only survived because they usually avoided Megalodon's warm, shallow seas, perhaps in part to avoid ending up as their next meal. Instead, they lived in cool, temperate waters closer to the poles – which were warmer than they are now, and more like the sea environments they inhabit today.

So was the Megalodon disappearing good news for us humans? Maybe not – when you remove large sharks, then smaller predators become more abundant and they compete for the same fish stocks we humans live on. Less Megalodons, means more whales, but less fish for us.

The case FOR:
Don't expect a Megalodon carcass to ever wash up – sharks don't float, they have no swim bladder to inflate after death, so would sink. And if they had adapted to deeper water, then sightings would be rare (though there are a few pictures circulating on the web, I'd view these with suspicion).

But then again, something that big should eventually makes its presence known, or at least leave clues. Well, of course – numerous sightings, and not just by rum-soaked seaman or overenthusiastic fiction writers. Here are few pieces of evidence for consideration:

• In 1918 a Port Stephens' fishermen refused to go to sea when an immense shark was taking the lobster pots (each around three feet across). This shark frightened the locals to the point where they refused to put to sea – this must have been something pretty substantial, as no fishing meant no food and no income. Many of the witnesses claimed the shark was over a hundred feet in length, and the monster hung around for weeks.

• In March 1954, the Australian Cutter called the *Rachel Cohen* supposedly ran aground, and when it was in dry-dock having its hull inspected for damage, it was found there was an enormous bite mark around the propeller that was far too large for any modern shark to make. The tooth marks were about five inches wide, and the largest Great

White has teeth only measuring two-point-five inches. The captain of the *Rachel Cohen* recalled an impact and shuddering on the ship as they were passing Indonesia, which he thought was the boat simply hitting a floating tree trunk.

All undeniable proof? Not quite. For every bit of evidence there is counter evidence. But then again, today we know more about the surface of the moon than we do about the depths of our oceans. Our oceans are vast and deep, and cover seventy-one per cent of the planet's surface and contain ninety-seven per cent of the planet's water. Yet more than ninety-five per cent of the underwater world remains unexplored (National Oceanic and Atmospheric Administration).

The final word:

Our seas are warming once again – it's a natural cyclic progression, and nothing to do with mankind. The heat is being captured in the deep layers of the oceans. It will lead to krill explosions, fish stock changes, and migrating pattern alterations of the huge cetaceans. With the krill come the massive feeders. With the fish stocks and the massive feeders come the super predators.

Keep your eyes open; I don't think it will be long now.

DEEP BLUE

Guadalupe Island lies a hundred and fifty miles offshore of the Pacific coast of Mexico, roughly south of San Diego on the Baja California peninsula. The island is surrounded by deep water, some of which attains depths of twelve thousand feet.

It is in these deep, dark waters that video recently emerged of what's thought to be the world's largest Great White Shark captured in the wild. The shark has been dubbed Deep Blue, and is estimated to be around twenty-one feet in length, and weighing in at twenty thousand pounds.

Deep Blue is a wide as a hippo and thought to be a fifty-year-old pregnant female. It was noted at the time that the slashes on her left flank indicate that she's probably been involved in fights with other sharks.

MOVILLE CAVE

Discovered in 1986 in Constanța County, Romania, a few kilometers from the Black Sea coast. The cave system is notable for its unique groundwater ecosystem and life forms that have been sealed off from the outside world for over five million years.

Forty-eight species of leeches, spiders, scorpions and insects were found inside the cave, living in a world of utter darkness. The food chain is based on chemosynthesis rather than photosynthesis, whereby there is methane and sulfur oxidizing bacteria, which releases nutrients for the fungi and other bacteria. This forms microbial mats on the cave walls and the surface of lakes and ponds that is grazed on by some of the animals. The grazers are then preyed on by larger predatory species.

The cave system with its unique and hidden life forms was the basis for the horror/science fiction movie 'The Cave', starring Cole Hauser (2005).

HIDDEN OCEANS

Earth's oldest body of water, found beneath Canada, contains more than all of the world's rivers, swamps and lakes put together.

Huge reserves of the oldest water on Earth are locked deep within the planet's crust and could be home to new forms of life, according to scientists. Geologists have revealed they have found water that is up to two-point-seven billion years old in sites all over the world. They now estimate there could be around two and a half million cubic miles of this water buried beneath the ground.

RICHARD GRAY, MAILONLINE. 18 December 2014

AND FINALLY

This was a real news story included in Channel 9's newsfeed from 2014 – Australian filmmakers contracted for a marine investigation are baffled as to what had taken a ten-foot Great White Shark they tagged as part of the study. The shark disappeared on the edge of Australia's continental shelf, with the electronic tag later washing ashore two miles from where the shark was originally tagged.

The data recordings from the tag shocked the researchers, as it seemed the shark took a high-speed deep dive down the side of shelf to a depth of fifteen hundred feet, and then the tag recorded a large temperature change from nine degrees to twenty-four and half degrees where it remained for eight days.

The film making investigators drew only one conclusion — the Great White had been eaten by a "super predator" of the deep – type unknown.

Channel 9 Technology News - 3:40pm June 8, 2014